DEARTH

Lynda Schor

DEARTH

LIBRARY OF CONGRESS CATALOGING-IN-PUBLICATION DATA

Dearth
Authored by Lynda Schor

ISBN: 9781734383546
LCCN: 2020947268

Acknowledgments

THANKS TO Nava Renek and Alexandra Carides for putting out a beautiful book and for not asking me to change anything. Thanks also to those generous friends and writers who read the final version, and offered suggestions, or wrote blurbs. And thank you to my two San Miguel writers groups, who read at least two versions of Dearth.

TO MY HUSBAND, the poet Halvard Johnson, who wrote the original outline with me over coffee in a restaurant in Baltimore that was shaped like a ship. And who introduced me to El Paso, TX, to Las Cruces, NM, and the border cities of Mexico. He died the day after I finished Dearth, and what seemed like the hundredth draft, and is hugely missed.

I'M GRATEFUL to the Virginia Center for the Creative Arts for all the residencies.

TO MY FORMER STUDENTS—it is so much richer having many of you still in my life, even if it's mostly on social media.

AND, AS ALWAYS, to Alexandra, Timothy, Amanda, and Zachary, and Hannah, Miranda, Noah and Ollie.

CONTENTS

ONE

Another morning and I wake with thirst
For the goodness I do not have.

Mary Oliver, *Thirst*

BY THE TIME THEY REACH THE MOTEL IT IS DUSK. The cottony cumulus have dissolved into a sky that is now rich royal, with just a thick line of peach along the horizon, blending into a thinner line of lavender. Skinny trees are black silhouettes, like cut paper.

Waiting his turn to register for a room, Ray has time to notice that the motel desk is just a narrow shelf of wood nailed under a thick plastic window separating the reservations clerk from a visitor, with six bullet-hole sized holes to speak through, and a mouse-hole to shove a credit card through. Behind the plastic is a woman with a large head and long blonde hair with three inches of black roots, which is either stylish or slovenly—Ray can't tell. She's wearing a bright red shirt, and nothing below her breasts is visible so it appears that her breasts are resting atop the desk like a statue. She uses an out-of-date credit card machine so Ray's receipt is mangled before the woman gets it right.

"Be thankful we didn't have to pay cash," says Stella, alongside him, nudging him.

Ray is so tired he can't think of the most elemental Spanish, and stands tongue tied when the woman asks what room he'd like.

Ray hugs Felix briefly, and kisses Stella on her smooth cool cheek. She turns a little and kisses him quickly on his mouth. He can taste her lip gloss—cherry, plus some chemical.

She takes his hand and squeezes it so hard his wedding ring presses painfully into his other fingers.

Alone in his room, Ray lies on the bed fully clothed and holds his breath. His large dark blue duffel lies beside him on the worn quilted magenta bedspread printed with red and pale pink roses.

Though the desk clerk reassured him it was a non-smoking room, and there's a little plaque on the door with a cigarette behind a red slashed circle, the place stinks of old smoke and ammonia, and there are two black plastic ashtrays on the dresser. There are cigarette burns on the bedspread, which Ray had immediately pulled down on one side so he doesn't have to picture all those who've been lying there before him.

He hasn't been on a bed with springs in ages, and every time he makes the slightest move, the bed whines and makes a grand gesture, as if it might throw him off.

Not looking too closely at the sheets, he pulls down the thin olive green pilled blanket that matches the leaves of the roses on the bedspread. He misses his computer, which Stella had convinced him to leave at home so he could really experience this trip and not be tempted to do any work, or look at messages. This place probably doesn't have WiFi anyway.

However he no longer wishes to experience this funky hotel, or look too closely at the moldy plastic tile in the bathroom alcove, the ratty maroon carpet, or the cruddy sink with the grout that looks like marshmallow. Stella is in a room with Felix and he's alone. It's amazing how much more fun it is to be with someone to share the motel horrors with. Ray is even too tired to read or even look through the magazines he's brought.

Or maybe he has changed. He's making a lot more money than he did when he was a T.A. in El Paso, and it's been a long time since he's been in a motel like this.

The one thing he does like about the tiny cabin of this pink motel with its office in the center and two rows of attached cabins like outstretched arms is that there are no neighbors, nothing around them at all, so he can pull aside the ratty red curtain and see the sky, rapidly turning black, so that now all Ray can see is his own image reflected in the window, on the bed, the lamplight brightening one side of his face. He reminds himself of John Turturro in the Coen brothers' movie *Barton Fink,* who plays a young indigent screenwriter, put up in a ratty hotel in L.A. so he can work on a script with a strict deadline. Unable to write despite spending all his time in the room, he lies in the saggy bed watching the wallpaper slowly melt off the humid walls, and listening to bizarre sounds emanating from other rooms.

TO GET TO THIS SEEDY, misnamed Agua Motel that Felix appeared to know of, they'd sped through those grimy Texas towns between the New Mexico border and El Paso, and then through El Paso itself where they rushed past all the landmarks of Ray's and Olivia's life. And suddenly he found he wanted to wallow in memories of Olivia. Olivia and himself. Olivia and Felix and Stella and himself.

Stella, thinking this route might be hard on Ray, had been willing to change the itinerary again, but Felix had been adamant, so they crossed the border into Juarez, speeding past the huge line of cars, trucks, and SUVs headed north, lined up to cross the border into the U.S.

"Thank god we're not on that line," said Stella, gazing at Mexican women and their children, or men, some in wheelchairs, sitting, wheeling themselves, or walking amongst the cars, and along the highway in the blazing sun, selling soft drinks, matches, Chiclets, newspapers, candied apples and other hideous looking sweets. The children were tiny and adorable and had lots of black hair. The littlest were carried in slings on their mothers' backs or over their shoulders, often with blankets covering their entire heads and bodies. The slightly older ones slept on, heads drooping, sweat beading on their wide foreheads and upper lips.

Here the Rio Grande—Rio Bravo on the Mexican side— was only about forty feet wide.

"Borders are dangerous places," says Stella, taking a deep breath.

Ray looks at her as best he can, as he's way too close to her.

"People are extra vulnerable at borders," she says.

"Is that some New Age wisdom?" Ray asks.

"Not new at all," Stella says. "There are many myths and fairy tales about crossing borders, passing over bridges, and moving across the border between life and death. Where whoever is crossing has to pay something, or lose something valuable—perhaps one's life—with the possibility of never being able to return."

In spite of the hot sun through his window, hotter because the car's crawling now, Ray feels a shiver run from Stella through his arm that's pressed against hers. Or is it coming from him?

Once in Juarez, beyond the dirty aqua, turquoise, green and lavender concrete buildings, with iron grills covering windows and protecting small patios, with a multitude of signs advertising *medicos, farmacias, abogados,* and *dentistas* galore, and past the paved streets of the city proper, were larger houses, some on hills along the highway, higgledy-piggledy, no order. The vacant lots with their dry yellow grasses were covered in plastic bags of every color, soda bottles, and a variety of paper, looking like small garbage dumps or recycling centers that hadn't been organized yet.

When Ray, standing on a hill near the Rio Grande in El Paso, got his first glimpse of Mexico across the river so many years ago, what had struck him was the disorder. No bulldozed hills to create level areas for building housing, no roads neatly running, squared-off, or curving, through planned developments. No neat landscaping. Just a chaotic jumble, made more so by distance and perspective. Almost as if a child had thrown down a huge set of brightly colored toy blocks and left them there.

RAY IMAGINES HE HEARS A RADIO OR TV playing Mexican music. He considers going back to the front "office" to see if there's any coffee or a snack machine, but he's too tired and afraid he might have to use his rusty Spanish. He thinks of the book he's brought, but he doesn't feel like reading. About to turn on the TV he recalls an article he read that said that the moment you arrive at a motel you should wipe the remote and the telephone with antibiotic wipes. He has no antibiotic wipes, and soon he realizes that there's no remote either.

He hears voices—maybe a television in another room, or people arguing. The voices get louder, especially the higher, he guesses, female voice. Then he hears bed- springs that aren't his, in no particular rhythm, just an occasional twang. By the time Ray finds the remote on the sink, the bedspring sounds have acquired a tempo. There are squeaks followed by bangs— maybe a headboard?—followed by bangs and squeaks, in a regular rhythm. He hopes these sounds aren't coming from Felix and Stella's room—but no, they aren't next door—they are at least three rooms away.

Ray doesn't want to think about Stella and Felix fucking. But he can't help it. He switches off the hideous lamp with the broken shade that's above his bed but not in the right place for reading anyway, and buries his head in his pillow. Squeak squeak bang.

He gets up to brush his teeth. No room for his Dopp bag, so he hangs it on the bathroom doorknob. He remembers to use only the bottled water provided by the motel—though it does occur to him that they could have filled the bottles with tap water so that they could reuse them. He looks for a place to put his toothbrush. The white towel looks gray. When he runs his hands through his dry hair and looks in the mirror above the sink he notices that he's already too sunburned.

Squeak, bang, bang. He goes to the window and looks out, and sees his own reflection. Bang bang-squeak.

He opens the door a crack, and the only car parked anywhere near Felix's Suburban are the two Toyotas in front of the office, that had been there when they arrived.

Ray lies down again, then he gets up to take his t-shirt off. Squeak, bang. He pictures Felix's firm body, taut as a bow, over Stella. She is naked and very white and plump, and Ray can picture her entirety because Felix is balanced over her like a bridge over a river.

Stella's hair is a dark reddish splash on the pillow and her freckled face is flushed. She's not looking at Felix—her head is way back—and each time Felix pumps into her, her head hits the wall. No, not the wall, but the fake wood headboard that bumps against the wall (bang).

Ray imagines Olivia under him. She is thin, with narrow hips, and her butt almost fits into his huge hand. When she lies on her back her stomach slopes in like a bowl. He pushes aside her dark bangs with his lips and kisses her forehead. Once in a while when traveling they'd stop at fancy motels for a good shower, a firm bed and great meal. But mostly Olivia loved funky motels that weren't catering to rich *turistas*. She's damp from a shower and smiling—happy to be here. She takes his penis and holds it. He feels the heat of her hand on him as if it's the center of his body, with a pulse, a heartbeat of its own. He runs his cock along her belly, her navel, then her underarm, and her ear, pretending he doesn't know where to put it. He hasn't thought of her giggle, her raucous laugh in a long time. Can one forget the sounds of a loved one who's died?

Someone in another room is laughing. Ray's room is now completely silent. Hadn't it occurred to him that Stella and Felix would be sharing a room every night? And if he hadn't, and why would he—so what—something like that wouldn't bother him because he loves being alone. But here he is, lonelier than he's been in a very long time.

 TWO

RAY WAKES SUDDENLY to what sounds like an airplane right above his room. The pounding in his temples is in synch with the banging on his door. It takes him a moment to realize that he's in a Juarez motel and not in his apartment in Boston. He feels the familiar ache, disappointment that feels like fear, in his solar plexus when he wakes and realizes Olivia's not there.

"Okay, okay," he mumbles, grabbing the magenta bedspread and wrapping it around his torso like an unwieldy towel as he rolls off the bed. Ray opens the door a crack.

A bit of his dream in which hundreds of Hell's Angels roar into town on their enormous souped-up Harleys and BMWs comes back to him.

He opens the door to Stella, whose hair, wavy and wild is now pulled back in a tidy bun, accentuating her cheekbones. Smiling broadly she holds out a Styrofoam cup. Her olive t-shirt and cropped pants are the same color as the *chamisa*, the dry rough grass along the paths between the cabins.

"It's not too bad," says Stella, handing Ray the cup and moving past him into the room. His bedspread, which he lets go of to take the hot cup, falls to the ragged carpet, nearly tripping him. He sips loudly. Stella has remembered how he likes it—with just a little milk and no sugar.

"Not bad," he says. In truth it's pretty bad—probably Nescafe—but it's hot and very welcome.

Stella looks Ray up and down, and then at the bedspread he'd had around him still on the floor like a huge puddle. "You must really be afraid of me."

Ray looks down at himself and sees he's fully dressed in his chinos and t-shirt.

"I forgot that I fell asleep in my clothes." He feels the blood rush to his neck and chest when he recalls the sounds he fell asleep to.

Inside, out of the sun, Stella's clothing seems brighter, lime green now, with very thin white lines, abstract meanderings, or a foreign alphabet on her Capri pants, which reveal ankles surprisingly thin for her size. The green reminds Ray of the chameleons he used to buy at the circus in Madison Square Garden when he was a kid, a cousin to the huge prehistoric-looking iguanas of Mexico and the Southwest.

"I actually feel the caffeine running through me, shoving my headache along in front of it," he says.

He heads to the sink with his coffee to rummage amongst his shaving gear for some aspirin.

"I woke up to the sound of an airplane or motorcycles, and now I recall that I was dreaming there was some kind of event for motorcycle enthusiasts, and Hell's Angels here in town. I was late for an important appointment—"he shakes his head—"I can't remember with who—but I remember my panic. I am on foot, and every time I try to cross the road, more bikes speed by. The noise is unbearable and the bikers look more and more ominous, overweight, naked bellies and legs, and huge arms, bits of black leather, lots of metal studs, chains and tattoos."

"Yeah?" says Stella.

"Then you knocked on the door," he says. "The dream, the noise, it just left me with this headache."

He doesn't mention the hugely ominous feeling that came with it. He finds his aspirin, a large bottle. In the dingy mirror above the sink he sees Stella behind him, coming closer. He's tempted to run.

"I have something better, something natural for headaches," she says. Ray watches in the mirror his face and neck turn pink, then red.

"What do you mean?" he asks, watching Stella reach around from behind him to feel his forehead. He sees her hands meeting in the center of his forehead looking like a strange Indian headband.

Her fingers are cool and once again he's aware of the lemony smell of her shampoo, or soap. Surely she will feel with her cool hands, how burning hot he is.

"You feel okay," she says. "Probably just one of those travel headaches—you know—new places, weird schedules ..."

"What time is it?" Ray asks. He feels as if he's slept too much, and at the same time, as if he's not slept enough.

"Felix and I discovered a surprisingly good looking restaurant attached to this dump," she says. "Shall we meet there in fifteen minutes or so?"

SHOWERED, AND DRESSED IN CLEAN CHINOS that look like all his other chinos, Ray, feeling much more together, easily finds the low-ceilinged restaurant behind the cabins.

It does look neat and clean—must be a recent addition—with a bright blue Formica counter and red Naugahyde booths. He's a bit late, so is surprised not to see Felix or Stella.

He slides into one of the many empty booths, and studies the paintings on the pale blue walls. Mostly dark, browns and dark blues, they have bright highlights of yellows, oranges, reds, and bright azure, all depicting romanticized versions of past and present Indians—Navaho, Apache, Aztec, Otomi, whatever, wearing full regalia: loincloths, beads, headbands, feathers, fringed leather bras and vests, ankle shells, necklaces, and large feather headdress. They carry spears, bows and arrows, some are in canoes, and others riding rearing stallions, with canyons and buttes and cactus in the backgrounds.

There's one painting of a woman, bare brown legs, on a white stallion, wearing a headband with one feather, long black braids hanging near firm round breasts that are bursting out of a tiny leather beaded vest. One arm is raised, brandishing a long spear.

This type of art depicting gorgeous hyper-sexualized Indians is so common in restaurants and motels in the southwest, New Mexico, Texas and Arizona and even parts of Mexico, and Ray wonders what's going on here, as most current residents of those places show no great love for the indigenous peoples they've displaced. There's something somewhat racist and even pornographic about these depictions, with their unrealistic Amazonian specimens, and their scant leather coverings over nearly exposed breasts and glimpses of genitals behind tanned hide, fringe and beads, but he can't figure out exactly what it is.

"Café, por favor, con poquito leche," Ray says to the very young boy, who may be anywhere between eight and eleven, and who's wiping the table with a very gray rag.

He doesn't see any other Anglos around. Almost no one in fact, except for one man with a sombrero hanging from his knee, and a very dark, maybe Mexican couple looking slightly rumpled.

Yes, Ray's ready for more coffee. His headache is gone, and he's hungry—starving—for his favorite breakfast, *huevos rancheros,* dragon's breath hot.

Ray's studying a blue Xeroxed menu when Stella, and then Felix slide in across from him.

"Dos mas cartas y mucho mas café, por favor," Stella nods at the child who goes back for the coffee pot and two more thick white china mugs.

Something seems off to Ray. Unlike earlier, both Stella and Felix seem stiff and maybe grim, as if both are in a bad mood.

Felix, wearing a blue and white striped dress shirt with a stiff collar buttoned all the way up to his large Adam's apple, more apparent than usual, especially as he's not wearing a tie, studies his menu.

Ray recalls that in spite of the funkiness of a bullfight arena, most people dress up for bullfights—they are considered grand occasions. He hopes he looks okay.

Stella, her hair plastered back in this new way, spine straight on her bench, studying her menu as if it's a prayer book, seems as severe as a matador. Ray wonders whether he's missing something. Not that unusual for him.

"Hey," he says. "Aren't you two talking to each other?"

"It's nothing," says Stella, not looking up.

Felix nods.

"Here's a joke I read somewhere or other, probably on Facebook," says Ray. He hates those things—funny photos or jokes, and can't believe he's going to tell one, but his need to break the tension wins.

"On an El Al flight, you know, the Israeli airline?" he continues, "there are always two flight attendants in a row." Ray has their attention. "One walks ahead serving the food, and the other follows close behind, saying, 'Eat, eat,'"

Felix looks blank. Stella smiles reluctantly. "Ha ha," she says.

"Hey," says Ray, removing his utensils from their napkin bunting, "We're on a trip. I came a long way." It takes effort to say this rather than sit quietly absorbing the mood, as is his habit.

"Well," says Stella, "are we going to have to act jolly when we don't feel like it just because you've flown here from Boston?" She absently runs the tines of her fork along the straw placemat.

"I hope you're not angry at me," Ray points his forefinger to his chest.

Stella stares at his hand, or his slim gold wedding band.

Their very young waiter returns to replenish their coffee. Ray watches to see that he doesn't spill anything, but the kid is dexterous.

He gazes into his mug of steaming coffee, now as tense as the others. He hates conflict and has always avoided it. He keeps away from fights, doesn't like to argue, and sharp criticism from anyone, even if not directed at him, causes his stomach to turn and his heart to pound in a kind of terror, something he's never outgrown.

He doesn't know why—he can't recall his parents ever fighting. There was no yelling, screaming or hysterics in the quiet apartment he grew up in, an only child.

Perhaps he'd be better off if his parents had fought. Maybe then he'd be used to it—and it would seem like nothing. Obviously, he thinks, they avoided conflict too, and he's read that not only can that personality trait be inherited via nurture, it can actually be genetic, like shyness, or empathy.

He remembers often suffering from feelings of injustice and being misunderstood, but whenever he tried to explain how he saw things to either parent, he'd begin to cry, making it impossible to speak.

"Of course we're not mad at you," says Felix, placing his red, large-knuckled hand over Ray's.

"We're just mad at each other," says Stella. It's nothing. Didn't you and Olivia ever fight?"

Ray didn't recall fighting or arguing with Olivia—but they must have. Most likely he wouldn't be fighting—she'd be yelling. But this didn't happen often. Even discussions where Olivia was angry felt like arguments. But Ray doesn't remember many of those occasions.

"We did have an ongoing fight while we were all living in El Paso," says Ray, scooping up his viscous *huevos rancheros* with tortillas rolled into fat flutes. The thought of revealing this makes him slightly sick, but he can't help offering it to change the mood.

"I remember a big argument," says Stella, wrapping a tortilla around some scrambled eggs, rolling it into a giant cigar, then biting the tip.

"Maybe it was when we visited you in your teeny ranch house on Fiesta Drive in El Paso. We were drinking wine. Olivia said that people who never have children always remain children. They always, no matter how old, think of themselves as children—the child of someone, but never the mother or father of anyone. And that keeps them immature. I remember you ended up shouting, spilling your wine on that horrible beige carpet, 'There's nothing wrong with being immature.'"

Ray does remember many discussions related to having children. "I think I meant 'childish,' not immature, he says. He does recall this now. But he can't imagine himself yelling.

"There are some good things about remaining childless; the ones I'm thinking of are you can continue to be needy. You can remain narcissistic. You can be as selfish as you wish, forever," Olivia had said.

Ray had felt attacked, not knowing whether to own up to those traits his wife had enumerated, each emphasized with a period.

He remembers now what Olivia looked like that particular evening—wearing a long narrow-skirted black dress, which made her look even thinner, her pale skin vampire-ish. Yet her straight eyebrows and high bangs made her seem always a bit puzzled, and vulnerable.

"We all met at the fertility clinic at the University, right?" says Ray. We were all in the waiting room that time."

"Yeah," said Stella, drinking her coffee. "Most of the people were women, much older than us," she says.

"Olivia and I called it the 'futility' clinic," says Ray.

He'd felt like a fraud the entire time they were trying to get pregnant because he was half-pretending to want a child. He'd never understood Olivia's desire for a baby. She was five years older than he, and maybe being in her thirties had something to do with it. But she was an artist—wasn't that enough for her?

Strangely, their diligent efforts to conceive didn't turn him off sex like it did for some couples—the temperature-taking, the hormone shots, the sex on demand, the emphasis solely on ovulation. He enjoyed the sense of purpose, the idea of sex for a reason.

Every month when Olivia got her period, she was depressed and while sad for her, and feeling like a betrayer, he was pleased.

Ray was taught to administer the daily hormone shot to Olivia's firm derriere. He recalls the initial resistance as he pressed the needle into her skin—then its surrender. He was not thinking, like her, of, please let this work, or sperm, eggs, babies, or even of sex. As he pressed the large needle further into Olivia's flesh he was imagining layers, and strata. Geology.

Ray says, unwrapping one last tortilla from the plaid cloth napkin keeping them warm, "How come you guys quit going to the 'futility' clinic?"

Not everyone is motivated enough to continue with the time commitment and the expense, he thinks. The cost was one reason they gave up. He can't imagine Felix or Stella with a child.

"I hope I'm not hitting on an exposed nerve here," he says. "But you lost your desire for a kid?"

Felix and Stella look at each other and laugh. "We never wanted a baby. You're remembering it all wrong, Ray," says Felix, sighing, and getting to his feet, "I was there for a vasectomy."

"Can that be true?" Ray shakes his head. How could he remember things so wrong? And if that's not the case, how could he have been so unaware of what was really happening, what his friends were thinking, doing? Unless they are lying. Or worse, kidding. He feels a sudden vertigo, and presses his fingers on the sticky table edge.

As the room settles, Ray, feeling with his tongue the small crack at the lip of his coffee mug, ventures, changing the subject, "What about those orgiastic sounds I heard from your room last night?"

Then he recalls his dream, and the image of the road he needed to cross. And the din of the motors.

Stella laughs. Felix shakes his head. "It wasn't us, that's for sure," he says.

"Though not because we weren't getting along. You can have fantastic sex with someone you hate," says Stella.

"I'm not sure that would work for me," says Ray, surprised.

Felix, just about done, looks all around the small diner, and then behind him.

"Think about it more, Ray," says Stella, pushing her chair away from the table.

"What's wrong?" asks Ray, watching Felix.

"Oh, Felix is being paranoid," says Stella. "He thinks we're being followed."

"Followed?" Ray looks up from studying the bill on the table. "Why would we be followed? You're kidding? Who'd want to follow us?" He feels his throat tighten. Is he once again missing something crucial?

"Don't ask," says Stella. "Felix is involved in border issues. I'm going to the john."

"Border issues. What border issues?"

"Well, Ray," says Felix, trembling slightly with fear, or with rage, "you may be able to ignore politics, but you can't live near a city like El Paso and remain pure."

"What makes you think I'm not involved in politics?" asks Ray, even though he's not. "And what do you mean by 'pure'?"

Stella is back and grabs her purse off her seat. "Let's go," she says, now in a rush.

"We'll talk more later, Ray," Felix says.

"Oh," says Stella, squeezing her lush body between two chairs near the cashier's booth, "are secrets being kept?"

Ray has a hard time keeping up with them. He already has his duffel with him, so he waits near the car, in the motel lot, while Felix and Stella go in to their room to pick up whatever bags and stuff they'd left there.

Somewhat alarmed, Ray watches Felix sidle cautiously along the motel wall, and peer through the window into his room, looking around him before opening his door.

What the fuck? thinks Ray.

THREE

If anything, these dry landscapes grow more powerful with time and increased acquaintance. The answers to things get shorter, with more room for the unknown built into them, and the unknowable.

Diane Keppel-Smith, *SALT*, Orion

AROUND NINE O'CLOCK THE PREVIOUS MORNING, the three of them, Ray, Stella, and Felix, stowed their gear in the back of Felix's ancient Suburban parked in the driveway of his and Stella's stone-colored ranch house, one of many similar homes, all of them various shades of grey and beige, colors echoed in the pebbles that substituted for grass in their small front garden, and climbed into the front seat.

Ray's flight had gotten in late so he didn't get a good look at his friends' house but he was kind of surprised, not imagining either of them would choose a house in a new development however upscale. Over a glass of merlot, the three of them spread across matching face-to face concrete-colored couches which made the undersides of Ray's thighs itch, he'd said something he can't now recall about them living in a nondescript housing development, and Stella had said, pouring an inch more wine into Ray's glass, "There's something to be said for living in a place where everything is brand new. And besides," she'd added, "there's something to be said for being invisible," a comment that at the time he'd thought was a joke.

He'd looked at her, her luxurious dark curls, her pale breasts just topping the curve of the neckline of her black t-shirt like cappuccino foam, the long silver chain earrings the ends of which played at skimming her shoulders, and said with a laugh, "You could never be invisible."

STELLA HAD SQUEEZED HERSELF in between her husband and Ray. The fit was moderately tight, but they'd decided they found the arrangement preferable right now to any of them sitting in the back, alone. The empty rear seat belonged to Olivia's ghost.

Maybe he should be sitting back there for a trip that the four of them had taken many times together. He's been on intimate terms with Olivia's ghost ever since she died of cancer, almost two years ago. It feels as if it was last week. He doesn't feel sorry for himself, and he doesn't feel deserted. He hasn't even wept, except when his wife had been in pain. It does feel as if she's with him now more than she was when she was alive.

In spite of how perverse that seems to most, he likes it. Ray's made no effort to leave Olivia behind and "make a new life," or all sorts of versions of that thought, as his few friends and his therapist Dr. Blankfein had suggested.

"I'm respecting my personal mourning speed," Ray had told him, thinking Blankfein a New Age idiot who might appreciate that way of putting it. "I'll make an effort to meet a new woman when it feels right."

But Ray suspected it might never feel right. The thought of trying to meet someone to be intimate with was terrifying and sickening. He'd just fallen in with Olivia somehow, as you do when you are young and don't think too much about what's happening, and how. Olivia had made most of the moves anyway.

He's known Felix and Stella since they were rookie teachers at The University of Texas at El Paso, while Ray was also getting his PhD in geology. They'd managed to convince him that a huge change of scene from his current teaching at MIT would be the best thing for him. But so far, seeing Stella and Felix has only made Olivia more alive for him, as she shared all his life during those years in El Paso.

Ray felt nauseous, a symptom of claustrophobia, from the proximity of his friends' bodies, and his fear of this visit. He shifted around on the already hot fake-leather seat, feeling that the front seat was much too tight for all of them.

"Got enough room?" asked Stella, shoving over towards Felix as far as she could.

Instead of saying he needed space, or telling them it was all a mistake and he's got to go home immediately, he wiggled in place and put his finger in a cut in the plastic seat near his knee.

"I'm fine," he said, watching Felix's tanned slender wrist, as he slipped the key into the ignition with an unconscious ease that made Ray think of sex.

Ray studied his friend. Felix looked the same. Red-faced from over-exposure to the hot southwestern sun, he still looked underfed. Bones showed everywhere—just beneath the tight, ruddy skin of his face and neck, in his shoulders and ribcage, at his elbows and the knee bones that were visible through his jeans, or the unsocked ankles bulging over the tops of his running shoes. He looked like someone who worked out far too much and never had time to eat.

Did he, Ray, look the same as he did years ago, in spite of feeling so different? He checked out his own long legs scissored into the tight space up front.

No matter how thin he got, he was still so soft he felt fat. He hated any form of exercise. His arms, squeezed between Stella and the door, were so white that even though he'd only been out in the sun for about five minutes, he could see his reddish hair looking bright blonde against his newly pink skin.

But some things do change. Ray had been pushing those thoughts away ever since he'd arrived. So young when they'd met, they'd had an uncritical relationship. But now they are solidifying into who they are, whatever, whoever that is. Maybe he didn't want to find out.

"Do you remember Placitas?" Stella asked, leaning away from Ray as Felix negotiated the curvy streets of their neighborhood.

"Of course," said Ray. "Do those friends of yours still live there? The poet and the painter?"

He couldn't recall their names, but Felix and Stella had once taken him and Olivia to visit them. Olivia had fallen in love with their small, whitewashed adobe house with timbered ceilings and a cactus garden courtyard.

"Bill and Pill," said Stella. Pill was her name for Bill's wife Naomi.

"They're still there," said Felix, "though they're talking about moving. Yet they complain that with only their adjunct teaching jobs, they can't afford to move."

Felix runs his right hand over his bald head.

"Californicators is what they call the migrating Californians, gentrifying everything, ruining the north of Albuquerque and the Sandia Mountains for poor poets, and building their huge ugly houses that they call Nouveau Trash."

Was Felix making fun of Bill? Or just being sarcastic?

Stella put her warm dry hand on Ray's knee. He looked out the window at an agave garden. "You remember that day?"

"Yes, of course," he said. "Why wouldn't I?"

"It was quite a while ago—seven—maybe eight years ago—just a few years after you and Olivia got married."

What might have been an ordinary silence became a silence Ray moved about in awkwardly, like an unfurnished house with too much space and nowhere to sit. He sensed Stella wondering whether she should have, once again, mentioned Olivia.

That day at Bill's, after looking at some unusual pale purple irises planted by Naomi, Bill had served them lemon tea in fragile bone china cups on a coffee table made from a thick plank of polished mahogany. Olivia and Bill had laughed about authors' photos, how hard it was for Bill to get one that he and his publisher both liked, and how, nowadays, all authors had to look like models.

"If the goddam photo is so important, why not just publish an entire book of photos of the author and forget about the poetry altogether," Felix had said.

Olivia had laughed. A loud guffaw, something rare for her, her lovely large mouth wide.

That day she wore bright red lipstick, which made her dark brown straight hair seem vampire black, her skin as white as the china cups.

Her eyes were not large, and were set fairly close together. Under her high bangs, cut straight across at least two inches above her dark eyebrows like a child's haircut, her expression often seemed puzzled, or as if she couldn't see well, or was trying to understand something difficult.

Ray recalled the photo on the back of Bill's published book of poetry, the book he had signed for them, and which Ray probably still has, but he didn't remember the poetry. He can see Bill's wide smile, his t-shirt open at the neck in a V, his arms out as if getting ready to hug you.

He wished he could recall what Olivia had said. He wished he'd paid more attention. He knows he tends to recall sensations or the general aura of events rather than exact details, or conversation. Luckily he doesn't write memoir or fiction—he'd be bad at dialogue. But now that Olivia's gone the details seem crucial.

Stella had inched her hand above Ray's knee and pressed. "We're really glad you decided to come."

She'd looked straight into his eyes with her own, almost orange in the sun, and black-lashed. Her dark wavy hair had brushed his cheek.

She was still slightly plump, maybe more so, and curvy. Maybe not the fashion, but to Ray her looks were lush.

He'd felt her warmth, and had studied her tan hand resting lightly on his slender chino-ed thigh, fingers spread like a starfish, radiating heat.

FOUR

This is the valley of the Rio Grande.
You are standing in the hot sun
at the intersection of two roads—one paved,
a yellow line down the middle,
the other dirt, angling off through the cottonfields.

A Cloud of Dust, Halvard Johnson, Dance of the Red Swan

"THERE'S NOT MUCH TO SAY ABOUT THAT," SAYS FELIX.

Ray is startled at the sound of Felix's deep voice, suddenly breaking what has been, except for the hum of the motor and the hypnotic hiss of the tires on pavement, a long reverie.

Absorbed in an inner landscape while registering the brown canyons with sudden pickets of tall saguaros and ocotillos, Ray's lost the thread of their conversation. But he is struck by Felix's gesture—a short arc of his bony hand and wrist, palm downward—that often went with his words.

The thought too is typically Felix, thinks Ray. Felix never made small talk. For him there was never much to be said about anything. It had always taken a long time to find out what was going on with him, and Ray knew that on this trip he'd have to be patient. But during long periods without having seen each other, this had the effect of compressing time so it always seemed they'd just seen each other yesterday.

Oddly enough, though it was Felix who Ray thought of as his friend, Stella was the one he talked to most. Maybe all Felix's news had been obtained from Stella—Ray can no longer tell.

He and Olivia had always thought of Felix and Stella as a ying/yang couple—each totally different from the other in every way that they could see, Stella, dark and voluptuous, in her silver bangles and other ornamentation, Felix, red haired, when he'd had hair, and toned, always in a t-shirt and black jeans.

And now that most of Felix's hair is gone, he appears even starker, as if he's finally gotten rid of every nonessential.

Of the two, Stella is the communicator. In the past he'd often grown impatient with her chatter, as he'd thought of it. But he realizes that Stella's talk isn't always to say something, it's her way of connecting, of generating warmth and intimacy, and now he welcomes her voice.

Strangely, since Ray had arrived at their house, Stella'd been pretty much silent, except for the usual warm greetings and hugs. Felix, with his bottle of wine and some tequila on their glass-topped coffee table, had talked on and on about what seemed his new passion, the plight of migrants crossing from Mexico into Texas and Arizona.

Ray had wanted to ask questions, and to ask Stella more about what was going on before retiring to their small bare guest room with its single bed like a monk's cell, but he never got the chance to grab her alone. And he'd been so tired from his trip he could hardly move or keep his eyes open.

He had to admit that his boredom about the issue didn't help keep him awake, or motivate him to extend himself.

RAY'S REMEMBERING Olivia's favorite trip when they'd lived here, the one they'd called Olivia's run.

They'd drive straight from home in El Paso, starting off at about nine in the morning to Las Cruces, New Mexico, and then on to Albuquerque, stopping at dusty jewelry shops on the pueblos while he and Felix waited outside watching the little boys playing basketball with some crumpled newspaper for a ball, and a bottomless fruit basket nailed to a wall, their feet kicking up the same brown dust that covered their sneakers and their legs. Or to try their luck at one of the new casinos run by some Indian tribe, their lights and gaudy signs rising from the desert looking like huge ocean liners on a calm sea.

They'd slip past Santa Fe and abandon the valley road north for a slower one that wound toward Taos through dry, mesquite and piñon-dotted hills, taking them through Chimayo, where they'd visit the Santuario.

Ray had marveled at those with great faith who left photos of themselves and loved ones pinned, or taped underneath portraits or sculptures of their favorite saints, along with intimate notes telling them about their grave illnesses, and with their wishes for recovery. He'd taken photos of a room full of crutches and canes, supposedly left there by scores of people whose prayers had been answered, and who were able to walk away without their aids.

Olivia saw these shrines as art installations, but all four, unbelievers, felt like voyeurs among those of great faith. Nevertheless, they each scooped a handful of the holy earth into small plastic bags they'd brought, to take back home and keep somewhere, just in case. And Olivia once posted a wish for a baby. Though not religious, they admit to being superstitious.

And now Ray's brought with him some of Olivia's ashes in a similar plastic bag.

They'd head on past Truchas, perched on its spiny ridge, with the sharp peaks of the Sangre de Cristos off to the east, sometimes stopping at one or two of the new art galleries.

Usually they'd make it to Taos just after dark—too late to see more than looming adobe structures at the pueblo on the outskirts.

Even in summer it would be chilly, and they would turn back to town, find a place to eat, and then bed down somewhere in some shabby motel.

Next day they'd head back to Santa Fe, spend a few hours wandering around the neighborhoods and peering over huge vine-covered gates into peoples' courtyards and gardens.

In the evening they'd drive back down the valley, the river a silver ribbon that flashed off the right of the highway.

NOW, BACK IN THE PRESENT, the car seems to be speeding. Ray's forgotten how fast people drive on the open highways here out west. The traffic speeds forward, but Ray can't keep his thoughts from moving backward.

Stella is telling the story of La Llorona, which Ray already knows. Stella had been uncovering and studying the folktales of the Southwest when they'd met, and by now has a treasure trove of them. She enjoyed telling them again and again, changing them around slightly in weird ways.

Ray studies her tan hands resting on her lime capris. Her wavy nutmeg hair smells of something lemony. If she leans into Ray a bit it's so that she doesn't get in the way of Felix's driving.

He's leaning forward, both hands on the wheel, his eyes, except for occasional glances at Stella or Ray, remaining on the road ahead. Always high strung, Felix seems unusually tense.

"La Llorona," Stella continues, "murders her three kids because she is too young to have children. Her husband has either died or left her. She has a handsome suitor, but she can't see him as much as she'd like because three children require a lot of her time. She can't afford a baby sitter and her boyfriend doesn't want to spend time with her if the kids are along. One day, stressed by the crying of the baby, she puts them all into a sack like a litter of kittens, and, hidden by the cottonwoods and salt cedars at the banks of the Rio Bravo, throws them in. At first their terrified screams don't bother her. I'm free, she exults. But later on she heard those screams whenever she attempted to do anything pleasurable. And when she died, God said to her: You've committed the greatest sin when you killed your children. So now and for all eternity you'll roam the rivers of the world, always searching, forever weeping."

"Last time you told this story La Llorona's boyfriend kills the kids," says Felix.

"Never," says Stella. "She has to be the guilty one."

"I like the story better the way you told it last time," says Ray.

Felix turns up the air conditioning and puts a hand over the vents. "The a/c's just about gone," he says.

"First of all," Ray says, "there was no God in your earlier versions. Once you mention God, that brings up many questions for those like me who have no faith.

"What do you care?" Stella asks. "You're not in the story. Does everything you hear or read have to mirror you—your experiences or your beliefs? It's about people who do believe in a god of some kind."

"A god who casts spells? Who punishes bad acts?" Ray says.

"You may not believe in God, but you have faith," says Felix.

Ray studies his knees, much closer together than if Stella wasn't pressed so close, and thinks for a moment.

"Right now I don't think I have any faith," he says. "Though maybe we should define faith. I have neither religious faith, nor general faith. I have no faith that things will turn out good, or faith in the future, or faith in our President. Or faith that our country will ever be anything but an oligarchy."

Felix laughs. He doesn't laugh out loud often, but when he does the volume is surprising.

"You sound like Stella, picking everything apart until things become so complex and all you know is how you can't possibly be left with any answer that isn't still questionable."

Stella pouts. "Well I like to think things out, Felix. And I communicate. Which is more than I can say for you."

Were they always like this? Ray can't recall. Without Olivia here as his social buffer he's paying much more attention. He pushes the car's sun visor to the side. His sunglasses are in the trunk.

"Here's how I remember the story," he says, to please Stella, who he recalls, enjoys rewriting these stories endlessly, uncovering various meanings.

Ray's delighted by her broad smile, and that he's pleasing her. He takes a breath and begins: "La Llorona is happily married, and has three gorgeous kids. Two boys and a girl, one of them still an infant. Tragically her husband dies from a work-related accident."

"At a *maquiladora*," adds Felix.

"At a *maquiladora*," says Ray. "And La Llorona, along with taking care of three kids, has to look for a job."

"Because," adds Stella, "there's no pension or reimbursement for the families of workers who are injured or killed at work."

"This was getting to La Llorona," continues Ray, "and it wasn't doing the kids any good. At work one day she meets a guy, handsome and charismatic, with thick black hair and a mustache, who is great in bed and wonderful with the children, reading to them and taking them fishing. The kids, after a short spell of acting out, grow to love him too."

"Yeah, so what now? Is that the new ending? The required happy ending for Americans?" asks Stella, poking Ray in his side as best she can with no distance for leverage.

"You can't accuse me of happy endings," says Ray. "No, I'm not finished." He pauses a moment, then goes on, "They get married, and are happy for a while. But the stresses of family life slowly get to him. First they have no time for sex. The kids get sick. Handsome begins to drink. He stays out later and later ..."

"This is trite," says Felix, smiling, beginning to relax, leaning back a bit and driving with one arm around the wheel, his other elbow out the window, which he's opened.

Stella leans forward so that Ray can see her roll her eyes, "Folk stories aren't trite. They're archetypal."

"Trite," says Felix.

"I'm not done," says Ray. "La Llorona, still very much in love, begs him to tell her what she can do to help the relationship."

"Why her," says Stella. "Why should it be only La Llorona who can help the relationship?"

"Because that's the way it was," says Ray. "Now I'm not sure whether he actually tells her she needs to get rid of the kids, or whether she just got the idea that the kids were once again ruining her life, or whether he meant maybe the kids could stay with some relatives for a while—but one day she fixes a picnic with tortillas, *frijoles refritos,* and plenty of soda, and they go to the banks of the Rio Bravo. The oldest boy, who is about seven, figures out that something is wrong and tries to run away. But with a huge effort, La Llorona manages to drown them all."

"I need details," says Stella.

"Ugly details? No. No one wants to see ugly details in a story," says Felix.

"When her children are gone, and they have more time for each other, La Llorona tries to recapture her romantic feelings for her handsome husband but she can't. She's too distraught."

"Distraught?" laughs Stella.

"It is too late," continues Ray. "La Llorona is surprised at how much she misses her kids. Her husband has discovered that he likes drinking, and isn't ready to stop. Whatever was handsome about him now seems ugly. It's clear that what she's done is evil. The only thing she feels is guilt, and longing for her children. She's nearly insane with grief and just roams along the river, her clothes in rags and her hair long and filthy, crying and moaning."

"Okay, that's definitely a gripping version. With no god and no spells," says Stella, pulling a bottle of Poland Spring from the large straw tote near Ray's long running shoes.

"This story disgusts me," says Stella. "It's unbelievable what women will do for men. But it's a lesson."

She hands to bottle to Ray, who takes a gulp.

"Are you still collecting folktales?" asks Ray.

Stella flushes. "I'm still interested … but I've done three collections … and …"

"Stella's trying to write something of her own," says Felix, swigging some water from the bottle Stella's holding up for him.

Suddenly subdued, Stella shoves the spring water bottle back in her bag. Hands clasped in her lap, she says nothing more.

Ray is curious and would love to hear more about Stella's new project, but because of the awkwardness, he remains silent, afraid to press her.

It's not even afternoon, the air is hot and dry, and Ray's already tired. He looks out the window at the mountains, mocha, black and mostly bare, their sharp crags exposed. Patches of cactus, or a scraggy bush here and there, or a small copse of stunted trees in the distance look like mange on a dog.

When he'd first lived in El Paso working toward his degree in geology, the mountains of the southwest were a revelation. So dark, so sharp and so stark, un-softened or smoothed by vegetation, there was no way he could avoid thinking about the earth in its earlier days of heaving, bursting, pushing and folding, and knowing they are still moving. Sometimes he'd look at them and find that he couldn't breathe.

He also appreciates how many varieties of grasses and cacti grow hiding with their subtle olive and grayish colorations that match the dusty earth. He loves their weird shapes. And the silhouettes of the canyons, the bizarre reddish plateaus.

His eyes grow heavy and Stella up against him feels relaxed. He hopes he's not going to be sorry he joined his old friends for this trip. He's determined to make an effort, if not to forget Olivia, then to get out of his rut.

But is this really going to be a trip into the future? Or back into the past, Ray wonders. Or is there any difference?

FIVE

That morning—when the day was new, when the sun slowly touched the sky almost afraid to break it—that morning I looked out my window and stared at the Juarez mountains. Mexican purples—burning.

"Exile," Benjamin Alire Saenz, *The Late Great Mexican Border*,
ed. Bobby Byrd & Susannah Mississippi Byrd

STELLA'S HEAD HAS FALLEN BACK against the seat and she's lightly snoring.

Ray is enjoying the amazing near mid-day sky, a bright flat blue, with small sharp-edged, sculptural cumulus clouds pasted on.

He hopes Stella's head, a few inches from his shoulder, doesn't fall limply over.

Felix is unusually silent and the car seems to be veering, making Ray feel slightly sick. He looks over and sees Felix trying to read a map he has folded in the center of the steering wheel, his eyes moving from road to map and back.

Ray can't bear to watch. He imagines the car going out of control and brakes the floor with his foot.

For one moment it does, swerving close to a narrow shoulder of rocks and dry grass, the right front wheel bumping over the stones. Felix pulls it back immediately.

"Hey," says Ray, feeling as if he's strangling. His fingertips tingle, and sweat tickles near his hairline.

"Hmm," mumbles Stella, before jarring awake with a small jump.

"This is a mistake," says Ray, his voice a croak. He thinks, I've got to get out of here.

"Pull over this minute," orders Stella.

"There's nowhere to pull over to—shoulder's too narrow," says Felix, calm, as if used to Stella in a panic or a rage. Only the muscle near his jaw twitches.

"I'm getting out," says Stella, pushing into Ray, who is between her and the car door as if she can just march through him and exit while the car's still moving.

"I should be driving," she says, realizing she's unable to get out. "He's always doing something else while he drives—phone, maps, reaching for things, reading …"

Ray sits stiffly, squeezed against the door, as far as he can get from this confrontation.

"We're in Mendoza now," says Felix evenly, ignoring Ray's unease and Stella's anger. "I'm pretty sure there's a gas station here, so we can fill up."

Ray doesn't see any sign welcoming them to Mendoza but he takes Felix's word for it. The one street that is Mendoza, Ray sees a restaurant or a bar and two more bars that look permanently shuttered, a bodega with a large For Sale/Se Vende sign across a shattered window, and, yes, a gas station with two pumps. If the rest of the town is any indication, that's probably closed too.

He can also see, without turning his head that Stella, arms crossed over her breasts, is still sulking.

Ray recalls that when there were four of them, they were all surprisingly amiable travelers. Olivia, Ray and Stella enjoyed an improvisational travel style, so planning, scheduling, and navigating fell to Felix, who was more interested in reaching their destinations than anything else. Ray was always happy to be on the move, nearly going into a trance, watching the flow of landscape, the geology—each layer of earth revealed on each mesa, hill or butte, revealed in stripes ranging from pink on through shades of yellow, orange, into the reds, siennas, and umbers.

Despite knowing the names of these layers, Ray cannot read maps. For him the various colored lines, and the tiny names, has no relation to the roads, the spaces and places of the three dimensional world. Or real life.

"Something missing there," Olivia had said about that. She'd also called Ray "passive," because he let Felix take over. But the dynamic had worked for them. At the time he felt hurt, but maybe Olivia was right. He realizes that he is somewhat passive but it doesn't bother him now.

So what's happening? Is Olivia a missing catalyst? Or is something going on with Felix and Stella?

THEY ARE STARVING AND DECIDE to have lunch there in Mendoza, in what seems like the only open cantina. All the tables are empty, as empty as the deserted dusty streets in this tiny town in Texas, not a good recommendation for the food, thinks Ray.

Stella, as if reading his mind, says, "Probably more customers will come later, during *comida.*"

They choose a table on the patio under a corrugated tin awning cantilevered out from the kitchen wall, well out of the sun. The other tables, all covered with bright flowered oilcloth, sit baking on the concrete patio, partially enclosed by a pink painted adobe wall curving around them like a protective arm around a shoulder. A clay planter, large enough for a small tree, with nothing in it but baked earth and dead weeds, sits at one end of the wall, like punctuation.

As if beaten by the molten noon in the short walk from the car to the table, Stella slides limply onto the same bench as Ray, while Felix, alone on the bench opposite, unfurls his map, smoothing it flat on the table with his long fingers the tips of which round over the tops of his fingernails. He seems unfazed by the heat and stands in front of his bench to better study the map in its entirety, fiddling a bit with his new frameless reading glasses he's taken from his shirt pocket.

Ray watches Felix stroke the map gently with two fingers along possible itineraries as if he's blind.

"I'm trying not to get a splinter in my ass," says Stella, pulling out the pale green fabric of her capris, avoiding rubbing against the rough wood of the bench, which Ray can feel through his chinos.

"Okay," says Felix, "how about this?"

Ray's having a hard time concentrating. Truth is, he doesn't much care about the details of the trip. When he feels cool drops of condensation dripping over his fingers, he realizes he's holding his cold bottle of Victoria as tightly as a child grips a comforting toy.

He swigs his beer and tries to relax. In spite of the good supply of bottled water Stella's stashed in the car, Ray's surprised that he's terribly thirsty. All three gulp from their bottles ignoring the pale blue plastic glasses provided.

"We're really glad you're here, Ray," says Stella.

"I'm not here," says Ray.

Stella looks into his grey green eyes. Hers seem almost black now, and piercing, as if she's searching for something Ray doesn't want her to find.

"I'd like to get back to Juarez in time for the bullfight," says Felix. "They usually start around three."

"What?" says Ray. "I don't know … I thought maybe we'd scrapped that idea."

"What makes you think that?" says Stella. "That's why we're all dressed up."

"Then why are we in Mendoza? We have to back track all the way to Juarez."

"It's not that far out of the way," says Felix, "if you think about where the bullring is."

He chugs his beer, his Adam's apple moving up and down as if in reaction to his tight collar. "We've already scrapped Olivia's run for this trip across Texas to Presidio, and from there, downriver to Big Bend, making side trips into Mexico whenever we want, right, then on to Lajitas? So we're pretty loose," says Felix. "For me, anyway."

He smiles broadly, lips thinning as they spread.

"I don't know …" says Ray.

"Come on," says Stella. "We've already decided. The last time we went to a bullfight was on a trip with you and …"

"And Olivia," Ray finishes, dipping a greasy *totopo* into a small dish of dark red salsa, which is so spicy he coughs.

"Let's just make a pact to talk about Olivia freely if she comes up. Otherwise this is going to be a pretty tense, no, horrendous, trip," he says. "Let's face it. She was here. Now she's not."

"You're sure you're ready for that?" Stella asks.

Ray laughs and coughs again. "It's been a couple of years now," he says. "Maybe if I think about her a lot on this trip by the time I get home I'll be purged. Something like bingeing and cleansing." He is sort of joking.

"Maybe you'll find closure," says Stella.

"I hate the word 'closure,'" says Ray, burping. "I don't think there is anything like what people mean by 'closure.'

And I don't want closure. I don't even like closure in the fiction I read.

Stella and Felix both look at Ray, surprised by his vehemence. He smiles at how they look, suddenly at attention, their eyes wide.

"When you are dead you have closure," he says. "But who knows, maybe not."

Felix nods and laughs, and Stella does too, as they make room for the three huge plates the waiter carries, his pale blue shirt glorious against his honey skin, two along one arm and one in his other hand.

"More Victorias, please?" says Stella. "Besides," she says, sniffing her food, "the reason we drove this way and now have to back track a bit is that we are trying to evade whoever Felix thinks is following him."

"What?" says Ray, "What do you mean? Are you serious?" His fingertips tingle and he looks around. He recalls Felix back at the motel, pressed against the wall.

"Oh, don't worry about it," says Stella. "Felix is paranoid."

"Yeah but unless you're totally crazy there's usually something behind feeling paranoid. Did you do something? I mean why would someone want to follow you?"

"Something like what?" Felix asks. "Hey," he says, wiping a bit of the deep red sauce his enchiladas are covered with from the corner of his mouth with a forefinger, "these are unbelievably great."

"Don't change the subject," says Ray.

"It's nothing. I'm always getting into trouble with people. You know that."

Ray thinks, is this true? Was it always true?

Felix wipes his mouth with his finger again, then with the napkin. Some sauce from the napkin gets on his shirt near his pocket.

"I don't remember how you were with people," says Ray, "but you always were a slob."

"Don't you remember that Felix was fired from UTEP?" says Stella, wiping her fork with her napkin before using it.

"Don't think I remember that. Was there some kind of scandal? Was it because he was a slob? Where was I?"

She's silent for a moment, and Ray looks up, interested.

"Nothing that exciting," she says. "The Dean hated him."

"The Dean hated everyone," says Ray.

She says, looking at her dish, "Mexican food looks so disgusting. All this gooey stuff all over, everything covered with melting cheese and white crema. Everything runs into everything else." She cuts into one of her enchiladas with a fork, checking out the shredded chicken. "Mexican food has no boundaries."

"Do you?" asks Felix, smiling. Grimly, thinks Ray.

When he looks at Stella to see how she's reacting, she seems miles away, staring into space, running a finger around the mouth of her beer bottle.

THE GAS STATION JUST DOWN THE STREET, squat, white-washed cinderblock, has a small square window on either side of its door, with two peeling red gas pumps symmetrically arranged in front, the whole looking like a young child's drawing.

Though they'd noted that it was open when they'd stopped at the cantina for lunch, it now appears to be closed. A dingy brown and white goat munches on the one clump of grass next to one of the pumps.

"What the hell," says Felix, looking at his watch. He swings himself up and out of the Suburban in one lithe movement.

"I'm going to take my chance with the bathroom," says Stella. "Maybe I should have gone to the toilet in the cantina. I'd hoped this one would be better, but up close I'm not sure."

Ray decides he can wait, the same decision he'd made at the cantina. He feels unable to cope with the possible overflowing pail of used toilet paper, no toilet paper left on the roll, a sink that has no faucets, and no soap anyway. In Mexico people don't flush paper down their toilets because of poor plumbing. But there's no reason for it in the Texas border towns.

From the car Ray watches Felix stroll back to the pump near the car, shading his eyes with a large hand. He towers over the dark-haired owner or manager of the station. Felix uncaps the tank, and the smaller man drags the hose around toward the back of the car out of Ray's view.

It is very hot and Ray dozes, perhaps for only a minute, and wakes to find Felix next to him, back in the driver's seat, turning the key and pressing the gas. He hears the dry cough of the starter, again and again, like someone trying unsuccessfully to bring up some phlegm.

A younger, taller version of the man who pumped the gas stands on Felix's side of the car. Ray can only see his yellow shirt now as he moves closer to Felix, who rolls down his window all the way.

"What's wrong," says Ray. "Where's Stella?"

The taller gas station man raises their hood and peers inside. Ray watches a tattoo on his cinnamon forearm that is blurry and looks self-administered, move back and forth with his flexing muscle as he fiddles with a wire or something, and indicates that Felix try again.

Which he does, again and then again, until the smell of gasoline catches in Ray's throat. "You've flooded the carburetor," he says.

Stella, her face flushed and her hair in front wet, as if she'd dipped her head into a sink full of water, gets in next to Ray, who moves over towards Felix, but trying not to get in his way. His knees are nearly at face level.

Up close the tall man's skin looks like bronze leather, as he adjusts something under the hood with a small wrench. No one can see what he's doing and not one of them cares enough to get out of the car, which is partly in the sun, and is stifling. They know it's worse outside.

"Try it," shouts the garage man from behind the hood, still raised.

"Right," says Felix, not expecting much. He turns the ignition, presses the gas, and the motor hums. Felix and Ray look at each other, surprised.

"Mexicans can fix anything," says Stella. "I'll be so glad to get out of here."

"Amen," says Ray.

Felix opens his door as the garage man slams the hood. "Thanks," he says, searching his tight pants pocket for his wallet. "How much do I owe you?"

Stella shoves her straw tote on Ray's hot feet. "Watch Felix pay this guy far too much. He's so saintly."

The man wipes his hand on a filthy rag. "A hundred fifty bucks," he says.

Felix laughs. "What?"

The man doesn't smile.

"What did you do?" says Felix. "Move a wire or something? We're very grateful—but what, it took you about four minutes."

"It's not the time. You're paying for my expertise." He speaks perfect English slowly and carefully, with just a hint of Spanish accent. He puts both of his thumbs in the waistband of his stained forest green very loose slacks.

"This is extortion," says Felix.

"I could have made you sit here for four hours pretending to wait for some special part for your car. Instead I'm being honest."

Felix mumbles, "Honest," and shakes his head. Then he raises his hand as if surrendering, and points to the gas station.

"What do you think he's doing?" asks Ray.

Stella doesn't answer for a moment, then, "I have no bloody idea what he's doing. Probably paying the guy, but inside, so we don't see." She wipes her hairline with the back of one hand.

Before long Felix is back, smiling. "Shove over," he says to Ray.

"Well? Stella asks.

"I gave him a twenty, which I think is fair," says Felix, raising and lowering his cramping shoulders.

"He was right about being an expert—at extortion," says Stella.

"Well he did exploit our ignorance of car engines," says Felix.

"How did you get him to take only twenty?" asks Ray, wondering if Felix is lying in order to avoid a conflict with Stella.

Felix slams his door and feels for his seatbelt. "I made him an offer he couldn't refuse," he says.

Ray hopes for something more, or that Stella will pry more information from Felix, but she seems satisfied, or done with the situation.

Mostly Ray has heard that kind of remark in gangster films, usually referring to some threat of violence, or even murder. Maybe Felix is joking? His friends are definitely not gangster types. Or are they?

He wants to see Stella's face, to see what she's thinking, so he turns toward her. But she's so close he can hardly see her. She's leaning her head against the back of the seat, which is pre-headrest era, and her eyes are closed. Her eyelids seem swollen. Ray leans back to study the long graceful line of her jaw and neck, the damp hair that curls around her ear. A tiny gold hoop glints among the dark tendrils. Ray is so close to Stella he can make out three other tiny holes along the edges of her rosy earlobe.

SIX

*The knowledge that the bull can be fooled into targeting a
cape instead of the man manipulating it, is, of course, central
to the* toreo *and the chances of any matador's survival.*

L. Kennedy, *On Bullfighting*

THAT AFTERNOON THEY WAIT ON A LONG LINE to buy the
more expensive *boletos* for seats in the shade. Though the
bright hot streets outside the bullring and the plaza in front
of the large church across the street are empty, the *corrida de
toros* is packed, bustling and noisy.

"Where did all these people come from?" Stella asks.

Along the concrete uphill path to the arena there are
two mariachi bands, one group in black suits embroidered
and sequined in silver, and the other in fancy white suits
with black and gold designs, both groups playing different
songs at the same time, to Ray's ears adding up to a kind of
energizing noise.

Many in the crowd wear dress shirts, or *guayabera*, and
quite a few women are dressed elaborately in bright dresses, or
colorful skirts and blouses, some holding colorfully patterned,
or white umbrellas to ward off the oppressive sun.

They talk loudly, and push into Ray, who feels as if he's
walking a ramp, as the bulls do, and will soon be in the center
of the arena, where everyone can watch him die.

This *plaza de toros* is enormous, with row upon row of concrete seating surrounding a huge sand circle—a Roman amphitheatre. Though they've come early they can hardly push their way through adults and kids who are shouting, talking, eating, and drinking from plastic cups or plastic bags closed around fat straws.

Ray's surprised to see so many children, some wearing faded logo t-shirts and jeans, some little girls in fancy tulle and silk dresses, their long hair braided or held smooth in colored barrettes. He's never noticed the children before at the few bullfights he's been to. He can't imagine American parents taking their young children and toddlers to bullfights, but these kids seem prepared for a celebration, rather than for horror. Small boys who look as young as seven or eight are hawking soft drinks, or peanuts.

Eventually they find room enough for three, which, in spite of their *sombra* tickets, are partially in the sun. And will probably be more so in a while, thinks Ray. There are plenty of seats at the top of the amphitheatre but Stella insists on being close to the action.

He throws the blue plastic covered foam cushion that Stella has rented for fifty pesos each under his butt.

"Corona, Corona, Corona, Corona," shrieks a vendor into Ray's ear.

The sun's glare, is almost like sound to Ray, like a saxophone high note, obtrusive, even painful. He may also be allergic to this harsh Mexican sun, the glare of which, through the car's windshield, has raised a red and itchy pinprick rash on the backs of his hands.

All the heat of the day appears focused telescopically enhanced on the sand and concrete of the *corrida*. The animal smells, the people, the sweat, the sweetish smell of caramel corn, the barbeque meat and the cigar smoke, are sickening. Ray's headache is returning too—he feels its stab behind his left eye, and knows it will progress to encompass his entire head, which will feel as if its in a vise, his blood beating like a hammer.

On the other hand, Felix seems elated, energized, jumping up and working his way through throngs to bring them cold beer, nuts, and bright orange fritos covered with red paprika.

They all hunch and dodge the flowers, jackets, bottles and half-eaten sandwiches hurled down into the ring. Someone's cane just misses Ray's head. His butt aches in spite of the cushions.

"Oh, god, the actual bullfight might not start for another hour or more," Ray says.

"This is the actual bullfight," says Felix. "This is all part of the whole ceremony."

Ray inadvertently presses this thigh against Stella's, and immediately pulls it away. She's fanning herself with some folded piece of paper or flyer, her cup of piss-colored Corona on the concrete floor next to her sandal.

People are settling down finally, the noise less oppressive. Ray can see, way across the stadium and near the top row, the judge, who may be the mayor, dressed in a shiny suit, surrounded by a bevy of local beauty queens, ravishing, dark-eyed, long-haired teens wearing sparkly rhinestone crowns on their shiny tresses. The mariachis in their fancy jackets play various fanfares as matadors, picadors and various *banderillos* troop around the ring in their glistening attire.

A wave of nausea, and everything suddenly seems cheesy, cheap and amateurish. Ray looks over at Stella, but she is looking straight ahead, rapt.

"I love this," she says.

"This what?" asks Ray.

"The ceremony, everything," she says.

"Like Hemingway?"

"The hell with Hemingway," she says. "Great story writer, but his novels are bullshit. Stilted, over-romantic."

She leans forward to avoid the knees of the tall man behind her. "No. I am thinking of Lorca, who followed the *corrida* and who had himself carried through the streets of Granada, costumed and bloodied as if he were a matador who had received a fatal goring."

Ray laughs. "Are you kidding?" He looks, to see if she's smiling. "You don't find that to be stilted and over-romantic?"

Stella smiles. "Lorca redefined the concept of *duende,* which is necessary if you want to understand the passion for the bullfight."

Ray tries to resurrect what he recalls about *duende.* "An imp or poltergeist?" he asks. "What does that have to do with bullfights?"

"Could be a goblin, or any malign spirit," Stella says. "But *duende* also carries the contradictory suggestion of being in contact with a higher self, the one who understands the tragic underside of the life force." Stella sips from her plastic cup of beer. "Maybe, rather than evil, or evil genius, *duende* is sadness, or the source for any work of art that is dark. A reminder that destruction has a close relationship with creativity."

Stella carefully places the fragile cup of copper liquid back on the concrete next to her foot. Her toenails are polished dark red, and some of the scarlet has cracked off.

A burp, then Felix's voice: "In spite of the struggle," says Felix, digging his forefinger into Ray's leg for emphasis, "the bullfight shows again and again that we are all animals. It's the same old thing—will the human, with skill, luck and courage, win over the dark force, the animal, the evil spirit? Will high culture, art and beauty, win over our animal natures, our smells, our fetid rank exudings, our lizard brain, our darker natures? The bull is always killed in this ritual sacrifice no matter what the matador does or doesn't do well."

He lifts his cup high so the dregs of his drink can flow into his open mouth. He burps again. "The problem is we now know the bull is just an animal, and not a symbol. And that our dark and animal natures are winning."

Felix places his empty beer cup inside the other empty cup near his large white running shoe, which is marked with a caligraphy of scratches and scuffs.

"Not always winning," says Ray.

He has also finished his beer and wishes he hadn't. It feels as if it's collected in his diaphragm area, and with his slightest movement he hears it slosh.

People squeeze in front of them, stepping on their feet, attempting to pass along their row toward the snacks, or friends, or whatever. He should get up to let them pass, but he fears that if he moves too much he will barf all over them.

A heavyset man clumsily bumps into their backs as he shoves his way to the aisle in the row above them. He nearly falls over on Felix, who jumps out of his seat, turning, red-faced.

Ray's afraid Felix might start a fight with the swaying obese Mexican man who smells like he's already had too much to drink, so he jumps up too, spilling Stella's beer all over her foot.

The Mexican safely past, Felix remains standing, and adjusts the baseball cap he's wearing to protect his shiny head, pushing the visor more directly over his eyes, causing them to disappear into shadow.

Ray, relieved, follows Felix's gaze around the arena, which Ray thinks is furtive rather than curious.

"Is someone really following Felix?" he asks Stella. "Who would want to follow him? What's going on?"

Stella leans into Ray. He feels her shoulder press into his upper arm, warm. "You never know with Felix," she says, wiping beer off her foot with an old tissue.

Still leaning against him, she whispers, "I'm feeling very bloodthirsty today."

"What?" asks Ray. Stella always surprised him. She rarely answers his questions directly, and he's off-balance with her most of the time. He can't figure her out. She lacks consistency, maybe, or some kind of gestalt. Perhaps because of her wild hair, her flip-flop style handmade leather sandals, all her bracelets, she seems to him like an out-of-time hippie. But what she says rarely goes along with that image. He can't figure out what her principles are, if she has any. Perhaps she's simply brilliant, able to be totally flexible and original about everything. There's something pragmatic about her; she's totally lacking in sentiment or sentimentality. But more—a selfishness that he admires, even envies, but doesn't like. A touch of cruelty that always startles him.

All heads turn toward the gate silently prepared for the entrance of the bull that the loudspeaker has announced is named Bruno. Still, they jump in their seats, startled, when the bull, black and smaller than Ray's expected, but far wilder, gallops in and charges around the ring as if his body can find a way out of his predicament. Slowing, he charges again and again at the *barerra*, the barrier protecting the matador, his horns bashing into the wood, resonant thuds that resound through the arena, giving the illusion that the concrete stands they are seated on, are shaking.

The matador, Ulysses Tresguerras, in spangled sequined blue jacket with black and pink embroidery, his sparrow thin legs encased in tight black jodphurs, pink tights below the knee, watches the *peones,* who are dragging their capes in front of Bruno, trying to discern his particular form and temperament.

Ray is sure this matador, so thin he's almost invisible when he turns sideways, is alarmed because Bruno doesn't seem to have any form. He either ignores the capes or runs around wildly kicking up sand.

Ray keeps his eyes on the bull's feet, or the red, purple and back ribbons of the *bandilleras,* the magenta capes, with their yellow linings, for if he watches the bull's face, already showing signs of panic, eyes rolling, mouth open, he won't be able to bear it.

When this series of tests appears to be over, the mayor, or whoever is up in the stands, waves a white hanky to herald the proper beginning.

Stella leans into Ray, whose skull feels as if it's lifting with each slam of the bull against the barrier. The crowd roars, including Felix, and Stella, on Ray's other side, standing now.

Bruno, who seemed so small for a bull, kicks and tosses his head, muscles jumping in the black gloss of his sides and back.

The *peones* dart and hide behind the wooden screens, the deceivers that fool the bulls, four placed evenly around the ring, to provide refuge for the toreros. The crowd shouts its approval.

Right behind Ray a tourist, who looks American, laughs. He probably enjoys that these people and the bull, seem out of control.

"Fucking gringo," says Stella, turning her head her hair tickling Ray's face.

Tresguerras tries his best to chain passes around Bruno's movements. Straight-legged he edges toward the bull and attempts, each limb tight, to control the animal's motion, to end each sequence with a finishing pass, which should fix the bewildered bull in place and allow the matador a safe retreat. Each pass comes perilously close to chaos.

The noise around Ray is chaos too—no concentrated "Olé"s—but an aggravated inattention.

Now feeling too sick to respond to anything, Ray is cold in spite of the hot sun, and nauseous. The vibration has moved into his body where it's turned into chills.

The picadors get to work, leaning hard on their *varas*. The cape work between pics is slight, while the crowd grumbles, then whistles as the blood begins to well thickly over the bull's *morillo*.

When Ray next looks up Bruno has stumbled to his knees. He can hear Stella's breath catch as the bull struggles up, and stands absolutely still.

Ray wonders why he identifies with the bull rather than the torero.

The *banderilleras* now find it hard to make him charge them. They place their sticks gingerly, with little response from the audience.

Tresguerras takes the *muleta* to face a sluggish, staggering bull. He advances his leg behind the *muleta* to provoke a charge, slips farther and farther forward, but is unable to create the response he needs.

Finally he takes the killing sword, the *muerte*, with its special artery-slicing curve, and pale and anguished-looking, sites for the kill. The sword goes into its hilt but doesn't quite find its mark. Bruno stands, urinating helplessly, sunken-headed, unaware that he is dead.

The *peones* use their capes to back the bull against the *barrera*, and there Tresguerras uses a heavy straight sword to deliver a coup de grace to the bulls neck, severing its spinal cord. The bull drops as if shot, and the matador, grim-faced, walks away. The crowd, including Felix, groans loudly in Ray's ear.

From the gringo in the back: "This sucks!

THE DAY HAS A BRUTAL RHYTHM, Stella becoming more rigid, stiff as a stick beside him, Ray becoming sicker, holding the late afternoon sun at bay with a piece of cardboard from some refreshment container held up to his head, as the next matador, the twenty-four year-old Roberto Morales Contreras, enters the ring wearing rich egg-yolk gold, with orangey-pink stockings.

His bravery looks faked as he confronts Extremeno, a mad black and umber massive primeval or prehistoric creature.

Stella murmurs, "Uh oh."

Contreras is kneeling in front of the Gate of Fear in preparation for a maneuver that has already stilled the plaza—a more than insane pass where the matador has to guess roughly how and where the bull will emerge from the gate, fix himself in a position of immobile vulnerability, and then, as the beast first breaks into the light, must swing the capote, one-hand over his head and to the side, causing the bull to either crash past him, or to leap his shoulder.

Though he has only seen this once before, Ray knows there's a good chance he'll get his face kicked in, or worse.

Contreras shifts a little on his knees, the strain telling, beginning to produce a fatal doubt—the crowd is relatively silent. But then the huge Extremeno is out—the pass elegantly completed—Contreras walks into the ring buoyantly, his flat black shoes seeming to float above the ground, while Extremeno gallops his five hundred and eighty kilos across alien sand.

Contreras, in his sunny gold jacket with black embroidery, black jodphurs, and peach tights, begins to perform, fanning and flaring his hot pink capote out into whipping *remates*, the two-handed media veronica which lifts and spins evenly from the matador's waist, revealing the capote's bright yellow underside. The bull stops in his tracks, rapt as the crowd is by the gorgeous passes.

The picadors however, are brutal. The crowd, now completely with Contreras, call out for him to stop them. He draws the now bleeding animal away into beguiling passes, but soon the bull's spirit seems broken. He will no longer charge the padded horses, but stares at them, panting, as if to say, Ray thinks, kill me, I'm done playing your game.

Contreras takes risks with the *muleta*, getting the bull engaged again, till it nearly catches him several times. The plaza seems to contract around Contreras and his work.

Then, while he attempts a chest-high pass to the right, his feet catch against each other delaying his retreat for just a millisecond too long.

And directly in front of them, maybe thirty feet away, Ray sees the matador's body jerked and hoisted into the air, shaken and bounced above the massive black head, his limbs turning and flapping against his will. His noiseless grimace, from a distance, looks like a smile.

Ray feels as if he's been unconscious for a moment. His cardboard sunshade is on the ground; the sun beats his head.

Thin female shrieks and screams mix with groans, and a single punch of breath from the plaza.

Contreras is down, flattening himself to the sand as the bull nuzzles in, trying to find a way to lift him again, and the *peones* leap forward, forgetting any danger to themselves, caping the animal off and to the right.

As soon as they can they pick Contreras up, sitting upright, cradled between two men who carry him off to the Infirmary Gate, in what seems a terribly primitive human embrace. His face is white, and below his waist he is entirely soaked in his own blood, his shining *talleguilla* now a slick crimson.

The crowd applauds him as he leaves, strange, because isn't this a failure? But maybe this is a respectful farewell.

The voice behind Ray says, "What the fuck?"

Stella stands, says, "Oh my god."

Felix is half out of his seat, in an awkward position, as if he's been suddenly shot.

"I have to leave," whispers Ray, rising unsteadily, hand over his mouth. He looks up at the stands. It seems impossible that he will every get out of there with the crowd milling, roaring.

Stella presses her body against his side, hot against him. He feels her heart pounding and smells the clean astringent citrus of her hair clearing his head for a moment. Sweat beads under the curls near her ear.

His sweat is dripping down his back, feeling almost like a waterfall. He's hardly aware of Stella taking his hand.

"What's happening to Contreras?" asks Felix, seeming miles away, his voice disappearing into the roars, his slender body standing erect trying to see something.

But it isn't over yet. Another matador must come out and finish the bull. Whoever he is, he goes quickly for the kill, placing the sword poorly. The bull stands there, its horns thick with human blood, pelt thick with its own blood which drips onto the sand, strings of saliva hanging in long strands around his grey tongue that hangs limply from his open mouth.

Swaying their capes at either side of the bull, the *peones* perform the *rueda de peones*, to make him shift his head from side to side, and hopefully work the sword through an artery as it moves.

This has no effect, and for a moment the toreros just stare at a bloody, dismally tenacious bull. They might almost be kids, mystified by something large they have set in motion but now lack the power to control.

Ray sways, and closes his eyes so he won't see the blood mixing with the sand down below and breathes through his mouth to mitigate the animal smells in the air, too hot, too thick, revolting. He's dizzy. Everything spins.

Finally the *descabello* comes and the bull finally sinks. There's not much reaction from the crowd—it was not an exciting, challenging heroic death but was sort of sad and disgusting.

Ray leans against Stella, who is still pressed to him. He wavers but remains standing. He tries to wipe away the sweat tickling the sides of his face and his upper lip, but is surprised when he realizes that the hand he raises to his mouth is Stella's.

SEVEN

*Bullfighting is the most difficult art form in the world. You are
required to create a work of art spontaneously with a semi-
unknown medium (the bull) which can kill you, in front of one
of the most critical audiences. And all it leaves is a memory.*

John Fulton, Spain's first U.S. matador

RAY FEELS THE COLD EDGE OF THE PORCELAIN TOILET along
the backs of his thighs as there's no toilet seat.

It cost two pesos to get into the concrete walled *sanitario*, and as
he begins to feel the relief of having rid himself of his watery bowels,
he can't stop picturing Extremeno's black eyes, the one remaining
ribboned *banderillo* hanging off Extremeno's neck with an air of
degenerate rakishness, as the bull, no fight left, is slaughtered.

He studies his sneakers, practically buried in the crumpled
mass of toilet tissue, a few modest folds of which were handed
to him by the man who'd collected his pesos at the door, and
wads of which overflow the white plastic basket in his stall.

When he leaves the stall, desperate to wash his face and
hands even with cold water, he tries both faucets, one of which
turns with a loud squeak, but there's no water. There are only
about six stalls in this bathroom and people are already heading for them, a line forming at the entrance.

He feels weak, as if he has nothing left inside, not even
flesh and organs. Eventually he finds Felix and Stella, milling
in a crowd waiting for news of the matador.

Dizzy, Ray squats in a triangle of shade near a wall, away from the mob. No one makes an announcement, but the knots of spectators slowly unwind and move funereally toward the exits.

RAY WANTS TO SIT in the back of the Suburban, but Stella won't have it, as if she's afraid he'll be horribly lonely. He's beginning to feel as if he's her special project. She points to the backseat which is full of some of the things they'd acquired—a woven poncho/wall hanging, a large sombrero, a striped straw purse, and some other junk including some disgusting candies that look like colored cardboard circles, and taste like them.

He sits in the front, in between them, feeling claustrophobic. What if he needs to get out in a hurry?

"I guess if a matador is killed, the rest of the show doesn't continue," says Felix, the only one who feels like talking.

"Let's find a motel," says Ray. "I'm beat."

"Do you know the origins of the word 'gringo'?" asks Felix, driving out of the parking area, and farther into this scraggly area of Juarez, with it's car repair shops and tire stores, its lots of *yonke*, and secondhand clothing stores, with their various dresses and pants hanging from awnings like so many ghosts.

No one answers.

There will be a few more hours of daylight, but Ray is relieved to see the deep gold of the late afternoon light, the long shadows. He loves this time of day wherever he is, but today he's pleased to count almost two days of this trip done.

He moves over a bit so Felix can scratch his bare ankle.

"Felix knows a lot of facts," says Stella, as if it's a fault.

"I'd like to know," Ray says.

"One Castilian dictionary says it's a perversion of the Greek, *griego*, meaning any foreigner. Or maybe it comes from the French, *degringolade*, meaning, downfall. Whatever, the term gringo always had a derogatory edge. In current dictionaries that list the word it's defined as 'one who doesn't speak the language intelligibly, or with good accent.' My favorite is that it's a corruption of the word *chingado*, one who is fucked."

"Okay, what's going on between you two?" asks Ray, after a long, uncomfortable silence. "Are you trying to hide something from me? Is all this just so I won't think about what's going on with you?"

"I'm not trying to hide anything," says Felix, taking both hands off the wheel and spreading his fingers.

"Something's going on—something with you, Felix—like why would someone be following you?"

"I'm not hiding anything. Ask me anything," says Felix.

"I just did," Ray says, looking at Felix, whose eyes remain on the road. He swings his sun visor down, and checks his mirror, but says nothing.

Stella looks at Felix too, as if waiting for an answer to something Ray is sure she knows.

He feels sick again, and doesn't think he can deal with this. His head pulses painfully, echoing through his body. He lets his head fall back, closes his eyes, and studies the bright scarlet insides of his eyelids.

"I'm involved in some border issues," says Felix. "As I said before. Nothing mysterious."

Stella says something—he isn't hearing details. About the Mexican women murdered in Juarez. Other things. Her voice is a pleasant buzz. He is missing some important information, but isn't capable of caring.

He can taste the way the air used to smell when the copper company's chimneys spewed polluted smoke. A taste, a smell that was everywhere, and which they all took for granted.

In fact he doesn't recall that any of them were especially political in the old days. Mexico was Mexico. They went there sometimes to drink. And to find a cheap dentist. Texas was Texas. The border was the border. There were poor people on both sides of the border—but what did that have to do with them? Yes, they were poor too, but they knew it was temporary. He flushes, embarrassed by what he recalls.

And now it seems Stella is defending Felix. From him.

Ray needs a bathroom again, but he's dizzy and too sick to do anything but breathe.

"You can't hide from politics," says Felix. He takes a swig from the huge water bottle Stella passes to him and the car swerves a bit, as he holds it out to Ray.

"Uh, uh," mumbles Ray.

"Hey, slow down," says Stella.

"There's no one around here," says Felix.

"I don't want to spend six months in a Mexican jail," she says, her hair suddenly ignited into dark flames by the burnt orange sun.

RAY'S WOKEN A FEW TIMES wrapped in a scary fog. He realizes that he's back in the motel in Juarez, with its familiar mildew-and-cigarette smells.

He recalls the rest of the trip in the car, listening to his teeth chatter, and trying to keep from breaching Stella's space, while listening to them argue. At one point, he recalls, he'd argued too, when Felix accused him of being passive and ignorant of all the horrors going on that need to be changed.

"Passivity and ignorance are evil," Felix had said. "At some point we have to ask ourselves what kind of country we are living in. What kind of people are we? What kind of country do we want?"

He remembers saying that he is political, and that he could have been making a high salary working for an oil company as a geologist, instead of a professor. And that no one person can fix all the ills in the world, and that they were being simplistic about something very complex. And even while he was arguing, wondering what difference any of it made, what difference anything made, and why bother talking.

Now he's amazed that he'd been defensive. It isn't like him. He must have felt ashamed, guilty.

He recalls the heat of the brown plastic seats, and the afternoon sun burning a triangle through his pants right into his thigh, which had no room to move. He remembers Stella, head turning away, staring out the window as if she's not there. He'd wondered what she was thinking, as he'd watched the wind blow her ponytail, an escaped curl flapping at her pale cheek.

HE KNOWS STELLA HAS BEEN IN HIS ROOM—she's been reading to him. Though he's tried to pay attention, he kept falling into a weird state, as if the boundary or border between being asleep and being awake has been erased. Still, he was soothed by Stella's new whispery voice that made no conversational demands, but reminded him of being read to as a child by his mother.

As Ray begins to spend more time awake, he wonders where Felix is. Ordinarily, wouldn't Felix be checking on his friend, keeping him company, even bringing him the chicken soup that is now cooling on the small night table, the odor of which is finally becoming more appetizing than revolting?

Thinking about it, he remembers Felix as the more nurturing of the two. Though he recalls once when Olivia wasn't feeling well, he came home from the University and found the two of them, Olivia and Stella, next to each other in the bed he shared with Olivia, so close that the rosy, voluptuous Stella's wild reddish hair nearly overwhelmed his tiny, translucent wife, under the one thin blue quilt. They gave him the creeps, so close and laughing at something—maybe at him. Was it the contrast between the two? Or was he shocked at their intimacy? At the time he didn't try to figure it out—but the image remains sharp as a color photo.

He smells himself, his sickly unwashed sweat and is suddenly ashamed. What a pain he's turned out to be, getting so sick right at the start of his visit. He props himself on the limp motel pillow and devours the soup, made from a package of dehydrated ingredients, but delicious all the same.

Leaning back, perspiring from his effort but feeling stronger and more awake, he can't help wondering whether Stella is trying to seduce him. Even worse, maybe Felix is in on it.

Or perhaps Ray's become different somehow, projecting a seductiveness, an openness to women, to sex, that he doesn't feel. Olivia's death has made Ray more attractive, more exciting to women. A recently dead wife seems to have transformed him from nerdy to needy, suddenly unaccountably desirable. But needy is the last thing Ray wants to be.

Since Olivia's death Ray finds it hard to know how to act in many situations. He realizes that he has little awareness of how he's behaving and why, and how he might appear to others. Some major portion of his identity is unrecognizable, or is gone. His marriage was like a transparent protective coating, like a caul. Without his wife he is raw and exposed.

He recalls the light pink snake they'd almost run over the other day—could it only have been yesterday? They'd stopped in time to watch how the pale snake crawled out of, and then rapidly away from, its own transparent skin.

EIGHT

No border town is anything but a border town,
just as no waterfront is anything but a waterfront.

Raymond Chandler, *The Long Goodbye*

RAY WAKES SLOWLY TO A LOW MOAN. Barely conscious, he wonders whether he's had a nightmare, has been groaning, or trying to yell. It is dark—even though the motel room is always dark—but the thin line of light around the plastic-lined drapes is missing.

He feels much better, except for a sensation of weakness, and a disgusting rotten taste in his dry mouth. No headache.

He wonders whether he'll be able to go back to sleep, given that he hasn't spent much time awake in the last day or so, when he feels something on his thigh through the thin blanket. He tries to push it away, and then nearly leaps out of bed, fumbling for the light switch.

There's nothing on his bed, but on the carpet beside his bed is an amorphous pile of clothing, or a blanket. Would he undress and leave all that on the floor? Wouldn't Stella have picked it up? He checks, and he is undressed, except for his jockeys.

From the corner of his eye, he sees the mass on the floor move. Is it his imagination, or a residue of vertigo?

Then he realizes it's a blanket, the same color as his, pale blue, and that it's covering something. Or someone.

He hears another muffled groan, and a thin, tan hand emerges—Felix's hand.

His heart beats high in his throat—he feels as though he will choke on it—and a gray curtain lowers over his vision till he thinks he will faint. What's Felix doing on the floor of his room?

He pulls the blanket aside just a bit, not sure whether Felix is even alive, and slowly uncovers just a sliver of Felix's face to see that his thin lips are swollen and dark red with dried blood, and that his cheek under his carved cheekbone is cut and is still bleeding. And the eye that's visible is swollen, and dark.

Ray places his fingers on Felix's neck, and when he feels a steady pulse, he pulls the blanket aside. Felix's clothing has black grease stains and his shirt and slacks are torn.

He moans loudly, and Ray jumps back onto the bed. Then he bends over Felix, who now seems awake, though his eyes are shut. Or can't open.

"What happened, man?"

Felix groans. His mouth is nearly swollen shut too.

"Hey, it's okay," says Ray, gingerly putting a reassuring hand on Felix. "Can you talk?" He puts his face closer.

"Yeah," mumbles Felix, without opening his lips.

"Should I get Stella? I'm going to get Stella," he says, getting up, heart still pounding.

"No, no, it's okay, man." Felix stretches out his armed, tanned and buff, but now covered in scratches. Ray involuntarily jumps.

"Ohhh." Felix turns, and tries to get up. Ray holds out a hand to him.

He sees Felix's face now, his black eye, and the large cut above his opposite eyebrow. And the deep cut on his cheek, his swollen and cut lips.

"What happened?" Ray asks again.

"I couldn't sleep. My back was aching from all the driving."

Ray can't make out the mumbles and bends his head close to Felix's. "So I decided to go running." He wipes his cheek with his finger and looks at it. "Am I bleeding?"

"I guess I went too close to the shoulder. I couldn't see it in the dark. An arroyo. I fell."

Instead of using Ray's arm to hoist himself, Felix falls back. He no longer looks like a pile of dirty laundry but Ray can see that there's blood on Felix's chest, and maybe more on the parts of his body still covered with the blanket. When he closes his eyes for a moment, he looks dead.

"You can tell me the truth," Ray says.

Felix is, or used to be, an athlete. He is a runner. Would he fall into an arroyo? His injuries look like the kind you'd get from a fight rather than a fall. But why would he lie?"

"Is there something you don't want Stella to know?" Ray asks.

Felix doesn't open his eyes.

RAY RUNS OUT IN HIS JOCKEYS, the gravel cutting into his bare feet. It feels sharp, and it hurts, but it's waking him up in a way that feels good. Bent, and breathing hard, he knocks on the door to Stella's room. However long he's been sick has taken its toll, and it's hard to stand. Where is Stella?

Finally she opens the door a crack, then farther, looking sleepy and disheveled, as if she's had a rough dream. Her eyes are swollen, and her hair awry. She's wearing a long t-shirt over underpants that hardly show below the shirt hem. Her legs are pale and surprisingly slender.

"Are you okay? You look like shit. You shouldn't be out of bed." She yawns.

"Come in."

"It's Felix," he says, reluctant to go into her room.

She turns on a lamp. One of the beds is still made and has her and Felix's bags on it, along with bags of snacks, and various other stuff.

"Where is Felix," she asks, surprised that he isn't in bed. Or is she?

"He's in my room."

"What's he doing there?" she asks, pulling out an indigo robe from one of the duffels on Felix's bed, and putting it on. She's left it open, its belt hanging perilously close to the floor.

"He's had an accident," says Ray. "Not to panic. He's okay. I mean he's not in really bad shape ..."

He hears her ragged breathing behind him and guesses she is, like him, terrified.

Yet once in his room, after an intake of breath, and the shock of seeing him on the floor partially wrapped in the blanket, she's quite rough with Felix, turning him to and fro, ignoring his moans of pain, checking out injuries and cuts, almost angry.

Without a word, businesslike, she fills the ice bucket with water, and, too roughly, wipes Felix's cuts and bruises with the threadbare motel washcloth, pulling him from side to side, ripping the blanket off his belly, his legs. So different from the way she'd just taken care of him, Ray, while he was sick and feverish. Perhaps she's exasperated and exhausted by the fallibility of the men she's with.

Ray, still weak, sits on the edge of his bed listening to the sounds of the water being wrung from the cloth as Stella endlessly dips, wrings and wipes. The water becomes pink, then red.

No one says anything. Ray's feet are a few inches from Felix. His legs begin to tremble. He'd love nothing more than to lie down again, fall asleep. But something tells him he needs to remain vigilant.

He'd love to believe that Felix fell into an arroyo. But even if scratched by some bushes, or cacti, where could he have gotten those bruises, those swellings, the black eye? If he fell on one side then his other side would be free of bruises. Yes, there might be a shallow arroyo, a small canal at a road's shoulder, but an arroyo deep enough to break a couple of ribs? Even in Mexico, where you'd pretty much have to watch out for yourself, he doubts the story.

In the past when he crossed the border into Mexico, wherever he crossed, he felt a sense of freedom, possibility, as if anything could happen. But this time, perhaps it was his impending illness, he felt that by crossing that invisible border, stepping beyond all the rational societal laws they were so used to living by, came to depend on, and took for granted, that something was going to happen. And this time it would be something bad.

NINE

If in doubt that today is not your friend, go to sleep and wait
for tomorrow. Then, if it's no better, consider yourself fucked.

Jenny Diski, *Harper's Magazine*, July, 2016

RAY'S RELIEVED TO BE BACK IN TEXAS, though close to the border. At the wheel of the heavy Suburban, he's getting used to the shift. He hasn't driven a manual shift since his first car, a black VW beetle.

He can't see what about this Suburban would be of interest to Felix, now in the middle, his head on Stella's shoulder, drifting in and out of sleep. Stella looks out the window or dozes too.

It's oddly silent except for the drone of the wind, or a whoosh of another car passing. The sky is a bright cyan, and it's cooler than it's been. If it weren't for Felix's injuries, Ray would be relaxed for the first time since he got here.

He's upset that both Stella and Felix had agreed that Felix would be fine without seeing a doctor. Ray thinks that there must be some reason they've made such an irresponsible decision, something they don't want him to know. Related to Felix's political activities that he'd hinted at?

When he got to ask Stella during a moment when he'd caught her alone, she'd just repeated something about a hundred and fifty young girls from the campo who'd come to Juarez to work in the maquiladores, murdered in Juarez and their killer or killers that hadn't been found. And something about corporations not cleaning up toxic waste, and some other stuff. That's all she claimed to know. Nothing new. Not that these aren't serious issues—and there are probably more—but what does Felix have to do with them? And why dangerous? If he's demonstrating, or being civilly disobedient in some way, would someone actually try to kill him? Is he searching for the Juarez killer or killers?

He glances over now and then to check Felix, who, sleeping, is soft, limp, very unlike the Felix Ray knows. His injuries look, if anything, worse than they did early this morning. Now a garish purple and magenta, his bruises have spread, along with swellings that are melting into each other. He should be in bed with ice packs, thinks Ray, but Felix and Stella were determined to move on.

Most of the dried blood's been washed away, and they've dressed Felix in clean clothing—a fresh pale peach long sleeved polo shirt, and pale blue, much-washed jeans. He looks like a small bald naughty bruised boy, dressed up for some event, curled softly into Stella, head on her shoulder, her head now on his.

Ray hadn't realized that being a third person with a couple would be so hard. He either feels ganged up on or marginalized. And guilty for even having these self-serving feelings when Felix is so messed up.

He suspects both of them of keeping crucial secrets from him. This trip no longer has anything to do with Olivia. Right now Ray feels as if he's taking Felix and Stella on a trip, but he doesn't know where they are going, or why.

Ray rests an elbow on the open car window. The Rio Grande is a thin green snake down the canyon on his left. The sun is so hot he can feel his sunburn-in-progress. He likes the idea of the sun burning the rest of his toxic illness out of his system, though he knows there's no medical validity to that. The hot air rushing through his hair, and the sun on his arms makes him slightly lethargic in a comfortable way.

He checks Felix's chest to see that he's still breathing. His sleeping so much is worrisome. Ray can count on the fingers of one hand all the times he's ever seen Felix asleep, even during the years they all lived in El Paso.

Stella's eyes are open now, but she doesn't look at Ray. He enjoys her new inattention to him. But he's pissed too, at her lack of response to this whole situation, and her husband's condition.

"Well," he says, "what are we doing now? Do we just continue our trip this way?" With an elbow he indicates Felix, who appears dead.

He smells Stella's strange scent, maybe her shampoo or her hand lotion, sort of vanilla, maybe some almond, and the sharper, ever present citrus.

Felix moans, and Ray suddenly recalls an image from the dream he was having when awakened by Felix at the motel. He and Stella on some rocky promontory, he's not sure where, but it's not a familiar place. So probably they are traveling. They are fully clothed, in jeans and shirts, but are passionately petting. He remembers noting the smell of her hair even in his dream, and how excited he was, though raw and swollen as if they've been kissing and touching each other for hours. Stella is pushing into Ray, into the granite surface. She's pulled down her jeans and underneath them, her white bikinis, just enough that he can see the top line of dark hair between her legs. The rocks under his back and buttocks hurt, but he can't bear the thought of stopping Stella from pushing down on him with her lush hips, her large round breasts slowly pressing into his chest, nipples first, then the whole soft warmth of them. No longer feeling the pain from the harsh terrain he's aware that he is now hard as granite. As Stella begins to lower herself on him, he moans. The soft sounds of someone in pain. The sounds Felix was making.

Ray looks over at Stella, who is flushed, her dark curls spilling over the back of the seat.

Felix, bald head with its new swellings sliding down Stella's shoulder toward her breast, is dribbling, a thick shiny line of saliva heading toward his chin, looking like a baby that has just finished nursing.

Heart beating too fast, Ray swerves suddenly as something runs in front of the car.

Stella and Felix jolt upright. "Shit," says Stella. "What was that?"

"Sorry," Ray says. "Some kind of lizard, or iguana. I didn't want to kill it."

"No, you'd rather kill us," says Felix, almost unintelligibly.

Ray laughs, but is thinking of himself dreaming of sex with Felix's wife, while Felix lies on the floor next to his bed, a beaten pulp.

Stella studies Felix's mashed lips. "How are your teeth?"

"Teeth?" mumbles Felix. "Not sure I have any left. Something in there aches like hell. Good thing I can't open my mouth to check."

"Another reason you should have gone to an emergency room, or to some doctor," Ray says. "You might lose some teeth, and your cheek probably could use a butterfly bandage, or stitches."

Stella rolls up her window. I wish this car had better air-conditioning. I'm so hot, and the air blowing around my hair and in my ears is hot too, and the drone is driving me nuts. I hate this car."

Felix mumbles something, his lips unable to move enough to wrap around sounds.

"What?" says Ray.

"He said," Stella translates, "He likes real air. He needs to be connected to what's real."

"Bullshit," says Stella. "Who knows what's real? Do you, Ray?"

"I no longer know what's real," he says.

"You love being uncomfortable," Stella says. Ray looks over at her, thinking she's talking to him. There's a faint blood-stain on her white blouse. But she's talking to Felix.

"If I didn't love being uncomfortable, would I have married you?" Felix mumbles, barely intelligibly. He tries to smile, and emits a groan, as he tries to sit up.

Stella groans at his comment.

"I think it's important to be uncomfortable," says Felix. "It's a way to feel alive. And a way to rebel against comfort-seeking which is all most people are interested in. We've become sad zombies."

"Speaking of discomfort, I wish I still smoked," Stella says. She takes a deep breath, as if relieved that Felix isn't leaning on her. "Seriously, we are just tourists in the land of discomfort. Because none of us have to be uncomfortable."

"Let's stop somewhere soon," says Ray. We can get out the aspirin for Felix, or whatever he's taking, and have a bite. I still think we should go see a doctor, or go to an emergency room," Ray says.

"Felix likes feeling as if he might be dying," says Stella. "It makes him feel alive."

"What can a doctor do for me besides give me a stronger pain-killer that I can get addicted to? Ohhh. I think some of my ribs are broken."

"A doctor could tape your ribs."

"They don't tape ribs anymore," says Felix.

"You could get checked for internal bleeding. Or a punctured lung."

"Yes, let's stop somewhere," says Felix. "Let's cross into back into Mexico for lunch."

"What?" says Ray. "I thought you were glad to get out of Mexico. I know I am. Remember you just fell into an arroyo, or you were being followed, or whatever?" This in a sarcastic tone. "Besides, just crossing the border is a pain."

"We can cross at Ysleta. Small town, no crossing to speak of, and no wait, I promise."

"What the fuck," says Ray.

"I'm with Ray," Stella says.

I'm with Ray. I'm with Ray. Those words bring back a warmth in his groin as he recalls his dream.

"Ray doesn't like Mexicans," says Felix.

"I don't dislike Mexican people," he says. "But I always have the feeling they don't like me. I feel guilty for all the evil the United States has done and is doing to Mexico and to Mexicans, even though I personally have nothing to feel guilty about."

Stella passes a bottle of water to Felix, who motions it away.

"You've always had your head in the sand," she says to Ray.

"What?" says Ray. "What do you mean? What the fuck are you talking about?"

Stella says nothing.

"Oh, so now you aren't going to answer?" he says. "Is there something here that I'm supposed to be doing?" he asks. "Come on," he adds.

"I don't want to get into it now," says Stella, looking out her window.

Ray looks out to see what she sees: bottle brush cacti the size of trees—a landscape from another planet.

Does he have his head in the sand? What does she mean? Is she referring to a specific incident? Is there something he should know about Felix's beating that he's hiding from?

So many questions. Yet the silence is such a relief Ray decides not to pursue it. Proof that Stella might be right.

THE TINY RESTAURANT IN THIS SMALL TOWN, has only four tables. Ray can see why Felix would feel comfortable here, with no one to stare at him, seated crookedly on the green plastic chair, sipping a fruit drink through a fat pink plastic straw the waitress, probably the owner, has given him without asking any questions.

Felix is beginning to look better, though his bruises are more colorful, green, yellow and magenta now added to the dark purples. He can sit in the chair, though he often places his hand on his side, which probably aches from his sore or broken ribs.

The waitress has also brought a bowl of ice in water, and colored fabric napkin, and Stella wipes Felix again and again with the cold cloth.

"This cheek," says Stella, studying the deep cut under Felix's left cheekbone.

"Oh, leave it alone," Felix says, speech slurred. He swipes Stella's hand away from his lips, still bloody and swollen.

"You look like the Elephant Man," says Stella.

Felix laughs, but it comes out his nose. A snort.

"Sure you don't want any?" Stella asks Felix when their fajitas arrive. "Does it hurt a lot?"

"My lips and tongue feel as if I've been to the dental surgeon, who has given me a number of shots of novocaine. I'm just not hungry. I can't imagine ever eating again."

Ray watches Stella cup a tortilla in one slender hand, then layer it with onions, peppers and small slices of steak. As she bites into the now-rolled, filled tortilla, Ray notices that her two front teeth are quite a bit larger than her other teeth—giving her the look of a very young person whose second teeth have just come in.

Since his dream Stella seems magnified, huge and detailed. The attraction he'd felt in the dream has drifted by osmosis into his waking life. This is not going to be possible, he thinks. Maybe he's been repressing something that has always been there?

He takes a bite of his club sandwich, but his hands begin to tremble, and his heart beats shallow and fast, like when he's drunk too much coffee, and he breathes deeply, too loudly, as if suddenly in need of oxygen.

"Are you thinking of Olivia?" asks Stella, her eyes, partly hidden by a shadow, searching his.

Surprised for just a second, realizing that for the first time he's completely forgotten Olivia, he looks directly into her hazel eyes, now umber in shadow.

"Yes," he says.

He thinks of himself as a person who is truthful to the extreme, so he's shocked himself at how quickly and easily he's lied.

TEN

"Now I realize why, when I was young, and leaving my father's part of the country, I headed straight for this side of the border; it felt like a powerful kind of speech. Mexico, like words themselves, yielded feelings so lurid and lovely that no one dared to deny its existence.

Philip Garrison, *Augury*

FELIX LOOKS BETTER NOW, though pale with the pain in his side. Though he doesn't complain about it, he sits leaning over, and places his hand regularly on the area between his chest and his stomach.

Stella grabs her shoulder tote off the fourth chair at their table. "I'm going to the john."

"Listen, guys," says Felix, shifting in his seat, making an effort to sit straighter. He breathes in deeply, then holds his side. "I guess you don't believe my story about falling into an arroyo?"

Ray looks up. Stella turns towards Felix and sits down again, holding her breath. "What?" she says on her exhale.

"Not really sure why I lied," says Felix. "It seemed simpler."

He runs his finger softly along the cut on his cheek. If he does nothing he'll have a deep scar. He has the attention of Stella and Ray, who are both waiting for him to say more. It requires attention to understand him. His lips look a little less mashed but are swollen, and must still be painful.

"I did go running," he says. "But I didn't fall. I was attacked. By three Mexicans—at least they looked like Mexicans—who wanted a fight." He pauses and breathes in through his mouth noisily.

The waitress places the handwritten bill on the table, and removes Ray's empty glass. "More tea?" she asks.

They all shake their heads. Maybe she'd like them to leave.

"I tried to run, but they were all faster than me, and very motivated. It took me what seemed like a long moment to realize they were seriously interested in hurting me. They were large guys, huge, really—and they surrounded me. I have no idea why they'd pick on me—they seemed drunk, and maybe they just wanted to fight. A gringo out all alone."

"A skinny gringo," says Stella.

"Do these guys have anything to do with your preoccupation that someone's following you?" Ray asks.

"Not a preoccupation. That sounds like I'm OCD, or worse, imagining something. I can tell that's what you think from the way you asked me—sort of gingerly—like you're afraid to mention it, afraid you'll upset a lunatic." Felix tries a grin.

"Why don't you tell us who you think is following you," says Stella, fixing her shoulder tote straps nervously, her fingers shaking. Is she scared wonders Ray.

"The person following me is a gringo rancher who tried to shoot me when I was helping migrants cross the border. He came after us with a rifle. It's his property. He didn't want migrants on it. He said they were filthy and left stuff, garbage, and feces, and once in awhile a dead person. He was ready to shoot everyone, and he probably would have gotten away with it."

Ray has a hard time believing all this, beginning with three Mexicans taller than Felix, and a rancher who wants to kill him, but says nothing, waiting for more.

"The only thing I could do with these three Mexicans was to fight back, and hopefully injure one of them enough to divert their attention from me."

Stella rubs a forefinger over Felix's tanned, scratched arm.

"The thing is," Felix says, "I think I hurt one of them pretty badly. This did get their attention but not until they got tired of knocking me around. I think they thought I was dead."

"I thought you were dead when I found you on the floor near my bed," says Ray, thinking of his dream, fucking Stella, while her husband, his friend Felix, lies injured not two feet away.

No one says anything. Stella gets up. "Let's go," she says. "I can't stand sitting any longer."

"In fact," adds Felix, still seated, "I think I killed him. In fact, I'm pretty sure I killed him."

"What?" says Ray, half out of his plastic chair, which moves across the floor. "You think you killed someone?"

"If it was dark, how could you tell you killed someone?" Stella asks. "They thought you were dead—but obviously you aren't."

"This story gets more and more bizarre," says Ray. It is a story, a commercial one. Not like real life. Do people really live this way, in the middle of violence, living close to people with guns?

Felix groans as he slowly gets to his feet, thin but muscular arms helping him push up from the fragile chair.

"I could tell. I mean, that I'd killed him. That he was dead."

"Shit," says Stella.

Ray has no trouble believing that Felix would stay and fight an aggressor, whereas he, Ray, would most likely make every effort to run away. If there were no way out, he'd try some verbal gymnastics. And if that had no effect, he'd probably just let himself be murdered—or wait until they tired of beating him—whichever happened first.

Felix on the other hand might just enjoy a good fight in the way he enjoyed hunting, football, bullfights and other somewhat violent sports. But could he actually kill someone?

"It can't be that easy to murder someone," Ray says, studying Felix's hands now supporting him by holding on to the edge of the table. Despite the scratches, and bruised, swollen knuckles, and one thin maroon cut between his forefinger and thumb, Felix's hands are delicate, with long, slender fingers—the hands of a professor.

"You should have called the police—it sounds like a simple case of self-defense," he says.

FOR THE FIRST TIME there are only two of them in front, Stella at the wheel. They haven't crossed the border, as Felix had wanted, and have decided not to mention going to a doctor, but to have an early dinner somewhere and go to bed early too.

Ray and Stella smile at each other as sonorous snores add a rhythm to the sound of the breeze.

Ray turns his head to see Felix asleep across the backseat, one knee up against the back, his other long leg stretched out, half on the floor, sneaker buried under some of the stuff they'd thrown there, one of Stella's straw hats resting rakish on his abdomen.

Ray feels like he could fall asleep too, even though it's only about two or three in the afternoon. He rests his head back, too lazy to even check his watch. The sun's in his eyes so he closes them, noticing the bright green insides of his eyelids slowly turn orange, then dark red.

"Oh, yeah," says Stella, "call the Mexican police. What a naïve, ridiculous idea," she says, her voice rising.

Ray isn't sure he hadn't been asleep.

"I'm not sure Felix ever told you this," says Stella, "but Felix spent six months in a Mexican jail when he was seventeen. He and a couple of friends decided to cross the border at Matamoros for a good time. Stupid kids, just wanted to hang around some bars, drink some beers, pretend they were going to get laid. Carlos was nineteen and still in high school, he had his father's beat-up Chevy. Apparently he also had some pot. The three of them sat on what passed for a curb, sharing the joint. Carlos, and the other guy saw a cop, rifle and all, got in the car, and left Felix with the joint. He was more scared by them leaving him than he was of the cop, who he thought would help him get home.

He was taken to a police station. At the time he understood very little Spanish—just what you'd know growing up in Texas. The cops didn't speak a word of English. If they did, when he begged to let him call his mother, they pretended not to understand. He figured they'd let him go after they scared him enough. Finally he got to call his mother. This was a small jail connected to the police station. Like a lot of places it looked small from the front, but went back forever, corridor after corridor. He thought they'd keep him for a night, maybe two. After a month, he wasn't sure he'd get out alive. The others in there were tough kids, mixed with older guys, with strange haircuts and self-cut tattoos, all drug dealers or gang members, or guys who'd tried to rob some sneakers or jackets. It was a tiny concrete bunker, with a shithole near the center, which sloped down into a drain, and a thin mattress made from plastic bags on the disgusting concrete floor. Parents or relatives brought food and treats, and money for sodas, and took their clothes home where they washed them and brought them back clean. His mother came down from Houston and rented a crummy apartment and got a Mexican *notario*. She thought her involvement would cause them to let him go sooner, but the lawyer told her that perhaps the money she brought, the cigarettes, and the food that Felix shared, might encourage them to keep him longer. The American Consulate wasn't that helpful because they were all being very strict about drugs— you know—the war on drugs—and Felix had been smoking a joint. Both he and his mother were terrified because there was no law, and no process, and that he could be in jail forever without any trial. And for what? One single joint—not even selling drugs. The lawyer was getting paid and it seemed he was in no rush. 'Don't worry, it will be okay, but it will take time,' he'd say."

"How did he get out?" Ray asks.

"Is she telling you that story?" ask Felix, who is now sitting, leaning forward, his head too close to Ray's, his breath sour.

Is this one of Stella's stories, like La Llorona, a folk tale?

"How did you get out?" Ray asks, moving a bit so that he doesn't smell Felix's breath.

"One day they just let me out. They even gave me back my penknife and my wristwatch. I never found out how or why. My parents gave the lawyer more money, though they never found out what he did for them, if anything. But we had to sign something promising we'd never return to Mexico."

"I'm surprised you never told us that when we were all at UTEP," says Ray.

"There's a lot you don't know about Felix," says Stella, passing a huge truck.

"What do you mean by that," asks Ray. "I'm getting tired of all your little innuendoes."

Ray looks at Stella. She's looking straight ahead, and blushing. "I'm sorry," she says, still not looking at Ray, who is surprised. He can't recall Stella ever apologizing.

"I'm kind of a nervous wreck with all this shit that's going on."

She looks tired now too, and pale. The little ridge of freckles over her nose and the tips of her cheeks are darker, as if they are standing out in front of her skin. Ray wonders what exactly the shit is that's making her nervous.

"What do you think we should do now, Ray?" offers Felix. "Aside from going to a doctor. Besides, I'm feeling much better now," he says, his arms on Ray's backrest. "I'm feeling great."

"Sure," says Ray, "I'm sure you feel great."

He thinks for a moment. "There's no reason why we can't continue as we planned, driving down along the river to Big Bend. It's gorgeous there and I haven't been for years." And we won't be in Mexico, he doesn't say.

"That sounds good," says Stella. "Let's find our next motel on the east side of the Franklins, up along the road toward Alamagordo."

"How about we take a vacation from the way we like to travel and find a very expensive hotel somewhere," says Stella. "A huge three-story La Quinta with a lobby, comfy chairs, a patio for margaritas, and lots of computers."

"And real blankets, not the rubber kind, coated with rat fur."

IN SPITE OF ALL THEIR TALK AND ANTICIPATION of a grand motel, Felix finds Mi Ranchito, another in the crummy genre— though perhaps a bit better than the last. There's quite a while till dusk, but they are exhausted, so they are happy to find anything.

For a moment it seems to Ray that Felix knows this motel—its location, and approximately when they'd arrive, but chalks it up to paranoia (not totally unjustified) and exhaustion.

They are checked into their usual two rooms by a teenager with a long ebony braid, the ends of which bob along the curve in the small of her back when she turns to check, on a chart, which rooms are available.

Ray watches Felix hand her his credit card to see whether the girl recognizes him, but sees no sign that either knows the other.

On their way out of the office there are a few bikers milling around the front of the motel. Bikers, or gangsters, Ray can't tell, but to Ray, with their shaved heads, and many tattoos, they look ominous and scary, like the ones in his dream. A chill runs up the back of his neck.

There are three guys, one tall and skinny, and an older guy with a pot belly, and another with a narrow head, bald on top, the remainder of his stringy hair tied at the nape of his neck, his arm around a young girl who is wearing shorts and a halter, and who is also covered with ink.

"I have a bad feeling about this," says Ray. "I don't think we should stay here."

"They're harmless," says Felix. "Besides, did you see another motel nearby?"

Then, trying to be reassuring, Felix adds, "Didn't you dress like this when you were young?"

Ray tries to picture Felix, in his Houston high school, dressed like these guys.

"Are you kidding? First of all, these guys aren't that young. And no, I was always preppy. But not elegant preppy. Just geeky. Conventional, but unfashionable."

Two of the men's muscles bulge from sleeves that look as if they'd just ripped them off.

They may not be Hell's Angels, and they are mostly young and skinny, but they look like Latino gang members with their ink, and their earrings and stylized dress. With the shaved symbols on their heads, and tattoos on their faces, milling around, they look like they are up to no good. Easy to anger, ready to explode.

Both Felix and Stella want to stay here, so Ray breathes deeply, trying to relax. It's true he's not that good at reading people so he could be completely mistaken.

And at least Felix no longer seems worried about being followed.

ELEVEN

The border is a word game. It is also grimy, hot and horrible. In most places it is ugly. The food is bad, the prices are high, and there are no good bookstores. The U.S. side is depressed by the filth and poverty in Mexico. The Mexican side is overrun by destitute peasants and roiled by American values. The border is transient. The border is dangerous. The border is crass. It is not the place to visit on your next vacation.

William Langeweische, *Cutting for Sign*

BLANKET AND BEDSPREAD PULLED DOWN, Ray lies on his fairly comfortable bed, damp towel around his middle, and covered with his sheet. The shower, though the water changed temperature now and again, felt great, and he's refreshed already, enjoying the air-conditioning, the cool current blowing at his wet hair, and is no longer the least bit lonely; instead he's very relieved to be alone.

He can't stop the images of Felix doing something violent to the Mexicans, kicking, or stabbing someone, as he'd described. The images remain cartoonish. He can't make them real.

He hasn't realized he'd been dozing until either the sound of the air-conditioning coming on again, or maybe a motorbike coughing outside, wakes him.

Holding the white towel around his groin, he tentatively opens his door to a cool breeze and the after-sunset royal blue sky. A sliver of moon and two stars are visible, and it's deeply still. In fact the motel seems deserted, as if he's the only person left on earth.

He dresses in clean chinos and a long-sleeve t-shirt, and heads, on the pebbly trail of the motel complex to find some ice.

Though only about seventy-five feet from his room, by the time he gets to the lobby, his white sneakers are covered with ochre dust, which he tries to stamp off at the door.

The young girl with the long braid has been replaced by a blonde woman who looks startlingly like the girl, except for her much lighter coloring, and a bit more weight.

Ray raises his ice bucket in greeting. "Are you related to the young woman who was here this afternoon?" he asks.

"She's my daughter," says the woman, smiling broadly. "There's an ice machine that's probably working, right behind this lobby, through the side door." She points behind her.

Ray thinks he's going through the correct door but he finds himself in a carpeted living room, where he probably doesn't belong. He backs into the lobby again, and hears the woman's voice, "By the way, we're having a party later, in the house—the one connected on this side." Ray nods.

"You and your friends are invited. You may as well join the noise rather than complain about it. It's my daughter's birthday. We're just having some of her friends for some booze and refreshments—nothing fancy—no dressing up."

Ray looks down at his clothing, as if seeing what he's wearing for the first time. He has no intention of going to any party. And he's pretty sure Felix isn't in any shape for any celebration—or even to be seen by anyone.

"Thanks," he says, holding the bucket awkwardly in front of his pelvic area, "I'm pretty sure we're all too beat, but I'll let the others know."

RAY KNOCKS ON STELLA AND FELIX'S DOOR, a few doors from his own room, and shouts to announce himself, "Hey, guys."

He waits a few moments, and is about to leave, thinking they might be asleep, but Stella opens the door. She's wearing her shirt, and a towel around her hips like a sarong. Her hair's a mess, she's flushed, and her eyes look tiny, like black-eyed peas. She looks as if she's been crying. Have they been arguing? Or screwing? Hard to tell sometimes.

"Hand me your ice bucket, you can have some of this," he says. It's pretty nice out. Should we go hunt for a place to have dinner?"

"I sure could do with a drink," says Stella, looking at the ice. "A margarita."

"Well, we were invited to a party tonight. The motel lady is making a birthday party for her daughter—the one who registered us? She's serving some alcohol. No dinner, though."

"Hmm. Sounds good," says Stella, hanging tight to the towel at her waist.

Ray tries not to look at the narrow naked band between her shirt and the towel, and says, "You're kidding. No way."

He looks past Stella to Felix, lying on the bed in his jeans, but with no shirt, arms straight out as if he's crucified, a small dark diamond of hair in the center of his chest. He looks quite a bit better, though the cuts on his face are still reddish, and he's got huge mauve bruises, though maybe most would be hidden under his clothes. Could he possibly want to go to a party?

"Come on, Ray," says Stella. "It'll be fun. And it's right here. We won't have to drive anywhere looking for some place to eat."

"You're not kidding?" he asks. "What about you, Felix?"

"Once I'm sure I can get up, I'm game," says Felix.

"I can't believe this. We don't even know these people," says Ray. "I'd rather watch sports news on TV, and you know what I think of sports," he says, "than be hanging out, maybe even dancing, with motel staff, maybe some teenagers, and some gang members. No thanks. I can't believe you'd want to go. But if you change your mind, knock on my door."

BACK IN HIS ROOM, less glad to be alone, and puzzled that Felix and Stella would rather go somewhere Ray so much doesn't want to be, he watches television—local news about tornados, and car crashes, high school football scores, and ads for local restaurants, where the huge portions of food look both appetizing and disgusting, and halls to rent for weddings. His stomach whines and complains so loudly he can hear it above the aircon and the TV.

Yet he doesn't feel like looking for a restaurant on his own, though the thought of exploring some of the edges of El Paso, maybe places he and Olivia had wandered in what was another life, seems enticing. The thought of eating alone in some strange restaurant or diner is not.

Ray must have dozed because he'd thought he'd been listening to a local TV station, but now seems tuned to a porn film with two men, one with a bath towel around his neck, and one naked, having sex with a large-breasted blonde, who looks something like the woman at the desk, all three lying or reclining on bath towels beside a small swimming pool. The woman's hair is long, and the ends reach the bright red and green stripes on her beach towel, her breasts huge, and perfectly round like Jello molds. As the naked man pene-trates her, they remain stiff and still, pale nipples pointed in opposite directions. They don't move even when the man, now inside her, begins pounding away. The other man, the one with the towel around his neck has blonde hair to his shoulders, but black pubic hair. He's hard, his long prick rests on his thigh, and he is watching, seemingly waiting for his turn to join in.

As the men change places, Ray sees that the woman has a bare childlike pubis, not a sign of pubic hair, and notes how strange that looks.

He can see the back of the blonde man's head in close-up, his stupid yellow curls at his neck, lowering himself clumsily, tongue stretched to an uneasy length, aiming for the woman's bare pudenda, now in close-up. She raises her hips to meet the large flat tongue, and moans.

Ray feels for the remote. He's vaguely disgusted. This kind of stuff was fun when he was young; he'd sought it out. It was harder to come by then, forbidden, and the shame was part of the pleasure. But he's suddenly aware of the poor quality of these films; they are either too ugly, or too silly to be a turn-on. He also can't take the faked screams and moans, and doesn't want those sounds coming from his room.

But suddenly Ray finds that in spite of his disgust with this porno, he's turned on. Seems the news that he hates the film and its stupidity has bypassed his brain—his penis makes a tent of his jockeys.

Ray joins the trio, creating a foursome. After they all climax, Ray falls into a slimy drowse.

He wakes to the sound of a screen door slamming, a familiar sound from childhood summers spent with his family in rented country cabins. His television is still on, and though the three in the porno film look mussed and bruised, they are still at it.

Ray is sick of sleeping, yet he must have only been asleep for a few minutes. He's as exhausted as if he's been having sex for hours, or has emerged partially from the fog of a dream.

He recalls an image from his dream. He is having sex with the blonde woman from the movie but this time they're both standing in the water, which is no longer turquoise, but an acid algae green. Her elbows rest on the blue tiled pool edge while he holds her floating yet weighty breasts, one in each hand, as if they are babies and he's teaching them to float.

About to bring his lips to the pale rose nipple, the breasts in his hands have suddenly become small, and berry brown. He pulls away when he realizes they're the breasts of the young Mexican girl, the end of her braid floating in the acid algae, and who he's obviously been having sex with all along.

"Shit." Ray jumps up and heads for the sink. He looks in the mirror, horrified at his dry hair, and the bags under his eyes, then hangs his head, hands braced on the edge of the porcelain.

He can hear the pulse of reggae music through the small high window near the ceiling. He spits into the sink, disgusted with his constant state of arousal and the fact that he's turned on by a child. The music, though not loud, beats in his chest.

He thinks about reading his book, but is pretty sure he won't be able to concentrate. And he certainly can't sleep.

He puts some ice in the bathroom glass and feels better after he drinks the cold water.

And he feels even better when he decides that in the morning, first thing, he's going to look into changing his plane reservation. He is done here, and looking forward to leaving for home as soon as possible.

TWELVE

The ghosts of wolves ring our hills
Those bird cries, Comanche songs drifting
Up from wartrails, the click of steel
In the night, prospectors or old soldiers
sharpening the darkness to a keen
wind that blows all the stories away

Keith Wilson, *The Voices of My Deserts*

THE SCREEN DOOR SLAMS BEHIND RAY, but no one acknowledges his arrival. Glad of this, and relieved, he looks around what seems like another ordinary motel room, its door adjacent to the office and lobby, but which is an entire apartment, with, as Ray can see even from where he stands, at least a few rooms.

The furniture is familiar, the same fake wood grain chipped particle board chest of drawers, the same light brown pottery lamps with the dusty beige linen shades as those in his own room.

Ray mumbles greetings to some unfamiliar guys relaxing with beers on the brown and black plaid couch and matching easy chair surrounded by empties, on the brown carpet, and on the small scratched coffee table. They nod, but speak Spanish to each other.

Parties make Ray anxious even if he knows some of the guests. In order to feel less awkward and self-conscious he morphs into a state of invisibility, and becomes an observer rather than a participant, as if the world is a film he's watching.

He scans the room for Stella or Felix. For a second he wonders whether the invitation wasn't for him, but just part of one of the many odd dreams he's been having.

Then he spots Stella, jam glass half full of some amber drink, standing next to a tall man in a sleeveless t-shirt, tight jeans, and pointy-toed alligator cowboy boots with high heels that make him look even taller.

Stella has to look way up to talk to him, and she's not short. Various dark blue and black designs emanate from where his sleeves would be if he had them, and continue sinuously down along sinewy arms. Tattoo bracelets, some thorny barbed wire design, encircle his wrists.

Ray moves closer.

"I bet I can drink this large worm," he hears the cowboy say, pushing his long stringy hair back with the hand not holding the bottle of mescal.

Who in their youth hasn't tried to impress a girl by drinking down the worm in a bottle of mescal?

Ray moves closer, intent on rescuing Stella from this immature posturing idiot, this Goth cowboy, until he notices her run her forefinger along his inked arm and wrist.

"Why don't you go get a drink," says Stella, noticing Ray. "And please bring me something—some bourbon or whiskey. I can't take any more of this." She points to the bottle of mescal her cowboy's still holding.

"Is there any food?" Ray asks. "I'm starving."

Stella shrugs. "You should have come sooner."

"Do you mean that in the larger sense?" He smiles.

He hunts for something to eat, wandering into the small kitchen area, where he finds nothing but a huge bowl with a few potato chips on the bottom, which he eats while searching other nearly empty dishes, one with a few stripes of guacamole that he scoops up with a chip, and another dish with a few pretzels, which he palms.

Maybe they are just physical types he recognizes from sometime in his past, but some of these people hanging around here seem familiar.

Ray picks up two bright red plastic cups of something he hopes Stella will be happy with, downs the contents of one, enjoying the sharp ting of the lime wedges he's found nearby, and finds that it's pretty good tequila. He doesn't see Felix anywhere.

Stella is seated on a bridge chair by herself, legs crossed. "Hey," she says, pleased to see Ray with the drink. He hands her the cup, which she sniffs.

"Thanks for the bourbon," she says.

"No need to be sarcastic. It's pretty good tequila. And here's some lime. If you don't like it you can ask that very young cowboy with the worm to get you a drink. Where's the food that was promised?"

"Pull up a chair. There are more over there." Stella points to a few folded chairs lined up against the wall as if waiting to be asked to dance.

"Well," Stella says, while Ray tries to open a chair without spilling his drink, "you missed some nachos with onion dip. And some cubes of some weird Mexican cheese without any flavor. Oh, and you missed the birthday cake."

Where is the birthday girl? wonders Ray.

He smells the gust of carbon from Stella's match as she attempts to light the skinny joint that's appeared between her red lipsticked lips. After a few tries the limp twisted end catches and Stella inhales loudly. Holding her breath, she passes the joint to Ray, her silver rings, one on almost every finger, sparkling.

"Where'd you get this? From your tattooed boyfriend? No thanks."

Stella exhales and Ray smells the musty musky weed. "Don't be jealous."

The joint, held delicately between Stella's thumb and forefinger, is in front of Ray. He takes the fragile spliff carefully between his thumb and forefinger, and careful not to squeeze it too hard, inhales shallowly. Then deeply. He coughs and gags.

"This stuff always made me cough," he says. "Never did much for me anyway."

Stella looks disgusted. "Here's your drink." She hands him his plastic cup of tequila. "You don't seem to be enjoying yourself. I'm just trying to help."

"You know me," he says, moving his chair a bit closer to Stella's. "I hate parties. I've always hated parties. The most you can expect is some good food, which is rare, or an interesting conversation with someone you'll never see again."

"We used to go to every party we could when we were in college," she says, inhaling and squinting. The roach is nearly invisible. When he takes it, it burns his fingers. He's afraid he'll inhale the whole thing and burn his windpipe.

"Those parties supplemented our diet of spaghetti with butter, or peanut butter on toast. Oh, and pasta with ketchup, which Reagan said was a vegetable," he says.

"Parties are important ritual gatherings of people of various sorts for a variety of reasons, which include networking for various purposes, and letting off steam by drinking too much, taking drugs, flirting, seducing or fucking. Even non-human mammals party," she says.

Ray tries to give back the roach but it falls on Stella's leg where it sparks. She brushes it off.

"I'm not a social mammal," says Ray. His head feels as if it will float off his neck like a balloon. "The trouble with parties is the people and their weird agendas." He raises his arm to point out those around them. His arm feels as if it will spin off into the air. He folds his hands in his lap to keep track of them.

"How did you meet Olivia?" Stella asks.

"At a party," says Ray.

"I thought so," says Stella.

They both laugh, Stella's sounding like a wind chime to Ray. They can't stop laughing. Ray's laugh turns into a coughing fit. His throat feels like a landing strip. There's nothing left in his cup.

"Pot's supposed to be good for asthma, he squeaks out, but I can't even manage to inhale."

"You have asthma? You never had it years ago."

"There's a lot you don't know about me," he says, trying to be sexy.

"Touché," Stella laughs.

Ray is about to ask where Felix is, when he spots him through a haze of cigarette smoke. He's standing far too close to the blonde motel manager, who is wearing a tight dress the same forsythia color of her hair. He can see that they're laughing, mouths open, her head back, but he can't hear anything because of a sudden trumpet version of Cielito Lindo played by one of the guests.

Ray looks at Stella to see what she thinks, but she doesn't seem interested in what Felix is doing, has gotten up, and is walking in the opposite direction.

Across the room the motel manager's daughter, her long braid now loose, a rippling black curtain, is making out with the biker with the long stringy ponytail. She's wearing a sleeveless white blouse and tight jeans that have a row of three large holes running down the front of each thigh, and bright green platform sandals.

The biker looks way too old for her, maybe in his thirties, and Ray's surprised that he feels indignation. Recalling the image of this young woman superimposed over that of the porn actress, he feels his blood rush to his face. Could he be jealous? He's definitely ashamed. This is all so not his thing. This apartment that looks like a motel. He's beginning to feel nauseous. Or maybe it's just a memory of nausea.

He's always thought of himself as someone, unlike most men, not at all vulnerable to women who are in the area of what he considers taboo—like the very young, a relative, a married woman. Or even the very old. Or the wife of a friend.

Ray thinks he's more attracted to a woman's mind than anything else. He's always fallen for women who have a kind of mental energy, a brilliance, unusual ideas, women whose conversation dazzles. Sexy minds. The opposite of himself. He'd thought he wasn't much interested in what a woman looked like—often that's not what he remembered about someone he'd met and found attractive. Yet Ray can't take his eyes off the girl. He almost feels her smooth beige skin, her shiny waterfall hair, the gentle swell of her arms and shoulders seem like soft tan suede next to the crisp cotton of her starched white blouse.

He's disgusted by the ugly biker, whose nose is buried in the girl's lush hair, and who is running a long skinny forefinger along the fine dark down on her forearm. And by the fact that she doesn't realize what an asshole that biker is. Or maybe he disgusts himself.

He looks around the room for her mother. She is alone on one of the many metal bridge chairs, staring into space, either a drink or an ashtray propped between her knees, pulling her dress up a bit, revealing a bit of her fleshy thighs. Ray hopes that her state, alone and somewhat dejected, signals the end of this celebration.

Feeling a bit woozy, Ray makes his way to where he thinks the kitchen is to see if there's anything to eat in the fridge, when Stella materializes beside him. Or has she always been there?

The office bell jangles above the country music on a radio. The motel manager leaves her drink teetering on the burnt sienna rug and walks toward the door that leads to the office.

"I was just talking to her," says Stella, her hand on his arm.

"Who?" asks Ray.

"The manager," says Stella.

"I just saw her sitting by herself," says Ray.

"Well just before that," says Stella. "She's half Anglo, half Mexican. She, Sara, owns this motel with her Mexican husband, the father of the girl who registered us?" She raises her voice at the end as if asking a question.

Ray puts his head close to Stella's to show he's listening, and so he can hear better.

"The dad is an alcoholic, who is mostly nice, but can get moody and depressed, and that's when he drinks too much." She pauses. "Or maybe drinking too much makes him depressed—and that leads to him turning angry, and sometimes violent. Both women love him but are afraid of him. They realize they'll have to be the ones to leave, but the motel is their only livelihood."

"How can you love someone you are afraid of?" Ray asks.

"Life is more complicated than you think," says Stella.

"Fuck you," says Ray. "Is that another one of your digs?"

"Just sayin'," says Stella. "Let's sit there." She points to the black, brown and orange couch.

"How did you manage to find out all that in the short time Felix wasn't flirting with her," he says, holding Stella's arm for balance as he sits. Feeling dizzy, he rests his head against the back of the prickly plaid couch. He imagines he can feel those ugly shades of orange, brown and black from the couch moving into his skull.

Music over, words from one of the chairs nearby waft into his head. "I feel big and handsome when I'm packing, and much safer when I know everyone around me has a gun."

Without raising his head, Ray says, "I feel just the opposite." He opens his eyes to see Felix lurch into view, limping, and hunched over, one arm protectively close to his side, probably in pain. Nevertheless, he looks much better—his purple and yellow swellings have gone down and their hues seem to have faded.

"Shove over," he says to Ray, who squeezes into Stella.

Felix has heard the gun comment, and adds, "Yeah, here's a quote from Mao, or maybe Sun Tze: "We do not want war, but war can only be abolished through war, and in order to get rid of the gun, we need to take up the gun."

"That's a bunch of crap," says Ray. "What about Gandhi?" He adds, I guess I'm one of those liberal commie city fags who believe in gun control. You should be glad the guy who beat you up had no gun." He recalls that Felix grew up in Texas and his dad took him hunting.

"You have a point," says Stella, her eyes closed, her head against the back of the couch, curls exploding onto the plaid. Her features look smeared, as if painted on, then wiped with a rag.

Ray leans back again, disoriented. Too much drink and pot, not enough food. Yet unlike before, he feels liberated, euphoric.

"I've decided to leave," he says to Stella, both their heads back, and eyes closed. "I'm ready to get back to my real life. I know it's early, but I think it's best. I'll check reservations tomorrow morning. Surely what's her name will let me use the office computer?"

Hearing nothing from Stella, Ray adds, "I really appreciate everything ..."

Surprised that Stella has nothing at all to say about his ending their trip—at least his part in it, Ray opens his eyes to see Felix talking with the thin pony-tailed biker who'd been smooching the motel manager's daughter. In fact both seem involved in intense conversation—their heads are close, Felix's hands are fists—too intense for people who don't know each other.

Ray tries to make out some words. He thinks back to how Felix found Mi Ranchito.

Sara reappears at the doorway with two dark men dressed in black pants and white shirts, one of them is wearing a jacket and a purple tie. Both look out of place. They are wearing what Ray calls "stockbroker shoes," shiny black dress shoes that look like beetles. Sara appears to be nodding in Felix's direction.

He can't make out a word they are saying. He tries to tell Stella that all these people are interconnected somehow in ways he can't figure out, and that they are dangerous.

Stella's eyes are still closed. Is she even awake?

"These people all creep me out," he says. "Something's going on, but I'm not sure what." It occurs to him that he is paranoid. Maybe from the pot? "I'm getting out of here," he says, not sure if he means the party, or the entire trip.

The music has been turned on again. Ray puts his head close to Stella's lips, which seem to be moving in reply.

"I'm seeing the most fantastic images," she says, her eyeballs rolling under her closed eyelids. "This one is pink, fading into purple, red and green. All the edges are gold, with tiny silver sparkles, like millions of stars …"

"Shit," says Ray, finding it very hard to move, "you haven't heard a word I've said. You're completely stoned."

THIRTEEN

We had gone through enough hard ridges and soft valleys for me not to just sense but to see the Paleozoic pageant played in the rock. For all the great deformity and complexity, the mountains now gone had left patterns behind.

John McPhee, *In Suspect Terrain*

RAY HEARS SCUFFLING AND SQUEALING. Try as he may, his eyes, which feel large and heavy as grapefruits, won't open. His sinuses are swollen too, and beat in rhythm with his pounding heart.

When he can, finally open his eyes he sees Felix on the floor scuffling with one of the dressed-up latecomers to the party. They're rolling on the carpet, clothing mussed, grunting like pigs.

Ray knows he must help Felix, already a mess and not in any shape to take another beating. But hard as he tries to rise from the couch, he remains inert. Stella, standing off to the side of the couch, mouth open in horror, eyes huge with fear, implores Ray to help. He tries again to move, and just as he feels freed, able to rise, he looks again at Stella. She is holding a large silver gun in one wobbly hand, propping her arm near her elbow with the other. Her wedding ring glints.

"Put down the gun!" Ray tries to shout, but no sound emerges until the loud explosion from Stella's gun as she shouts at the struggling pair, who disengage in slow motion.

Who was shot? Ray holds his breath. The man in the suit jacket, tie open and askew in on his knees clutching his chest. Ray waits forever for him to fall over, but it's Felix, on the carpet who cumples into a tight fetal position, and then opens slowly, like a flower.

Suddenly and without thinking about moving, Ray rushes towards Felix and lies down beside him. The rough brown carpet seems to crawl towards Ray as he puts an arm around Felix.

"Are you all right? Felix, answer me," he says, panicking because his arm around Felix feels cool. "Bring a blanket," he says to Stella, whose brown leather sandals he can see. When they don't move, he looks up. Stella's legs are spread wide, and her gun is pointed at him.

"No!" he shouts.

RAY WAKES, teeth chattering, goose-fleshed. He's wrapped around Felix, but he's naked, and there's nothing, not even a thin blanket, covering them.

He recalls what happened and retches, and then forces himself to check for gunshot wounds, and to see if he's even alive. There's no blood anywhere—odd, but good.

He begins to extricate his limbs from Felix's when he realizes Stella's legs are tangled with his and that he has his arm across her shoulders. She's as naked as he, except for the red panties wrapped around one of her tan calves. She's still asleep, curled in a fetal position, just as Felix was in Ray's dream, and is probably chilly. He looks for a blanket to cover her with, and sees his clothing tangled with Stella's behind the couch.

Throwing her blouse over her, and, holding his own clothing over his genitals, he tiptoes out of the motel owner's apartment, across the gravel path with his bare feet, and into his own room, which is, surprisingly, unlocked.

His head pounds, a default condition on this trip. So much for loads of tequila and pot. One of his goals was to loosen up, but now he's pissed for getting talked into doing all sorts of things he knows aren't good for him—things alien to him, and which he doesn't even like.

Before he has both legs in his chinos, the pounding in his head turns into banging on his door. He hurries to finish pulling on his pants, then stops for a moment, his head expanding to the four walls of the room, straining to make out whether the pounding really is his door, Felix's door or someone else's.

He considers not responding—he doesn't feel like talking to anyone—but the banging continues and sounds urgent. Noting his boxers are missing, he zips his fly, and hurries to the door, expecting to find an angry Stella, a puzzled Stella, maybe an outraged Stella who will demand some explanation for why they were sleeping together naked behind the couch. What really happened last night? He has no idea, no answers. He remembers nothing after he'd decided to go to bed.

"Okay, okay," he says, pulling the door towards him reluctantly.

Sara is there, blonde hair mussed, black roots visible, still in her yellow dress. Up close, Ray sees that there's a tiny pattern of finely-drawn champagne flutes on the fabric.

Behind her the Mi Ranchito sign, blue and pink neon glowing dimly in the grimy dawn, proclaims vacancies.

"My daughter, Vanessa, she's missing. Maybe you've seen her? She's never not come home to sleep," she says, her eyes scouring the room behind Ray, who moves aside so she can see the entire room.

"I haven't seen her," he says. He doesn't feel comfortable telling her that he's just gotten back to his room, wondering whether he sounds as flustered as he feels, as if he's guilty of abducting the kid.

"I'll help look for her, but I've got to shower first and take some aspirin for this horrible hangover. Meanwhile, try not to panic. She could be anywhere." He hates that he always tries to console.

"That's what I'm afraid of," she says. "A lot of girls have gone missing here."

"Missing? Here in this motel?"

She's already running along the gravel path when Ray wonders whether she means here, not far from Juarez.

RAY DRINKS THREE GLASSES OF COLD WATER and takes a delicious shower. The better he feels, the sorrier he is that he's promised to help find Vanessa, along with the guilt he feels for just wanting to get out of the motel and find a great breakfast. And then make his travel arrangements.

He's pretty sure the kid will turn up soon, he justifies, in spite of recurring images of the tattooed bikers she was hanging with. It must be hard to tell when a teenager is missing, just gone somewhere she doesn't want her parents to know about, or has run away. And they're so vulnerable to getting involved with seemingly fascinating but evil people who wish to do them harm.

He pauses in front of Felix and Stella's door, before knocking, remembering waking tangled, naked, with Stella. And although he did tell Stella last night that he was planning to go home, he doesn't relish telling Felix.

Stella opens the door dressed in tan linen shorts that reach almost to her knees and a fresh white sleeveless shirt, hair combed back, still damp from a shower, looking as fresh as if she's slept in her own bed for eight or nine hours, instead of drinking, smoking weed and whatever else happened. Could he have imagined waking up intertwined with her? Or was it one of his weird dreams?

"You look great," says Ray. "Is Felix awake?"

"You seem surprised that I look great," Stella says. "I heard someone knocking at your door."

"Oh, that was Sara, looking for her nubile daughter. Didn't she knock on your door?"

"Maybe, while I was in the shower. Or maybe it was an excuse to get into your room."

"What?" asks Ray. "Why would she want to get into my room?"

"Maybe her nubile daughter was in your room," Stella says, snapping on a leather waistpack, and grabbing a sweater off the messy bed.

Is Stella jealous? "I would never never sleep with a kid like that," says Ray, blushing. Luckily Stella's too busy to see his face.

"I'm starving," he says. "Can you please hurry? Remember I didn't eat anything for dinner? But I promised Sara I'd help look for her kid. Vanessa." He makes a sour face, and shifts from foot to foot, still in the doorway, but tired of standing still.

"While we're looking for her we can look for Felix."

"What do you mean? Isn't Felix with you? I thought maybe he was in the shower or something. I assumed you knew where he was."

"I have a feeling we'd better not check out yet," she says, looking around inside to see if she's forgotten anything, then closing the door. "If I knew where Felix was we wouldn't have to look for him," she says. "I think he was in our room last night. His bed's messed, and his stuff's all over."

Ray pushes away the thought that maybe Felix and Vanessa are together somewhere. Why not? He could have ended up with her somewhere, especially if they'd had too much to drink, just as Ray found himself with Stella.

Can Stella not be wondering whether the two missing people are together? And so far, if Stella knows that when Ray awoke he was practically lying on top of her, both nearly naked, she's not saying. Her face, freshly made-up, red lipstick neatly applied reveals nothing.

"How come you're not worried?" asks Ray, thinking she's very calm, not like her, and especially given her husband has just been beaten up by some thugs, one of whom he thought he'd killed.

They wander the gravel paths along the row of rooms shaped like a square with one side not attached to the other three sides, like arms, that hug the parking lot, peering into dark and mostly uninhabited rooms where the drapes are open.

The office, and whatever lies behind it, Ray notices, is situated in the center of the section with the arms, like a head with a hat that says "Office." Near the one row of rooms that is separate is the large free-form sign, the tall pink and blue neon "Mi Ranchito," and some bushes, which they check behind, as if searching for bodies.

"Should we check all the rooms? We can get keys from Sara," says Ray.

"If she's looking for her daughter she must have checked the rooms that are empty," Stella says.

Ray is still thinking about food—eggs, toast, and coffee. Stella doesn't seem too worried, and he takes his cue from her. Though each time they approach a window to peer in, Ray is filled with dread. And each time there is nothing to see but one or two beds, and identical furniture, as if they are in some multiverse.

Stella checks the few pickups left in the lot. Felix's car, still parked in front of his room, offers no clue. Not one motorbike is parked there.

Sara is behind the desk in the office looking frazzled and distracted, her hair pulled back, but much of it escaping its green scrunchy. The TV is on, tuned to the morning news.

"I've already checked all the vacant rooms, which is most of them," Sara says.

Ray has no idea whether she knows that Felix is also missing. Stella, standing beside him, doesn't say anything, so he takes her lead.

"We're going to get something to eat, and then we'll help you look some more," he says.

They check Felix and Stella's room once more, hoping he's arrived back from wherever. Ray gets a better look at the room now. The blankets are awry, and the pillows askew. It looks as if both beds have been slept in. Yet wasn't Stella with Ray all night in Sara's motel apartment?

"Is all Felix's stuff here?" he asks, looking around for the familiar royal blue sports duffel, and other things he might recognize.

"His bag's here," says Stella, "and one of his running shoes. Where can he go with one shoe and no car?"

Ray can see from where he's standing near the bed that Felix's shaving stuff is on the sink.

Stella sits on the bed fiddling with the blanket.

"Did he leave his wallet? His car keys?"

"I didn't find them," says Stella, trying to gather some errant strands of hair into her ponytail.

"Should we be worried yet?" asks Ray. He thinks better of reminding Stella that the last time Felix disappeared he came back a mess. The only thing worse would be if he didn't come back at all. She seems distracted rather than panicky with worry.

"Why wouldn't Felix leave a note for us if he was going somewhere. With some idea of when he'd be back."

"We can leave a note for him, telling him to wait here for us. Let's get out of here and get some breakfast."

"How stupid of us to leave our cell phones home. Even if only to use for an emergency," says Ray, feeling for the small pen he always keeps in his shirt or pants pocket. It's not there.

His own room is neat compared to Stella's, and dark and silent. He feels like lying down, but finds his pen near the phone, and searches for something to write a note on. He rips the last page, which is blank, from the paperback he'd been trying to read, and writes, *Hi Felix, We went for breakfast. We'll be right back. Wait for us here.*

He runs back to Stella, gravel crunching. She places the paper carefully in the center of the bed that she's made up just enough that the paper is visible. Ray checks it from the doorway. It would be hard to miss on the maroon, navy and green striped background—the same bedspread that's in Ray's room.

FOURTEEN

Frontier means border, and the history of the line where America and Mexico meet is rife not only with wonder, but with speculation.

Debbie Nathan, *Women and Other Aliens*

"LET'S SIT HERE," RAY SAYS. "I want to keep my eye on the car."

Stella rolls her eyes, throwing he straw bag on an empty chair at their table near the window. The small café is not far from the motel. "Why do you want to see the car? What good does watching it do?" She slides onto the chair next to Ray rather than across from him.

He shrugs. He's not really sure. "Maybe because it's my only immediate way out of here?" He shrugs.

There are only four tables in the entire place, each covered with a bright flowered oilcloth, the kind he recalls at his grandmother's house and which he hasn't seen for years.

The round man, perhaps the "gordo" of "Gordo's Café," wearing a bright green shirt with the sleeves rolled to just above his elbows, has brought their coffee right away.

"How did you know we were dying for this?" asks Stella. To Ray she seems inappropriately, and stupidly flirtatious.

"I guess we do look as if we need coffee," says Ray.

Stella, in spite of trying to be playful, does look distraught, and he, Ray, probably doesn't look great either, with the remains of his hangover. He brushes his hair back with his hand.

Stella says, "You do look greenish, and you have huge bags under your eyes."

Her fingers tremble as she turns over her white mug so "Gordo" can pour her coffee.

"I wonder—did you happen to see a thin bald guy, maybe running, maybe wearing, wearing—a running suit, you know, with pants that have a white stripe down the side?" Her hands clasp the full mug between them, steam rising around her words.

Ray recalls the one sneaker on its side, on the worn rug in the motel. What would Felix have on his feet?

"I'm sorry," the man says, thinking for a moment, while pouring Ray's coffee. "I'm in the back preparing the food and making coffee until someone comes in," he says.

When he goes into the back, Stella says, "This coffee is burnt. How could you say it's good? You're a fine liar, I'm finding out."

"What do you mean, 'a fine liar'? When have I lied? This coffee is a bit burnt, but it's hot and it's strong, and it's just what I needed." He sips loudly, "What do you mean, I'm a fine liar?" he asks again.

"Boy that really bothers you. Why?"

"Not sure," Ray says. "Maybe because it's always been important to me to be told the truth and to tell the truth. When I was a kid I didn't even tell white lies, the kind that make people feel better in social situations."

"I remember. You were always polite and passive, but once in a while you'd shock with a comment that could be considered nasty. I'm trying to think of examples."

"I'm much nicer now," says Ray. "I've mellowed. I can lie like everyone else. I still don't enjoy it."

His coffee is already cold, and now he can taste how bad it is. He looks around for the waiter.

"Olivia told me what a fuddy-duddy you are," says Stella, rubbing his arm just above his wrist with a shaky finger. Her nail is bitten.

Ray pulls his arm away and looks out the window past the protective wrought-iron bars, at the car. He doesn't want her to touch him. She's far too close as it is, but he can't bring himself to ask her to move to the seat opposite him.

"I'm sorry," says Stella.

"You can call me a fuddy-duddy, or worse," he says, "but the idea that Olivia was telling you stuff about me that she never told me …"

He wants to believe that he and Olivia had the kind of marriage in which neither of them shared personal tidbits of their life with anyone else.

"If you think I'm unaware, or old-fashioned, or stupid, or passive, just say so. Why the hinting and niggling? And own up to it. Don't pretend they're Olivia's thoughts, or Felix's."

"You're right," she says, looking down at her hands.

Ray's stomach contracts with hunger when he inhales the steam from the blue napkin covering the tortillas the café owner has brought. He lifts the napkin, and scrunching a steamy flour tortilla between two fingers, gobbles it in two bites.

The café owner, seeing them absorbed, silently leaves their *huevos Mexicanos,* eggs scrambled with onions, tomato and chiles, and some tiny dishes of red and green salsa in case they like the eggs even hotter.

"I know I'm sort of not a big experimenter, and I'm kind of passive. I accept that," he says, mouth full. I'm not sexy, and I'm not an explorer, or even a traveler. I'm not a go-getter, and I'm the opposite of aggressive," he continues, putting some green salsa on his *frijoles refritos.* "To be like me, an introvert, passive, is un-American and anti-male, too. It's always to be inferior," he says. "I'm accepting it," he says, "but I don't need to be niggled."

He doesn't tell her that he'd rather observe his life than participate. That he often lets something uncomfortable continue just so he can see what will happen, or how it will turn out. He doesn't want to control his life—he wants to watch how it goes.

Stella looks up from her dish, fork in her hand. "I'm sorry," she says again. "I'm just upset about Felix being gone. And other stuff."

She leans close again. He feels the hairs on his arm rise towards hers as if magnetized, and he shifts on his chair as far from her as he can. He's now so close to the window that he has to eat with his left hand.

"What other stuff?" he asks.

"Felix is so goal-oriented that he can't enjoy anything anymore. I don't know, maybe he was always like that. Maybe I liked that he took over and was so driven. I didn't have to do anything. But now I'm a grownup," she smiles. "Sort of. And I can take care of myself."

They both eat, silently and ravenously.

"Ahh, that's good," says Ray.

"Felix is now totally driven, interested only in challenging himself."

Ray is curious about their relationship, yet feels guilty hearing about Felix. He imagines Stella might want more attention from Felix.

"But he's very political. He's driven to help people—to do good."

How can you complain about that, he thinks.

"I always remember this movie I saw, with Barbara Hershey. She had two children (I think the story was narrated by one of them, now grown). But she was part of the revolution in South Africa, doing very dangerous work with the anti-apartheid groups.

She's put her family in danger of being killed, and there's also the danger that she will be arrested and taken from her children. And she does have to leave them for a while—I can't remember why. And so here's the question—do you owe society, your country, your life? Or is taking care of your own children, your own family, enough?"

"Interesting conundrum," says Ray. It is interesting, but he's watching Stella finish her breakfast, running a huge chunk of her roll across what is left on her plate in a way he finds kind of disgusting. Yet he feels a tug of pleasure in his groin.

He remembers waking up intertwined with Stella, both of them nearly naked. His neck pulses with the quick rush of blood to his face. Perspiration prickles at his hairline.

What did they do, if anything? What does Stella know? It's possible that she wasn't totally awake and aware until after he'd covered her and left the party apartment. He could be reading her wrong, but she seems a bit more fey and flirtatious than usual, in spite of Felix being missing. Can it be possible that Felix left her? Maybe she kicked him out.

Ray forks the last of his eggs onto the last tortilla, putting some red salsa on top. Stella must have moved while he was engrossed in food, as she's now leaning on the table nearly across from him. She leans forward, and he leans closer too, sure that she's going to say something about last night.

"I read," she says, "that you shouldn't eat any salsa that you find on the table. Because people dip chips they've already bitten."

"You know what?" says Ray. "I don't trust you. I think you're not telling me everything about you and Felix. And about Felix. I'm beginning to think the two of you planned this whole thing—the party, the disappearance, whatever it is. You're acting weird. Not like someone whose husband could be dead."

"What am I not telling you? What more can I tell you? I don't know everything Felix is into lately. It's always changing, and frankly I need to keep separate from it."

"It sounds like you resent that he wants to help people. He is empathetic." Ray had never noticed that about Felix years ago—but they were young.

"I once read about a man who had so much empathy that he donated a kidney to a stranger. It felt so good that he couldn't stop. He wanted to donate more body parts. He donated a section of his liver. Then he donated bone marrow. And blood. And more blood. And more bone marrow. Then he wanted to donate his other kidney."

She takes a last sip of her coffee and makes a sour face. "There's a place where empathy has to stop before it destroys you. A boundary. You need to have boundaries."

Stella leans towards Ray again, her breasts grazing the salsas, and places a hand over his. "Don't look over there," she says, her green eyes traveling towards the door, but her head not moving. "I think the two guys coming in here are two of the bikers from the party last night. I think they look familiar."

There are now two huge bikes parked next to Felix's car. How had he not heard them?

One of the two is gaunt with high cheekbones and small deep-set eyes hidden under a beetling brow. Long sideburns outline his bony jaw. His hair seems pulled back in a ponytail, but Ray can't see it. He's wearing a short sleeve shirt and a vest over it.

His narrow upper bicep is encircled by a tattoo of black interlocking triangles. He's blocking the other man from Ray's view, and he doesn't want to stare. All he can see of him is a wide back and sinuous Elizabethan curls to his shoulders. They are both so large that the table nearby looks like doll furniture.

They could have been at the party. There had been a steady stream of biker-types, and Ray had stopped checking them out.

Stella gets up and unhooks her bag from the chair. The two guys look over, studying Stella, and then Ray with their pinhole eyes.

"Let's get out of here," she says. "Where's the bill?"

"I remember how much our meals were—I'll just pay." His hands shake as he retrieves the correct amount from his wallet and his pocket full of change, both Mexican pesos and U.S. currency.

Stella is outside, leaning on the car waiting for him appears small, frail even, as if she's been sick. The round collar of her lacy white blouse adds to her childlike appearance.

"Let's pick up Felix and get going," says Ray, fumbling with the key in the lock. He's used to his car's remote. "Hurry."

"You don't have to tell me to hurry," says Stella. "I'm sick of bikers. They may be completely benign but somehow they want to be seen as outlaws. And groups of outlaws are scary. It's like they can do anything."

Back at the motel, Ray stands behind Stella, staring at the backs of her knees just visible under her long linen shorts, while she hurriedly opens the door to her room.

"Felix," she calls out, even though it's easy to see at a glance that no one is there.

The note they'd left is still in the middle of the bed. The room feels desolate, as if it's been uninhabited for weeks. The mess of clothing and stuff strewn around doesn't make it feel homier, just that it had been left under suspicious or sad circumstances.

Stella, arms at her sides, straw bag hanging limply from one hand to the floor, is like a sad, disappointed child. She sits down at the edge of the bed and studies the note. But it's nothing more than their note to Felix, on the same crappy paper ripped from the paperback book. Her face turns red and crumples.

Ray sits next to her at the edge of the bed. Her sudden very real grief, or fear, reassures Ray that whatever's going on with Felix, she's not part of the plan. Usually dumb and immobile in the presence of any display of emotion, especially crying, Ray folds Stella in his arms.

Suddenly Stella, who'd seemed so diminished and in need of protection, feels large and warm against him, and it's he who feels protected. They are still for the moment, as Ray feels her body heat melt into him, aware of her citrus scent. He thinks she's about to move away, but instead she buries her head into his neck, where he feels her cool lips on his tender sunburned skin. A tendril of her hair, loosened from its clip, wraps across his mouth like a gag.

After a moment Ray is aware of her breasts pressing against his chest and one upper arm, and her warmth turns into heat, then electricity.

No, he thinks, no, no. He recalls movies in which comforting after shared disasters often lead to sex. Not here, uh, uh, he thinks—but he's powerless to let go—instead he pulls her closer, kissing her forehead, her moist eyelids, and tear-salt cheeks. His hands caress her back, searching for her skin under her shirt.

Stella moans and bites his neck a little too hard. Ray hardly notices that they are sliding down, clutching each other, soon prone on the bed. Ray feels soft and hard at the same time, expansive, spreading, yet focused on his swollen penis that seems as if it will push out on its own right through his clothing, until, lying back a bit, he feels Stella opening his fly, exposing him, now hard as bone. Her clothes fly by as she throws her shirt, her bra, into the air.

Enveloped in the humidity of her, tangled in her hair, her mouth on his belly, her nipples grazing his upper thighs, over-whelmed by her usual scent, along with something deeper, he is gone.

Half under Stella, aware of cooling liquid on his thigh, wrapped in the blanket and bedspread that before he'd deemed too bacteria-laden to allow near his skin, Ray hears a timid knock at the door.

He sits up as far as he can. Felix. Oh god.

Stella is up and pulling on her shirt and shorts. He's never seen anyone dress that fast.

"Felix! Thank god," she says. "And thank god he doesn't have his key."

Ray stands on shaky legs, and hunts for his chinos.

There's a sound from outside, but not another knock. They both stop for a moment, Ray on one leg, his other leg half into his pants. Stella tilts her head, and holds up her hand for Ray to stay still.

After another moment, Ray breathes again, relieved.

"If it were Felix he wouldn't leave after one or two knocks. Though maybe he'd been knocking for a while." Stella lies down, pillow on her chest. She's unaware that their note to Felix is stuck on her shoulder.

"I thought we wanted Felix to come back," says Ray. "I'm so sorry," he adds, zipping his fly, then trying to straighten the creases.

"What for? Screwing? Or coming too fast?"

"Both," says Ray, smiling now, glad that Stella's not upset. But he doesn't feel good about it. In fact, he's disgusted.

"What if that were Felix," he says. "What then?"

"Felix wouldn't care," she says, getting up, pulling the stuck paper off her shoulder, then absently organizing the clothing on the bed. "We've always had an understanding." She throws Ray's shirt at him.

"What do you mean, 'understanding?' That's bizarre. When we were teaching at UTEP, getting our degrees, and spending lots of time together, do you mean to tell me that you and Felix had an open marriage?"

"I'm all sweaty," says Stella. "And your cum's all over my legs. I could use a shower."

"If so, how could we, Olivia and I, not have noticed?" asks Ray. "We were sure you were as monogamous as we were."

Stella is getting undressed again, ready for a shower. She stops what she's doing to give Ray a strange look. "Are you sure Olivia was monogamous?"

Before Ray can absorb this comment, there's knocking on their door again; this time it's insistent. Ray looks around the small room for a place to hide.

Stella has the bedspread wrapped around her like a toga.

As Ray makes for the small bathroom, he sees that Vanessa, the missing manager's daughter is at their door.

She doesn't seem the least bit surprised to see Stella wearing a bedspread, and Ray, in the same room, half-dressed, heading for the bathroom. She's wearing jeans, her hair back in her neat business-like braid. Her shoulders are much wider than her hips, and she reminds Ray of some Egyptian, or Pre-Columbian statues.

"Are you okay?" asks Stella. "Your mother was frantic looking for you," she says.

"I know," says Vanessa. She sighs. "My mother is frantic about everything I do. She's worried about rapists, killers, kidnappers, robbers, drunk drivers, gangs, drugs ... whatever." She sighs again. "She told me to let you know I'm okay," she says.

Standing outside the doorway in the late morning sun she doesn't look so young anymore. She's at least eighteen— maybe nineteen, or twenty—young, but not a kid.

"Are you checking out?" she asks.

Can she possibly be mistaking Ray for Felix? But Felix had been talking to her at the party. Even flirting. So how would that be possible?

"Have you seen Felix anywhere?" Stella asks. "You know, the other guy we came with? Do you have any idea where he might be? Maybe you saw him out running?"

"I haven't seen him since last night," says Vanessa. But she looks uneasy and flushes a deep rose.

"Would you keep an eye out for him? He seems to be missing. He wasn't here this morning when we woke up," Stella says. "He didn't leave a note. Please ask your mom to watch for him? I'm not sure we can check out yet. We'll let you know," she says, closing the door fast. She pulls the door open again immediately, "Hey, was that you knocking before? Like maybe fifteen, twenty minutes ago?"

Vanessa, already heading for the office, turns, "Uh, uh. It wasn't me."

Ray, in the bathroom, hears Stella say something so low he doesn't hear. Is she talking to him, or to Vanessa?

"What?" he asks, opening the bathroom door, toothbrush in his cheek.

"That wasn't her before," Stella says, bedspread falling away.

"It wasn't Vanessa knocking before. Maybe it was Felix. Or someone with news of him. Oh, why didn't I answer the door right away," she says, collapsing onto the bed.

"If we hadn't been screwing we would have answered the door right away," he says, toothbrush in his hand, foam around his mouth like a mad dog.

He remembers he was planning to change his plane reservations. He'd be traveling home by now—or pretty soon.

"I think we'd better not leave here yet," Stella says.

FIFTEEN

Then we go to the river. We take off our clothes and put them in a bag. We get into the water and cross the river naked. If we crossed wearing clothes, when we got to the other side, we'd be wet and people would notice. If La Migra sees that, they'll say, Look, there goes another wetback, and they'll nail you.

Daniel Rothenberg, *With These Hands: The Hidden World of Migrant Farmworkers Today*

IN SPITE OF EVERYTHING GOING ON, the shower feels great, as if something as simple as hot water can fix one's entire mood, one's life, swish away Ray's disgust with himself. He can almost pretend that everything bothering him now, and all he feels responsible for, is running out of his body and streaming away.

When Ray thinks about it, though much is happening that's totally unexpected, whatever he's uncomfortable with, the worst is the fact that he's slept with a friend's wife—who is also a friend.

Perhaps he's completely freaked that he seems to have no control over anything, including himself. Ordinarily he enjoys going along with events rather than controlling them, but perhaps his no-risk lifestyle lately has kept him from getting into too much trouble. Any trouble, for that matter. Or maybe he never noticed temptations before? Can he be as closed off as Stella seems to think? So unaware? While married to Olivia, he was never tempted to have an affair. And mostly all he did, or does, is think about ways to teach the very few impassioned geology students in his classes, to keep them excited by finding articles for them, films, sharing his own excitement, which is less and less frequent. He has never had an affair with a student, something he finds unthinkable.

Yet the unthinkable is happening. I must get out of here while I can, he thinks. Then he wonders what he means by "while I can." As if he is on the verge of some quicksand, or is swimming too far out in some ocean. As if his volition will be destroyed.

But can he go home now, with no answer to the mystery of Felix's disappearance? Will he really be able to leave Stella to hunt for Felix on her own?

Water drips from his hair into his mouth. He doesn't bother to spit it out, as if he's more comfortable now with the malignant bacteria that he was afraid of just a couple of days ago. The water remains very hot, a small thing he is grateful for.

He feels around for the tiny bottle of motel shampoo, and feels nothing but sandy grout where he thought he'd put the shampoo. He pulls the slightly slimy shower curtain from his hip, where it has stuck, and tries to lather his hair with the remains of the tiny soap the motel provided.

"Forget something?" says Stella, pulling aside the curtain and stepping over the curb of the shower. She hands him a tiny bottle.

"Shit!" says Ray, protecting his genitals with both bony hands. "Does our accidental intimacy mean we are a couple?"

"Sorry," she says. "I desperately need a shower and I didn't know how long the hot water would last."

Ray turns around. So far he hasn't seen Stella completely naked. Nor does he want to. "Don't you have a shower in your room?"

"I can't bear to stay in that room," she says. "I'm scared to take a shower there. What if Felix was kidnapped? Someone could come back there. Besides, the shower reminds me of the movie Psycho."

Ray, without turning around, raises his head, eyes closed, to wet his hair and wash out the soap he'd been using. He spreads the shampoo through his hair. "Isn't that bizarre? Who'd want to kidnap Felix? It's not like you are wealthy. Who'd pay a ransom for him?"

He jumps, dropping the shampoo, when he feels his balls cupped from behind. He doesn't want Stella touching him again, and the shampoo's burning his eyes, still, he's getting hard.

Thinking to push Stella away without having his balls pulled off, he instead backs up into her until he can feel her entire coolly wet and soapy body, breasts, stomach, her thighs, plastered along his back. He tells himself to move away and out of the stall; instead he turns to face her, pushing himself into her as hard as he can. Or is she pressing into him? Somehow she's holding on to his cock, maybe trying to guide him into her, but the silky, soapy rubbing makes his prick feel enormous and still swelling, as if it's become his entire body. With a loud groan, he comes.

"Ohh," he gasps. "Sorry."

He hasn't felt this way, or this out of control sexually since he was thirteen. Yet, though he hates feeling this way, he's getting hard again. Stella, looking at him, pushes him roughly toward the wall so he can feel the faucets at his spine. He pulls her wet hair back and wraps his other arm around her thighs, just under her butt. His prick dips to find her, like a divining rod searching for water. Is he holding her up or is she holding him up—he can't tell. The faucets dig into the small of his back and his thighs are shaking. Their rhythmic grunts, loud and harsh, sound as if they are working hard at something difficult, tedious, like digging a grave.

After, Ray stands in the shower, arms hanging limp at his sides like an infant, the water already cool, as Stella rinses some soap off him with the rough white washcloth

"I can't help feeling that Felix is in some kind of bad trouble," she says.

Ray pushes her hand away, and throws a threadbare towel around his hips. "I have to lie down for a minute. You can at least wait a few moments before bringing up Felix."

"Why do men always have to rest after sex," Stella asks. Uninvited, she lies down, damp and naked, alongside Ray.

"Everything points to it," she says.

"To what?" asks Ray.

"Felix. In trouble. Wish I had a cigarette," she says. "He always had a tendency toward paranoia—but nothing like the last couple of days—thinking he was being followed. Maybe he was being followed. I should have paid more attention. I should have taken him more seriously. Especially after his beating. And thinking he'd murdered someone ..."

"Let's try to get organized here," says Ray, moving away from Stella. "It's time to tell me what you know, what you suspect is going on, and what you know Felix is involved in."

He's relieved that Stella doesn't seem inclined to discuss their sexual stuff and whatever's going on there, a lack of acknowledgment that keeps it oddly unrelated to anything else. Right now he's okay with that.

Stella crosses her legs and wiggles her toes. Her toenails have chipped scarlet polish on them.

"Felix has always been secretive," she says. "You couldn't get along with him if you needed to know everything he was into. I got tired of trying to keep up, to figure out his mysteries. I needed to take care of myself, do my own thing. I mean, he could reel off speeches about this or that political thing, or this and that horrible injustice—but to really find out what, if anything, he was actually involved in, well, you never knew what was really going on. Lately he'd been getting calls that weren't from women."

Ray looks down and sees Stella's dark pubic hair, and the stubble on her legs, and can't help thinking of Olivia, and suddenly feels nauseous.

Stella's lower lip trembles and tears run down the sides of her face into her hair.

He squelches an impulse to wrap his arms around her, comfort her. "So what do you think was going on? What could get him into trouble? Anything with drugs?"

"You can get into trouble doing good," says Stella, obviously upset that he's mentioned drugs.

"That's true," he says. "But drugs is a border issue. That's, I think, how Felix described what he was into. Border issues."

Stella wipes her eyes with her forefingers, and sniffs. "I need to blow my nose," she says, going into the bathroom.

"I think you know that Felix isn't very happy with teaching these days. He wasn't doing the publications thing. He said he wasn't a writer. But then, using some of my folk tales for inspiration—this was quite a while ago—he wrote a beautiful short novel from the point of view of a native Apache. Two faculty people not only voted against his tenure, but they accused him of cultural appropriation. They got others on board. When the book went out of print, the publisher, with Felix's blessing, let it go."

"How come I never knew about the book?" asks Ray. "I'd love to read it."

"I think it's great, but Felix is humiliated by it."

Ray can't picture Felix humiliated. Angry, maybe.

"I always thought he didn't get tenure because some faculty members hated him. At least that's what he told me. And somehow I believed that if anyone could cause some faculty to hate you it would be Felix. Now that I'm teaching I see how easily it could happen. And how political the whole tenure thing is."

"I do know this—Felix is working with some anti-pollution group. They call themselves Good Anarchists. Lately they've been working to keep the Arcco Copper Smelter from starting up again in El Paso, spewing their pollution into the air. Last time they got closed down they let the government pay for a huge cleanup. Now they think it's time to re-open."

Ray remembers the smell of the copper smelting. You just took it for granted then—it was how El Paso smelled. Juarez smelled that way too. No one seemed aware of the toxicity.

"Unbelievably, it seems Arcco Copper has the law on its side."

"What are they doing? I mean the Good Anarchists?"

"I don't know—they have 'events,' like sit-ins, and marches with signs. They annoy the city politicians, the state senators ... nothing really too destructive. Nothing too illegal," says Stella, now rubbing lotion on her calves and her heels.

"They'd love to be rid of the Good Anarchists. And Felix."

"Yeah, but they're not going to off someone. For them it's like a gnat you keep swatting. They're big. A person against them, or even people against them, is small."

"Are you kidding?" she says, rubbing moisturizer on her hands, spreading it up her wrists, and then her arms. She retrieves her bra, and underpants from the pile of blankets.

Ray's amazed that her underwear, looking like nothing more than large rubber bands, can fit a human body.

"What else?" he asks.

"Not sure. But he's told me some stuff, not much. I think he's become part of some movement, Sanctuary. They help migrants get across the border alive. Helping illegals—who would care enough about that to kidnap him, or to want to hurt or murder him. The Border Patrol? The FBI? I mean, it's a great political issue for prejudiced people, but isn't it all a pretense? Politicians pretend and the border agents pretend, and they torture Mexicans to show Republicans how much we don't want them in the U.S. But don't they, all along, really love the cheap labor?"

Ray gets up. "That's a beginning," he says. "We need to check out his phone and his computer." He finds his shirt, then his pants. "We can call some of his friends, his cohorts, anyone who's Felix has been hanging out with lately."

"It could be," says Stella, that the person Felix thinks he killed has some friend who wants to get even. She puts on the long linen shorts she'd been wearing earlier. The aroma of her skin lotion lingers.

"He even used his office at the college to harbor some illegals from San Salvador, or Guatemala. Not exactly sure where. He let them sleep there."

"That could get him fired. But I doubt anyone would want to do him physical harm," says Ray stepping into the wrong leg of his chinos. All his clothes are dirty. "I find it kind of hard to believe you don't know more about what your husband was doing. I'm not sure what we can do with all these bits and pieces."

Stella looks as if she might cry again. But this time Ray doesn't care. He's frustrated, and frayed.

"Did you really know everything Olivia was doing? Do you really think you know what she was thinking?"

Ray doesn't respond. He'd thought he did. Now he's not so sure. It's not something he wants to think about right now. Or ever, if it requires re-thinking everything in their life together.

When he'd first heard Felix talking a bit about what he was doing, why didn't Ray pay more attention? His first response was embarrassment at Felix's passion, and his anger. What can one person do? Did it pay to get that enraged? He hadn't wanted Felix to barrage him with that good Samaritan stuff, the rage at injustice. Yet he thinks that maybe he'd been a bit envious. Lately he'd been feeling nothing much. He was even beginning to hate his students, and their lack of passion. What about himself? His own lack of passion.

He watches Stella brush her hair into temporary submission.

"I couldn't possibly be involved in every aspect of Felix's life," she says. "You know what kind of energy he had. And he was always secretive, but he became more so. Maybe because he could see I wasn't the least interested. I wanted him to be passionate about me, not about some Mexicans he didn't know. I began to see that the less Felix shared with me the more freedom I had."

She puts down her hairbrush and looks in the mirror. "That kind of marriage can be fulfilling in ways, but it can also be kind of lonely," she says, wistful. She bites a cuticle on her forefinger.

The loneliness—did some of what Felix kept secret have to do with lovers? Is that also something she didn't want to share? Did they really have an open marriage? Is that why she was susceptible to Ray? Why she seduced him? The more he finds out the more questions he has.

"The last thing I want to do is see any of these people again," he says, "but we must go to the motel office to ask some more questions about Felix. I'm not sure he stopped here by chance. It seemed to me that he knew what he was doing and where he was going. We can't leave before we see if anyone here has a clue, or any information we can convince them to divulge. Aside from that, and going to find his computer and his phone, we have little to go on." He said "little," so Stella wouldn't get too upset again, but he means, "nothing."

Sara is at her desk wearing a white lace blouse that would look better on her daughter, eating what looks like a couple of tacos off a bent paper plate that she holds in one hand.

Vanessa, and the Latino handyman who'd said he thought he'd seen Felix go running are seated behind her, legs crossed and looking uncomfortable on two bridge chairs watching the news on TV. It seemed to Ray that they'd glanced at each other when Ray and Stella opened the screen door. Maybe they know something about Felix. On the other hand, they know something about Ray and Stella that might provoke a glance as well.

"We're checking out," Stella says. "But my husband hasn't returned. Are you sure you don't know anything more about where he might have gone? Anything you might have forgotten to mention? Or anything he might have said last night?"

Stella's hand shakes as she places her room keys next to the purple plate, now on the desk. None of them say anything.

"Remember the two guys, the well-dressed ones who came to the party last night late? They wanted to talk to Felix. Do you know who they were, or what they wanted?" asks Ray, impatient.

He'd like to shake these three, who shrug and look at each other stupidly, Sara with a forkful of chopped beef, lettuce and salsa halfway to her lavender lips.

"Let's go," says Ray, pulling Stella's arm, pinching her.

"Wait," she says, pulling out of his grip. "If Felix comes back here, can you let him know we're looking for him? We'll be going back home—to our house—for a bit?"

She's at a loss, not really knowing where they'll be.

Ray slams the screen door behind them. "What was that weird look the handyman gave you?"

"What? What are you talking about? You're not going to get all paranoid too."

"You know what's going on here, don't you," Ray says.

"What are you talking about?" Stella asks, stepping away from Ray as if he's suddenly become her enemy.

"I'm sorry," says Ray. "I have to get out of here before I become Felix. He begins to walk very fast.

"Ray," Stella shouts, rushing to catch up, hair wild. She turns her ankle on the lava-colored gravel walkway, but doesn't stop.

Suddenly Ray hates this whole southwest landscape that feels so niggling, so ungenerous.

"Ray, where are you going?" Stella limps after him, her voice high with panic.

"I have to get out of here," he says, running towards the car, which is already packed.

"We have to get out of here," pants Stella. "We will get out of here." She runs after Ray, her sandals kicking up sharp gravel that bites into her bare ankles and calves.

SIXTEEN

The boundary between morality and depravity intersects at la frontera. *At their junction, narcotics and weapons pour between the Americas. The political division itself adds to their value. Danger heightens and profits increase. As they do, hopes decline and drag the future along with them.*

Alan Weisman, *La Frontera*

RAY IS AT THE WHEEL. Dry, bare mountains are on their left, pale and empty desert on their right. Above the mountains the bright cumulus clouds have flat bottoms as if they're sitting on shelves of air.

Ray's inclination is to speed, but Stella's demanded that they stick to forty, forty-five miles an hour so they can look for Felix. He thinks finding Felix along the side of the road is a ridiculous fantasy.

"We have no idea which direction Felix would be … traveling. Even if he had a choice. And if he's in someone's vehicle, would we even see him?" Ray asks. "The quicker we get to Felix's computer and phone the faster we'll find him."

Stella is quiet; she fiddles with her hair blowing around her head, and looks out the window, concentrating. The landscape is so bare that a person, walking, running, or even lying down would be visible for half a mile.

The car is roomy with only two in front, and Ray enjoys the solitude of Stella's non-attention. It feels good to be driving. He's been feeling as if he's being led somewhere he didn't want to go, and now he has the illusion, anyway, of being in control.

"The Mexican, the motel handyman, said he saw Felix running south, towards Juarez," Stella says, not looking away from the window. "Though Mexicans often want to please so they'll say anything, rather than say they don't know."

They are driving north, to Felix and Stella's house to look for his phone.

"I'm pretty sure he was in no condition to go running," says Ray. "I'm surprised he went to the party. But you don't go running with a possibly broken rib. And wouldn't he take his motel key? And two running shoes?"

Stella is unusually pensive, which Ray welcomes. If they have to be driving they might as well remain calm until the next crisis.

When a police car passes them he feels Stella's tension level rise.

"I know we've discussed this before," he says, "but don't you think the police could do a better job of finding Felix? Especially if he's in trouble? I mean the United States Police. They have ways of searching for people who go missing. They know better where to look, and they have the manpower to cover greater distances. They aren't going to have any record of Felix being in Mexican jail fifteen years ago."

He looks over at Stella, who doesn't answer. She doesn't even look at him. It's as if he hasn't said anything, which annoys him.

"What about the Border Patrol? Can't we trust the Border Patrol?"

She takes a long time to respond. "Ray, I don't want to discuss this again. We'd probably end up spending a whole day at some dinky out-of-the-way police station and we'd probably have to pay them some money to let us go. That's all we need right now."

"I know you don't think the police would be helpful, but I'm wondering whether you're afraid of the cops because you suspect Felix did something wrong ... something illegal? Because we sure could use some help here."

Stella doesn't respond.

"Why are you ignoring me?"

For the first time, she turns to look at him. "Because you are stupid and naïve, as always."

Her lips curl down in disgust, and Ray thinks how ugly she looks, and how he hates her right now.

"If Felix has been helping illegals cross the border into the U.S., wouldn't he be in trouble with the Border Patrol? Or the U.S. Police?"

"Is that an actual crime?" he asks. Then, "Are you hiding something? Your excuses, your sudden lack of enthusiasm for finding your husband"—he chokes on the word "husband," something feels off here."

He waits for an explosive reaction. Any reaction would be welcome.

"What are you looking for at the side of the road? Do you think Felix, beaten-up Felix, would be jogging five hours after he's supposedly left the motel?"

He jumps when Stella grabs his arm and shrieks, "Stop!"

Ray slows, pulls over. There's almost no shoulder. Before the car has fully stopped, Stella is out, looking at something hidden from Ray by dry pale grasses, along the edge of the road—maybe a dog that's been hit by a car?

"Look" she shouts, cradling a filthy, battered sneaker. "I'm pretty sure it's Felix's, right?"

Ray hasn't studied Felix's sneakers closely enough to know whether that's his. Millions have the same sneakers. The running shoe she holds up was once white, but is now coated with dry, pale umber clay where it isn't scuffed and scraped.

"I'm not sure," he says, feeling as if he's failing Stella. "You'd be better able to recognize his footwear."

He doesn't say how doubtful he is. It's his experience that the roads are often littered with running shoes, high heels, even underwear, causing some wonder about what happened to their owners. Small clues to lots of mysteries.

Stella bites her lip and places the filthy shoe carefully on the back seat as if it's a fragile, precious object. He can't help thinking about how it's dirtying the seat.

"We can check it later to see if it matches the other shoe in Felix's bag," she says, snapping her seat belt.

Ray's aware of how the seat belt cuts between Stella's ample breasts, accentuating her cleavage, and then thinks about her relationship with Felix. Now he knows that Felix has had lovers. How many has Stella had?

"Now that I know that you and Felix were unfaithful to each other, what else haven't you told me."

"We weren't 'unfaithful,'" says Stella, "as I said, we had an open marriage. We didn't lie to each other about who we were fucking, or what we were doing." she says. "We didn't lie to you either. I can't believe you had no clue. You were always kind of obtuse," she adds.

"How could I have known what was going on with you two? Why are you blaming me for not knowing things like that? Would it have mattered? You're angry with me, but shouldn't I be pissed at you? What sort of friends have secret lives? Are you really a friend? Besides, though I thought we used to be close, the four of us, we haven't seen each other in quite a while, so obviously, or it should have been obvious, we're very different now."

"You just don't know," says Stella. "You didn't want to know anything. You were afraid to know."

"Are we in the past tense here?" asks Ray.

Stella doesn't respond. She rests her head on the head-rest, where it moves involuntarily from side to side as if she's saying no.

Ray's disturbed enough to know that maybe she's hit on something. He realizes how much he's stopped himself, even now, from asking questions. But he doesn't want to give in.

"It wasn't something I should have discovered. You and Felix were lying to us all those years ago."

"The truth was there to see. We weren't making an effort to hide anything."

"You and I have different ideas about truth," says Ray, trying to keep his voice steady.

"Yeah?" Stella says. "What's your idea of truth?"

"Truth is truth. Exactly that," he says.

"Are you kidding? First of all, what the fuck does that mean?"

"For you truth is relative," says Ray. "Truth for you seems to be whatever it suits you to say at the time, whatever gets you through, or gets you what you want."

Stella bites her cuticle, after picking at it for a while. "Doesn't everybody lie, Ray?"

"Doesn't everybody lie?" Ray tries to keep from shouting. "No." he says. No wonder he didn't ask too many questions. The more he asks, the less he understands. The less he knows her.

He glances over and when she's looking out the window he studies her profile, the thick, unruly hair blowing around her face; the strands that stick up are reddish in the sunlight. He imagines pulling that hair back hard. He feels like throwing her across the backseat, and pulling the crotch of her shorts aside, and, as if sex with him is punishment, pumping her secrets from her.

THE BAR THEY'VE STOPPED AT IS DARK after the glaring afternoon sun. Ray can hardly see. It's cool too, from huge ceiling fans, their long black blades slicing through the air with a soft rhythmic whoosh. Ray sits on a high stool at the bar, rubbing his cold moist El Sol bottle across his hot forehead as if it could cool the riotous growth of confusing thoughts and impulses germinating there.

Returning from the toilet, Stella hoists herself on a stool next to Ray, sighs, combing her hair from her face with her fingers, and takes a long swig of beer from a glass dripping with condensation.

"This is great," she says. "I was thirsty but I didn't realize it. That's how people die in the desert."

They watch the bartender, bald, with a long black beard, a large hoop earring in one earlobe, and a lot of hair in his nose, wipe wine glasses with a red rag, carefully hanging them upside down on the overhead rack.

There's a daytime serial drama or *telenovela* playing on one TV screen at the end of the bar, near the ceiling, and a football game on another TV at the other end, just above an array of liquor bottles. The sound has been turned down on the TV nearest them, the one with the drama.

Ray watches a beautiful, overdressed couple fighting, but the sounds he hears is the sports announcer from the ballgame on the other screen, and the cheering crowd.

The man in the drama has lost his temper and smacks the woman across her face. Her hands fly up, then to her cheek, and she flushes, surprised, hurt, then, angry. She throws her wine glass, the red liquid splashing against a pristine periwinkle wall, where it drips like blood, and storms out, slamming the door.

Ray has seen this scene, or scenes like it, countless times in movies and on television, which makes it trite, yet also causes it to seem real. But do people really act this way? He doesn't think anyone he knows does. But what does he know?

He looks over at Stella, who's also watching the screen, absorbed. What is she thinking?

"If you don't believe there's a real truth, then what do you believe in? How do you trust anyone? Don't you begin to lose a sense of what's real?"

Her eyes still on the silent drama on the screen, she says, "Wow, where did that come from? Oh, I remember what we were talking about before. So many questions. Did you really trust Olivia?" Stella asks, finishing her beer.

"Don't change the subject to Olivia, and our relationship," says Ray. "Of course I trusted her. We trusted each other." If there's one thing he's sure of is that he and Olivia had a relationship based on trust. How on earth else could you continue living with someone?

"Olivia told the truth. There was no relative truth for her, no partial truth, no truth based on an interpretation of truth, or truth that changes over time. Or truth that's thought up at the moment for some kind of gain."

"But supposing she didn't always tell you the truth?" Stella persists. "And what if you found out much later that she'd lied? Would that change how you feel about her? Would that change your relationship?"

"Yeah, you always get out of answering questions by asking questions," says Ray, rubbing the well-worn dully-sheened mesquite bar with his forefinger, as if to rub out the faint initials carved there. Could new information about Olivia change a relationship that lives only in the past? Would Ray have to go over everything, and revise it?

Before he can say anything, Stella grabs his arm, causing his beer to slosh over his hand holding the bottle.

"What the hell ... He follows Stella's eyes locked on the TV; her hand grips his wrist. There's still no sound, but Ray recognizes the motel they'd stayed at—the office, the grounds. But don't lots of motels look alike? Especially those old, rural ones from the fifties?

"Please turn the sound up," Stella pleads of the bartender, who bends his hairy ear towards her, his round stomach swathed in a lavender apron, swinging a bit too close to Ray.

Next is a shot of a body on a stretcher, the kind with aluminum legs that fold, being lifted into an ambulance by two cops. The body is covered with a white sheet, head and all, except for the feet, which are bare. No socks, no shoes.

"Those are Felix's feet," says Stella. "I know those are his feet," she says, shaking.

Her ragged breathing is louder than the sound of the football game on the other TV.

The bartender fiddles a bit and the sound comes on.

"Police on both sides of the border are looking for an Anglo couple, late thirties, early forties, driving an old Suburban with Texas plates."

"What does this have to do with us?" Ray asks, looking at Stella, who is staring at him, her eyes wide with fear. Her mouth opens. She's trembling. With her hair now all wild around her face, and her terrified expression, she looks like a lunatic.

SEVENTEEN

The border was the crossing to the underside of our consciousness, a passage from all things rational—law and order—into a surreal cultural landscape, where real Indians still wandered the streets, the Virgin Mary in the guise of a deified brown woman was the equal to Jesus Christ, and seat-of-the pants economic improvisation was a way of life. The border in this North to South scenario was a thin, porous membrane through which cultural explorers slipped into our collective unconscious.

The Late Great Mexican Border, ed. Bobby
Byrd & Susannah Mississippi Byrd

RAY WAKES WITH A SOUR TASTE IN HIS MOUTH, trying to recall how he got here. He feels as if he's been asleep for days, yet he doesn't feel rested. He forces himself to look over at Stella. He's relieved that she's still asleep beside him on the king-size bed, so he can orient himself. Or just think. Even when married to Olivia, he loved waking up before her, to know she was there, but to be alone for a while. But waking up with Stella in the same bed reinforces his fear that they are now a couple, and his heart races, fingers tingling.

A room service menu near the phone says they are at a Holiday Inn. The room is very clean, if you don't think about strangers' bacteria, and fairly spacious, with a couple of comfy chairs, a small couch, a round table, and even a desk. A large glass door opens onto a small private terrace. He scares himself with the thought that he could probably be comfortable here forever.

Stella is covered to her neck with the pink sheet, her lush dark hair spread over the pillows, one under her head, and another she's hugging under her chin. He's reassured by her pure repose, the regular rise and fall of her chest—calm breathing. No sign now of how terrified she'd been. She'd scared the shit out of him.

HE'D TRIED TO REASSURE HER AT THE BAR. "So what if the cops are looking for an Anglo couple? An Anglo couple, no description, except approximate age? How many of those are there? Hundreds? Thousands? And the body on the stretcher? It could be anyone."

He'd put his hand on Stella's shoulder hoping his warmth could comfort her, stop her shaking, which was scaring him.

"And even if it is, god forbid, Felix, which I'm sure it isn't, what did we do that would cause us to be arrested? Maybe they are just looking for someone to inform of his death? To identify him?" It was hard for him to say this—"Unless you know something I don't."

"They'll want to question us," she'd said. "I'll have to identify him. They'll hold us there forever, asking about what he's been doing, who he's been seeing. We don't know how he died. Maybe they'll blame us."

"Blame us for what? What did we do? Nothing. Nada. We don't even know anything much about Felix's activities. Right?"

His words didn't help. She looked down at her lap, hyperventilating.

"Two tequilas," Ray'd said to the bartender.

"What kind?" he asked, wiping his hands on his apron, large silver belt buckle visible underneath.

"Anything strong," said Ray, grateful that he seemed totally uninterested in Stella's hysteria.

Back in the car Stella was calmer, more together.

"Let's get rid of this car," she'd said, suddenly, rubbing Ray's arm. "I hate this car. I've always hated it. The seats burn like hell when it's hot, and the car stinks of something. Something plastic. Besides," she'd said, "the car is the only way we can be identified. The only thing that distinguishes us from any other couple driving together who appear to be around forty years old." She ran her forefinger along Ray's thigh.

Ray resisted the strong urge to push her hand away. Wherever she touched felt as if he'd be left with a permanent scar. He wondered whether he was more disgusted with her or with himself. He pulled as far away from her as possible.

She pinched his thigh, angry. He felt, along with pain and surprise, an internal flow as if all his internal organs were flooding into his prick. He looked out the window to make sure no one was anywhere nearby, and then, any thought useless, volition suspended, he was lost in Stella's softness, enveloped in her vanilla and lime-scented breasts. His mouth found her slick lips, kissing, then biting, and then, her nipples. He ignored her requests to bite harder. Soon her shorts were down, his pants around his hips, his black leather belt flapping. He penetrated her quickly and hard, her breathy groan in his ear, as she bit his earlobe hard. Her moans morphed ugly and harsh, and her sweat dripped onto him, merging with his own, until he felt an unbearable sweetness that became fluid, as if he were melting all over the hot fake leather seat. It felt like they'd both turned to oily liquid.

HE WATCHES STELLA SLEEP, the soft sheet exposing a pale shoulder with a dark red bite. Images of their voracious, almost vicious, sex in the front seat of the car, like sex between strangers, or people who hate each other, run through his mind.

His own white chest and pink, sunburned arms seem to belong to a stranger. What on earth is he doing here, at this Holiday Inn, with Stella.

He dresses quietly, praying now that Stella doesn't wake. He's going to the El Paso airport, and would rather not confront her—or have her convince him to stay. He wishes he'd brought his phone and computer. Leaving their tech stuff seemed like a fun idea at the time. Whose idea? Felix? Stella? Was there some ulterior motive?

Dressed and ready to leave, he looks at Stella again. She hasn't moved. He can't believe she slept through his washing up, his zipping his duffle, and all the other sounds he'd made. He's glad—but disappointed too. Leaving her like this without even a goodbye, and in the midst of this situation with Felix, feels too much like desertion. Almost as if, by not waking in time, she's deserting him, rather than the opposite. Well, she'll do all right, he thinks. She's pretty good at taking care of herself.

ALONE, DRIVING, Ray is less anxious than he's been in days, even though he feels like he's someone else in this large vintage vehicle. He takes a deep breath because he begins to realize that he's left Stella with no car and hasn't left her any message about where to find it. Though she'd wanted to get rid of the car anyway. And she can always get someone in the office to call for a rental.

His plan is to leave the car in long-term parking, and to then exchange his return ticket for whatever's available.

There's a hint of dawn in the reddish hue at the horizon, though it's still dark. He smells of Stella, her skin, her lotion, her secretions, mixed with his own. The entire car smells of sex. He'll be glad to get rid of it.

Though energized to be fleeing, the farther he drives, the more he is aware of a soft thud of longing in his groin, in his chest.

There are plenty of spaces in long-term parking. Ray drives around for a while searching for a spot that's out of view of the shuttle bus stops. Once parked, about to grab his duffle off the back seat, when it occurs to him to wipe his fingerprints of the wheel, the doors, the dash with the bottom of his shirt. He can't say why, as he doesn't believe Stella's fear that they're being hunted by the police, or even that it's Felix's body on the stretcher on TV.

He's well aware that he's acting like a criminal, and the more he acts like a criminal, the more he feels like he's committed some crime.

But maybe Felix has. This is Felix's car, and there's no way to identify Ray's connection to Felix when and if it's discovered by the authorities.

Before Ray closes the car door, he notices the worn, grimy white sneaker in the back, on the floor. Looking at it he feels queasy, but chalks it up to hunger.

He walks away, then goes back. He's decided to use some of the tools in his trunk to remove the license plate. He hunkers down, working furtively, hiding whenever he hears some wheelie on the concrete, the clack of high heels, or the shuttle bus on its route around the lot.

Felix's plates are almost impossible to remove. They are bent and the bolts have rusted. None of the socket wrench openings seem to fit them. He uses the tire iron to knock the bolts loose, trying not to make noise. It doesn't help that his hands are sweaty and shaking. It isn't that hot yet, but perspiration drips into his eyes, stinging.

Finished, he wipes his face with the bottom of his shirt, and, with it, opens the car door so he can sit inside for a moment and pull himself together.

Now he has committed a crime—removing the license plate of a car he's going to be deserting in an airport parking lot.

More relaxed, Ray wipes some of the grime and rust from his hands with a tissue from the glove box, and thinks about Felix. Can he really just leave not knowing whether Felix is alive or dead, or what sort of trouble he may be in? Wouldn't it be best to try to help his friends rather than run? And the way he left Stella—sneaking out without leaving a note, or waking her up to say goodbye—nothing—in fact, leaving just the way Felix did?

The more he thinks about it the more he realizes that he's going to take the airport shuttle to a rental car place, and then drive back to the Holiday Inn near downtown El Paso, and back to Stella.

DRIVING THE RENTED, nearly-new silver Toyota Corolla, Ray's feeling pretty good, and clear about this latest decision. For a second he pictures the scraped running shoe he'd left in the Suburban. He knows it's ridiculous, but he thinks about going back for it. He'd thought, when Stella'd found the shoe, and had thrown it into the back of the car, that maybe by some magic it could attract its mate, and ultimately, Felix.

When Olivia died it took him forever to pack up and give away her clothing, her art supplies, her things. It felt natural for them to be around—they'd always been there.

When he'd invited Mayra, one of the few women he'd dated, to his apartment, she'd been surprised that he, a tenured professor, had a roommate. When he'd said that the clothing and paintings, and practically everything in the apartment had belonged to his deceased wife, she'd looked horrified. He never called her again, and she never called him, but he realized it might be time to do something about it.

As he went through Olivia's clothing, he spent too much time thinking about each item, to see whether he remembered when she'd worn it, or used it, and to who or where he'd like to donate it. This process was agonizing, and he ended up throwing everything into huge black garbage bags even without looking at them.

These he brought, a few at a time, to his neighborhood Goodwill donation box, behind the small shopping center. One of those times, as he was driving away, he saw that one of his black bags had opened and some of Olivia's clothing had fallen out. When he'd arrived home and was already parked in his building's underground parking garage, he kept seeing one of the items, a cobalt blue silk blouse, strewn on the ground near the donation box, one sleeve resting on a small hill of dirty, black-edged leftover snow.

He hadn't cried much during the period that Olivia'd been treated for cancer, or even after she'd died, but the vision of the blue blouse carelessly deserted near some filthy melting snow set something off. He felt a horrible ache in his chest that for a moment he thought was a heart attack, and which rose into his throat. Then he wept and wept.

When he recovered, not until evening, he drove back to the Goodwill donation box. As he picked up the damp, stained blouse a woman in a red puffer coat got out of her SUV with a small plastic bag. Slamming her car door, she said, "You piece of shit—stealing from the Goodwill box!"

Ray, startled, didn't know immediately what she meant. She came close enough for him to smell her sweet perfume, and began to pull at the cobalt fabric in his hands.

Very suddenly he let go of it, and drove out of there as fast as he could, his car's beams lighting the woman, her maroon hair framed by the Goodwill sign, eyes wide with surprise, Olivia's bright blue blouse hanging from her hand.

WHEN RAY ARRIVES AT THE MOTEL, the pale sky is streaked with peach and rose.

Unbelievably, Stella is still in bed, in nearly the same position as when he left. He removes his shoes, placing them each soundlessly on the carpet near his side of the bed, and carefully climbing into the cool space that seems to be waiting for him.

He pulls the soft pink sheet over himself, places his arm gently across Stella, and settles comfortably against her warm back as if they have been intimate forever. Stella stirs and sighs, but doesn't wake.

EIGHTEEN

Our crossing of any border owes, after all, as much to what we abandon as it does to what we anticipate.

Philip Garrison, *Augury*

RAY JUMPS, STARTLED. He looks around, disoriented, and finds himself in bed, facing the motel table with the lamp on it.

In his dream he is sleeping next to Stella. He's woken because she's causing the bed to move, as if she's shaking, or crying. Or masturbating. He just lies there, trying to see which it is. He's concerned that she might be terribly upset, yet the idea of her masturbating is turning him on. He's also humiliated for her—for discovering her in some very private act. And with all the screwing they've been doing, why would she need to masturbate? He pretends to be asleep, riding with her regular movements, listening to her breathing accelerate. He considers turning over and placing his hand on her, and then joining her if she's up for it. When he does turn he sees that there's a woman on top of her (or maybe not a woman?) and they are moving rhythmically, and beginning to moan.

Seeing he's awake, Stella says, "You can join us if you'd like."

He pulls the blanket down and nods a welcome to the stranger, who has very short, dark hair slicked back behind delicate ears. Just as the woman (or man) has given Ray's penis a long slow lick along its swollen underside, and is about to wrap it in his/her large warm mouth, Ray wakes. He can still feel hot breath on himself, and he's tingling all over, his cock so hard it's bent way over his flat belly.

HE HEARS STELLA IN THE SHOWER. The sheets already smell of both of them as if they've been using the bed for weeks.

In his dream, Stella screws someone else, but Ray doesn't care. It feels right that she invites him to join her and whomever she's fucking. Is he beginning to feel comfortable in a world where everyone betrays everyone else? Is he himself in his dream? Or does he represent Felix? Perhaps Stella represents him? Or maybe he's the stranger making love with Stella?

He's gotten into bed in his clothes, he realizes, sitting up. "Stella," he calls. She doesn't hear him.

He opens the bathroom door. Stella wrapped in a white towel, leans way over, her hair hanging in front of her face, cascading toward the white tile floor, moving the hair dryer above her head.

She hasn't heard him behind her, but she hears his pants, with his keys and wallet in the pocket, dropping to the floor, his belt buckle clinking on the tile. She continues what she's doing until Ray grabs her from behind, pressing against her.

He wants to tell her about the Suburban at the airport, and that he's rented a car. But he says, "I was dreaming about you."

He grabs her flow of damp thick hair. The dryer falls to the floor with a crash and continues its loud wail, vibrating against the ceramic tile. With his large hands he covers her face. She nips at his palm and fingers like a school of sunfish.

"What did you dream?" she asks, muffled.

"You were fucking someone," he says, moving his hands to hold her breasts, soft, with their hard nipples.

"Who?" she asks, pressing her butt into him.

"I don't know," he says. "I think it was a woman."

"Interesting," she says. "What does it mean?"

"Beats me," he says.

"That you don't trust me?" she muses. "That I have a secret life? That you think I'm gay?"

Her warm nakedness melts him as he pushes into her, pressing her taut stomach with the one hand around her.

RAY SITS ON THE CHARTREUSE EASY CHAIR next to the small round table, drinking the coffee Stella has made with the coffee pot in their room.

"There's not enough coffee here for two full cups," she says, pouring some for herself. She sits on the other chair. "I can't believe you still don't trust me after all this," she says.

"What do you mean by, 'after all this?' You mean, after all this fucking?"

The coffee is hotter than he'd thought, and he's burned his tongue.

"I meant, after all these years. We've known each other for so long." She smiles. "And all the fucking."

"We've known each other," says Ray, "but we obviously don't know each other." He runs his sore tongue along his upper teeth.

"Unfortunately the sex makes me feel as if I do know you, but all I'm getting to know is your body. It's an illusion of closeness that helps us to feel as if we trust each other, until something strange happens, and you do or say something entirely weird, or you lie to someone, and then the doubt returns."

He doesn't add that their growing physical intimacy makes their real life feel that much more uncomfortable. At the same time, this discomfort, or anxiety, and the guilt, seem to be making him more desirous—and more passionate, an admission to himself he's not ready to share.

"Look," says Ray, pulling aside the thick plastic-lined maroon motel drapes a bit.

There's a sudden slice of light, and a bright triangle across the table. "I do wonder whether you know more than you are saying. Both about what Felix is into, and about your relationship and your marriage. And what you are into. And whether you are using me. You've made it clear how dense you think I am, and how much I haven't noticed, even in my own marriage and with the four of us in the past. Yet, aside from your snide remarks you're holding back on letting me know anything. For instance, why would the police be after us. If that (he doesn't want to say 'body') was Felix under the sheet, would the police think we murdered him? Isn't it possible they just want to find out who he is?"

He runs his finger along the edges of the triangle of light on the tabletop. "Given all this, I have only a few choices: I could leave you here and go home." He doesn't mention that he very nearly did that. "I could go to the police on my own. Or, if we can't agree on an agenda, I could simply follow your every decision."

His coffee is now tasteless, and hurts his burned tongue.

Stella looks into the stripe of sun behind Ray, and squints. She runs her forefinger over the top of her cup, clockwise, then counter.

"I'm not hiding anything." She adds, "From you. I'm not using you, but I do need your help now."

Her face turns pink; her features crumple.

"No crying," says Ray. "And definitely no more sex." These sound like the terms of a commitment from him. "So let's follow through on our plan."

"Yes," says Stella, sniffling. "We'll go home ... to our house."

"Our house," says Ray, eyes wide. He thinks for a second that she's referring to some house that he and she share. "Oh, you mean your El Paso house. To find Felix's phone, his computer."

"What other house?" she asks. "Though if the cops suspect us, and if they have any information on Felix, wouldn't that be the first place they'd look?"

Ray still doubts that Felix's body was found. That it was Felix under the sheet. He doesn't believe the cops are looking for him and Stella.

"If you want to find Felix, what else can we do? We'll have to chance it," he says.

He expects an argument, but Stella says, "Maybe that body wasn't Felix. Maybe he's gone home. Maybe he's home, needing our help." Re-energized, she sits up straight, one sandal hanging from her hand. "You're right, Ray. I'm sorry. I was just so frazzled, and I got so freaked."

He's surprised by Stella's apology. Yet relieved. He's hoping the police will be at their house—and that perhaps they'll help find Felix.

Ray pulls aside the curtain and points to the silver Toyota and tells Stella about his trip to the airport where he's left Felix's Suburban.

"Where was I?" she asks. Then, "You left me sleeping. You were going to leave me. Right?"

"I didn't, though."

She's throwing everything that's on the bed into her suitcase. He can't tell whether or not she's angry.

"There's no way anyone can trace us now," he says. He unzips his duffel, and holds up the Suburban's license plates. "It will take the authorities quite a while to realize no one's picking up the car, and then to find out whose it is," he says.

Stella laughs. "What should we do with those plates? You don't want them in your bag."

Ray stands there, plates in his hand, paralyzed.

Stella takes them and puts them between the mattress and the box spring of one of the beds, shoving them in towards the center.

"So," she says, "we'll sneak into my house and I'll get Felix's stuff. And we'll go somewhere and check it out, right? Is that the plan?"

"I guess so. Since I have no bloody idea what's really going on, and no matter what we do we'll be making mistakes, like everyone does in mysteries. We can try to figure out a plan, or we can throw dice."

Ray's about to hoist his duffle, and look around for anything they may have forgotten, when Stella says, "The gun. If Felix didn't have the gun with him, then it's either in the house or it was in the car," she says.

Ray pictures the glove compartment, and the small declivities they kept change in. There was no gun, for sure.

"I'm sure I got everything. I didn't leave anything in the car," he says, picturing the running shoe in the back, on the floor. But did he really look carefully on the floor of the back? He could have missed seeing a gun if there was one back there.

"I can't believe you and Felix had a gun," he says. "What do normal people need a gun for? I mean real law-abiding people, like writers and professors? Not people in movies? Guns are for weird Republicans, gun collectors, hunters, and criminals," he says, "or insane people."

"Felix wanted one," she says. He thought he'd need it. I thought that was a bit paranoid, but now look. He taught me how to use it." She looks dazed. "Our fingerprints are on it, so I'd love to know where it is."

Ray remembers the dream he'd had at the crummy Mexican motel. Felix's blood, deep carmine, splashed all over the ragged ochre carpet, and Stella's wobbly hand gripping the silver pistol, trying to keep it from shaking, as she aimed it at Ray.

NINETEEN

As the Interstate swings to the northwest again, it closely follows the course of the Rio Grande all the way to El Paso. Serrated Laramide ranges on the Mexico side of the river are outlined against the sky while the green fields on the river floodplain nestle at their base. The road runs on a high terrace level above the river; much of the surrounding landscape is windblown sand and dune deposits. Abundant sand in the dry flat of the river bottom is readily available for the wind to distribute. In some places the dunes are stabilized by the sparse vegetation, but look for rounded sand dunes, and wind ripple marks on free sand faces. They are especially obvious in low sun angles of early morning or late afternoon.

Darwin Spearing, *Roadside Geology of Texas*

RAY PARKS HIS SILVER RENTAL CAR at the end of a cul de sac in the development where Felix and Stella's house is, about half a block away.

It's dusk, which he thinks will be great for not being noticed. But soon he realizes that in a place like this where not a soul is when it gets dark, they'd probably be less conspicuous in the middle of the day. If police are looking for you, there is no good time.

They are silent. Ray is tense, and he guesses Stella is too. He'd tried to convince her, and he really believes so, that she's imagining that the police are looking for them, yet her fear, like a virus, has infected him.

"That was probably the victim of some hit and run driver, and maybe a couple was noticed driving the car that hit him," says Ray. This is just one of his explanations for the barefoot man on the stretcher, and the police search for a man and woman.

Ray would be home in Boston by now if he hadn't returned to the motel and Stella. Is he simply following some paranoid fantasy of hers? Perhaps recent stresses have caused in her some kind of breakdown? Sometimes it seems that they are both crazy.

However, Felix is missing. And Ray is going to try to find him.

He takes a good look around. He'd only been to their house the night he'd arrived, exhausted from the flight from Boston, which now seems as if it had been eons ago. He'd been a different person. He'd hardly noticed the outside of their house—only that the houses around seemed similar.

Each low concrete house is ranch-style, except for the ends of streets, each of which sport a fancier house with a second story. All the houses are painted a pale pinkish or a pale yellowish variant of beige. They are planted on sand, or pebbles, a huge rock set here and there as part of the landscaping, which includes small round cacti, young century cactus, or, here and there, a tall ocotillo. It will take a while till these houses look as if they belong there, no less unique, or personalized.

That evening of Ray's arrival they'd had wine and brie, crackers, and olives, and something else, some sort of salami. He hardly recalls what their house looked like inside.

They'd sat on a very plain modern brown leather couch. Or was it black? The snacks, and the wine bottles and glasses had been laid out on a long, low mesquite coffee table. He thinks the walls were beige, but he's not sure. He can't recall if they had any art on their walls. If they did, he didn't notice it.

The houses Felix and Stella, had lived in when they were all teaching or getting their advanced degrees at UTEP, were in an old, funky, low-rent neighborhood of small ranches, or blocks of narrow brick houses, with porches, and tall trees. Those neighborhoods had seen better times, but even then gentrification was beginning. Diverse and interesting, full growth old trees, coffee houses, and small stores, with sidewalks, it was perfect for students and young faculty. They all had framed posters on their walls, and bookshelves constructed of piles of bricks and pine boards.

"Wait here," Stella says. "I can do this alone. I need to remember that going into my own house isn't a crime." She grabs her straw bag, and searches for her keys.

"I'm coming with you," Ray says, peering around the fast-darkening area.

The house they've parked near (not in the driveway) is about five or six houses from Stella's. There are no lights showing through anyone's windows, so either it's still too light out, or no one is home. They hope it's the latter. Their silver car parked along a curb, seems very visible.

As it gets darker, the houses now appear gray, silhouetted against the very deep cobalt sky. To the west there's one final bright coral streak half hidden by a lavender cloud. Soon the streetlights will come on. Any lamp Stella turns on in her house will trumpet her arrival if anyone's keeping an eye out for her or for Felix.

"Head towards the backyards," says Stella. "There's an alley behind all the back gardens."

Ray, out of the car, follows Stella, feeling like an idiot sneaking around, walking along someone's driveway in order to get behind the houses. The gardens are as bare as the front of the houses, mostly cactus and scrub grass, a mesquite tree here and there, and more pebbles.

There are wooden porches behind many of the houses, and Ray hopes no one is out on their deck having cocktails, or dinner. The alleys Stella mentioned, are narrow back streets that connect all the houses, as a way to deliver packages, and pick up trash.

"Let's just walk straight to your back door," says Ray. "You do have a back door?

His heart's beating too fast. He squats for a moment. "I'm having a heart attack," he says.

"You have some issues you need to deal with," says Stella.

"I have some issues?" says Ray, too loud. "The fact that we're crawling around your neighborhood to sneak into your own house after your husband disappears under mysterious circumstances causes me to have anxiety symptoms. Is that something I need to deal with?"

"Shhh," whispers Stella. She seems to be smiling, but maybe it's a grimace. They both jump when the streetlights go on, bright bluish white.

"I'll go in myself," she says. "You keep watch from that garbage dumpster area where you won't be seen. I'll be quick. I'm just getting Felix's laptop, phone, and the gun."

She points to a large dumpster disguised from looking like a garbage area with a low concrete wall that has an opening just wide enough to get into with one's trash, a cactus or two planted alongside the wall in a further attempt to disguise it. Parked right next to the low wall is a black car that Ray hopes is abandoned.

Ray stands in the entranceway to the bin area watching Stella move lithely, soundlessly to her house, now three houses from Ray. His heart pumps so hard that the top of his head vibrates. He prays no one comes to throw out trash.

Once Stella has disappeared into the house, Ray decides to check out the black car, right at the alley side of the concrete wall he's hanging next to. From where he is he doesn't see anyone in the car, yet he keeps low, out of range of the slightly tinted windows, feeling like a character in a movie.

Now close to the dark car, Ray stands up high enough to see inside, peering through the driver's side window—and jumps, heart pounding. The passenger seat is in reclining position, and there's a body in it, either sleeping, or dead.

He immediately ducks, panting. Hearing nothing, trying to regulate his breathing, which sounds like a buzzsaw to him, he raises himself to look again.

The body is wearing a forest green running suit, with white stripes running along the outsides of the arms and legs. For a second he thinks maybe it's Felix, but a second glance at the man's face makes it clear that it isn't. This man has thick black hair, a low forehead, and a huge nose, which looks larger because the man's mouth is open, lower jaw slack.

Ray looks for some movement, some sign of breathing. Then he notices, perched on the dashboard, a cop light, the kind undercover police throw on their car roof when they get an emergency call.

He grows bolder and stands up straight, studying the sleeper. Just then the body slowly unfurls and stretches its long limbs. Is it possible the man, who may be a cop, woke because he senses Ray's presence nearby?

He yawns, stretches, and gets out of the car. Ray is stuck squatting on the driver's side, near the rear tire, panting in terror. He burrows as far under the carriage as he can get, and tries holding his breath.

Can Stella be right? That someone's following them? The police? He hopes he doesn't have to run because there's no cover here in this desert landscaping, and he's also out of shape.

After a couple of moments of nothing, Ray calms a bit, and raises himself to see what's going on. The man's standing there, still, and appears to be studying something in the distance. Ray sees what he's looking at—Stella—inside her house—just shadowy movements as she passes the high, screened window of what is most likely her bedroom. There's probably some small lamp on in another room giving off a faint glow, and soon a light, low and pinkish, goes on near her.

Ray's hands squeeze into fists. There's no way to warn her. Doesn't she realize that with the lights on, and translucent curtains, she's as visible as a movie screen in a dark theater?

But Stella isn't stupid. Maybe she's making herself visible on purpose, as a distraction from something—maybe to protect him, Ray, so he can get away?

But what does she know about any policeman in the black car? And it is her house. Why should she have to sneak around in her own house?

He has to let her know someone, someone with a cop light on his dash, is watching her. His throat is dry, and he suppresses a cough.

The man turns and looks right at Ray, who drops to his knees. If the guy just walks around his car he'll see Ray, kneeling in the pebbles. If he hasn't already seen him.

Unbelievably, he hasn't. It's gotten darker, and Ray feels less visible, which is comforting, even if it's not true.

Fortunately there's no streetlight near the dumpster, maybe another attempt to make it seem as if the people who live in these houses produce no garbage. Nor does the area smell of garbage. It is dusk sweet, with a hint of night-blooming jasmine, and ozone, as if it might rain.

The man turns away from Ray's side of the car, distracted by Stella walking out her back door straight towards both men, her purse and a computer bag over her shoulder, and pulling a large black wheelie.

The man in the running suit walks towards Stella. From the back, walking, he looks incredibly like Felix. It's all Ray can do not to call out to him. But the hair, no, it can't be. And Ray has seen his face, slack with sleep.

There's no way he can warn Stella. Nothing he can do but wait and see what happens, what she will do.

He might confront the guy outright, ask him what he's doing hanging around the area. Or even, whether he's seen Felix. But this is too bold for him, and he simply stands and watches, feeling helpless.

Stella sees the man in the dark green running suit, moving slowly, calmly towards her, the white stripes on his sleeves and on his legs standing out in the dark doing their own dance with each step he takes, and she stands still.

Ray hunches, expecting the man to grab Stella, but he stops about a foot away. Stella stays where she is, placing the wheelie, maybe with the gun in it, at her feet n the thin strip of concrete walk.

She seems angry at the cop. Ray watches her gesticulate, he hands moving wildly, her dark hair rippling. She appears to know this person, whoever he is.

Ray can only hear hints of her voice, broken like ragged clouds. He tries, but can't make out any words. What can she be talking to him about?

TWENTY

It is not what happens to people that is significant,
but what they think happens to them.

Anthony Powell, *Books Do Furnish a Room*

THIS IS IT, THINKS RAY, his body and this thoughts working together for a change. He moves out of cover of the black car, and walks, determined, over to where the policeman and Stella are standing. He's walked straight across a few properties, crunching loudly on gravel, or pebbles.

The cop is involved with Stella and doesn't turn around. Another few steps, though, and he'll see Ray, who's making no effort to be silent or invisible. He's going to confront this guy, see whether he's really a cop, and see what he wants. And maybe they'll be able to glean some information about Felix, and whether this visit from him has anything to do with the man on the stretcher, or the man and the woman they are searching for.

He feels good, released, physically and psychologically, for jumping out of the shadow of Stella's paranoid world, and taking over.

He is about eight feet from the two. He expects the guy to turn towards him at any moment, and is prepared. Instead the man moves closer to Stella. Too close.

Behind the cop's back, Stella's hand almost glows in the dark, motioning to Ray not to come further. Stopping in his tracks, Ray watches the guy grab Stella's suitcase, and walk together to her back door, the door she'd just come out of.

Flabbergasted, Ray sees Stella fumble with the computer bag and her purse, find her key once again, and open the door. She nods for the man to enter, leaving Ray near her driveway deserted and exposed.

He makes his way to the front of the house, hoping to see what's going on inside through the front picture window. There's no light on in the living room, but there's a faint glow from another room, the foyer, or maybe the kitchen, in the back.

What could they be doing? Maybe he's questioning Stella—or maybe she's questioning him. Somehow he expects something worse, something violent.

He's so close to the window his breath moistens the glass whenever he breathes out. He hopes that because he's in the dark looking into the light he won't be seen from within. But what does it look like from outside, a man so close to someone's living room window, peering inside?

He can see almost as far back as the kitchen, but the foyer leading back there is long, until it opens into the fairly large open kitchen and dining area, not visible from the front window. He doesn't recall exactly how the rooms are arranged, but he knows he probably won't be able to see anything unless he goes again to the very back of the house, where, hopefully, the windows won't be too high to look through.

The bedroom windows begin at least six feet above the driveway, and the same for the bedroom facing the backyard.

He only vaguely recalls how the house is laid out, as, when he'd arrived in the evening they'd spent time in the living room, and then, because he'd been tired from traveling, with only a cursory tour around, he'd gone right to bed. Now he wishes he'd been more observant.

Feeling like a thief casing a joint, Ray walks towards a slightly bayed window that might belong to the dining room. He can see the cop, as a tall black shadow, near what is possibly the doorway to the dining room. For a skinny guy, this shadow has a lot of heft.

And where is Stella? His heart lurching into his throat, he realizes that they are one shadow. They are in a clinch.

"Hey, you over there." Ray turns, startled. A husky man, not bothering with driveways or paths, is striding towards him.

"What in hell are you doing here sneaking around? I've been watching you. You don't live here," he accuses.

Ray raises his arms as if surrendering. The man has shirt-sleeves rolled up over hairy forearms as if he's been relaxing, but is now ready for business.

"You've been slinking around here for a while. What is it you want? Are you a peeper? I'm going to call the cops."

Ray wonders whether he has a gun—a concealed carry—or whatever you call it in Texas. To protect them from geology professors like Ray. He remembers that in some American states it's perfectly legal to shoot someone if you feel threatened by them, and you can find out what was really going on only after they're dead.

"I'm waiting for my friend," mumbles Ray. "It's her house. She's just getting something. She'll be right out." He points at the house.

The man moves closer, menacing.

"I'll wait for her in our car," says Ray, moving fast in the direction of the silver rental five houses up the street. When he doesn't hear anyone following he begins to run.

He cowers in the driver's seat, comforted to be back in a car that isn't even his. This feels familiar—cowering.

He has little time to worry about Stella or to wonder about her in a clinch with the running-suit guy before he hears the crash of his back window, the sound of metal on metal, glass cracking, then cascading like a waterfall. This time he really cowers—hands over his head, head down between his knees.

"Get the fuck out of here, asshole."

Is it the same man? No, this one is even larger, wearing a faded lavender wife-beater that shows off his considerable shoulders and biceps, covered with ink.

"I'm waiting for my wife," says Ray.

"When the enormous man, legs apart, raises the huge tire iron, Ray starts the car.

HE DRIVES AROUND AND AROUND outside the area of the cul de sac, hoping Stella will find him.

Finally, his heart still racing, he parks near a low bush a few blocks away. The silver car seems to him to radiate the light and heat it's absorbed during the day.

What if she can't find him? But is it his fault she's chosen to live in a neighborhood full of unwelcoming thugs? Let her stew a little, he thinks, until he remembers the large shadow he'd seen through her window. The two of them, too close together.

He looks behind him. There's glass all over the back seat, he has a few nicks from flying slivers on his arm. He gets out and cleans himself off, and with one arm wrapped in Stella's sweater, he swipes most of the glass shards off the trunk.

Why did he say he was waiting for his wife? It came out so naturally—he didn't even have to think. He recalls the shadowy image of Stella and the cop, entwined.

This isn't the first time he's either seen or suspected Stella of using sex to get something—or to get out of something. Very different from an open marriage.

He looks around, wary, hoping no more of Stella's hideous neighbors have followed, and glad he no longer lives in Texas.

He breathes deeply, studying the sky, now full of stars, trying to calm down, but starts at the low growl of wheels on the narrow strip of sidewalk. "Open the trunk," orders Stella.

Ray pulls the trunk lever, but lets her struggle with the suitcase, and whatever else she's carrying. He hears some left-over glass tinkle to the ground.

"I had a hard time finding you," she says, pulling back her hair, getting in beside him. "What the fuck happened to the back window?" Her voice is compressed, as if she's having a hard time not exploding. Her breathing is too loud.

"I had to move the car because I didn't want my head to look like that." He turns his head toward the smashed rear window. "What did that guy want? What were you doing for so long?" He feels as if he's whining.

"Just taking care of things. I found Felix's computer, and his cell phone. I got my computer too."

He starts the car. "I bet you took care of things," he says. He moves away from Stella as if she's an insect that's too large to kill with one's hand.

"You don't know anything," she says. She looks as if she's about to yell insults at Ray, but her face shrivels and he sees tears on her cheek.

"Who is that man?" asks Ray, swerving as he grabs her upper arm, squeezing. "You seemed to know him."

She pulls away, rubbing her arm. "Ouch," she says. "I don't know him from Adam. He's just a cop."

"Just a cop! I thought we were keeping away from cops. Aren't they after us? What did he want?" he asks, through clenched teeth.

"He asked some questions about Felix." She wipes her nose with her forearm, like a kid. There are red marks on her freckled arm where he'd grabbed her. He waits to hear more, but she says nothing.

"Why would he ask about Felix? Did he have any information about him? Whether that was Felix on the news?"

Stella sniffs. "They are saying the Mexican embassy in D.C. is asking questions. They say Felix murdered a Mexican national."

"Really? What sort of Mexican national. Hundreds, maybe thousands of Mexicans are killed, or disappeared, each year by Mexicans, and no one seems to care," Ray pushes.

He asks, "Did it look as if Felix had been home? Was there any sign of him?"

"Not really. Hard to tell. It's not like he made dinner and left the dirty dishes. There were no messages, no notes. I didn't take the time to look at his emails—but if he'd been home he'd surely have taken his computer—and his phone."

She leans against her window, away from Ray.

He wonders about returning a car with a smashed rear window to Enterprise. Did he take the insurance? He can't recall much of anything anymore.

Stella hunches into herself. She's weeping, hard, but soundless. He wouldn't have known she was crying except for regular involuntary gasps.

Ray's impulse is to comfort her. Instead, he's so mad he just keeps driving, head straight ahead so he can't see her. He feels paralyzed, like those people who appear brain dead, but can see and hear everything.

In his peripheral vision he sees her shoulders heave. Suddenly she turns from the window and wraps her arms around his stiff body.

"When I couldn't find you, I thought you'd left me," she wails.

TWENTY-ONE

Nothing is less passive than the act of fleeing, of exiting.
Paolo Vino

THEY PARK IN THE LOT OF THE 7-ELEVEN, where they buy disgusting sticky donuts, huge cups of bad coffee, an El Paso Times, and a USA Today.

"It's disgraceful how few good newspapers there are in the U.S.," says Stella, putting her cup into the holder, in a better mood. "No wonder our citizens are so ill-informed." She opens the El Paso Times, her donut resting on its waxed tissue on the seat, next to her, and licks her fingers. Even this paper is crap."

They've already returned the silver Honda to Enterprise. Ray let Stella handle everything while he sat in the molded orange plastic fake Eames chair and watched her charm the man behind the counter.

They've been up all night driving, except for a short nap in a Target parking lot, when Ray could no longer keep his eyes open. There were few cars on the road at night, but quite a few very large trucks, looking like ocean liners, their edges festooned with lights.

"I used to love the vintage look of this car," says Stella, indicating their newly-rented black P.T. Cruiser. "But now it looks to me like a mini-hearse."

The donut is sticky, too sweet, and gummy, but it's just what Ray needs. He licks his fingers.

Stella leans close to him so he can see the newspaper she's reading. Her hair tickles his nose, and all of a sudden its citrus smell repels him.

"I saw you kissing that guy—that cop—or whatever he is," says Ray. "I watched through the window. I thought I could let it go because we don't owe each other anything like sexual fidelity. In fact the idea in our situation is a joke. But as friends we do owe each other honesty," he says. "And I'm not sure I can even expect that. However I am curious about what's going on—after all, I'm spending my vacation here looking for my friend Felix. And I can't seem to help feeling jealous."

Stella pulls away. "We're finally able to do something about finding Felix, and you're bringing that up again?"

"Yes," says Ray. "You do stuff that seems crazy to me. Yet I have to trust you, or I can't go on with this. It feels like you're manipulating me, that you know more than you're telling me because you need me here for some reason."

"You're wrong," says Stella, taking her large coffee out of the cup holder. "I mean about the cop. It was probably just an illusion of perspective."

Ray is silent for a moment. "You mean it just seemed as if your bodies melted together? Not possible. This is just one example of why I can't trust you."

"I'm sorry," says Stella, looking down into her lap covered with newspapers.

"There was nothing else I could think of to get out of that horrible situation. I was terrified. And it worked—we got away, right?"

Ray squelches the urge to wipe a small piece of cream filling from her lower lip.

"You don't care how I feel, you just think about yourself," she says.

He's disgusted by her pleading expression, her corrugating forehead, raised eyebrows, eyes seeking his. Luckily she makes no move to embrace him.

He looks away, at the sections of the newspapers that she's handed him. They read in silence for a while.

"Look at this," Ray says. "This article." He reads aloud, "A Caucasian, early to mid-forties, found dead in a Juarez motel." He reads more, silently. "Says they think it was drug-related. Looks like an overdose. Well that's not Felix. Felix didn't take drugs. Right?"

Stella looks around the parking lot, anxious. She grabs the paper from Ray, nearly ripping it, and continues the article.

"The police are looking for a male in his early forties, and a female, same age, traveling in a Ford Suburban with Texas plates. The three may have been involved in the murder of a Mexican national. The deceased has not been identified."

"It could be anyone," says Ray, swallowing the sudden bitter taste in his mouth. "But an old Ford Suburban with Texas plates? How many are there?"

"It didn't say 'old' Ford Suburban," says Stella, now taking on Ray's role of cooling their fears. "Let's think for a moment. We're acting as if we're guilty. Of something. We have no idea who this article is about. Felix is missing. That's all."

"That's all?" Ray asks. "Didn't he admit to maybe killing a Mexican before he disappeared?"

"We're not even sure he killed anyone. He said he thought he may have. And we're not even in the car they're looking for—thanks to you," she says, removing an invisible bit of donut from between her front teeth with a pinky nail. She throws the newspapers into the back seat.

"I'd like to get started looking at Felix's phone" Ray says. "Is there somewhere we can go? A Starbucks? A motel?"

Stella laughs. "A Starbucks here? Let's drive around a bit. Go somewhere. I can't bear being cooped up in cars and motels."

RAY DRIVES TO A SMALL PARK at the highest point in El Paso, part of the Franklin Mountains, the end of the American Rockies that stretch behind them all the way to Canada.

They make an effort to stroll, like normal visitors to the park, to an overlook called "The Point."

At their feet lies the sprawl of El Paso, a much larger spread than when Ray was last here. Some new, modern glass houses now hang from the cliffs. The Rio Grande, a tarnished copper, snakes through the mountains. On the other side of the river lies the chaos of Juarez, beyond which they can almost see the same Rocky Mountains stretching south through Mexico, where they become the Sierra Madre Oriental.

At one time Ray thought he'd love nothing more than to live here, on this mountain, in one of these houses perched above steep cliffs. Looking down and across at the incredible vista, thinking about mountain ranges that have no borders, he suddenly feels dizzy, and leans into Stella for balance.

She puts her arm around him. He feels as if he's become very tiny, and Stella has become huge.

Though they never made it to Chimayo, where Ray was planning to leave the small amount of Olivia's ashes he'd brought along in three plastic sandwich bags, each inside the other, he thinks that this would be an even better place. He fumbles for the bag, just as small as a pinch of tobacco, and probably too much handled, and pulls it from his pocket. He realizes he's been fiddling with it when he's been anxious or upset—a tiny piece of Olivia that he's brought along as a security blanket.

"What's that?" Stella asks.

When Ray puts his fingers in for a pinch, she says, "Oh, no. Olivia?"

He feels the grittiness between his fingers, then turns the bags inside out way in front of him, and shakes it empty into the air. The small amount of grey ash sticks to the bag at first, then begins to fall out. But instead of dropping down the cliff most of the ash blows right back into their eyes and mouths.

They cough, spit, and rub their eyes. "Any on my face?" says Stella, laughing.

She wipes some ash off his cheek and off his hair. "Just like Olivia," she says.

Is it just like Olivia? Ray wonders.

THEY'VE DECIDED TO VISIT DORY, an old friend of Stella's, though someone she hasn't seen in a while. Ray remembers her vaguely. They hope they can stay with her for one night to go through Felix's phone and his computer.

Ray would much rather go to another motel; he doesn't want to talk to, or visit anyone, especially someone he hasn't seen for years.

Neither he nor Stella say what they are thinking—that they'll be hiding out at Dory's, at the other end of town from where Stella and Felix live.

"Have you heard from Daniel since their divorce?" Ray asks. "I haven't. Olivia and I weren't really that close to them."

"Not at all. I haven't even seen Dory. She and I kept up a bit by phone, but you know how it is—we got involved in other things, and we don't live near each other anymore—so it's easy to be too busy to actually get together."

Ray thinks for a moment about how easily Daniel, Dory's former husband, disappeared from their lives.

"And I haven't even seen Dory's new husband, Miguel, since their wedding. Which was a couple of years ago," Stella says, checking the directions given to her by Dory, who she's called to see whether it's okay if they visit.

Dory's new home is in another new development, quite a distance from downtown, on the west side of the mountains, practically out in the Mesilla Valley. On this side of town the houses are small, cheap ranch-style houses with little more than a narrow driveway in between each, fake wood siding, and spare earthen surroundings with little vegetation. Some of the houses rest on small lots of bare earth.

"Dearth," Ray says.

"What?" says Stella, squinting. She is driving slowly, searching for addresses.

"This area makes me think of the word 'dearth,'" says Ray.

"Well," says Stella, signaling with her hand out the window. "Asshole," she mutters at a driver going even more slowly than she is. "Dearth has 'death,' and 'earth,' in it."

"It also has 'dear' and 'ear' and 'hear.'"

"And 'read', 'head', 'had'," adds Stella.

He knows she loves this sort of game. They've played it before, with Olivia and with Felix. He does better with paper and a pen.

"Okay," he says, 'At', 'the', 'tea.'"

"I'm great at this," says Stella. "'Rat', 'tread', um, 'eat', … uh oh." She points to a blue Ford pickup.

"Look at that driver, Ray. Wasn't he at the party at the motel? He came in near the end with someone?"

"With a woman?" Ray asks, craning to see through the tinted glass of the blue truck.

"No. With a man. Maybe the man he's with now."

Ray does recall the two men who came in late. Well-dressed compared to all the others at the party. But he can't see anything much through the truck windows except the reflection of their own car.

His eyes on the cab, Ray sees that the driver's plaid shirt is unbuttoned at the neck, revealing a white t-shirt. Like too many guys he's seen lately, he thinks this guy has a scraggly ponytail gathered at the back of his neck. The only thing that Ray can see of the passenger is his bright white t-shirt. And possibly a beard.

"Did you ever notice," he says, "that guys who are bald often grow beards? It's as if they turn their heads upside down."

"I'm not amused," says Stella, shivering.

"I don't think we have anything to worry about," says Ray. "We're in our third car. Even if someone wanted to follow us, how could they keep track of us? On the other hand, maybe they just want to tell us something. Something that has to do with Felix?"

"There's something about these guys I don't like. Something dangerous."

Can you tell if people are dangerous by their looks? Ray has no idea. The bikers had looked like trouble to him. Yet he says, "That's silly."

"I can tell," Stella says. She turns off at the next exit, looking behind her through her mirrors, speeding up instead of slowing for the curve.

Ray brakes with his foot, even though he's the passenger. "Hey," he shouts, grabbing Stella's knee.

TWENTY-TWO

Everywhere you went you left something behind.
Benjamin Alire Saenz, *In Perfect Light*

"MIGUEL?" STELLA HUGS THE SLENDER, handsome man who's answered Dory's doorbell.

She's not sure she recognizes him from the wedding a few years ago. She doesn't recall that he was so young. His dark hair curls around his ears and shoulders.

"Dory didn't tell us you'd be here. She said the door would be unlocked, and we should just go inside and wait for her to get home from work."

Miguel looks puzzled, his onyx eyes wide open. He hugs Stella warmly, though Ray notices that he's not smiling. In fact he looks displeased, as if they'd interrupted something.

A thin black straight-line mustache hovers above the sharp shapely bow of his upper lip. He hasn't let them inside.

"You remember me?" Stella asks. "I was at your wedding. With my husband Felix?" She holds out her hand. "Stella."

She looks over at Ray and blushes. "It's been a while," she says.

It's no wonder he doesn't want to let them in. Stella's clothes are wrinkled, and wisps of hair escape from her makeshift bun. Perhaps they, so frazzled, look like a homeless couple.

Miguel studies Ray. It's apparent that Stella isn't going to introduce him. Most likely he thinks he's Felix.

"I'm Ray, a friend of Stella's. And of Felix. Dory knows me too," he adds.

"Come in," says Miguel, offering a thin arm, over the threshold.

Ray notices some blue line drawings tattooed on the delicate and much lighter skin of Miguel's inner arm.

He looks like a kid. Dory, a few years younger than both he and Stella, has to be at least twelve or fifteen years older than Miguel.

"Dory should be home in about a half hour," he says.

Inside there are cartons piled along the sand-colored walls of the small open living and dining area, with a few pieces of furniture here and there in the center of the space, as if they are still in the process of moving in. Or maybe out?

The carpeting is also sand, the same as the dry earth outside. The only spots of bright color are a white plastic table with two dark green plastic garden chairs, a child's yellow chair, a red truck, some multicolored blocks, and a bright blue tricycle.

"Can I get you a couple of cold beers?" says Miguel.

He seems edgy, Ray notes, standing on his toes, ready to be on the move.

"Sit anywhere," says Miguel, pointing to the two green chairs.

"Sounds great," says Ray. "The beer, I mean. It feels good to stand. Too much time in cars."

"What the hell," whispers Stella, as soon as Miguel has turned a corner into the galley kitchen, separated from the living/dining area by half a wall topped with a beige Formica counter.

"Something's very weird here. Dory doesn't have a kid. Especially not one old enough for a tricycle."

She pulls her hair out of its bun, and stretches the elastic she's removed, over her hand and onto her wrist, like a bracelet. "I have to go to the john," she says.

Miguel comes back with three bottles of Coors in one hand. "Do you need glasses? I'm not sure they're unpacked."

"This is fine," Ray says, taking the cold, moist bottle closest to him, trying to make out the tattoo on Miguel's inner arm. Are those needle marks he wonders, thinking he sees swollen dots, like mosquito bites in and among the dark, thin lines of the intricate design. He sits in one of the green plastic garden chairs, surprised it's so comfortable.

Miguel sits in the other chair. His expression is lethargic, but his body seems electrified. He crosses one leg over the other, pumping it up and down like the oil wells all over the flat land of the Texas countryside. He's wearing tan shorts a few shades lighter than his skin, and his legs are smooth and hairless.

"Do you have a child?" Stella, returning, asks, taking the third bottle of beer off the low table. She looks refreshed, her hair combed. "Have you been together that long?"

She takes a long swig. "Ahhhh. That's good," she says. "Dory never mentioned a kid."

Miguel rises rapidly, as if on a spring, and opens a frail bridge chair that had been leaning against the wall. He offers Stella the other plastic chair, and hunts amongst some of the cartons, pulling out two framed photos.

"This is Stevie," he says, showing the first, in its brown leather frame, to Stella.

Ray waits his turn, suddenly very sleepy. He'd love to crawl into one of their bedrooms and curl up. An evening of socializing, even with someone from his El Paso past, seems beyond him.

Stella passes the photo. A blonde child, about three years old, smiles at him. The kid is adorable, but looks nothing like Miguel, except maybe around the eyes, which have an Asian tilt. But Stevie's are bright blue, not black.

"Handsome boy," says Ray.

Stella is studying another photo when they hear someone at the door. Stella jumps, dropping the photograph in her hand. The knob rattles, then a key.

Ray gets up to greet Dory, who he hasn't seen since he and Olivia moved from El Paso, almost ten years ago.

Miguel jumps back. Stella is already at the door, arms out for a hug.

Dory looks exactly the same as she did all those years ago, though she's flushed from the heat, her clothing is creased, and there are damp circles under her arms.

She gives Miguel the evil eye while balancing herself on the doorknob and kicking off her black pumps into the room as if they are missiles of aggression.

Stella's arms drop. Ray steps back. One shoe has just missed him.

"You aren't supposed to be here," she screams at Miguel. "Get the hell out!"

Her eyes on Miguel, she says to Ray and Stella, "I have a restraining order out on him."

Ray's mouth is open in dumb surprise.

Miguel, head curled into his skinny body, as if trying to disappear, reminds Ray of some long-legged bird, head under its wing. He looks far from dangerous to Ray, who's tempted to put an arm around him.

"He's not supposed to be anywhere near this house," Dory says, her straight blonde hair flying. "Get out!" she screams, even louder, her voice cracking.

Miguel, blushing a deep maroon, grabs a worn leather bomber jacket off a hook near the door and silently slinks out.

"Bastard," says Dory, the word coming out as a cough. Her voice nearly gone, she flops down onto Stevie's small plastic chair, and, looking like a distressed child, bursts into tears.

Stella running over to comfort her, kneels beside the tiny chair, not knowing what to do.

Dory looks around the half un-packed room, the cartons, opened, but full, lining the walls, and weeps hard, wracking sobs.

"I can't take it anymore," Dory says, her voice soft and hicuppy.

Ray stands still, arms hanging, feeling too heavy. He's still shocked by the surprising outburst, and embarrassed, and has no idea what to do. Finally he sits on the bridge chair vacated by Miguel.

Stella brings a wet paper towel from the kitchen for Dory, who says, sniffling, "I'm sorry you have to see this." She looks at Ray. "Sorry, Ray. I know you have your own issues."

Ray guesses she's referring to Olivia's death. He doesn't want to think about or talk about it. Instead he thinks about how people now use the word "issue," instead of "problem."

Dory grabs her thick straight shoulder-length hair in one hand, twists it behind her head and pins it up with something that Ray can't see.

"I moved here to get away from him," she says. "Now I guess we'll have to move again." Her mouth twists as if she's going to cry again.

"Are you sure it's a good idea to keep moving? Isn't there some other solution?" Ray asks.

Stella rolls her eyes. "If someone's after you, restraining orders don't work. You don't know what it's like to be stalked by someone who's violent."

"And you do?" asks Ray.

"Where's Felix?" Dory asks, maybe to change the subject. She seems to have just realized that he's not there.

Ray is going to let Stella answer that question. It feels as if minutes go by before Stella says, "He's missing."

Dory gets out of Stevie's chair. "Missing? What do you mean?"

Dory looks at Stella. Ray wonders what she's going to say. Will she tell the truth?

"He disappeared from a motel," says Stella. "We have no idea where he is."

Now Stella's face reddens, her freckles stand out. Is she putting on an act for Dory?

"What makes you think he's missing?" Dory asks. "Is it possible he just went somewhere, and will be back?"

"I can't go into it now, but we've looked into everything. We were hoping we could visit you, and spend the night here, so we can go through Felix's phone and his computer and stuff," says Stella. "I'm sorry—I had no idea you were having all these problems of your own."

To Ray's surprise, Dory doesn't ask why a motel or hotel won't do. Stella says nothing about the police being after them. She doesn't need to.

"I guess you could sleep in Stevie's room," Dory says. "He can sleep with me." She looks in one of the cartons and finds a glass ashtray. She places it in the center of the white plastic table, and feeling around in her large leather purse, she pulls out a crushed pack of Marlboros.

"I'm trying to stop smoking," she says, "but this horrible stuff going on—it's impossible." She searches the narrow windowsills and feels along some high empty shelves, finally finding a book of matches.

She places a broken cigarette between her thin red lipsticked lips, not lighting up right away, but fiddling with the matchbook, turning it round and round, as if it's part of some strange ritual. She lights the match the way Ray used to as a kid—by ripping one out of the matchbook, planning the tip between the sandpaper strip and the top cover, and pulling the match hard. A sudden odor of sulphur, and Ray desires a smoke.

"We could sleep on the couch. One of us could," she says. Dory doesn't ask any questions about details of Ray and Stella's sleeping arrangements.

"May I take another beer?" asks Stella. When she opens the fridge, Ray notes that aside from a few beers there's nothing much in there.

"I'll take one too," Dory says.

"Who's Stevie," Stella asks, sitting on one of the green plastic chairs across from Dory.

"Stevie is Miguel's kid. Miguel's girlfriend Cristina had custody of Stevie but after she OD'd about a year ago, Stevie came to live with us. Miguel had been clean for quite a while, but lately I started noticing things … one of which was missing money. Mine."

She takes a drag of her limp cigarette, and blows the smoke out swiftly, turning her head to keep the plume away from Ray, on the bridge chair.

"He's hit me—he's violent sometimes when he's using. Or maybe it's when he's not using. There seems no time that things are good any more. How long will it be before he starts hitting Stevie? When he kept forgetting to pick Stevie up at daycare, I began to make an effort to get custody of the kid. Which is making Miguel even crazier."

Yeah, thinks Ray. He can see how it would make Miguel livid to have his kid taken away by someone who isn't even the child's mother. Yet if he's not capable of caring for Stevie, shouldn't he be glad to have his boy well taken care of, even if it's by someone else? Yet he can see Dory's point. Her desire to protect Stevie from violence, an addict dad, and a life of unpredictability, at best.

As if reading Ray's mind, Dory says, "He doesn't deserve Stevie." She picks something invisible, making a tiny piece of tobacco, off her lower lip. "He's a liar, and a cheat. He's totally unreliable. And he's violent."

"Has he ever hit Stevie?" asks Stella.

"So far, no. He's loving to Stevie. And I do appreciate how much Stevie needs his father, as he's lost, or maybe never had, his mother." Dory puts out her cigarette, pressing the butt harder than necessary, into her ashtray.

"I used to think loving someone was enough, that that, and the fact that Stevie loves Miguel very much, made him a good enough father. But does a good father steal from his wife? Does a good father lie? Or hang out with drugged-out sociopaths, or people who sell drugs? Does a good dad sit around strung out, head hanging, saying nothing for hours on end, while his kid plays at his feet? Stevie has seen his father lie, and he's seen him smack me. Oh, and he can't provide for his son. So, is that a good father? What's left? The fact that he donated the sperm?"

Dory's eyelids and cheeks redden, her lips tremble.

To Ray it seems pretty unclear what makes a good father. An incredible person, it seems. So really, who is up to that standard?

"It all seems so complicated," Ray says. Right now he's pretty glad he's never had a child.

"Complicated! Complicated?" shouts Stella. "It's pretty clear to me that you're right, Dory."

Ray's startled by her vehemence at his ambivalence.

Stella and Dory huddle at the small table, excluding Ray, a blue haze of smoke around Dory, who is on her second or third Marlboro.

He can't hear what they are saying, and he makes no effort to. Dory seems to be complaining about Miguel, and men in general, and Stella seems in agreement. Once in a while one of them will look up at Ray with a scowl, as if he's a representative of some hideous species.

Does he really care? He's having a hard time keeping his eyes open. He may have even dozed, because suddenly Stella is talking to him.

"We were talking about the time Felix and Dory had an affair," she says.

Suddenly Ray's awake. He looks at Dory, who is stubbing out another butt. "What? When you were married to Daniel?" Are they teasing him?

"I wouldn't call it an affair," Dory says. "More like a couple of unsatisfactory screws."

More stuff going on that he'd never noticed? Wouldn't Felix have said something to Ray? And what was Daniel doing at the time?

"You never knew that I had an affair with Olivia?" says Stella.

"Yeah," he says, sure she's putting him on. He does recall them lying around together, once in awhile on Stella's bed, sometimes just on the floor. So what does that mean? They were close friends. So, are all his memories false? If so, what does anything mean?

When Ray looks up, Dory is in a short, flesh-colored slip, rummaging through a pillowcase full of clothing. She steps into a creased pair of shorts she's pulled out. "These are clean," she murmurs.

"I have to go pick up Stevie from daycare," she says. "Why don't you two go out for dinner? I'll just order a pizza for me and Stevie. It will give me a chance to get myself together. And I won't have to worry about feeding you guys." Dory smiles.

"Are you sure?" Stella asks. "We can all have some pizza here."

"You're sure you'll be okay?" asks Ray.

"You're really leaving him? Miguel." Stella says.

"He has a court date tomorrow, and by the time he gets back we'll be gone from here," says Dory.

Stella grabs her purse, and goes over to hug Dory. "I'm so sorry you're having all this trouble," she says, her own troubles forgotten for the moment.

Dory sucks on a lock of her hair, looking small and forlorn, barefoot and in her shorts. "It's all my fault. I should have left him long ago. I should never have married him. I knew more about him than I could admit," she says. "But I'm weak."

"Maybe we shouldn't stay here," says Ray. "Maybe it will be too much trouble." With all their own troubles, what are they getting into now?

"No. No," says Dory. "Do come back. You are helping me by staying here tonight. Your being here will keep Miguel from coming back," she says at the door, one bare toe scratching her other arch.

Stella seems reluctant to leave Dory, and stands looking at her.

Ray practically pulls Stella out the doorway, so anxious is he to get out of there.

TWENTY-THREE

*Dreams would come and go intersecting with and disintegrating
the wall between my surroundings and my subconscious.*

Jim Feast, *Long Day, Counting Tomorrow*

STELLA IS EDGY, QUIET, fiddling with the bottom of her blue
sweater. Ray doesn't feel much like talking either, in that Mexican restaurant in one of the older El Paso neighborhoods. He
doesn't want to be there at all.

"Drink, Ray," says Stella, her hand and wrist trembling as
she holds out the large, sweaty pitcher of sangría they'd ordered.

Ray stares at the glimpses of orange and lime in the deep
crimson. He watches Stella stick her fingers into her glass,
extract a slice of wine-stained orange, and devour it.

"How did we get into this?" he asks. "There's always something new with you. I don't want to spend the night with Dory.
I don't want to have anything to do with her husband. I want
to go to a motel, and start looking at Felix's stuff."

He looks at the menu. Nothing looks good. His appetite
is gone.

"We are masquerading as a loving couple who are eating dinner
out, and will soon go home and maybe fuck, and go to sleep."

Or are they masquerading as a couple of friends who
are looking for the husband of one of them, and are going to
maybe go home and fuck? Ray doesn't say this.

He watches, disgusted, as Stella attacks a pair of huge fried chilis, breaded, and layered with steaming melted cheese.

She points her knife at him. "Yes," she says, rerieving a string of cheese caught on her bottom lip. "We maybe are in a scary situation—but we are also a loving couple who are eating dinner out and may soon go home and fuck, and go to sleep."

Ray's own dinner, also *chilis rellenos,* sits in front of him while he continues to watch Stella eat so that he can feel more and more disgusted with her.

"Don't you care about Dory and her boy eating a crummy Pizza Hut pizza on those two plastic chairs, afraid of her violent husband? One night. Just this one night that they need some protection. And then we'll be on our way," Stella pleads.

Ray looks down at his dinner, the aroma of which begins to stir his appetite. He's hungrier than he'd thought.

"I feel," he says, cutting his chili pepper, "as if my plane to El Paso got sucked into a huge black hole and I've come out into an alternate universe."

The waitress has lit the two candles on their table, and when Stella looks up at Ray he sees a tiny flame reflected in each of her dark eyes.

Their table brighter, the rest of the room has receded.

"Huh?" she says.

He'd thought she'd get it without needing an explanation.

"You mean your life is nothing like this ..." She waves her magenta napkin.

He has no idea whether she's being ironic. He notices that her nails are dirty.

"No. I mean, yes, my wife just died of cancer ... but what's been going on here for the last few days ... is like genre fiction. Or soap opera."

"This is real life," Stella says. "You're just very good at tuning things out."

Here it is again. The complaint of this trip to hell—that he has hidden from life, from troubles, from darkness.

Perhaps it is the sangría, or the events of the last days, but Ray doesn't feel the usual shame at this suggestion. It doesn't make him feel good, but maybe it's true. Maybe it's something worth thinking more about.

But he says, "Yeah, my life is really like this—beatings, people going missing, betrayal, sex, police looking for me—but I've just closed my eyes to it all, and continue to get to work on time, eat my meals, and brush my teeth, and pretend nothing is going on." He takes a deep breath. It's all a little funny.

Reaching over with his fork, he pushes it past Stella's refried beans, to scoop up a mound of olive green guacamole. "You're not going to eat this?"

Stella smacks his hand and they watch the fork go flying, guacamole and all.

"You pig," Stella says.

"I'm not oblivious," said Ray. "I just have good boundaries." He's trying to be funny, but it sounds like something Olivia, or Stella might say. Had said.

"Your boundaries," she says, playful, "are not boundaries. They're walls. Like the ones we are building to keep out the dirty, poor, and brown immigrants, and which will also destroy America, and a lot of wildlife and vegetation."

Stella's wide smile, her lush lips. He feels a sudden, unwelcome surge of desire.

She places her bunched-up napkin on the table near her dish. "Seriously, there's a big difference between blocking out life—the parts you don't want to see—and, making choices about what you want to get involved in."

"True," he says, after thinking about it.

He finishes his meal with the fork the waitress has replaced. He doesn't say that perhaps Felix and Stella, definitely Stella, are people he should have chosen not to get involved with.

Finished, he wipes his mouth. "I feel as if I'm just following you. This is your life. I've just become a character in your life."

IT'S AFTER TEN WHEN RAY AND STELLA RETURN to Dory's neighborhood. There are very few lights still on in the houses, making it seem much later. The pink fluorescence of sodium lighting makes the street appear darker rather than lit, colors altered; just a few doorways here and there spotlit, roofs an ugly purple. The block looks like a painted stage set for a sad play.

He almost drives right past Dory's house, which is surprisingly completely dark.

"I assumed she was going to wait up for us," Stella says. "Or at least leave some lights on."

Ray sulks, and says nothing.

Suddenly they recognize, behind a low bush, a green and white border patrol car. Stella jumps, but a further look shows there's no one around. The car is just parked.

Stella parks in the driveway behind Dory's Ford Fiesta. She gets out to see whether Dory's left a door open for them, while Ray pulls out their duffels, and the large black wheelie that Stella's retrieved.

"Shhh," says Stella. "The back door's open." She grabs her huge purse, and Felix's computer from the trunk.

Ray is thrilled that apparently Dory and Stevie are asleep, and his mood lightens. He is almost cheerful.

"Doesn't it seem strange that she didn't even leave a night light for us? Did she forget we were coming back?" whispers Ray, breathless from hauling their gear. Maybe she's changed her mind and doesn't want us here.

Stella holds the door open while Ray throws their bags over the threshold, returning to wheel in the black bag, which squeals horribly in the neighborhood silence.

He stands near the doorway for a moment to catch his breath, and to allow his eyes to adjust to the darkness inside the house.

When he moves, he trips over the bags Stella's left in the space between the back door and an outer screen door he hadn't recalled. Soon he can see the half wall between the kitchen and the dining/living room, and he watches Stella moving around there. Trying to be silent, he moves the bags in and closes the screen door very very slowly.

"Looks like Dory and the kid are in that larger room," Stella points with her chin, "so we're probably in there."

She's pointed to two doorways, probably the two bedrooms, and an open bathroom door off the small foyer he's standing in. He tiptoes after Stella, squeezing through one of the doorways with the duffels, which he'd thought were small, but now seem too large for this house.

Once inside the room, Stevie's room, he can see better. Pink light from a streetlight comes in through the red and green plaid curtain, onto what must be deep blue walls, creating a lurid purplish glow.

If he were a kid, this room would be terrifying, he thinks.

Though maybe only eight by ten feet, Stevie's bedroom is more furnished than anywhere else in this house, with a small bed, and a white chest of drawers that has some decals plastered all over it. Near the bottom of the bed is a wooden toy chest, painted red, open and vomiting a batch of undefined objects.

"Help me get all our stuff in so we can shut the door and turn on a light," Ray says. "There are still some things—your purse, and the wheelie—by the door."

"Dory's bedroom door is shut, so I don't think any light is going to bother her," says Stella, switching on the fire truck lamp on the chest, which now he sees is covered with Shrek and Batman stickers. It occurs to him that the bed isn't nearly large enough for two, nor is it even long enough for an adult.

He fishes in his Dopp bag for his toothbrush and toothpaste and tiptoes into the bathroom shared by the two bedrooms. He's suddenly so tired he could sleep on the floor.

Stella squeezes past Ray at the sink to get to the toilet.

Ray gets into the tiny bed and curls up, his naked back (he's just wearing his jockeys) against the chilly wall, leaving as much space as he can. He curls into a semi-fetal position, trying not to take up Stella's space with his knees, yet doesn't want his long legs hanging out into midair. He pulls the small square quilt over his stringy legs. He's uncomfortable, but the sheets smell clean—of kids' soap and shampoo. By the time he hears the toilet flush, he's half asleep.

"Ouch." Stella falls on top of him.

"Shhh. Move over."

"Are you kidding? Get off me. I'll sleep on the floor," he says.

"Just move over as far as you can, and I'll squeeze next to you back to front, like spoons," she says.

"That's a cliché," he says.

"Okay, then, like dishes."

After some effort and adjustment, they somehow fit, Ray's outer arm over Stella, his hand hanging above her naked breast. He's a little surprised she's come to bed naked, but he's too tired to care.

"I like this," he mumbles. "Feels cozy. Reminds me of my baby crib." Feeling Stella's warm body alongside his, and the rhythm of their tandem breathing, lulls him.

Suddenly Felix is there on the bed too, which has gotten wider. They are all looking for a book that Stella has, something like her collections of folk stories, or maybe a book she wrote about Olivia. Ray wants Stella to tell him something about Olivia that's in the book, but she just gives him a strange look—one he can't read—and moves closer to him, so close that he can't breathe, and soon feels himself gasping and choking.

He wakes to find Stella turned, as much as she can, towards him, and her lips are on his. In order to do this, she's partially on his chest, smothering him, their bottom halves still spooning. Somehow he no longer needs to breathe. He feels Stella's back and buttocks all along his front, his penis hard along the center of her behind.

Then he remembers where they are.

"What's going on?" he asks.

"Shhh," she whispers. Her hand, behind her back, searches for the opening in his jockeys. She strokes him, pulling his penis out. She turns her back to him again and places his hard prick between her legs.

Ray has no desire to fuck in this bed, in this house, but once again, it's too late. There's no stopping now. He doesn't know if he's in her or not, in her butt crack or just between her thighs. They are pressed so close he feels as if his entire body is inside her, inside-out.

He runs his hand along her side, feeling the edge of her breast as it curves into her rib cage, and moves along down her waist. He closes his eyes and sees the curving Rio Grande. Their breathing is the breeze. He moves as much as he can, which is almost not at all, pressing hard against her as she pushes back. He feels for her breasts and she moves so he can feel more of their smooth roundness, the hills, arroyos. Are they still driving? Is he dreaming?

Stella's breath catches, and Ray, with the vertigo of being dragged down into something deep, an arroyo, a cave, explodes with a grunt.

Head buried in her hair, which smells like grass, the arm he's lying on is asleep, so numb it's begun to ache, Stella's elbow sticking into his ribs, he feels her breath catch, feels her go still.

He's become aware of some rhythmic thumping sounds not coming from them, and now, Stella is holding her breath, so he knows she hears them too.

Another heavy thump, and a small, high-pitched scream. It definitely sounds like someone having sex. Would Dory do that with Stevie right there in the same room?

Stella struggles to sit upright, and she pulls the small blanket off Ray and over her shoulders like a huge shawl. There's another thud, and a muffled groan. Stella is sitting up against the small padded oval headboard of the narrow bed. Somehow she's gotten her knees up to where they nudge her nipples.

"There's something about those sounds," she says.

He shrugs. "Sex."

"Ray," she says, pulling her knees up closer to her body, "I'm scared."

They listen, as if paralyzed, to more of the same noises, till Ray leaps off the bottom of the bed to avoid jumping over Stella, and bangs his knee on the toy chest.

"Ouch." He grabs his knee and hops on one leg.

Stella giggles nervously. Ray looks at her to see if this is all a joke, but her arms are crossed over her knees, and she's shivering in spite of her blanket shawl.

More struggling noises, louder, but muffled, as if under blankets. As if they are struggles, and not just sex. It's amazing how closely sex can resemble violence.

"Is Miguel's car here?" asks Stella.

Ray peers out the high window. It's lighter outside than it was before.

"It's right beside our car, on the … whatever you call a lawn when there's no grass."

Stella gets out of bed, pulling on her t-shirt and underpants.

Ray kicks some toys out of the way. "Sounds as if someone's getting killed," he says. "Sex would be over now."

"Ray!" Stella grabs his arm, pinching him hard. "Don't go in there. It's none of our business."

Ray's surprised. "You were the one who wanted us to come back here to protect Dory and Stevie. We can't let her get beaten up." He pulls away.

"Maybe no one can help people like this. Aren't we in enough trouble?" she says, now down on her knees, searching amongst the toys and old pairs of tiny dirty socks for her sandals.

"At this point, we are people like this," Ray says. There's no time to remind Stella that she's now voicing the same objections he'd had, at the restaurant.

The screaming, louder now, is unmistakably violence.

"Ray," shouts Stella, turning the fire engine lamp on.

From their bedroom doorway, looking past the foyer, Ray sees Stevie sprawled on the living room carpet, still.

Moving closer to the living room, beyond Stevie, Ray sees Dory, pinned between some cartons and the couch. He can't see her face, but she moves, and groans.

On his way to her, he spots Miguel in Dory's bedroom doorway, blood running in a scarlet stream from his nose onto his yellow t-shirt. Wild-eyed, ready to spring, he reminds Ray of an animal, a panther, or a hyena.

"Hey, man," says Ray, hands out in front of him for surrender. Or protection.

Then he sees the knife in one of Miguel's hands.

The Ray who always avoided violence is gone. Something tells him he'd better leap first, as he jumps straight into Miguel, keeping as far from the knife as he can.

Miguel is much smaller than Ray, but his wiry strength is surprising, as Ray attempts to keep one of Miguel's arms behind him, and force him to drop the knife. He's vaguely aware of Dory trying to get up, and of Stella, nearby, a whirl of nervous energy.

The knife flies across the room, and Ray feels as if he's diving for it, but he's still holding on, with all his strength, to Miguel.

Stella gets the knife close enough to Ray that he can grab it from her with one of his hands with which he's been holding Miguel.

Desperate, hanging on to Miguel, but knowing he won't be able to for much longer, he tries to stab Miguel's upper arm to get him to calm down, to get him somewhat immobile, and into another state where he is not beyond the reach of reason. But they are locked together; Ray's got no leverage. He misses the spot he's aiming for, and the point of the knife jabs, but not deep, into Miguel's bony chest.

Miguel is shocked, and for the moment unguarded he stands still, pale, arms out. Then, with a terrifying roar, he moves forward. Ray hears the knife drop, but has no idea where it is. The two wrestle, silently, except for their loud, ragged breathing, as they move together as if underwater, into the living room, where they seem to be trying to avoid the body of Stevie, immobile on the stained carpet.

Miguel must have been wounded by Ray even though the knife didn't penetrate, because there's blood all over his arms and his bare bony and childlike chest, and he's drops to the floor.

Unless it's Ray who has been injured?

Is that Stella over behind the cartons near Dory, and moving towards Stevie?

Ray's still wondering about all the blood and whose it is, when Miguel throws a punch at Ray's nose.

An explosion of light without sound, then darkness for a moment—then fireworks, and nausea. He leans over, trying to keep from fainting, watching huge drops of blood fall and nearly disappear into the beige carpet. He doesn't even know how to throw a punch like that.

Miguel moves close again—two shadows. Ray's seeing double. Police sirens in the distance. Maybe Stella's called the cops? He hopes they get here in time, before he's beaten to a pulp.

Suddenly he's pushed to the floor by an enormous weight. He tries to breathe but can't get any air. He's being buried alive and his last heartbeats pound in his head.

As blackness fills him, there's a sensation of sudden light—then sound—so loud that for a moment Ray hears nothing but the whoosh of blood through him. Air rushes into his lungs as he hears himself gasp.

Through a veil of red, Ray sees the small silver gun in Stella's wobbly hands. Trembly as she is, she can't seem to drop her arms, which are out in front of her. She appears paralyzed. He moves, groggy and with a hum in his head, towards Dory.

Again he hears sirens. Stella hurries over and grabs Ray's shirt. "We have to get out of here."

"Looks like you may have killed Miguel, and we have to see how Dory is, and whether she's able to take care of Stevie." He doesn't mention anything about what sort of state Stevie's in. Ray hasn't seen any movement from Stevie since he came out of the child's bedroom.

He pulls away from Stella.

"The cops can take care of Dory and Stevie. Will it really help if they find us here?" Stella asks, breathless.

Ray trips over Miguel. "What do you mean, will it really help? I think Miguel's dead. We have to wait."

He's nearly dead himself. A wreck.

"Let's go, Ray. We've got to go," says Stella, dancing in place.

Should he stay? Or get out now? Ray can't decide. He feels as if his nose is his entire head or his head has become nothing but a nose, which aches and throbs horribly.

He wipes his upper lip with his hand, which is covered with blood. Looking down he sees that his t-shirt's bloody too. He still has no idea whether it's his own.

Stella grabs his arm and pulls him along, and out to the car, where she helps him into the front passenger seat. He hears the car door slam; the sirens get louder. So loud. It seems they won't get out of there in time. If not, no choice has to be made.

Where is Stella? She's back, lugging their bags, which, like in some silly comedy, have remnants of clothing sticking out in various places.

Neighboring houses begin to light up, and there's a deep pink line on the horizon indicating the coming dawn.

Maybe a siren will get these neighbors moving in a way that screams and sounds of distress and violence, a neighbor in trouble, won't.

"Please, please, please, please, please," says Stella, a senseless litany, a prayer, while trying to start the car.

Finally the motor hums and Stella manages to drive slowly and steadily, counter to instinct, so they don't attract attention.

Adrenaline surge gone, Ray, wiped out, is completely limp. Even his pain is a now a dull throb, a bass drum he's getting used to.

His body feels as if it's asleep, yet his mind's in high gear. The car clock says 4:24, and his watch says 4:40. But he wonders why he's checked. Does it matter what time it is?

Somewhere in the deserted desert east of El Paso, Stella pulls onto the shoulder. It's still dark except the pink at the horizon has expanded and glows weirdly.

"You'd better get out of those clothes," she says.

When Ray moves he feels sick. He leans over and retches out the door.

Stella comes round to his side and hands him some clothes. "Just don't barf in the car."

He retches again at the smell of her Handy Wipes. Then the sharp odors of alcohol, disinfectant and soap in the wipes clear his head. How can he even smell anything with his nose smashed in? He washes his face, hands and hair, dabbing gently at his nose.

"You don't look too bad." Stella smiles, and studies him. "Most of that blood wasn't yours. You only have a few cuts and bruises. And your nose is broken."

"That's news," he says, gingerly touching his nose. "And are you asking yourself whose blood it is? And how that person is?"

He is about to throw the pile of used wipes, and his blood-stained clothing, which he's managed to change out of without any other car passing, into the nearby shrubbery. Stella grabs his wrist.

"Ouch. Fuck."

"We shouldn't leave that stuff here. Should we put them in the trunk? I don't know," Stella says.

Ray tries to recall the detective movies and programs he's seen. What would be best? He can't think, yet it seems he's leaving everything up to Stella.

His headache's back, the pounding in and out of the top of his skull as if still an infant with a delicate membrane there. He knows that on TV detective programs criminals can be caught because of one small, misplaced item, or one tiny hair with some DNA. Even just a few cells. But he doesn't think that real murders or crimes get solved with the same frequency and skill as fiction. However he notes that now he's thinking like a criminal, and has been for quite a while, rather than identifying with the detective.

He hears the sound of the trunk lever opened by Stella, who is back in the car, and that decides it. He throws all the bloody clothing and waste in behind their luggage, trying not to get blood on his hands again. After he slams the trunk closed, he wipes his hands on his pants legs.

Stella drives. Ray leans against his door, hand holding up his head, which weighs about three hundred pounds. He'd love to blow his nose, clogged with so much blood and mucus that he can't breathe through it, but he's afraid it will begin to bleed again.

"You act as if I have some disease," says Stella.

It takes a moment for Ray to get what she means. "My head aches," he says. "It has nothing to do with you. I need to lean and rest my head."

"I saved your life, you know," she says.

"Yeah," he murmurs, not wanting to get into it. Nothing at all would have happened if they hadn't gone to Dory's in the first place, and if they hadn't gone back. And if they'd minded their business. He concentrates on the white line on the road so he doesn't throw up.

"You would have killed ... him ... too ... if I hadn't done it first. Or he would have killed you."

Yes, Ray thinks. He remembers that he was trying to kill Miguel, so enraged was he that Miguel was forcing him to fight for his life. He recalls that at that moment he didn't give a shit if he did kill him.

He hasn't felt like that since he was seven or eight years old. On the concrete front stoop of his house, his best friend Victor, a good-looking, athletic boy, had teased him, punching his arms, seemingly just dying for some reaction from Ray, who finally grabbed a handful of Victor's thick dark brown hair, and pulled. He would have pulled the hair, along with a chunk of scalp if he could have—he just didn't care. Luckily an old woman who lived nearby pulled Ray off. He doesn't remember anything afterward, as if it had been involuntary, like a seizure, but Victor never teased him that way again.

It felt the same. As if, pushed to a limit far in the distance for him, he could be capable of anything. This is horrifying. At the same time he feels liberated, relieved of a great burden, and excited that, yes, he can be capable of anything.

TWENTY-FOUR

Mirages that look like puddles stretching across dry highway pavement are produced when the boundary between superheated and normal air reflects the sky onto the ground producing a very believable image of water on the ground. More complicated mirages result when viewers look at the distant horizon through the abrupt hot air-cold air boundary. It's like looking across the surface of a mirror; mesas seem to float free, separated from the land by a blue sky. Mountain ranges clone themselves, growing upside-down mirror images attached at the peaks.

Susan J. Tweit, *The Great Southwest Nature Factbook*

"THERE'S A BORDER PATROL CHECKPOINT a couple of miles ahead," Stella says.

"We have a trunk full of bloody clothes," says Ray, thinking he should have thrown them away into the bushes as he'd instinctively wanted to do. To get rid of them as quickly as possible.

Stella seems calm. "They don't usually bother gringos. Once they look at us, and hear us speak, they won't search anything."

"Though there's an alert out for a gringo couple—and we do have a gun with us, don't we?"

"Yes, I still have the gun," says Stella. "God, I'd love nothing more than to be able to go home, have a cup of coffee or a beer, and go to bed. Or read a book. Just be normal."

"I thought this was a normal day for you," says Ray. "You can pretend that Felix will be home soon."

"We shouldn't have left them," he says. He's haunted by the image that appears when he closes his eyes, of Dory, looking sickeningly rag doll-like lying near the cartons of her own possessions, and Stevie, in his Batman pajamas, one small fist on either side of his head, like a baby who's played so hard he's fallen asleep on the floor. But who'd been ominously still during the entire fracas in the living room.

Can Stella really believe they're okay? Is she just concentrating on the road or pretending?

"We should have made sure they were okay. We should have called an ambulance, and waited there." His face aches, including his front teeth. He wishes he could pull his face off, like a rubber mask.

When she finally turns to look at Ray, her eyes, dark and incomprehensible, show no anguish, nor even a sign of doubt. She looks somewhat excited by their situation, with her hair half up in a ponytail, the rest in a multitude of messy strands framing her flushed cheeks.

She's driving, a madwoman, and he's her willing passenger.

"You've left fingerprints all over Dory's house. And on the knife. The police will think you killed all of them."

A flicker of panic flares in his chest. "How come it's 'my fingerprints'? Not, ours? Besides, haven't you been telling me that Dory and Stevie are alive, not to worry about them? Or is that more of your manipulative bullshit, to reassure me? Or do you just say whatever comes into your head at the moment?"

Stella, driving up onto the shoulder, turns to Ray and places a hand on his arm. He cringes. The memory of the smells at Dory's, of blood and fear and the bitter copper taste in his mouth become unbearable. He pulls away.

"You're afraid of me!"

"Why did we stop?"

Ray looks around, and then at the road. Not a soul around, even though it's nearly dawn. Just gray road, straight, into the peach horizon, and tall, dry, olive green grasses.

"I have to pee," Stella says. "This looks like a good place, as we're not near any town or anything."

She turns the car off, and the motor ticks like a metronome, then dies. It's absolutely silent. No crickets, no birds, no breeze.

"Where's the gun, Stella?" Ray tries to undo his seatbelt, which is stuck.

"You don't think I'm stupid, do you Ray?" She grabs his hands and holds them. Ray imagines it's to comfort him, reassure him, but she's gripping them painfully.

She's going to kill me now, he thinks.

She glares at him, shadows making her cheekbones look like shelves that her eyes, dark marbles, rest on.

He tries to pull away, surprised at her strength. She brings her face up close to his, too close—he feels her hot breath. His sore nose throbs. Terrified, he's also strangely excited. Her breath is repugnant, yet he's stopped struggling, and he looks down at his tented chinos as if there's something there that isn't part of him, a small disgusting animal or insect, perhaps.

His heartbeat feels as if it's thumping outside his body, against his skin. He thinks about pulling away, but he doesn't move.

"Put your arms up," orders Stella, in a tone he's never heard her use. She releases his wrists from her grip, which are circled in rose. He surprises himself, and obeys.

Slowly, so slowly, Stella unbuttons her white blouse.

Ray is afraid a car will drive by—it's been a while since any has passed on this road. He wishes she'd hurry. He notices that the buttons on her blouse are tiny pearls, light glancing off each. One breast is now visible, so pale compared to her suntanned neck and chest.

He remains still, watching her every move. He no longer feels any pain in his face and nose.

Slowly she unbuttons the fly of her shorts with fingers so slim it isn't possible that she could have had the strength to hold his wrists so tightly. His penis seems to want to move closer and he exerts himself to remain still, where she has pushed him, on the front seat of the car, knees, calves and feet hanging down somewhere, he couldn't care where at this point, his arms still raised.

Stella's door is open, he's leaning his back against his. He worries for just a moment about a passing car, then not at all.

He hadn't noticed what she did with her shorts. He sees her black bush against her slightly convex white belly. She moves over him, while he remains still except for his noisy heartbeat, and the sound of his blood creating a tsunami in his body.

"Good boy," whispers Stella, and for a moment Ray is turned off. This kind of game is too stupid and never works for him. But then he feels her hands under his butt, stretching him towards her until he's taking up the entire front seat, knees near Stella's door, calves and feet hanging outside the car.

She hovers above him, a luminous ghost. He raises his hips, as Stella, taking all the time in the world, unzips his fly and pulls down his jockeys. He stops worrying how she's balancing. His dick, liberated, jumps out.

He moans and tries to sit up to take Stella in his arms, to pull her close, but she grabs hold of each of his hands and pulls them back up over his head, where for a moment they flap against the window like birds. Only then does she lower herself on to him.

He moves, wanting to find his way inside her, but the pressure on his sore wrists warns him to be still. She's balanced above him—her upper half, her belly gently touches the tip of his cock.

Holding both of his hands up with one of hers, supporting herself with her other arm, she pushes down on him so suddenly and so hard he feels nothing—maybe pain? Yet he's so excited he hardly knows what he feels.

She moves up along his shaft so slowly that he aches with the painful sweetness. Another eon and she moves slowly down. He's learning about patience and about paying close attention.

She continues this endlessly. Her head drops and Ray feels her soft hair on his face and neck.

Their bodies are gone, dissipated, and only sensation remains and expands to fill the world around them.

He hears a howl and wonders whether it's a coyote. Coyotes, he's relieved to note, don't bother anyone unless they're disturbed. He soon realizes he's the one howling.

Stella grunts like she's lifting heavy cargo. When Ray can no longer bear the sweetness, Stella comes down on him hard, with all her weight.

You're hurting me, he wants to shout. Stop!

"Please, please," is what he hears himself say, as he gets fucked faster and harder. His surprise at the change of pace holds him off a moment. Then he's about to explode. This time his entire body will burst. He roars.

He tries to pull Stella close, but only when he's still and silent, does she drop onto him, limp, her tangled hair around his neck.

Slowly he becomes aware of his discomfort—his neck twisted, his head pressed into the door, his face and stuffed nose aching, his arms having nowhere to rest, hands flapping above his head. His torso twisted with one leg hanging off the seat, the gearshift sticking into his kidney, Stella's hair, strangling him.

Now he's afraid to hold her close. Still draped over him, one of her knees digging into his inner thigh, she seems unaware that he's there. She's in her own world.

He waits for her to get up—to release him.

TWENTY-FIVE

No one has ever succeeded in domesticating the coyote. Sometimes they
mate with dogs but the offspring can never be trained nor trusted.

Philip Garrison, *Augury*

DRIVING FOR HOURS THROUGH THE MOUNTAINS, their goal
is Lajitas, once an old Wild West town that the four of them
had visited many years ago, when the mayor was a goat who
drank beer, before it was developed into an upscale resort that
still looked vaguely like it used to.

The car windows are all open, and Ray, driving now,
enjoys the breeze. His hands are so tired he's having trouble
keeping them on the wheel. His forearms are wrapped around
it, supported. He hasn't slept all day and all of the night before.
His eyes close every once in awhile, then, startle open.

He knows he should stop, find a motel, or even a rest stop,
but there's nothing in sight, not even much of a shoulder to
park on. He gets a whiff of ozone, and sees the lightning strik-
ing the mountains ahead of them. The craggy crests appear
to ignite when lightning strikes behind them. Then the low
rumble of thunder, like a dog's wary growl.

Stella leans against her door, her head slowly drooping. When her chin hits her chest, she jumps slightly, and
raises her head again with a small snore. But she doesn't
completely wake.

Ray loves the peace, and the feeling of being alone. He's almost forgotten how much pleasure it gives him. He tries not to think of the disturbing scene at Dory's. And he doesn't want to think about his sex with Stella, and the fact that in spite of feeling so distraught, she was able to get him to respond to her. To her ordering him around.

How he feels when he's with Stella is familiar. Nothing to do with sex so much as about fear, anxiety. But more complicated.

Did he ever feel this way with Olivia? He thinks back. No, not at all. His mother? He's pretty sure no. But sometimes she didn't get mad at something he thought she would, and sometimes she'd explode in a rage at almost nothing. It was as if they spoke a different language, one that no matter how he tried, he wasn't going to learn.

He does recall feeling misunderstood and hurt. He'd go into his small room and lie down on his narrow bed with the scarlet bedspread with the blue baseballs and beige baseball bats, run his fingers over the soft, much-washed flannel, and sulk, nursing feelings of betrayal.

RAY IS LYING ON HIS NARROW BED with the maple headboard, drawing lines with his new Swiss Army knife on the matching maple chest of drawers nearly up against the bed. He's carved other letters and pictures into the wood, below mattress level, so they aren't visible unless one looked, or moved the furniture. He's wearing his favorite pajamas, flannel, laundry-smelling, with black and white stripes that look like a prisoner's uniform.

His mother surprises him by entering his room without knocking. He flinches and drops the knife.

"What are you doing to the furniture?" she asks. She has small even features, something like his. She's wearing a bright caftan dress that Ray hates because in it she looks like a huge bat. From its folds she lifts one hand, which holds a small silver pistol, shiny, like jewelry.

He can't believe his mother would shoot him, or do anything to intentionally hurt him. He wonders whether she's playing some kind of new game.

Still, he can't help cringing, keeping his eyes on his mother's face and on the gun in her hand, hoping he can figure it out.

She is sweating, though it's autumn and not hot out, her lipstick smeared, she resembles La Llorona, wrapped in La Llorona's robe, Llorona's wild long tangled hair over her shoulders like a raven shawl.

"I have to do this," she says. There's a loud bang, and a bright explosion that is jagged and gold, like lightning.

"Oh, god, says Stella. "What happened?"

The odor of gunpowder is transformed into that of pre-storm ozone and creosote.

"Sorry," Ray says, flustered. "I think I may have fallen asleep." He shakes his head to wake himself, bringing back the pain and some vertigo.

"Driving while asleep. Great." Stella rubs her eyes. "Maybe I should drive? But I'm still too exhausted. Where are we?"

"We're almost there. I think," Ray says.

"Okay," says Stella, combing her hair with her fingers, and squeezing it into some sort of hair clip or rubber band. "I'm waking up. Talk to me, Ray. So we stay awake."

"Do you remember when Felix and I were taken on a small plane through Big Bend National Park so I could research some geological stuff for my thesis?"

"I think I remember," she says, pulling a bottle of water from her purse near her feet. "Want some?"

She opens it and hands it to Ray. "Felix told me that you were airsick the entire time, and never saw anything."

"Thanks," says Ray, laughing, handing back the water. "I needed that. No. I was somewhat airsick, but I did see a lot. What an unbelievable place."

Unlike any landscape Ray had ever seen, Big Bend, which got its name by being surrounded on three sides by the great southward swing of the Rio Grande, on the West Texas-Mexico border, hundreds of miles from anything, is seven hundred thousand acres of arid, cactus-strewn, mountainous topography. It has an extra-terrestrial look with is shockingly sharp beached mountains, and desert plants that looked like outer-space creatures, or drawings of trees by Dr. Seuss.

"According to Indian legend," says Stella, taking a swig of water, "when the Great Creator had finished making the Earth, his big main job, he had a large pile of stony stuff left over that he'd rejected for one reason or another. He didn't want it to go to waste so he got the idea to throw all this material into one huge heap, and made the Big Bend country."

She wipes her chin with her hand. "Water. We have to remember to drink. You can become dehydrated without feeling it until it's too late."

"Is that like falling asleep when it's freezing cold, and not realizing you are freezing to death?"

"Sort of," says Stella.

"Funny that it took the Great Creator a few minutes to get the whole Big Bend area together, yet it took about thirty years, from the time of Pancho Villa, to get Big Bend the status of National Park," says Ray, smelling under his arm.

"I desperately need a shower," he says, feeling filthy, though he can't smell much except for the tinny odor of dried blood in his nose, which reminds him of his bloody clothing in the trunk, and then he pictures Stevie, lying there so still. He puts one hand in front of his eyes as if to wipe the image away.

"Want me to drive?" Stella asks.

"Almost there," he says. But he feels sick and exhausted, and tired of breathing through his mouth.

He's sure his nose is broken and wonders whether it can heal without his seeing a doctor. Maybe he'll end up with an intriguing crooked beak, or one with a hook. A nose that will make him sexy.

One of his wrists is red and swollen, and throbs. And his ears are clogged. Or just reacting to the steady buzz of the car on the road.

He knows they need to talk. He's surprised Stella doesn't mention anything—about what they've done—and what their plan is.

As if reading his mind, Stella says, "We need to rest, then make a plan. We'll be okay at the resort, where we can study Felix's stuff." She adds, "You do need a shower."

She stretches her neck round and round. "Boy, I'm stiff. The resort's called The Badlands Hotel. I like that," she says.

She looks at Ray. "By the way, you're getting a couple of black eyes. Does that mean your nose is broken?"

YEARS AGO THE FOUR OF THEM, Felix and Stella, he and Olivia, were visiting Big Bend National Park on their way to Lajitas. But only Felix and Ray took the plane ride to see the canyons from above, a trip he'll never forget, though he's already forgotten the thesis he'd been working on, and which changed many times till he finally got his degree.

Felix had his camera equipment—a lot of stuff pre-digital days. He was working on some kind of book, maybe his own thesis, about the border.

They'd climbed into the small Cessna-182. As Felix settled himself and his equipment into the small space, the pilot complained about not being able to use a tiny Piper Cub that day for some reason or other, so they could fly between the canyon walls.

To Ray the Cessna was small enough, and he'd whispered a "thank god."

Their pilot wore a leather bomber jacket and a peaked leather cap resembling a Lindburgh-era uniform, and he had a lot of black hair on the backs of his hands, which Ray would stare at when the view made him sick.

From eight-hundred feet the Rio Grande appeared a rich chocolate color as it prepared to enter the massive canyons of the Big Bend, with islands of silt, built up and washed away again and again, appeared in the middle of the river. Sheer rock rose from the river on both sides, carved by centuries of flowing water. Sun colored the upper walls, the lower remained dark, a sharp line dividing them. As the canyon walls lowered, more light reached the river, and both sides of the canyon were verdant with lush greenery.

Felix and Ray remained completely silent, hardly breathing, squeezed into the small seats, awed by the view, Felix snapping photos, and Ray getting sick from sharp dips the pilot purposely made to entertain them.

The walls of Mariscal Canyon, which mark the actual bend where the Rio Grande begins its flow northward, are so close together, and so straight, that Ray felt he could lie down on top of them, across the river, with his head in the United States, and his feet in Mexico.

Between Mariscal's sixteen-hundred foot walls, they watched the Rio Grande's transformation from a docile flow to a wild hurricane of a flood. It almost seemed that they could feel splashes in their small aircraft. Ray's stomach turned and rose into his chest. The canyon walls got lower again, and ended, the river seeming to heave a monstrous sigh of relief, and became calm. Free again.

Their pilot had the Cessna fly slowly above Boquillas, to show off what to Ray was the most spectacular of the canyons. Its gently sloped walls were tinted with brilliant reds, browns and yellows, an occasional strawberry cactus brightening the plateaus above the canyon.

It was peaceful for miles, except for the steady, very loud drone of the plane, which they almost no longer heard, as if it had become a part of their bodies.

"I have a surprise for you," screamed their pilot. "I saved it for last."

"Uh oh, one of your airplane tricks?" said Ray.

"It's coming up right below us."

They looked down to see the most magnificent land formation they'd ever encountered—a seemingly endless series of canyons more grandiose than some caverns they'd seen and more colorful than the Painted Desert. Narrow slivers of rock pointed straight up, shaping into formations only imagined in science fiction—moonscapes, or other planets. At the sides, fingers of parched desert were frozen in the middle of odd gestures.

Ray felt transformed and transported, as if he'd smoked pot. He recalls that Felix was more interested in San Vicente, a crossing where candelilla wax for chewing gum is smuggled into the United States. He'd wondered whether Felix was considering some risky money-making venture.

When they crawled out of the Cessna, Ray's legs trembled, and his stomach seemed to be searching for its place in his body. His knees buckled, and he grabbed Felix's arm.

"Hey," shouted Felix, adjusting the straps on his shoulders of his camera case, and balancing his bag of lenses, and films and other equipment, "watch out for my stuff."

Later that same day Felix signed on with some other company to go rafting on the Colorado Canyon section of the Rio Grande, near Terlingua, while Ray met up with Olivia and Stella at their campsite. He can't recall ever having seen any of Felix's photographs from that day.

"I had a dream," he finally tells Stella, "during the one or two seconds that I may have fallen asleep at the wheel."

"You actually had a dream while you were driving," Stella says. "That's pretty fucking scary."

"It may have been that state, you know, right before you actually fall asleep, when you are in both worlds."

Yeah," Stella says, sighing, pretending to prepare to be bored.

"I dreamed that I was shot by my mother. That my mother shot me. It was her, I'm sure, but then she turned into La Llorona."

"Your mother shot you?" says Stella, her voice sharp.

And then she turned into you, Ray remembers, but doesn't want to say, recalling, in the dream, Stella's shaky hands, arms straight out, trying to keep the shiny gun steady. He's replayed that image quite a few times. Hopefully it will lose the power to horrify.

Stella doesn't ask for a more detailed story. She says, "Poor Ray. We may be having nightmares for a long time to come.

He recoils from her sympathetic touch on his upper arm. She doesn't seem to notice. Or maybe she doesn't care.

"See?" she says, holding up her hand near Ray's on the wheel. Her fingers spread apart in front of him tremble.

"See? My hand is still shaking."

TWENTY-SIX

Behind us, as the rain begins again, a funeral procession winds its way down the narrow mud tracks, men in wet cowboy hats and boots pull shovels out of a station wagon and wrestle a coffin over the hillocks to a likely spot; ladies with lace veils are buffeted by the wind; endless plastic bags blow between them like fleeing ghosts.

Luis Alberto Urrea, *None of Them Talk About Their Dreams*

"OH, GOD, SORRY," SAYS STELLA, LIGHTING A CIGARETTE.

Ray watches her eyebrows curve upward as she inhales.

"I was so exhausted but I couldn't sleep," she says. "I knocked over that crappy lamp reaching for my purse."

The lamp from her night table is on the floor, but it's still on, casting weird misplaced glimmers, lighting everything from below, deep shadows in unexpected places. The room upside down.

Her large straw tote, or purse, whatever you call it, is on the bed between them, the same one he's seen beside her throughout their trip, at her feet, on a nearby chair, thrown casually on to a motel bed. Would she keep the gun in there?

He looks around. Another ugly room. They were both so exhausted that driving straight through to Lajitas became less and less of an option. So—Starlight Motel.

"Do you have to smoke?" asks Ray. "This is a non-smoking room."

"Yes," says Stella, turning on to her side, "I have to smoke." She laughs hoarsely, and smashes the cigarette out against her fake mahogany night table, pulling her tote bag off the bed and down to the floor on her side.

"I'm glad we decided to take a different route and bypass that Border Patrol checkpoint," says Ray, rubbing his eye. "Ouch."

"There will be more checkpoints if we hang around the border," says Stella. "Oh, you poor baby." She leans over, looking as if she's going to touch Ray's nose.

"No," he says, backing away. "Don't dare touch it. Don't ever touch me again. I ache all over."

He thinks of Miguel. The fight. I saved your life, Stella had said.

His gaze rests on the smooth arc of Stella's lower back— the curve towards her shapely bum in her yellow bikinis.

But he sees the dark maroon of blood on the beige carpet, the feel of the knife hitting Miguel's breastbone. The particular limpness of the bodies they'd left.

He leans over the side of the bed and dry-retches.

"Are you okay?" Stella asks, propping herself on an elbow. Her ample breasts, suddenly exposed, curve sideways against her breastbone. "I need some tea. Would you like some?"

"Mmmm. Yeah," says Ray. He thinks of Felix, missing him suddenly. His stomach aches. He's hungry, but the thought of food is sickening.

"There's nothing here to boil water in. I thought we might have a coffee pot," says Stella. "I'll go see if I can get some boiling water and some tea bags at the office."

Ray watches Stella pull on her jeans and a shirt. He intends to look for the gun, and get rid of it. Somewhere.

He hadn't realized how scared he is of her. He knows he doesn't trust her. But Stella with a gun? If she'd give it to him, or even let him know where it is, would he have to sneak behind her back? If she hadn't been hiding it, maybe he wouldn't be thinking about it. Maybe she doesn't trust him. Maybe she thinks he'll shoot her? That's totally ridiculous. He smiles at that thought. Or, maybe she thinks he'll hand the weapon to some law enforcement person as evidence against her?

As soon as she slams the door, Ray pulls on his chinos. He's sweating. It isn't in her purse.

He bends over Stella's soft black duffle, the bag she's had with her since they left on this trip, which is on the floor near the bathroom. He knows he has to hurry, but he's between the bed and the door, and if Stella comes, he'll just shut the bag and stand up.

He rummages through clothing he vaguely recognizes, finds a flowered cosmetics bag, and a velvet jewelry bag, both too small for the gun. No need to be neat, or worry about getting it back the same way it was, as by this time most of her clothing has just been thrown in, a result of their current life of emergencies.

A kick at the door, then Stella: "Can you open the door? I've got two teas here."

Even though he knew she'd be back in a few minutes, Ray rises rapidly, flustered, then bends again to zip the bag.

He opens the door to Stella, who holds a small plastic tray with two white, steaming mugs, strings and labels hanging down their sides, and two white plastic spoons.

She looks at Ray, who blushes, then her eyes go right to her bag on the floor.

"You won't find the gun in there," she says, placing Ray's mug on his night table, and walking around the unmade bed to her side.

"Then where is it?" he croaks, startled, and ashamed.

Stella pulls the pale green sheet and bile green blanket up so she can sit on the bed, and looks around. "This motel is just as revolting as all the others," she says. "But it has good air-conditioning. It's going to be pretty hot today."

Ray's tea smells good. He breathes in the steam, sipping too fast, and burns his tongue.

Stella dunks her teabag up and down in the mug. "We have to trust each other," she says.

"Well, I'm trustworthy," says Ray, the tip of his tongue numb, "but you are noticeably not."

"How do I know you're trustworthy? Anyway, what choice do we have?"

"If you get to the point of having no choice, isn't that a sign that you've made many poor choices up to that point?" Ray asks. He notes that she hasn't claimed to be trustworthy.

They both sip their tea to the hum of the air-conditioner. Apparently Stella has no answer. Or doesn't want to discuss it.

"Let's do what we came here for," she says, and she and Ray lift the large black wheelie Stella had brought from her and Felix's El Paso house, onto the bed.

"Shit, what the fuck's in here?" Ray asks. "Felix's body? I thought you just went to pick up his computer and his phone."

"Hey," says Stella. "That's not funny." She moves close to him, and he imagines she wants to open the bag first, so he moves back. After all, it's her husband who's missing, and whatever's on the computer is her business. But instead of opening the suitcase, she puts both her arms around him, and gently hugs.

She's warm, and her breath carries the sweet odor of tea. After a moment he tries to pull away, but then leans into her.

"Let's get started," he says, feeling her lips on his neck. He feels the tip of her tongue, sharp and wet, and then her teeth, as she bites the tender flesh there just a bit too hard.

"Ouch, fuck. I'm all bruised. Remember?" He moves away, rubbing the bite.

Stella ignores him, moving far too close, pressing into him too hard. He's too close to push her away. He can only shove her hard, or move back. When he tries to move away, she moves forward—her aggression is intentional.

"Get the hell away," he says, pushing her as hard as he can.

She lands on the bed. He doesn't know if she's hit the suitcase.

"I'm sorry, sorry," he says, going over to her. "I hurt like hell, and I'm not interested in your games." But he lies on top of her, trying to make amends. "I'm sorry. Did I hurt you?"

He tries to get up, but she turns quickly, and is now on top of Ray, holding him down with all her strength. He feels her teeth bite hard right above his nipple, the pain sudden and sharp.

"Ouch, you cunt." He's startled himself; it's not a word he uses often if ever, and never to curse a woman.

Stella laughs. He bites her neck, but she holds him tighter, clasping her two hands together behind his slender back. Her legs are around his lower back, like some kind of wild animal climbing a tall tree. He has no idea how her pants get pulled down, or off, but he pushes her down with his body, and enters her hard, his body a weapon, and loudly growls.

"Ahhh," groans Stella, biting his ear hard.

WHEN RAY WAKES he has no idea what time it is. He may have only fallen asleep for a moment, but the dark green drapes are still closed. Stella's lamp is now back on her nightstand, still lit. There's a fluorescent glow from the bathroom. Stella has moved up on the bed and is lying alongside the suitcase. Ray still lies across the bottom of the bed.

He gets up, gingerly, as he aches all over, almost the same as when he'd fought Miguel. Stella doesn't move. He studies her, at first to make sure she's really asleep. Which she seems to be, her knees drawn up a bit towards her chest, her dark curls spread out behind her on the pale green pillowcase as if blown back by a headwind. Asleep, she could be a child. Her mouth is open a bit, her two front teeth show under her upper lip. Her skin is smooth, except for a tiny vertical line above the bridge of her nose, not quite in the center, which deepens when she's worried, or trying to be earnest. The room is cool but there are minute drops of perspiration along her hairline. A tiny rivulet of spittle runs from the corner of her plump lips to her fist, which is partly under her head, between her mouth and the pillow.

He thinks he heard her whisper, "I'm sorry, Ray. I'll give you the gun. But maybe it was a dream.

Ray zips up his chinos quietly, and pulling aside the skanky viridian rubberized drapes, he sees it's daylight, though outside all is still. There are now two pickups parked near their rental car, which beside them looks tiny.

It's unusual for Stella to be asleep when Ray is moving around. He's itching to get into Felix's stuff, and he'd love to do it without Stella hovering about, or distracting him.

He stands beside the suitcase, which is on his side of the bed, and releases the center clasp, which snaps open loudly, sounding like a small explosion.

He waits a moment but Stella doesn't move.

Given how things are going, Ray expects some trouble with the suitcase. Like maybe the lid won't open, maybe there's a special lock with a secret combination, or something. So he's surprised at the ease with which it yields. He has to hold the top of the suitcase to keep it from falling onto Stella.

There's a mess of clothing—why did Stella pack more clothing? Underneath a couple of layers he spots Felix's silver laptop. He finds two phones stuck in along the sides, and near the laptop, a pile of mail, a computer power cord, and a couple of small notebooks. Cautiously he lowers the top of the suitcase, and, using it as a desk, plugs the power line into an outlet and into the computer.

Another snafu—would this motel even have WiFi? He turns on the computer and waits as it boots up. He clicks on gmail and sees that he needs the motel password. Welcome to Starlight Motel. The last thing he feels like doing is going to the office for the password. Then he recalls the tiny slip of paper that came with the room key.

Felix's mailbox loads. Hundreds of messages, most of the ads or political messages asking for donations to help save the world. There are advertisements for items Felix may have checked out.

He sits down near the door, back against the wall, feeling the rough carpet through his chinos, computer on his lap, and begins to read.

TWENTY-SEVEN

As the Interstate swings to the northeast again, it closely follows the course of the Rio Grande all the way to El Paso. Serrated Laramide ranges on the Mexico side of the river food plain nestle at their base. Much of the surrounding landscape is windblown sand and dune deposits. In some place the dunes are stabilized by the sparse vegetation, but look for rounded sand dunes, and wind ripple marks on free sand faces. They are especially obvious in low sun angles of early morning or late afternoon.

Darwin Spearing, Roadside *Geology of Texas*

THERE ARE SO MANY MESSAGES, hopefully an indication that this is the only computer Felix used to keep in touch with anyone, but there's so much to delete. Or, of course, he shouldn't delete anything.

He takes a deep breath. Will he really find anything here? He'd been feeling excited to finally begin, but feels more hopeless by the minute.

Maybe he should let Stella do this. She knows who his friends are. She'd recognize some names for sure. Or would she? She's claimed to know little—close to nothing. Yet he feels as if he's wasting time looking at junk.

Ray writes, on the back page of one of Felix's notebooks, the names that show up more than a few times. Oskar, Alberto Carlos Ramirez, Al (maybe a nickname for Alberto), Roberta, Chase Grinnell.

From a month ago (Ray can hardly remember what the date is, or how long he's been here) from Oskar: *It's screwed up. Supposedly the Marines were assisting the Border Patrol with some drug smugglers. Turns out the Border Patrol shot a Chicano kid in the back of the head, one of a group just playing there near the border. The kid had been running back to the Mexican side. They said the kid had a weapon, but no one saw anything. Yeah, a ten year old with a weapon?*

More from Oskar: *Sucked up, man. What about Mexico? They'd rather die of thirst in the desert. We are forcing meatpacking plants to check workers' IDs.*

Oddly, there are no responses from Felix. Bizarre, Ray thinks. But the issues are familiar. Ray pictures Felix, tight and tanned, enraged, long fingers splayed, expounding in his loud deep voice—too loud, and too angry—sometimes embarrassing Ray.

Is Oskar Mexican? His name seems to be, but his English is perfect.

A moan from Stella, and Ray closes the computer.

He stands, and rubs his sore back. "Are you okay? I've been checking out some of Felix's emails."

Stella wipes some stray spit near her cheek with her fist. "I have a splitting headache," she says. "Maybe it's meningitis."

He thinks she's joking, but she hurriedly gets out of bed, feet tangling in the sheet for a moment, threatening to trip her as she runs the two steps to the john.

He stands, awkward, not knowing whether to give her privacy, or follow her to make sure she's okay.

He hears retching, then the toilet flushing. She emerges looking as if she's run a marathon, damp strands of hair stuck to her cheek, and collapses on to the bed. "Can you find me some aspirin in my drug bag?"

"I see two bags here. One has makeup."

"And the other has meds," she says, impatient. "So far the makeup bag is the larger. As I age my meds bag will take up more space than my clothing."

"Ha, ha," says Ray, bringing her some water, and sitting on the small space between Stella and the edge of the bed. He pulls the sheet up over her legs.

"Ugghh." Stella's white tongue is out, two aspirin on the tip. She drinks one sip, and lies down.

"Try to drink more water," Ray says.

Stella closes her eyes.

"I've begun looking through Felix's computer, says Ray, making sure her water glass is within reach.

"I can't deal with that now," she says, not opening her eyes. Yet a moment later she asks, "Have you found anything yet? I mean anything helpful?"

"Just a lot of spam ... and some angry messages." He doesn't say who sent them. "Do you know anyone named Oskar? Or Bob?"

"No Oskar. I know at least four Bobs, Robs, or Roberts," she says. "Maybe more."

"He's been so angry lately," she whispers. "Felix."

"More than usual?" asks Ray.

Stella is silent. Ray listens to her breathe. Or maybe the breathing is his?

"What's happening to Mexicans, and Americans, and poor people, and black people, and Syrians, and Nigerians, and slaves, and traffic-ed women, and abused children, and victims of wars, and pollution, is unspeakably sad, and horrible and totally unjust," Stella says, straining, raising herself a bit, looking at Ray. "But what's the good of getting so angry about all these things, all the injustice and cruelty in the world? Injustice that we have no power to alleviate? And then to be angry with oneself for not doing more, and more? Does it help to be so enraged that you ruin your health, and destroy your family and your marriage to spend all your time doing dangerous stuff to help people you don't even know—and probably not even succeeding?"

Stella is white with a greenish tinge, and seems to have used up any energy she had. She closes her eyes again.

"And what about you?" he asks. "Don't you care about illegals dying in the desert? Or young *maquiladoras* being murdered by sexual predators who never get caught? Are you saying that because there's too much evil going on in the world, and we can't fix everything, that we should do nothing?"

It seems that her last effort has exhausted her and that she may have fallen asleep. All the better. What the fuck is wrong with him anyway? He agrees with everything she's said, so why is he accusing her of not caring? And what about himself? He reads the news. He's not unaware. He's felt guilt at not doing more, not doing something, anything, beyond sending small donations to a coterie of charitable organizations, all the while wondering if any of the money gets to the needy, and signing a slew of online petitions. And then just going about his life. He really does think that because there's so much that needs to be done, why bother. No, he doesn't think it, but he acts or doesn't act as if he thinks it's so.

He likes to think that if each of us lives an aware life and acts in a moral way, that's also a crucial form of activism. But isn't that, while true, something he's made up or read about, and adopted in order to assuage his guilt? Because there will always be those who don't act in a moral way.

Stella's face has gone from greenish to rose. He feels her forehead to see whether she has a fever. She feels warm, but isn't burning up.

He'd like to find somewhere to sit outside where he can check Felix's phones. He's still having trouble breathing, and the airless room is smothering. He imagines he can smell Stella's vomit, though he can't really smell anything with his nose still a mess.

He touches her forehead again, and her neck, worried.

She grabs his hand. Hers is hot.

"Please, Ray, please. Don't go anywhere," she mumbles, eyes still closed. "Stay here with me, don't leave me."

"I won't," he says, doubtful, trying to pull his hand from her surprising grip.

"Please," she whispers, "please. I need you."

LYING BESIDE STELLA ON THE BED, with sheets and blankets an unruly mess, Ray feels headachy himself. He's checked out Felix's phone, which has more than seventy-five contacts, and no tweets or texts. Good, Ray thinks, you are, like me, not a tweeter.

There are, however, lots of photos, many of people Ray doesn't recognize. He sees none of Felix, or for that matter, of Stella—or maybe a couple of them taken in some restaurant, but just part of her head. Stella may recognize the people in some of the photos. There are photos of restaurants, dining rooms, and photos of food. There are photos of the desert and some of cacti.

The other phone is locked. Ray's tried a few possible passwords, but nothing's worked. Why would Felix need a locked phone, anyway?

He's checked the contacts, and is surprised that he doesn't recognize any names or numbers at all. How is that possible that they have no friends in common anymore?

Some of the messages on the phone, but mostly on the computer, are from Ray, preparations for this trip. Reading them feels odd. They seem to belong to a stranger, from a Ray he scarcely recognizes, a person pretending to be more cheerful, and more excited than he recalls ever being. Like the first time he heard his own voice played back on a tape recorder. A voice that sounded like someone else's. A voice that was somewhat embarrassing in its strangeness.

There are more messages to and from Oskar, and others to strangers that have to do with water in El Paso, Mexican and United States policies and laws. Lamentations about corruption, both of Mexico and the U.S. Angry messages about the Border Patrol, and roundups of immigrants. It seems that Felix belongs to a group of people who leave water along the desert routes taken by migrants. Ray is surprised at what looks like much more involvement by Felix than he'd ever thought. How could Stella know so little?

She's still asleep. He's remained there as she'd requested, but there's been nothing he could do for her except adjust the air-conditioner. He's brought her tea, and some dehydrated chicken soup, still on her night table in its polystyrene cup, a yellowish green scum, like algae, on top.

He can't decide whether he should wake her up to eat, or drink, or if letting her sleep would be best for her. She hasn't even gotten up to pee.

"Stella," he whispers. Then louder, "Stella."

Facing the bathroom, she lies on her side. Her color looks a bit better, if pink is better than pea green or dark rose. Her mouth is open and her lips are dry and pale. Her forehead is shiny with sweat or oil, and her hair is as stringy and limp as if she hasn't bathed in a month.

Ray watches her ribcage under the thin blanket to see whether she's still breathing. It takes some concentration to see whether or not he's just imagining she's alive, so minimal is the movement of her chest. He touches her cheek, which is not as warm as before.

Half the time Ray has no idea whether it's day or night, and it seems as if he's been in this motel for a week. He's finding it harder and harder to motivate himself to move. He pictures both of them, him and Stella, just lying here on this bed, slowly forgetting to get up, or no longer able to move, or to eat—just slowly dying.

The thought is so horrifying he stands right up. But there's nowhere to go.

TWENTY-EIGHT

Walls are not just about whom a country wants to keep out, they
are a mark of what it is trying to preserve, its idea of itself.

Tony Estrada, Sheriff of Santa Clara County

RAY IS IN THE CAR, happy to be out of the motel, and moving.

He'd taken a shower, leaving the bathroom door open in
case Stella called for him. Hair dripping, a ragged white towel
around his middle, he'd opened the drapes to a blue and cloud-
less sky. The light blinded him.

The sight of a green and white Border Patrol car parked
in front of the office cause his knees to buckle, but on second
thought it probably meant nothing—there were Border Patrol
cops everywhere around here.

Stella had changed her position while Ray was showering,
so that was reassuring.

He left her a note near he chicken soup, saying he'd gone
to see a friend of Felix's, and would be back soon. He didn't
mention Oskar's name. Though she'd said she didn't know
an Oskar, maybe she doesn't want Ray to know she's had a
relationship with him, fucked him.

He'd slipped Felix's phone into his pants pocket, which
sagged from the weight of the small notebook he's also taking,
his keys, and pesos mixed with U.S. change.

For an instant, closing the door quietly behind him, the wish came, unbidden and unexpected, that Stella would be gone when he got back. Yet a moment later, he was filled with dread at that possibility.

His hands on the steering wheel feel good, as does the dry wind whizzing past his ears, drying his hair. The only thing he wishes for right now is his sunglasses, as his eyes are sensitive to bright light, and ache from squinting.

He runs one hand through his damp hair, getting longer, he notes, feeling curls at his neck and ears. His plan is to get rid of the bloody clothes still in the trunk, and then drive to El Paso to meet with Oskar, who he's sent an email to, and who has blessedly responded.

Ray tries to recall an Oskar in their life when he was at the University of Texas. It seems odd now but he doesn't remember doing much socializing at all except for parties and dinners with couples. Because he was married, that seemed natural. Though there were many Mexican students, married and unmarried, he and Olivia had never become close with any of them—not even those on the faculty. Oh, maybe one or two, but he'd always thought of them as gringos. Oskar, or Oscar, a name more common in Mexico than in the United States, is still a bit unusual, and he imagines he'd remember it.

He feels good that he's still able to find his way around El Paso, and this neighborhood where he is to meet Oskar. Five Corners, the older part of town, bears street names of American states. He is looking for "Tennessee".

This area of El Paso resembles the neighborhood where Ray grew up, in upstate New York, with its tall spreading trees, plenty of bushes and grassy lawns. The houses, not very far apart, but most with roomy porches, seem very well kept. It had been a lower middle class neighborhood that has obviously gentrified.

At "Kentucky" Ray is aware of a Border Patrol car half a block behind him, the usual white and green Ford Bronco. Could it be following him? It looks the same as the one at the motel—an SUV, not a sedan. Why would a Border Patrol agent follow him when he could just confront him? And why would the BP be trolling a neighborhood like this, driving just as slowly as Ray, who is not sure where the house he's looking for is.

Unless of course the agent lives here somewhere; this is just the sort of neighborhood a BP officer might live in.

Ray thinks he's near the four-digit address he's been looking for. When he parks he'll see what the BP agent does. Could he be leading the agent to Oskar? Maybe it's Oskar he's looking for? Maybe, if Oskar and Felix were up to something illegal together. Like what?

A startlingly thin man emerges from a royal blue doorway on to a narrow porch with an unpainted wood railing. The address is invisible, hidden by overgrown bushes so tall they cover most of the windows on both sides of the porch stairs, which are also unpainted wood, and seem to have been recently added to the house, an afterthought.

The man waves to Ray, his long arms rearranging the air.

Ray wonders how the man knows he's the person he has an appointment with? But there aren't that many people around at all, no less one who's parked on the street right near your house.

Then he realizes that Oskar, if that is Oskar, is waving to the man driving the Border Patrol vehicle, now passing Ray's car, moving slowly along the street.

Ray runs up the stairs to shake Oskar's long, leathery hand. He has so many questions he hardly knows where to begin, but he's surprised at the welcome, given Stella's, and even Felix's, secrecy.

"Come in, come in," Oskar says, with a wide, thin-lipped smile, bending over to get through the threshold. Ray follows, ducking through the door too, though he's half a foot shorter than Oskar.

"Thanks for seeing me right away," says Ray.

"No problem," Oskar says, deep voice booming in the small space.

Oskar's voice sounds familiar; has Ray heard it somewhere before?

Ray follows Oskar as he takes the white and black tiled foyer with two steps, his long legs in their faded stove-pipe jeans, and nearly knee-high, pointy-toed, ostrich skin boots into a small living room overstuffed with furniture that looks as if it's come from a much bigger place.

Oskar indicates where he'd like Ray to sit with a tilt of his chin in the direction of a large, too large, chartreuse couch, with a pattern of huge dark green leaves and vines crawling over it, as if it's been taken over by jungle.

Ray sits, guessing that someone other than Oskar picked out this furniture.

Seated, Ray can see through a wide doorway into a bedroom with a low platform bed and a modern chest.

"Can I get you a beer? Some coffee? I have some tequila," says Oskar, noticing Ray's glance into his bedroom.

"Yeah, when my wife lived here, we enlarged the bedroom, made a glass wall, and added a modern bathroom. But it wasn't enough to keep her here."

Ray smiles, "Yeah, sometimes creating a lot more space can save a marriage. I imagine," he says.

"She was the gardener," Oskar adds, indicating with one hand the huge amount of uncared-for vegetation pushing in at the glass wall in the bedroom.

He hands Ray a very cold Negra Modelo. "My grass," he says, bending into a low, fat, jungle green easy chair, "is illegal."

Ray assumes Oskar is talking about a crop of marijuana he's growing.

Oskar continues, "I could be arrested, or at least fined, for letting my lawn and all the grass grow past the limit of what the city rules, which is, I believe, only two inches. As you might guess," he adds, "I'm not someone who finds it easy to follow rules."

Ray sips his beer, wondering why Oskar would make sure to tell him that.

"Are you a close friend of Felix Mann's?" asks Ray, as Oskar places a white mug, coffee for himself, on the ornate, possibly antique, cherry coffee table in between them, which leaves little room for their legs.

If the table is valuable, it doesn't matter to Oskar, who has left his mark with a multitude of cigarette burns and intersecting circles and rings.

"I'm a good friend of Stella's too," he says.

Ray hides his surprise. Stella had said she didn't know any Oskar. He studies Oskar's expression for any sign of irony, for instance "good friend" meaning we were lovers. Possible, since it seems that Stella fucks almost everyone and anyone.

Oskar reminds Ray of Robert Redford—the handsome bone structure still apparent under all his many wrinkles. Or even more so, Clint Eastwood, with his tall ranginess. They both wear their skins like jackets that have grown much too large.

"Tell me why you're here," Oskar says, an unlit cigarette in the corner of his lips, distorting his speech.

He looks directly at Ray with small, very light blue eyes, his long legs straight out, pale boots disappearing under the ornate coffee table. He removes the cigarette from his lips with his thumb and forefinger and places it behind one ear like a pencil, crosses his legs at the ankles, and leans forward.

Ray sips his beer, which gurgles loudly in the silence. "I'm looking for Felix," he finally blurts. "I found your information on Felix's computer. There were a lot of messages to and from you."

He expects Oskar to react to the fact that Felix is missing. Instead he says, "He-ey," sounding like a Texan for the first time, "why would you be looking through Felix's messages? What's going on?" Though he's speaking slowly, he is angry.

Ray sighs. "I'm not going to be able to begin at the beginning—wherever and whenever that was," he says, leaning forward until his belt buckle bites into his abdomen. "So I'll summarize."

Oskar's small pale eyes look directly into Rays larger green ones with a laser stare.

"The three of us—Stella, Felix and I—were taking a trip along the border. I hadn't seen them for years—since we were teaching and studying at UTEP. On the third, or maybe the second day Felix got beaten up pretty badly. He said he'd been in a fight with some drunk Mexicans who attacked him. And he thought he might have killed one of them. By accident. Or maybe he killed one of them by accident and then they came after him. I may be forgetting some of the details because I'm summarizing—and because, frankly, Felix seemed to be lying. Or it seemed a ridiculous story at the time. Though at this point I'd believe anything."

Ray looks down at his amber bottle. He's having a hard time maintaining eye contact with Oskar's piercing orbs. He looks up again, and studies the wrinkles around Oskar's eyes.

"The next day when we woke up Felix was gone—missing—from our motel in Juarez. We thought he might have gone for a run, which is what he said he'd been doing when he got beaten up the day before, so we waited for him, but he never came back."

For the first time since Ray began his story, Oskar lowers his eyes.

"He's been missing ever since. About two days."

Ray waits for a response. Oskar returns the cigarette from behind his ear to his mouth, where it dips slightly crookedly, like an old drainpipe off a roof.

Already intimidated by Oskar's penetrating gaze, and his intensity, he feels a need to fill the silence. "We've been looking for him, but frankly, we don't know where to begin. That's why we checked out Felix's messages."

He notices he's using the word "frankly" a lot. Is that because somehow he's not being frank?

"We need to find out if Felix was into ... was doing something dangerous. Can you give me a clue? Something to go on?"

The story, summarized for Oskar, conveniently leaves out whatever bothers Ray, such as his relationship with Stella, and the events at Dory's. But Oskar doesn't need to know that.

Again Oskar removes the cigarette from his mouth with his thumb and forefinger, just holding it. It's beginning to unravel, and a string of tobacco hangs from its tip.

Ray wants to hear from Oskar, but he can't seem to stop talking, filling the deep uncomfortable silences. He's about to ask if Oskar knows Dory—but what does she have to do with Felix's disappearance?

He sips his beer to keep himself from talking.

Oskar says, "You look as if you've been in a fight. Maybe you've killed Felix."

Ray's eyes open wide as they can. Then he remembers his nose, and his swollen and blackened eyes.

"Have you looked in the mirror lately?" asks Oskar.

"Oh," says Ray, carefully touching his nose, "that's another story."

"Doesn't Stella have any idea where her husband is? She knows him better than I do. Where is she? Didn't you say she's looking for Felix too?"

Oskar runs his fingers through his thick yellowish-white hair. With his hair back, his forehead is long, and there's a deep indentation where or ridge where perhaps a hat or sombrero usually sits.

Surprised at the questions, Ray feels the heat of a blush. "She's at a motel on the other side of town," he says. She's not feeling well or she'd be here. I came without her because we can't afford to lose any more time."

Ray fiddles with the label on his beer bottle, now empty.

Oskar points to it. "Another?"

"No thanks," says Ray. "So you know Stella?" Oskar has said he knows Stella, but Ray is pushing for more information.

"Of course I know Stella. I've known her for years." Oskar almost smiles. "She introduced me to Felix, and taught me about El Coyote.

"What? El Coyote?"

Oskar smiles broadly, his wrinkled cheeks parentheses within parentheses. "The Trickster, to the Paleo and Apachean hunters. The Greeks, the Chinese, the Japanese, the Hebrew, all had a similar trickster character in their legends. A character who embodied all these opposites—creator and destroyer, giver and negator, one who dupes, and the one who can be duped. She doesn't know the difference between good and evil, possesses no values—either moral or societal—and is totally at the mercy of her passions and appetites. Yet through Coyote's actions, all values come into being."

During this narrative Ray is restive, wondering where this is going, away from his concerns, certainly. But Oskar seems transformed—he's practically glowing. This is definitely the kind of story Stella might be telling—and maybe Oskar is telling Ray something important about Stella, which is maybe the key to finding Felix.

"Coyote made the earth, but then he fucked up and also gave us death. One has to wonder how a character like Coyote came to life in such a variety of cultures," says Oskar, untangling his legs and rising. "I'm getting more coffee," he says, this time not offering another beer.

Ray thinks about Stella. He's been away longer than he thought he'd be, and it looks like he's not going to find out much more. But he doesn't make a move to leave.

"Coyote is always out there—and he's always hungry," laughs Oskar. His ratty cigarette is back behind his ear. He returns with his mug.

"Quit smoking recently?" Ray asks, smiling.

"Yeah," says Oskar. "Four years ago."

Ray laughs. "Yeah," he says. Then, "Look, we're desperate. Aren't you concerned that Felix is missing? Do you have any thoughts? Any ideas?

Oskar's pale boots have a pinkish tinge, and remind Ray of the snake they'd seen on the road, shedding its skin.

"Stella thinks that Ray may have been kidnapped, and that a body she saw on a TV news program is his, even though it was covered. Except for the feet. She says she doesn't know much of what Felix was into—but maybe she's just not telling me. Must be some pretty bad stuff if she thinks he'd be kidnapped, or killed. And she also said she doesn't know anyone named Oskar.

Oskar doesn't seem surprised by anything Ray's said, moreover Ray can't read him, in spite of his lined, expressive face and the attentive gaze, with his dark pupils in irises that appear nearly white, outlined in cerulean. He's been here for about forty minutes, and has no information except that Stella has lied about knowing him.

"Maybe he just ran away," says Oskar. "Perhaps because you were there, and he sensed something between you and Stella, it was easier for him to leave. Maybe he thought it was his moment?" Oskar sips loudly. "Not hot enough," he says.

"If so, wouldn't he leave a note—something? Especially if he didn't want to be searched for? And what about the beating? Is Felix the kind of guy who gets into fights?"

"Or," Oskar continues, ignoring the questions, "maybe he's on some mission ..."

"What sort of mission?" Ray asks, thinking he's finally going to get something useful.

"Felix is an angry guy," Oskar says. "It's impossible to tell what people will do. Do you think you know Felix?"

Ray almost nods, but the more he thinks about it, he thinks better of responding.

"For instance, my wife," says Oskar, pulling his knees up from under the coffee table, and turning slightly so they are high, pointing towards Ray. "I thought I knew her. We lived together for almost twelve years. We slept together every night. I knew her breathing, her snoring, her skin—the sounds she made during sex. Her smells. I thought I knew her thoughts. After she left me—and I was never sure why—I found out she'd been lovers for four years with someone I'd worked with on a ranch, someone I'd been friends with for almost as long as my marriage." He shakes his head, and holds up his large, tanned hand, thumb curled in so Ray can see the four long digits.

Ray doesn't know what to say. How can you live with someone and miss signals for four years?

"I know what you're thinking," Oskar says. "That somehow I'm dense. Or too trusting. But don't you have to be trusting to be married? I maintain that no one ever really knows anyone completely."

"That's your experience," says Ray. "I don't know. I'm pretty sure I knew my wife." Even as he says it, he's no longer sure.

"Did she leave you?" asks Oskar.

"She died," says Ray.

"Sorry," Oskar says.

Ray runs his finger across the rings on the coffee table, feeling the slight roughness. He takes a deep breath. "Stella thinks maybe Felix was involved in drug smuggling."

He studies Oskar, who says nothing.

"Do I take your silence for assent?" Ray asks. "That you think it's possible?"

"Take it for whatever you want," says Oskar, squirming in his overstuffed chair, and unrolling himself until he's standing.

"I have no idea where Felix is. If I did I'd probably tell you," he says, moving the cigarette from his large red ear. He bends over to tap it on the coffee table as if getting ready to light it, then places it in his mouth, where it sticks to his lower lip. He stretches, leaning backward, pressing his hands there as if he aches.

Ray stands too, wondering whether he's fucked everything up here. Has he approached this all wrong?

He follows Oskar to the door, feeling in his pocket for his car keys. At the door, he walks past Oskar, then turns to say goodbye.

"Hey," Oskar says, "Felix has morals. And values. He can't live without fighting for something. But like Coyote, he's not all good. Illegal aliens aren't bad—but they're breaking the law. The Border Patrol aren't evil, but they're in a position to be cruel sometimes. Cops do a lot of good, but some of them are violent. Or corrupt."

"You don't need to tell me that," says Ray.

Oskar smiles, shrugging his bony shoulders, long thin legs apart.

Ray pictures Stella standing with her legs apart, on Dory's sand-colored carpet, her hand with the gun in it shaking, her other trembling hand holding her elbow straight. He's going back to the motel. To Stella. Who has told him she doesn't know any Oskar.

His stomach turns.

TWENTY-NINE

I confess that I am often lost in all the dimensions of time,
that the past somehow seems nearer than the present and
I often fear the future has already happened.

Deborah Levy, *Hot Milk*

WHEN RAY APPROACHES THE STARLIGHT MOTEL with
its fifies-style metal sign studded with neon stars, some of
which no longer light up, he sees the stocky desk clerk running
towards his rental car, her raised arms waving at him in her
black blouse like grackle wings, her pale abdomen above the
waistband of her dark slacks, suddenly exposed.

His heart pounds in fear. He manages to pull up next to
her without hitting her.

"Is something wrong? Stella? My wife. She's okay?"

Though her voice is calm and she's making an effort to
be polite, she's panting, and above her low neckline, the tops
of her breasts tremble. "The maid and I thought you'd gone
without checking out, but we heard strange sounds from your
room, and she was afraid to open the door with her key."

"What sort of sounds?" asks Ray, panicking about Stella.
Wouldn't she open the door if she could? How could he have
left her when she was so sick? His legs buckle as he gets out
of the car, and he can't find the key card in the jumble of
his pocket.

The first couple of passes don't open the door. He feels the woman from the office waiting behind him, some distance away to appear as if she's giving him privacy, but needing to see what's happening.

Inside the odor of dead air and barf is gone. The room is full of steam emanating in clouds from the bathroom, the door to which is half-open. The shower sounds like a heavy rain.

He breathes in the steam, instantly relieved. It smells of Stella's shampoo—coconut and lime.

But the room looks as if it's been pillaged. Either Stella, or someone else has been into everything, and has thrown all their belongings around. The bedding's on the carpet, and the contents of all their bags are on the floor too, or the bed.

The pictures on the walls, which Ray hadn't noticed before, prints of summer cottages covered with ivy, under tall oak trees, are now very crooked. On the opposite wall, two drawings of cattle skulls with enormous horns look as if someone had looked for something behind them.

Ray's mouth feels dry. Maybe that's not Stella in the shower. He tiptoes into the bathroom. He can see through the translucent shower curtain that someone is there, but not who it is. He tries to see through a narrow slit where the shower curtain doesn't meet the wall, and he sees two dark eyes.

Stella screams. Ray jumps.

"Fuck, Ray," Stella shrieks. "You scared the shit out of me. I thought I was about to be stabbed by Norman Bates."

"I'm sorry," Ray says, gripping the plastic towel rack, "I wasn't sure who was in here."

She turns off the shower, and pulls the curtain aside. "Really. Who the fuck would be in our shower?" she asks.

She's tanned burnt almond on her face, arms and legs below the line of her shorts. Her hair, wet, looking almost black, frames her face and neck in dripping tendrils.

"I don't know. You could have been dead in the shower, you know—the motel owner or attendant, whoever, said she heard strange noises from this room, and the maid was terrified. And then when I came in it looked as if we'd been robbed, our stuff all over the place."

"I was just looking for something. Hand me that towel, please."

"Looking for something! Looks like you had a party. You got better pretty fast," he says.

"You sound jealous. And disappointed. Did you want to come back, after leaving me all alone, to find me still lying there, sick as a dog?" She bends over, wrapping her hair into the towel, tucking and folding it into a turban.

"The opposite. In fact I was feeling guilty for leaving you, and I was worried about you the entire time. I just felt we had to get started finding Felix."

"I don't know how it happened, but I was asleep for what seemed forever, and then I finally woke up feeling great." She pulls the towel off her head and her damp hair spills out, a snaky mass. "I mean I felt great in a weird way. Like, not just good, but great. I feel a little weak, but empty, purged somehow, like this is a new beginning."

"Another new beginning," says Ray.

"Did you eat? Stella asks. "I'm starving. Can you wait outside? You're using up all my space."

"There's nowhere to wait out there. It's a mess."

"I was looking for Felix's phones and for his notebooks. Which I guess you have?"

Ray looks at the chaos, not knowing where to begin. He should begin to pack, he thinks, since they are leaving. Order will be created as he folds and puts items into their bags. He looks under stuff for their gym duffels. Felix's large black wheelie is wide open on the bed, vomiting its mass of papers along with some of Stella's clothing. He closes it. He'll deal with it last.

He finds his duffel near the window, and pulls the drapes part way open to let in some natural light, when he notices the white and green Border Patrol vehicle is pretty close to their door. He jumps back. What the hell, maybe Stella's right, and someone is following them. Or maybe he's going nuts and it's a hallucination. If he didn't feel so guilty he wouldn't think twice about Border Patrol cars, or police cars.

"Who's this Oskar you went to see?" Stella asks, pushing aside some clothing so she can sit on the bed. She bends over, rummaging for something, probably her sandals.

"Did you find out anything?" she asks, without waiting for an answer to her first question.

"You mean the Oskar who is a good friend of Felix's and a better friend of yours? The person who long ago introduced you two? Can we stop playing games?"

The disorientation he feels makes him feel light, as if his skin isn't holding all his organs together, and they're floating. "Oskar says you taught him all about Coyote. And that you are very good friends—which if I know you means you had a sexual relationship."

Stella has combed her hair, still damp, back from her forehead and behind her ears, causing them to stick out and her features to appear larger, as if carved.

"Oskar is probably Felix's friend, if you found messages from him. What reason would I have for pretending not to know him?"

"That's what I'd like to know," says Ray.

"Did you ever think that perhaps Oskar had some reason to lie to you?" she says, pulling the strap of a sandal over her heel. "If it's the Oskar I'm thinking of, he's a bad drug guy."

"I thought you didn't know an Oskar," says Ray. "And how would you know a 'bad drug guy'? Why would Felix be messing with a 'bad drug guy'? None of their messages to each other included anything about drugs. Not one word. Though Oskar did imply that Felix might be into that. He didn't include himself in the implication."

"I recall one name, the person working with Felix to help migrants cross the desert—Aureliano," she says.

"Aureliano," Ray repeats, trying on the sound to see whether he remembers the name from Felix's messages.

"I've already checked our bank records," Stella says, folding clothing into her bag. Nothing at all has been withdrawn since we took out money the day before this trip," she says. "If he's alive, wouldn't he need some money? Unless he had some secret account."

"How can he withdraw money without his bank card?" Ray asks. "I wouldn't assume he's dead."

"By the way," says Ray, "there's a Border Patrol car outside our room. There was one here this morning, when I left, and one that may have been following me when I went to see Oskar."

Ray hadn't mentioned the BP car because he was afraid Stella would freak out or get paranoid again about being followed. So he's surprised at her response.

"BP agents sometimes need to sleep in motels," she says. "Or maybe one of them is meeting up with a lover. They're human too." She pulls a royal blue polo shirt, one Ray hasn't seen before, over her head.

He doesn't remind her how panicky she'd been about being followed. He does remember, while straightening the prints on the wall, that he's forgotten to get rid of the bloody clothing in the trunk—so stupid of him. He's not in a hurry to tell Stella that.

"I'm starving," says Stella. "I have to go eat. We can leave this mess till later."

"We have to check out," says Ray. "I want to get out of here."

"Let's stay one more night. We can eat. And then pack, and then we can read more of Felix's messages and check out his notebook."

Stella has her straw bag strap over a broad shoulder. The only sign of her illness is her pallor, and maybe she looks a bit thinner.

THE RESTAURANT RECOMMENDED by the motel clerk is a small yellow low-ceilinged dump about a mile down the road from the motel that appears to be held up only by sagging pieces of plywood at each corner. Ray's stomach turns looking at it.

"I don't care what the place looks like, as long as it has food." says Stella. "I'm starving."

They are surprised that there are quite a few people at the tables inside. Walking past a smeary mirror that makes them look as if they are disintegrating, framed with dusty fake magenta roses, they sit at a table near the dirty front window.

"What do you think of this heat?" asks a woman at one of the tables of the waitress behind the counter near the entrance.

"My lawn's dried up," says the waitress, picking up some menus. "When I water it I just get big dust balls that sizzle and evaporate."

"Did she ever think that maybe this is not the climate for a lawn," says Stella, too loudly.

The waitress hands them sticky, plastic-coated menus. Her nails are polished with cerulean polish, but bitten down past the tips of her fingers. She's younger than Ray had first thought, maybe still a teen, kind of pretty in that too-made-up way that Texan women like, with too much blue eye shadow, and too much rouge, her hair too high, and too smooth.

"What looks good?" Stella asks.

"Nothing," Ray says, looking at a sign on the wall that says, "Deer antlers for sale," then noticing the dust on the windowsill near him. However, the restaurant's smells are appetizing.

"Hmmm. Maybe the chili? I'll have a bowl."

"Pot roast for me," says Stella.

"I forgot," says Ray, calling back the waitress, "a large glass of orange juice."

When he turns back to Stella, she's standing next to a stool near the counter, talking to a Latino-looking guy in a Border Patrol uniform. His straight ebony hair falls over one of his heavy eyebrows in spite of an application of shiny hair gel that Ray imagines he can smell from his seat. Most notably his thick black moustache frames his mouth ending in sharp points just below his full lower lip.

What the hell is she doing now, Ray wonders, as he leans back to let the waitress put their water glasses on the table. Could he be the same Border Patrol guy she thought was following them? What is she doing, talking to him? Last time she spotted a BP they ran.

The BP hands Stella a thin newspaper, and she passes it to Ray, who's not sure if he should take it. He does, and Stella turns farther toward the uniformed guy, still engaged in conversation.

Just as he feared, the agent slides off his stool lizard-like, and slinks over to Ray.

"Where you from?" he asks.

"We're from Baltimore," says Stella, before Ray can respond.

He makes an effort not to look surprised. It seems Stella can make up lies without even having to think about it. Blood rushes to his head. "Yeah," he says.

The food has arrived, and smells delicious. The orange juice looks fresh squeezed. Ray wishes the guy would leave.

"Long way from home," says mustache man. He stands with his legs slightly apart, one hand on his thick black leather belt, a leather holster hanging below his waist. It's the stance of an older man, or a bully. Or a gangster.

"Right," responds Ray. He tries to smile but can feel how forced it probably looks.

"And what about you?" Stella asks, friendly, but too coy, thinks Ray.

"Just having a little breakfast before I go to work. I'm on the evening shift," he says.

"Where do you work?" asks Stella.

Ray begins to eat. Get done with this already.

"Well, I patrol a couple highways hereabouts and today I'll also be manning the checkpoint down the road a ways. You'll come by it if you're heading east." He pulls his large-brimmed gray felt hat from the counter beside his empty dish, and places it gingerly on his head as if he's afraid of messing his hair, and with a wave to Stella, puts some change on the counter and leaves.

"What was that about?" He sips his juice, grim.

"I just think it's a good idea to be friendly to BPs." Stella folds her flour tortilla multiple times until it's a small origami-looking triangle. "I asked him if I could see his newspaper after he finished reading it, and he gave it to me."

"I think it might be a good idea to avoid Border Patrol agents so they don't notice us," says Ray.

"That's your way," Stella says, not eating, but riffling through the newspaper. "I'm more proactive."

"Look at this," she says, her finger on a small square of type. "Looks like someone found Felix's car at the airport."

"Why would his car be found so soon? It was parked in the long-term lot?" says Ray. "Can't be."

"See," says Stella, "if I hadn't talked to that agent I wouldn't have this paper."

"Well we can't be traced to that car. Or you can't, anyway," Stella says. "Did anyone at the rental agency see you with that car?"

"I told you, no one saw me park. In the long-term lot. It's a shuttle ride away from anywhere. But when and if they trace the car to Felix, they'll find you. You are his wife, no?"

Ray has finished his chili and is drinking coffee, which is cool, and burnt. He studies the delicate black scratches in the white glaze of his mug and looks up at Stella to see whether she's worried.

She's eating her pot roast and potatoes with gusto, concentrating, seeming completely unbothered.

THIRTY

THE SKY IS PALE PINK with shreds of lavender and rose. Now Stella drives.

Ray relaxes for the first time in what seems like ages. They've packed, cleaned up, and have gotten an early start on their way to Lajitas. He's read more computer messages and some of Felix's notebook, and has a list of people to check out once they reach the resort. One is the owner of a huge ranch on the border, who shoots any migras on his land. The other is a gringo priest who helps by placing gallons of water along the migrant paths, so they don't die in the desert, and has even built a small safe-house. For these he endures lawsuits, and even death threats. Stella is vague about whether she knows any of those on Ray's list. He's still freaked out that she hasn't admitted knowing Oskar, and insists that he was lying. Yet "coyote" seems like an interesting and apt description of Stella, the storyteller.

"Well, do you know any of them?" he asks. "Did you hear me?"

"I'm thinking," she says.

"Thinking about what lie to tell me next? Thinking about Felix? About Dory?" He can't bring himself to mention Stevie.

Stella sighs.

Ray begins to feel sorry for being so nasty, when Stella says, "I wish you could live more in the moment, Ray."

"What the fuck are you talking about?" he says. He'd love to strangle her. "I mean, I know what that means, but what do you mean?"

"I mean," says Stella, "that it does no good to go over those things in the past." She holds the wheel at its bottom with both hands.

"Well, you're pretty good at living in the moment," says Ray. "You don't bother to think about anything you do, whether it's moral, or any of the consequences. But isn't that what makes us human? Isn't that how we learn from the past? Past, present, future, they are all part of us."

"If you can't learn to live in the moment, you aren't living," Stella says. "Because if you aren't aware totally of what's happening in the present, there is no memory. You need to be here for it."

"New Age crap," Ray says. "I know what you mean," he adds, "but that doesn't mean we always need to, or even can be, in that state of awareness."

"What about cultures, collective memories, all of culture? What about writing, what about stories, myths and fables?" Ray asks, registering that Stella is driving with one hand, arm wrapped over the top of the wheel.

"You can't have a memory unless you are in the moment," says Stella.

"Can you have a memory and be in the moment at the same time?" Ray asks.

"I think you're just being contrary. You are jealous of Oskar, who I don't even know," says Stella, swerving out of the path of a dog that is already nearly a part of the highway.

"I wish I still smoked," says Stella, opening her window more.

"I've seen you smoke," says Ray.

"No, I mean still smoke. Like all the time, with all the desire, and the guilt."

"For humans, maybe memory is more important than the moment," says Ray, watching a lock of Stella's hair blow crazily in the breeze.

Now that the windows are open it's noisy, so they stop talking, which is fine with Ray. He wants to think about the stuff in Felix's notebooks, about the border. About the slums of Juarez, the factories he's never visited though he's lived not too far away. About the vans that pick up the *maquiladoras*, and leave them off, about the fifty-gallon water drum in the slums that the city fills with water once a week. About the naked children, and the skinny, sick dogs.

"We're not murderers," says Stella, picking at a piece of dried skin on her lower lip.

"We should have called the police in El Paso," says Ray.

"See? This is what I hate. Going over things endlessly. We did whatever. Even if it was stupid, there's no re-doing it. You have to move to the next thing." Stella sighs deeply.

"Yeah, the next thing, based on a stupid choice, into a spiral leading to a black hole."

Stella laughs. "Dark, Ray, dark. Seriously," she adds, "do you think American police are much different from Mexican cops?"

"I sure as shit hope so," he says, laughing now too.

"This is just a way to blame me," says Stella.

"I'm blaming myself," Ray says.

"Well that's kind of useless. Let's just get out of this mess without dwelling on anything," Stella says.

Ray looks out at the yellow and beige hills, blue and hyacinth mountains in the distance. He likes to think he takes responsibility for his actions. That's different from feeling guilty.

"Looks like someplace we could get coffee up ahead," Stella says, her wedding ring glinting in the sun.

"It looks more like a Border Patrol checkpoint," says Ray, putting down his sun visor to see better, his body tensing.

And, shit, there they are, two BPs with their olive drab uniforms and their huge rifles.

Ray looks at Stella. She looks as if she's going to gun the motor and make a run for it—and maybe that crosses her mind—but she stops just beyond the two officers, one on each side of the road. The two BPs walk slowly up to the car. The motor, turned off, ticks in the silence.

"This is it," thinks Ray. "Done for."

His vision blurry with panic, he's about to get out of the car near the gray cinderblock structure, but Stella grabs his arm.

Ray's mouth opens and closes without saliva. He feels like the huge lizard, big as a dragon, which lay at the side of the road. In the dream he was trying to speak, to warn Stella, but nothing came out; he had no voice. He woke hearing his own inarticulate sounds, his mouth feeling like sand.

The officer on Stella's side of the car bends so he can get close to Stella. But he looks across her, at Ray. The brim of his hat hits the top of their car. Stella flinches.

"Any illegals in your trunk today?" he asks.

"Nope," says Ray, his voice hoarse, picturing the bloody clothing that is still in the trunk, now moved up toward the opening, in front of their luggage, bagged, ready to be thrown away. Except they haven't done it.

It takes Ray a few moments to realize the officer is joking. He's never heard anyone joke about this before. In fact, isn't it illegal to make jokes like this at airport security or at border crossings?

The officer stands, one hand on the small of his back as if it aches, holding his rifle loosely, as if it's weightless as a toy. "Sorry," he says, "but I'm going to have to take a look anyway. Mind opening it?"

Stella is more flustered than Ray's ever seen before, her hands with their bitten nails searching for a lever that unlocks the trunk.

"Sorry," she says. "The car's rented, and I've only opened it from the back using the key."

Ray's about to get out, but the officer indicates with a large hand that he should remain in the vehicle.

Stella, like Ray, stares ahead as if paralyzed, wanting to appear totally disinterested in the search of their trunk. Ray holds his breath.

Suddenly there's a huge head right near his face, so close Ray can see the roots of the mustache hairs, the dots of his pores. He smells his shaving lotion, sharp against the heavy oily odor of hair gel It's the officer from the restaurant last night, the one who gave Stella his newspaper.

"Sorry I'm late, Enrique," he calls to the officer standing in front of their now-open trunk. Then to Ray, "Leave it open, please."

"He already checked us," says Stella. In spite of the heat, she shivers, the hairs on her arms standing up. Does he remember them? He's all business today.

"I'm sorry," he says. "I have to look. Oh, I remember you," he says. You're the couple from Baltimore."

As he moves toward the back of the car, Ray asks, "What are you looking for?"

The officer shouts so Ray will hear, "Oh, we check for contraband, drugs, stuff reported stolen, weapons—illegals. We don't check every single car—just random spot checks. You guys are lucky."

His voice sounds weird now, coming from behind, inside their car. Another joke?

Ray can't bear the suspense any longer and turns around. All he sees is the trunk hood up, and the officer standing alongside their car. It looks as if he hasn't touched anything, or even pushed their bags aside. The plastic bag with his bloody clothing is the first thing he'd see.

"What's in the bag?" he asks, touching it gingerly with a rubber-gloved hand, the other on the raised hood. He has a huge sweat stain under his arm that looks like a dark green planet.

"What bag," asks Stella, swallowing hard. Her heart's beating so fast Ray can see her shirt tremble.

"That's just our dirty laundry," she says.

"Okay," he says after a moment. "You can close it."

Ray's so astounded that he can't figure out how to close it without actually getting out and shutting it. But Stella is out, suspiciously fast, and has slammed it.

Now the BP looks as he did in the restaurant, smiling, ready to banter, or tease them, Ray isn't sure which. "You guys on your honeymoon?" he asks.

"At our age we really don't think about a trip as a honeymoon," says Stella.

"Where you headed?"

"Lajitas," Stella says.

Ray, still in the car, has the door open and watches them. Something sleazy about the BP playing with them like a cat with a bird. But he is so relieved about the clothing he could pee his pants. He no longer gives a shit whether the two of them flirt—he can't wait to get going.

Stella says, "Can we go now?"

She turns, ready to get back in the car. The BP doesn't answer, but follows her to the car door, as if prepared to wave them off, or shut the door behind her. He slips one side of his mustache into his mouth with a fat forefinger.

"Wait here a minute," he says, an afterthought. He turns suddenly, walking to the entrance of the low gray building, his black boots loud on the concrete path.

Ray holds his breath, eyes on the amoeba-shaped sweat stain on the back of his grey-green shirt.

After a moment the BP is visible inside the small office. Through filthy half-closed venetian blinds, Ray watches him pick up a phone.

THIRTY-ONE

One Thursday I saw some Border Patrol throw some men into their van—throw them—as if they were born to be thrown like baseballs, like rings in a ringtoss at a carnival—easy inanimate objects, dead bucks after a deer hunt. The illegals didn't even put up a fight. They were aliens from somewhere else, somewhere foreign, and it did not matter that the somewhere else was as close as an eyelash to an eye.

Benjamin Alire Saenz, *Exile, El Paso, Texas*

"WHAT DO YOU THINK'S GOING ON?" Ray asks, his heart beating up in his throat so he can't swallow. "Who's he calling?"

Stella sits in the front seat, biting her fingernails and staring out the window.

"Are you thinking what I'm thinking? Should we just split?"

"Split?"

"Yeah, make a run for it," whispers Ray, impatient.

"If we do that we'll have the entire Border Patrol and the Texas State Police after us. We won't have a chance." She runs trembling fingers through her hair. "Let's wait and see."

The BP is still on the phone, and looks at them through the window.

"Wait and see is what I usually suggest," says Ray. "But this looks bad." He hunches as if he can hide.

Stella touches his knee, maybe to reassure him. The car is getting hotter, the sun, more annoying. A trickle of sweat runs down his spine, tickling. He wants to scratch it, but can't reach. He rubs his back against the seat. How long will they have to wait?

"I have to get out," she says. "People die in cars in heat like this." She wipes her forehead with her hand.

"Sorry," says the BP striding toward them, slightly bow-legged, running his forefinger and thumb first down one wing of his mustache, then the other. "This is more complicated than I'd thought. Mind coming inside for a bit? It's cooler there."

Ray, head down as if he's a naughty kid following his teacher to the principal, and Stella behind, follow him into the bunker. He's about to find out what evil thing he's done, and what the punishment will be.

The entire concrete structure turns out to be a one-room office, with a door off a dark alcove that Ray guesses is prob-ably a toilet.

He and Stella sit in two brown leather captain's chairs in front of a grey metal desk with a mess of papers, and a many-level plastic organizer, also overflowing with papers and envelopes. A grayish-green (almost the color of their uniforms, Ray notes) leans against the back wall, opposite the window, the top also covered with papers.

"Behind on your paperwork?" asks Stella, smiling. Provoc-atively, Ray thinks, annoyed.

The BP, in a black office chair, puts his feet up on the desk, filthy boots and all, on top of a pile of manila folders. There's a flat brown area on the sole of one boot that Ray is sure is dog shit. He pats his computer monitor, a huge old-fashioned thing. I spend a lot of time on this—mostly playing solitaire," he says.

Ray, on the edge of his chair thinks, who the fuck cares about what you play? He knows he's being played right now.

He's going to have to pay something before they are released. He notices a glass cabinet near the toilet displaying guns and rifles. He's shaking, and having a hard time keeping his teeth from chattering in the sudden air-conditioned cold.

"But sometimes I get some interesting information," the BP continues.

Ray can't see the screen. He can only imagine what the BP might say next.

"For example," Mustache Man says, not looking directly at either one of them, "before I went to breakfast at the Café, I saw this notice from the El Paso po-lice," emphasis on the first syllable, "are looking for a rental car similar to the one you've got there." He points a shoulder toward the window.

He fixes his dark eyes on Ray, who finds his gaze too intense to meet. He stares at the BP's classical nose instead, then lightly touches his own sore, still-swollen one. Despite his shivering, some sweat drops from his forehead to his left eyebrow, itching.

"They didn't have no plate number, but the car description—PT Cruiser, four door, black, Texas rental plates, fits pretty well. You two match a couple they're looking for too. What puzzles me is why you, if you're they ones they're looking for, aren't hundreds of miles away by now."

He looks from Ray to Stella, who says, "Isn't the fact that we're not running proof that we haven't done anything that would make anyone want to find us?"

The BP's onyx eyes fix on Stella. It doesn't seem he has any response—this is a sexual stare—pinning. Bullying.

For a moment Ray feels irrelevant, as if he doesn't belong there—a voyeur. He avoids checking to see how Stella's responding.

"What do you—or the El Paso police—want with us?" Ray asks. Because he doesn't really know if they are wanted because someone found Felix's body? Because Dory is dead? Or because of Dory's drug dealer husband Miguel? Or maybe something else? Something Felix was involved in?

The BP is in no hurry to enlighten them. Though he doesn't seem to be enjoying himself as much as he did a moment ago. He pulls his dusty boots off the desk, scrunching some of the paperwork under them, and leans back in his chair, taking a sip from an ugly plastic travel mug that has a burn scar on its side.

"We're just traveling," says Ray.

"Where to?" asks BP.

"We told you," says Stella. "Over to Fort Davis, and then down to Big Bend, to Lajitas," she says. "Can we go?"

The BP looks out the window, maybe at their car. Ray follows his glance. He can't see much as the blinds are partially closed, but the sun glares off the car's window into his eyes. Ray pictures the black plastic bag with bloody clothes in the trunk, and wonders whether the officer, now caressing his mustache, can see a picture of it above his head, as a thought, like in a cartoon.

"You two married?" the officer asks.

"That's irrelevant," Ray says.

"I'll decide what's relevant," says the BP, unnaturally slowly.

"Sure, we're married," says Stella. "I told you."

The interest of the BP, who leans forward, chills Ray more than the air-conditioning. Lying about anything before they have any information about why anyone is interested in them could be their undoing.

He's about to tell his story, from the moment he arrived in El Paso, when the BP says, leaning back in his chair precipitously, "Look, I can have the police here in one minute by hitting that key," he says. "I don't even have to get up."

"Tell us why you're interested in us," says Ray.

He rocks back even farther, as if to show them how calm and in control he is.

"Okay," says Stella. "My husband and I are taking an anniversary trip. He's got a grant to study geological formations. In Juarez we met our friend Felix, who got separated from us, and is missing. We're looking for him, hoping he'll meet us at Lajitas. My husband's a professor," she adds, touching Ray's arm.

Stella has the officer's full attention. "Did you call the police when your friend went missing?"

"Oh, no. We're kind of used to it. He's known to wander and then reappear again. We were a little concerned because he didn't leave a note, which he most often does. But, also, we didn't feel good about calling the Mexican police."

Stella looks cool and comfortable spinning these lies, all of which could be checked out if anyone were interested. Ray hopes he's affecting the same cool and credible demeanor, but is failing. For one, he's so nervous his breathing is audible.

"And you're going on to Big Bend without your friend?" the BP asks.

"He knows where we're going, and he can always find us," Stella says. She looks at Ray for support, or corroboration, but Ray can't speak. He has no idea what Stella has in mind, or how to continue her story. Lies need to be covered with lies, a stratified mountain of them. All he can do is nod. And what if they're being tricked into lying?

"You know," says the mustache man, "An Anglo was found dead in Juarez. Did you see that? Maybe you saw it on TV, or in the newspaper? Did you wonder whether it is your friend?"

"We haven't seen any news," Stella says.

Ray is surprised there's only one Anglo dead in Juarez.

"You didn't read the newspaper?" Ray pictures the BP watching them begin to look through the newspaper he gave them at the café. How can they get away with this?

The officer gets up with a groan, holding his back. He sips from his plastic mug and wipes his mustache with his hand.

Ray hope this is almost over. He'd like some water himself—and a piss. He's about to ask if he can use the head when the BP says, "Why don't you wait in your car for a bit while I chat with your lady—your wife."

About to say no, he sees Stella shaking her head yes. She waves him away.

"I'd rather not," he says.

The BP lays his hairy hand on top of the holster near his waist and stares at Ray.

Back in the car, Ray's relieved to be out of there. He considers getting away on foot, but there are a few cops around the area, and nowhere he can sneak away. He also realizes he's not ready to leave Stella, and he wishes he knew what was going on in the office bunker. He imagines that BP with his disgusting mustache intimidating Stella.

Car after car passes through the checkpoint. Once in awhile a car is pulled over to the side and searched, then let go on its way.

What can they be doing in there for so long? Ray thinks he's going to have to go inside to the bathroom. He looks at the office window. The Venetian blinds are completely closed.

He gets out of the car. Apparently no one is interested in him, probably leaving him for the mustache man to play around with. He walks toward the office door, and looks through the rectangular glass at the top, which also has a very small Venetian blind, which is partly open enough for Ray to glimpse Stella's back. She's kneeling in front of the agent, who, seated, is in his favorite position—leaning way back, mouth open as if he's had a heart attack and Stella is attempting to revive him.

He can't see very much, except for Stella's blue shirt and black Capri pants, a tiny slice of flesh showing at her waist. Ray jumps back, shocked. He bends a bit to avert sudden vertigo, and forces himself to walk normally back to the car.

Before he gets there, Stella has opened the office door, and is behind him. He turns to see the BP in the doorway, rubbing his arm and leering at Ray, his thick black hair mussed.

Stella grabs Ray's arm and pulls him towards the car. "Let's get out of here," she says. "Disgusting pig," she says, from the driver's seat.

"What's going on here?" Ray asks, getting into the car. "We're just going to be allowed to leave?"

"Hurry up" she says, wiping her mouth with the back of one hand, her silver bracelets jangling.

Ray grabs her arm. "What's going on? What went on in there, Stella?"

Stella stares at him, pulling her arm from his grasp. Her face is flushed and there are tiny drops of perspiration, like blisters, along her hairline.

She rubs her arm where Ray had squeezed it, perhaps too hard. "What do you think happened in there, Ray," she says, her voice shaky.

THIRTY-TWO

I will not follow language like a dog with its tail between its legs.
Margaret Randall, *Immigration Law*

"HEY, SLOW DOWN."

Stella drives what seems like a hundred miles an hour.

"I can see why you want to get away from there as fast as possible, but do you want to get picked up for speeding?" He presses an imaginary brake with his foot.

He feels as if the top of his head is about an inch above where it belongs, floating. He can't get the BP's final leering smile out of his mind.

"Look, Ray, I just want to get away. Remember, this is Texas. We're only driving a few miles above the speed limit." She smiles, and slows down. "At least I got us out of there. We're free for now. We just need to get rid of the bag of clothing."

Ray would love to grab Stella and shake her like a dog with a possum. "What the fuck. You pretend to be my, our savior, but you end up doing the most ... the most horrendous things. And each one gets us into more trouble."

"What have I done, Ray, what have I done," says Stella.

Ray's head's ready to explode. He pulls back his arm, and to his own surprise, smacks Stella across her face.

Stella is shocked; he car swerves wildly. She gets it back in control, and rubs her cheek with one hand.

"God, Stella. God. I'm so sorry. I can't believe I did that."

He knows he didn't hurt her much as he's too close to have any leverage. But he's upset that he's even tried—he's never done anything like that in his entire life. Nor has he ever wanted to.

"Stella." He moves close, trying to see her face. She won't turn towards him, or respond. "I'm so sorry," he says again.

"You're getting more like Felix every day," she says, sniffling.

"Are you crying?" Ray asks, touching her cheek with a forefinger. "Does it hurt?"

"No to both, asshole," says Stella. "I was just shocked."

"I'm sorry, Stella," he says. "Did Felix hit you? Was he violent?" She doesn't answer.

"Did he? Did he? I'm so sorry."

"Stop apologizing. You're getting on my nerves."

"I can't believe I did that," Ray says. Ashamed, and scared, he shakes his head as if things in there will get back into their right places, and he'll be the Ray he knows. "Did Felix hit Stella? He can't imagine being friends with anyone who'd smack a woman. Yet he, Ray, has done just that. He'll never really know about Felix because Stella lies so much. He can begin to see how Felix might have been driven to it.

He breathes deeply, looking out at the low cacti, the dust devils, the pure cerulean sky. He's always felt that there's no excuse for, no provocation enough to justify violence. He's detested the idea that a victim may have been "asking for it." But he's now in that place where he's actually thinking he's the victim.

He turns toward Stella, who's looking straight ahead, seeming concentrating on driving, or lost in her own thoughts, as if nothing's happened, but also, as if he's not there. What is she thinking? Her silence seems fraught with the unspoken, while her cheek, flushed, bears the mark of his hand.

"I'm sorry," he says again.

She turns towards him a bit, eyes still on the road. "Okay, you're sorry. I really believe you. Let's stop somewhere soon for some gas. And I need to pee."

Ray, relieved, looks out his window again. "Nothing here to indicate civilization," he says.

MORE THAN TWENTY-FIVE MINUTES PASSES before they see a gas station attached to a small grocery, and the kind of outdoor bathrooms Stella can't stand, the kind that require a key, yet which always seem as if they've been vandalized anyway.

Ray says, "Sorry, kiddo." Stella gives him a weird look, and he realizes that she thinks he's apologizing again for the slap. "No, I mean these are the bathrooms you hate."

"We can't stop here anyway," she says. "This is Exxon. I'm boycotting them."

"Very funny," says Ray. "I'm boycotting them too. But it looks like we have no choice. So let's go back to boycotting them after we get gas and go to the bathroom."

Ray looks up the street at pretty much nothing—a few shabby concrete stores at both sides of the road, most of which appear to be out of business, their signs, and photos of food, covered in graffiti, their tiny graveled parking areas edged with windblown debris. Some parts of Texas would be great for shooting an apocalypse movie.

Ray heads for the john while Stella fills the tank. The door opens without a key, and Ray enters the small room that has a sink with a frightening red stain in it. Where the faucet might be is a ragged hole in the wall. There's one toilet without a seat. The room is so small that while he's peeing he can hold the door, which has only part of the lock, closed. In a corner beside the toilet is a used paint can overflowing with used toilet tissue.

He notices that he's standing on some of the paper that's missed the can, and is stuck to the concrete floor with some indefinable liquid, and wonders why the need for the can in Texas, where the sewage pipes are built for toilet tissue as well as waste. Perhaps for those coming from across the border in Mexico, where you can't flush paper.

Ray flushes, and as he zips his fly, he's horrified to see the water keep rising, past the orange rust stain, and higher. Just as it looks ready to overflow the bowl onto his feet, he gets out and shuts the door.

He looks for the car near the gas pumps, but it is no longer there. Where has Stella parked? She's not near the small grocery, nor is she anywhere he can see. He walks around the entire place just to make sure, as if maybe their car has shrunk and might be hiding behind some skinny cactus. Could she have left without him? Or maybe someone kidnapped her? Or that fucking BP? Maybe something with him?

Ray's hyperventilating and feels faint. The last thing he wants to do is lose consciousness on this hot gravel, tar and concrete rest area with its small circle of dried yellow grass and two cacti, like some bum, with no luggage, and no car.

He's about to ask anyone around whether they've seen Stella. He's so freaked he can't even remember what kind of car they'd rented, or the license plate—just that it's black. He's sweating profusely, and if he hadn't just been to the john, he'd probably be peeing his pants. Breathing so hard he can hardly walk, he moves from the pump area to the grocery. He doesn't want to seem like a crazy person when he asks anyone inside whether they'd seen Stella. Or the black car. Surely someone would remember her as there's hardly anyone around, and only one pickup getting gas. He wipes off some sweat, then wipes his hands on his slacks, and is about to open the door, when he sees their car parked near the bathrooms. A mirage?

He knocks on the door that says, Ladie's.

"Hey, are you in there? Are you okay?" he calls. There's no answer so he pushes on the door, which, surprisingly, opens. Stella is on the toilet, studying her knees.

Ray rubs his eyes. "You're here," he says, grabbing at the wall for support. "I looked all over for you. You were gone. I thought you were kidnapped or something happened to you."

"I saw a pile of garbage down the street, some old furniture and a few bags of trash, black plastic, like ours, so I thought I'd drop the bag of bloody clothes there. Which I did. What a relief."

"God, I was so worried," he says, leaning on the sink.

"Oh, Ray, poor Ray. I'm so sorry. I just drove down the street, and came right back. I'm sorry."

"Now you're apologizing. It's fine. I'm fine now. Aside from you possibly getting kidnapped, I was terrified to be left having to hitch a ride from this place."

"This toilet is no cleaner than the men's. I thought women were much neater," he says, looking around. There is a faucet in this bathroom, and a filthy mirror. Even some toilet paper, for drying his hands after he washes them with cold water. He presses the soap dispenser in vain.

Stella wipes herself and flushes.

She stands behind him, and he looks up from the sink to see both their faces in the mirror, their edges blurred. Who are they? They look like strangers, both of them flushed pink, looking sad, exhausted and lost.

"Poor Ray," Stella says, pressing into him. "You were so scared."

He turns so she can hug him. But she puts her hands behind his head, pulls him closer, if that's possible, and kisses him gently. He is upset by her inappropriate intention, and is smothered by the heat in the tight bathroom, and Stella, far too close. Still, he feels his cock hardening against her.

He pulls away. "You're disgusting," he says, wiping his mouth. "You just sucked off a BP. This place is disgusting. I can't believe you. That you'd want to fuck now. You're an animal."

Stella ignores him and turns to lock the door. "I am an animal," she says, her breath buzzing around him like some drunken insect. Her hairline smells of sweat and shampoo.

"Uh, uh," he says, pushing her away. He hangs on to his chinos, as Stella, her thick curls in his face, tries to pull them down.

"You want to," she says. "I can tell."

"Really? That's what men say when they're raping some-one," he says. "I'm serious."

She pins Ray against the grimy wall alongside the sink.

Stella, kneeling in front of the BP officer whose head is way back, mouth open with pleasure, involuntarily fills his vision. For a moment he feels as if he will puke. Instead of becoming sick, he's never felt so aroused. He turns them both around so that Stella's against the wall. He enters her fast, and bangs her in a hard rhythm punctuated by what sounds like angry barks. He turns his head and sees himself in the mirror, smeary red face, teeth bared, hair awry, and isn't at all surprised that he's become a wild animal.

THEY DRIVE ON. Stella at the wheel seems relaxed for a change, leaning back now, her fingers of one hand hooked around the wheel, her other elbow out the window. Buzzing frantically around them is a fly searching for the open window.

Ray is weary, sweaty, and disoriented. He can't help looking out for cars that might be following them.

Feeling the need to walk, they join a tour group at Fort Davis, and wander around the half destroyed fort among strangers, pretending to be normal tourists, only half listening to the guide. Ray keeps his distance from Stella.

Then they head toward Presidio and the Rio Grande. Simply moving, no matter where, calms Ray. Yet he can't completely rid himself of the sensation of being followed. Someone, or something, is creeping up on them.

THIRTY-THREE

Before you learn the tender gravity of kindness
you must travel where the Indian in a white poncho
lies dead by the side of the road.
You must see how this could be you,
how he too was someone
who journeyed through the night with plans
and the simple breath that kept him alive.

Naomi Shihab Nye, from *Kindness*

"PRESIDIO TONIGHT?" ASKS RAY.

"Presidio's a dump," says Stella. "Let's just continue on till we get to Lajitas. There's still plenty of daylight, and the valley here is spectacular."

Ray's fine with that. He's remembering the valley when Stella was with Felix, and he was with Olivia. Are those memories even real? Are they even memories? Maybe just a bunch of snapshots? Or old stories he's told himself too often. What would he remember? Only what he knew at the time. What are they doing, trying to recapture a past that may not have existed? Did Stella and Felix have lovers? Did Stella seduce Olivia, as she's implied on this trip? Did they have an affair? Was Felix really at the Fertility Clinic for a vasectomy?

Rays stomach rolls, the same feeling he gets on a roller coaster. And now he can't stop seeing Felix everywhere. Felix is driving a car that's just passing. Ray can tell by his sunburned face, his bald, freckled head. But no, it isn't him—just someone who looks like him. Felix standing with a rifle among some uniformed guards at Fort Davis, his long face, and thin long mouth. He's Felix's height, and just as slender—but no, it isn't him. Felix is loading something into that crappy blue Ram pickup. Maybe it's Felix in that large trailer truck hauling forty wetbacks he's picked up to drive to a safe house in the U.S. He imagines Felix being kidnapped, and tortured by Mexican drug smugglers. He imagines Felix smacking Stella. He imagines Felix fucking Stella.

Images of the BP, alternating with those visions of Felix creep up on him anywhere and everywhere. An immigration official is the BP. The border patrol guy is amongst a group of soldiers with rifles, and strange hats. He is after Felix. Or he knows where Felix is. Or he's coming after Stella, with his thick black mustache, and shiny hair.

By the time they get to Lajitas, it's dusk and he's exhausted.

"I can't believe this," Stella says, driving through the renovated resort looking for the hotel.

"I knew about this, about the entire mining town having been bought by a wealthy developer, and I've seen some photos, but I never imagined this!"

Since they'd last been there the whole funky town has gentrified into an upscale tourist resort—a complete replica of an Old West town, with a Western movie-type fancy hotel, some cabins, a large restaurant, and at least two bars, all of fake gray weathered wood, including the long street of shops selling souvenirs. They've already passed the shooting range, a riding stable, and a replica of an old ranch where you can pay admission to see roping and rodeos.

"I hate this so much but I'm so ready for it," Stella says. "It's so fake, but I love it."

"I was sure you were going to say you hated it," says Ray. "Can a replica of something that was real be fake?"

"It's fake because it's all fixed up so that it looks real, but isn't," says Stella. "It's all redone so it's aesthetically pleasing, and comfortable, with modern fittings and fixtures, like lights, refrigerators, good gas stoves, comfy beds, so that it's comfortable."

Ray is glad too—he'd love nothing more than to be comfortable for a change. Why did they decide to relive their old trips? Why did they used to like trips with funky, disgusting cheap motels? He's so far from that he can hardly remember. But then it was so important. They were downwardly mobile. It was revolutionary, fighting capitalism, and consumerism, and escaping the middle class, and your grasping parents. You didn't endure uncomfortable disgusting surroundings then, you loved it all, and embraced the funkiness, the deprivation, with a passion. The illusion of living real life.

But in the end they haven't escaped the middle class. They have the educations, even with the debt. They begin to want things. They begin to collect things. They can't help it.

"Doesn't it seem fake that we were staying at these crumbly, uncomfortable motels? I mean, our lives aren't like that," Ray says.

"Our lives should be uncomfortable," says Stella. "Remember we felt that we were in touch with real life. Our parents kept working to be more and more comfortable, cleaner, farther from dirt. Farther from what we thought was life, humanity."

"Is dirt real life? Our parents came from hard lives in Europe to escape that."

But for a moment Ray feels again that hunger, that desire he'd had to experience everything. The difficult, the disgusting, the ugly. Especially the difficult, the disgusting, and the ugly.

He breathes deeply, and the air smells delicious. Ozone.

"It's going to rain," says Ray, watching the ultramarine evening sky rapidly taken over by enormous roiling dark gray storm clouds forming and turning black, obscuring the tops of the mountains, then moving downward, disappearing the entire landscape.

Lightning spears burst through the new dark like silent rockets, leaving the air a smoky and sickly purple. Then a loud crack of thunder.

The rain begins before they are out of the car, pelting down, cold, and heavy on Ray's hair and clothes. More lightning, and rolling rumbles.

It's pitch dark now and the lightning's far away, jagged and all over the mountains at once, with no order or design, like runaway fireworks.

They run into the restaurant, a huge open room, and choose one of the heavy wood tables, wet shoes squeaking, dripping water. Ray wipes his face with the cloth napkin and shivers, the air suddenly too cool on his wet clothing.

Ropes and harnesses, chaps and saddles hang on the wall alongside the bar, along with ancient black and white photos of the old Lajitas, and of the Rio Grande, looking much grander and fuller than they've ever seen it. The other two sides of the large room have glass walls so, when seated, they can see the mountains all around them, the clouds, and the lightning, as if they're outside.

A waiter brings them each a towel, and they dry off as much as possible. Stella's wet hair, sleek as a seal's, outlines her head, making her cheekbones stand out. Her nipples are visible through her shirt. She dries her hair with the towel, and now it curls, messy, around her face, which suddenly looks thin and frail.

Ray notices her hand, white with chill, resting on the thick rough plank of a table near the upside-down glass on the white linen placemat, and covers her slender fingers with his own large hand. With the other, he turns over his wine glass.

"Let's have some wine," he says.

Stella is staring at something, or nothing. She turns to Ray. "Yes, let's," she says, her eyes glow amber, like a coyote's he thinks, pushing away his anxiety.

In this clean, beautifully designed new place pretending to be old, it's not hard to pretend they are simply new lovers who don't know anything about each other, out on a date. So far the best their relationship offers.

"I'll tell you a coyote tale," she says tasting her wine, the liquid golden with reflected lights.

Ray, sipping his wine, which suddenly tastes sour, coughs. Can she read his mind?

"Sure," he says, though he wonders whether he's alert enough to concentrate. He doesn't want to be alert. But maybe, he hopes, her story will tell him something. Something he needs to know.

THIRTY~FOUR

Your body wakes
into its quiet rattle.
                    Ropes & ropes . . .
How quickly the animal
empties.
            We're alone again
                    with spent mouths.

Ocean Vuong, from *Scavengers*

RAY IS EXHAUSTED BUT HE CAN'T SLEEP. He wonders how Stella can drop off so fast. Why is he lying awake worrying? She's been driving all day, true, but he's tired too. So how can she be instantly dormant?

He twists and turns in the clean-smelling, silky linens on their grand and comfortable bed, and watches Stella's breathing change subtly, her pink, sun-warmed skin, with the row of tiny freckles sprinkled around her cheekbones, morphing, as she falls more deeply asleep, into a wrinkled idiot, open-mouthed, slack-lipped, air stuttering in, then out, irregular, as if she's forgotten how to breathe. He can't remember how it feels to desire her.

BEFORE THEY'D GONE TO BED, while Stella was in the shower, Ray had gone out to the lounge to get one of the USA Today newspapers he'd seen earlier. When he'd opened the door to their room, newspaper in his hand, Stella'd looked surprised. He saw his duffle open and half-emptied on the bed, next to Felix's bag. In her underpants and the t-shirt she often slept in, her hair all wet, and just standing near the large king-size bed, she'd looked guilty, but also defenseless, as if he'd caught her in some private moment. Then he'd seen the gun in her hand, pointed at him. He'd jumped back, hitting his elbow on the doorknob.

The newspaper had dropped, and he'd rubbed his elbow. "What the fuck, Stella?"

"What do you think, Ray? How would I know it was you?"

"Who were you expecting?" He'd been pissed. "What are you doing? Why are you going through my things?"

"Nothing. I'm not," Stella'd said, backing up, gun still in her hand, but pointing toward the edge of the bed.

"Give me that gun," he'd said. She hadn't moved. "Put that thing away. I'm learning that everyone has a weapon in the U.S., and you have to depend on people being civilized enough not to shoot you."

He'd sat on the opposite side of the bed, numbly pushing aside some of this own clothing, clenching his fists till the skin of his knuckles had felt tight enough to burst.

Stella'd seemed miles away, though only on the other side of the huge bed.

"This isn't going to work, Stella. We're as intimate as we can be, but you won't let me in on what's going on. I've touched the most private parts of you—but our relationship is a lie. This dichotomy is too painful for me."

When he'd looked up, she was seated beside him. She'd placed her cool white hand on his thigh. He'd felt the cold through his chinos. She'd removed her hand quickly, and began to fold some of the clothing she'd thrown out of his bag.

Ray had placed his own hand over the cool spot on his leg. It felt wet but wasn't. He'd kept his eye on the gun, which looked like a child's toy, near the bottom of the lush cream quilt.

Stella had stopped folding a pair of Ray's jeans, and had reached over toward him. He'd jumped up, heart beating hard, sparks shooting at the edges of his vision.

"You're terrified of me," Stella'd said, standing, surprised. She'd reached out again, tentatively, and Ray had moved closer to hug her. He'd felt her body along his, her chill cheek against his, her damp hair dripping on his shoulder and chest. Her soft breasts pressed into his bony chest, her stomach against his groin.

"So this is our life now," he'd said.

STELLA'S NOT AWAKE YET, so Ray goes to the restaurant, which looks like a completely different place in the morning—informal, more like an elegant coffee shop.

It's not raining, and is cool and clear, and Ray sips some coffee, watching through the glass wall, mauve shadows underlining discrete cumulus clouds, each about the same size, that march in rows over the sharp edged mountains, which this morning are completely visible.

Before he cracks Felix's red-covered notebooks, which he'd glanced at before, but only just, and which he's brought with him to read, he tries to remember more fully the disturbing dream he had after he'd finally fallen asleep. He thinks his anxiety around it will disappear if he goes over it, clarifies it.

In the dream, he and Stella are sleeping. He can't place where, or whether it's one of the motels they've stayed in, but they are both in one bed. He's woken by a sound that gets louder, and as he wakes more fully (though he's still dreaming) he realizes that someone is using a tool to pry open the door to the room.

The bottom of the door swishes against the carpet as it is opened. Even with his eyes closed, Ray can see the change in the light.

Stella's gun would come in handy now. Where is it? He has no idea. Aggression not an option, he pretends to be asleep. If the intruder is a thief, hopefully he'll find something he wants, and will leave.

All he hears is his heartbeat, and Stella breathing. Maybe she's awake too, also pretending to be asleep? He opens his eyes and sees a huge mound where Stella is lying, covered by the blanket. Someone must be on top of her. Maybe the intruder, murdering her.

His fear a hot bolus in his throat and chest that he can't rid himself of by swallowing, he shouts, "Get off her," which sounds only like a small croak.

Soon he understands, from the rhythms of the blanket, which is falling off, and the sounds, that they are fucking.

He would like to think that Felix has returned, because even in the dark he can see that the person on top of Stella is wearing light blue running pants with a black stripe, pulled partially down, the elastic pressing into those straining thighs.

He tries to say, "What the hell," but it just sounds like metal scratching on glass.

"Shhh," says Stella, turning her head toward Ray. "Don't disturb him." Even in the darkness he sees her flushed face beside him, "I'm doing this to save your life," she says.

"Who is that?" he asks, as someone is obviously writhing on top of her—Felix? The BP? Whoever it is, is pressing into

Stella's chest, his body arching sharply. Partially blanketed, knotted together, they look like a giant tortoise.

As Ray tries to make out who is with Stella, her white hand emerges from the blanket, holding a silver pistol.

"I'm saving you," she says. But the gun is pointed at him.

"Tell me the coyote tale," she says, still holding the gun. "Your version of the one I told you last evening," she says.

"What?"

"Come on."

"You're kidding. Put the gun away,"

She aims the gun towards Ray's face, so he begins, but he's so nervous and upset he can hardly recall the story, and can't figure out its meaning, or even why she'd told him that one.

"It's about the coyote marrying his sister." He watches the gun. He can't think, his brain is muddled and fuzzy.

Stella nods, and the gun moves along with her head.

"Coyote is tired of his wife—they've been married for a long time, and she's old. Of course so is he. He becomes interested in his beautiful sister who is just beyond puberty—so basically, he's thinking about incest and child molesting. He knows his family will be looking for a mate for her soon. He knows it's wrong to marry your sister, so he tricks his family into thinking he's died—I forgot how—and gets them to move to a new location—mmm. I forgot how?"

"Go on," says Stella, still at the bottom of the unmoving tortoise lump, still pointing her gun at Ray.

"The gist is—Coyote pretends to be a young suitor for his sister, he is accepted, and they are happily married. But that's not the end. In the end he has to get caught—but I can't remember the story—how his wife finds out—I forget how he's punished? If he is. Or whether there's a happy ending. And what's a happy ending? For Coyote it may be the fact that he's punished. Is that happy? Should an ending be true? Or falsely happy?"

"I want a happy ending," repeats Stella, with two hands now holding the pistol. As if he's incapable of fulfilling her demand.

THIRTY-FIVE

Sometimes I catch myself saying those words in the street, as if hearing someone else's voice. And yet, it was no dream.

Patrick Modiano, *The Black Notebook*

RAY ONCE AGAIN OPENS ONE OF FELIX'S RED NOTEBOOKS, thinking that if he were Felix or Stella, he would have written down that weird dream.

He feels a tickle at the back of his neck, almost a fluttering of his hair there, as if someone were breathing on him. He turns quickly and sees only a man he doesn't recognize, seated alone at the nearby table, studying him. The man nods, and touches the khaki baseball hat hanging off the back of the unoccupied chair next to him, as if to make sure it's still there.

Ray can't help staring, wondering whether this guy looks familiar. To be honest, most Latinos look somewhat alike to Ray, partly because he's better at distinguishing various forms of rock than he is at recognizing human faces. Could this man be one of the guys from the party at Mi Ranchito, or whatever the motel was, right before Felix disappeared?

The man, long thin legs encased in tight jeans, gets up out of his chair, as if called up by Ray's stare, and grabs his khaki cap.

The large silver buckle on the man's black leather belt looks familiar—though a huge ornate silver buckle is far from unusual throughout Western Texas.

No escaping now, he thinks, as the man walks the few steps to Ray's table.

"I was thinking maybe we've met," says Ray, trying to justify his stare.

Close up the silver buckle is an ornately designed skull.

"Maybe we have," the man says. "You look familiar." He has an accent that could be Texan, or maybe Southern. Hard to tell.

Ray's impulse is to make some excuse and get out of there. But why? He has no reason to be afraid of him—or all the reason in the world. While he's thinking about escaping, the man pulls out the chair across from Ray, which shrieks a protest, and sits, his long legs straddling the seat. His longish hair, which may once have been blonde, but now is colorless, wraps around large ears with deeply-creased lobes, one of which has a small dangling silver hoop earring.

"Revel," he says. "I know who you are." His breath smells minty over tobacco. He holds out a hand with long thin fingers.

Ray is so surprised he ignores the outstretched hand. "What?" he says. At first he doesn't get that Revel is the man's name.

He looks a bit like the Border Patrol officer who remained outside that office, checking cars. But he's not in uniform, and Ray isn't sure.

"What?" he says, realizing he sounds like an idiot.

"I know you're looking for your friend Felix Mann. We'd like to find him too."

"What!" Ray says again. "Who the hell are you. Why are you looking for Felix?"

"You're not giving me any more information," says Ray, studying Revel's small eyes surrounded by sparse colorless lashes, still trying to figure out if he's familiar.

"Your friend Felix is a troublemaker, you know."

304

"I don't know," says Ray. "I'm not taking your word for it. So tell me how he's a troublemaker. I'm trying to find out what he's into."

Does this guy have anything to do with Stella? Did she send him here, to this restaurant? Is he the cop she was kissing in her house? A plainclothes cop? Or maybe—this cause him to suddenly sweat—he has something to do with Miguel's body—or Dory and Stevie.

"Come with me," Revel says. "I have some ideas."

"I bet you do," says Ray. The last thing he'll do is go anywhere with this man. "Who are you?" he asks again.

Revel puts his fingers in his back pocket. For a moment Ray thinks he's going for a gun. His jeans are so tight it takes a few minutes for him to pry out a wallet, his fingers seemingly aiding a difficult birth. He opens the brown leather bifold so Ray can see a Border Patrol badge that may or may not be authentic.

"I'll go with you," says Ray. "I have to get my wallet—all I have is some cash in my pocket—in my room—and I need to tell someone I'm going—she'll panic if I disappear—"

And he needs time to think. It seems fishy, like everything else.

"We have to leave right now," says Revel, putting some money on the table. He pulls his chair out with its complaining screech, and stares at Ray. His eyes, like his hair, have no color.

Ray is about to run, but Revel grabs him by his elbow and twists slightly, not enough to cause Ray to yell in pain, but enough to show he means it.

"Are you arresting me?" Ray asks. "Are you kidnapping me?"

"Just convincing you to do what's best," Revel says.

"What's best for who?" says Ray, as he tries to keep from tripping on Revel's long narrow feet in the ubiquitous cowboy boots, these with extended pointy toes, like witch's shoes in scary fairy tales, trying to keep pace as Revel pulls and pushes him along, out of the restaurant, and towards a silver Honda SUV.

"Let me go," shouts Ray. "I have to get something." He's remembered Felix's notebooks, left on the table. "Just for a minute—I promise."

"No going back now," Revel says between his teeth. You want to find your friend, don't you?" He sounds like someone trying to get a young child to do something he doesn't want to.

Ray is either pushed, or he gets into, the back of the SUV. He sees no way of escaping the strong grip of this tall, skinny man so he figures he will go along with things until there's a better chance of making a break. And though he doesn't for a moment believe he'll be taken to Felix, or even that this guy is trying to find Felix, he can't help but hope it's true.

But the notebooks. Gone.

Once in the back of the car, free of Revel's boa constrictor grasp, Ray sees another man up front, in the passenger seat. He is wearing a Border Patrol army green uniform, which relieves some of Ray's anxiety. He'd rather be kidnapped by the Border Patrol than many of the other options, such as drug dealers, Mexican cops, ransom-hunters, or just plain murderers who are seeking revenge for something Felix has done.

Ray calms a bit and looks closer at the BP insignia near the man's shoulder, his shaved cheek with some dark, five o'clock shadow, and the usual thick black hair of a Latino, smoothed into a semblance of order with some strong-smelling gel. He can't see much unless the man turns, as his headrest blocks anything more.

"If we did anything, it wasn't on purpose," says Ray, rubbing his elbow and wherever Revel had gripped him. "I was trying to save Dory from being beaten, maybe to death, by her drunken husband."

Neither man reacts to what Ray has said. No one responds.

Revel is so tall that even with his seat pushed all the way back he has a hard time squeezing his legs into the driver's seat of the SUV, and into the right place once they're in. When he finally starts the motor, his mate, or partner, turns slightly, and Ray sees the bottom of a thick black mustache.

"Where are we going," asks Ray, breathing deeply, making an effort to relax. Nothing good can come of his current state of fear. He realizes that he's said where are we going, rather than where are you taking me, pretending that he has some agency in all this.

"We're going back to El Paso," says the mustache guy.

"Is Felix in El Paso?" asks Ray.

"Glad to see you've decided that hostility isn't useful," he says.

"I guess I just wasn't up for being kidnapped today," Ray says. "It was really nice of you not to put a hood over my head."

"You watch too much TV." Mustache Man laughs.

Ray recalls that laugh from the border checkpoint office. His skin crawls. But he keeps himself from saying out loud what he's thinking—that this BP blackmailed Stella into sucking his cock. And here he is again. Why? What has he figured out? What more does he want? From Stella, or from him?

THIRTY-SIX

*Things are always what they seem and never
what they seem to be. Rivers flow upstream
and down. Light travels at the speed of light and
then applies the brakes. Silence speaks volumes,
and noise, as always, is silence in our ears.*

Halvard Johnson, *In Reality*

BY THE TIME THEY GET TO EL PASO IT IS EVENING, and because nothing bad has happened so far Ray has lost some of his fear of these two, though he still doesn't know what they're up to.

Talky and Gawky, he thinks of them now, though Revel, he's found out, goes by the nickname Estrecho, is mostly as quiet as a hired driver, while Mustache Man, Manuel Martinez Acosta, nicknamed Bigote, is the designated talker.

"We are going," says Bigote, "to a checkpoint at the border. We want to show you something."

"Why would you want to show me something?" Ray asks.

"Because you seem like the kind of know-nothing idiot who needs to learn a lot."

"What you and your friend Felix don't know is that the border is a word. This kind of border is everywhere. You can put a line between the Mexican side and the American side, but without one side you cannot have the other."

"Why are you telling me this? What does this have to do with me? Does this have anything to do with Felix?"

"Because you are a stupid gringo," says Bigote. "Think about your words, 'What does this have to do with me?'"

"I'm getting some supper," says Revel, stopping the Honda near a block of half-built brick houses, with a forest of long iron rebar that stand a few feet up above the unfinished walls.

He extricates himself from the car with the same difficulty he had getting in, and stretches his arms behind him, his shirt tightening across his narrow chest, his no-color curls sagging along his skinny neck and large ears. He pushes his sunglasses up to the top of his head, leaving shiny red indentations on either side of the hooked bridge of his nose.

The unfinished houses they've parked beside look uninhabitable, and there's no sidewalk, but a woman and two small children emerge from one of the rough doorways that look like dark mouths, another of which Revel has entered that has a small hand painted sign, "Brisa's Gorditas" on top.

"Get in front," orders Bigote.

"So what are we doing here?" asks Ray. "I mean, besides getting some food." He's afraid they're playing with him before arresting him. Reluctantly he gets out of the car and into the driver's seat, which is farther back than Bigote's because of Revel's long legs, and leaves the car door ajar. Now, with Ray sitting beside him, Bigote for once, is silent.

Ray settles his sneakered feet amongst the crumpled wrappers and Styrofoam cup trash on the floor up front. He's surprised at the mess.

"You ask why you are here? Yes, this is about Felix. This is all about Felix. You may think, what does this have to do with me? Well it does have to do with you. We are here because I want to us to be here. I want to show you some things. Why? Because it gives me pleasure to show you some disgusting things," Bigote says, turning slightly at the arrival of Estrecho, who hangs on to a large pale pink plastic bag, and grips three brown bottles by their necks in his other hand, which he holds out to Ray, who takes two and gives one to Bigote.

They've already been opened, and Ray gulps his. He hadn't realized how hot, thirsty and hungry he was.

Revel folds himself into the back seat, careful of his steaming pile of Styrofoam boxes encased in the large plastic bag.

"Fried chicken gorditas with lettuce, tomatoes and jalapenos and stuff," he says, opening the bag, removing plastic forks, and some napkins. The smells of the food wafting around the car are heavenly.

Ray's surprised he was given something to eat and drink. He'd thought he was going to be questioned, tortured, brought to the police, or even kidnapped—some horrible treatment related to Felix's, or his own crimes. So, can this simply be the private whim of a Border Patrol agent?

Bigote turns sideways to take his container of food from Estrecho.

"So you're just a couple of sadists, out to show a gringo what awful things you have to deal with? Am I that important that you'd go out of your way and take time off work to teach me?" says Ray, biting into his sandwich.

"I'm going to show you that you are not important. You are nothing." Bigote opens his sandwich. "We have the hard job," he says.

"If the border is not real, is a myth, it is our job to play along," says Bigote.

He takes a small bite and looks at his food. Satisfied that it's edible, he takes a huge bite, a third of the sandwich, and chews. For a few moments there is only the sound of the three of them eating, and a dog howling in the distance.

"Here's something," says Bigote, wiping some drips off his chin with the too-small paper napkin. "I was on horse patrol with some other agents. We caught a group of muds and made them lie on their bellies, on the ground. One of them was this old woman, maybe fifty or sixty—who knows—maybe older. She calls to me, '*Official!*' 'What?' I go. She says, pointing to this small three or four-year-old boy she's got with her, 'Know anyone who would want this kid?' I go, 'What!?' She's Salvadoran. She says, 'My son and my daughter-in-law were gunned down, dead. I'm the only family this boy has. I thought I'd come north, give him a chance—give him a life. He's a good boy. Come on, why don't you take him?' I looked at the little boy. He was a beautiful boy. If I could have taken him, brought him up, I would have. But we can't do that. I looked again at the old woman, who had tears and dirt in the lines on her face. She looked desperate. 'What's going to become of him?' she asked me."

"That happened six years ago and I still think about it. Most everyone who comes to cross the border is desperate. Like that woman. But some, mostly young, just want more stuff. And one way to get stuff without working hard is to smuggle drugs."

Bigote wipes his hands with what's left of the napkin, sucks his teeth, and checks his lap for crumbs.

Ray takes his sandwich out of the box on his lap, pieces of lettuce and tomato hanging off the small round roll, and bites into it. He'd been so scared he hadn't realized he was starving.

It's delicious and messy, filled with chicken, potatoes, shredded salad, mayo, and some other salsas, half of which drops on to his lap, and wonders what Bigote is trying to tell him and why?

Does he want Ray to feel sorry that he can't do anything for the desperate people who he catches crossing the border? Or is he giving him some hint about Felix, about drug smuggling? What is he showing Ray? Does he want his sympathy? Why would he care what Ray thinks?

"An alien sees me, and what's the first thing goes through his mind?" Bigote asks, indicating that Ray should change seats with him, not so easy with the sandwich.

Ray doesn't respond. He's concentrating on getting out of the car and into the passenger seat without dropping his food. And, he doesn't know the answer.

"Respect," says Bigote.

Sure, Ray thinks. Respect for Bigote, the agent. Not terror. Or disappointment.

Bigote pulls the driver's seat forward. Ray is pleased to see a string of lettuce hanging from his macho mustache.

"Here's my life story," Bigote says. "Born, grow up, go to school, join the army, get a job. Vote. I wanted to be a cop in New York. Became one in the Bronx, then joined the Border Patrol. I'm a happy man, married to a beautiful woman. We have two kids, a boy and a girl."

This sort of stripped-down bio doesn't interest Ray, who is getting nervous about where they are going and the fact that it's getting dark. They're driving through the outskirts of the city, passing longer and longer deserted stretches, to where a fence ends and a steel cable strung between two poles marks the boundary between Mexico and the United States. The cable, meant to keep cars from going across the border in that area has been cut, and a family perhaps, a man, a woman carrying an infant, and a small boy, is walking across.

Bigote calls to the little boy, and hands him, through the car window, the long green chili peppers that had garnished his sandwich.

"These people are not migrants," says Bigote, "they are just taking an evening walk."

"How can you tell the difference between a family taking a stroll across the border, and a family of aliens?" asks Ray. "And when are you taking me back?"

"I can," says Bigote.

It's nearly dark, and it's getting cold. Ray, in just his t-shirt, shivers. "I get your point," he says, even though he doesn't have any idea what's going on, or how to process any of the information Bigote thinks is important. How does it relate to anything? Estrecho has been silent. Is he asleep?

At another section of the border, at the top of a hill, Border Patrol agents stand in two-man teams, wearing camouflage jackets, and working infrared scopes.

"There are twenty-three agents that I've deployed and am in charge of, to guard three miles of the boundary," Bigote tells Ray.

"They will radio other agents, directing them to their quarry, with instructions, like 'Four meters down, behind the bush.'"

Ray gets out of the car, and looks through a scope as directed by Revel, into a bright greenish landscape of gullies and bushes, and watches phosphorescent figures moving north. These are people actually trying to sneak across into the States. He remembers the same bright various greens on his television screen when the U.S. began bombing Iraq.

Bigote and Revel become more intense as night wears on, Bigote talking more, and Revel ever more silent, yet more apparent in spite of his silence. Or because of it.

Bigote parks in a gully, and indicates for Ray and Revel to get out of the Bronco, and to move away from it. He switches off the car lights and his flashlight, and it's very dark.

"Don't leave me out here, please," Ray says, his arms goosefleshing.

"Don't worry," says Bigote.

"You are an agent out here alone," says Revel, as if he's memorized a script, as if this is an act they perform together often, as a team. He clears his throat. Perhaps his voice is rusty from not being used. "What do you see? What do you do?"

"I don't see anything. I don't know."

The bushes rustle.

"What do you hear?" Revel asks. "Animal or alien?"

Ray shrugs, annoyed, yet curious to see where this is going. "I don't know."

"What about your nose? Do you know you can smell the presence of aliens?" He switches on his flashlight. "We need to use all our senses," he says.

Bigote now stands, short and stocky next to the very tall Estrecho, continuing for him—"the Border Patrol this, the Border Patrol that"—Ray is so tired he doesn't hear half of what's said.

"There's people who think all we do is beat on Mexicans," says Estrecho, waving his flashlight. "Did you know we only get one allegation for every seventeen thousand arrests?"

Why are they making such an effort to show Ray how fair the Border Patrol is? And how misunderstood and mistreated they are?

Ray won't say another word. He's hating this lesson, and he hates these two assholes. If he's so unimportant, why are they making such an effort to impress him, and to justify themselves? Also, to scare the shit out of him?

He's afraid he'll say something accusatory, nasty, or sarcastic, something that will get him into trouble, because his hostility and hatred is bitter in his chest and his throat, and he isn't sure these guys are nearly done. They might still find some pleasure in finding more painful ways to torture him.

Maybe Bigote reads the silence sensing Rays indifference.

"What's an agent to do? We have to defend ourselves. Put yourself in our position. You're out here doing your job. You apprehend some aliens. A fight ensues. Someone picks up a rock. A rock can kill you. It's a missile, like a bullet. People will say how can you compare a rock to a bullet? Well let me throw a rock at you. I'll give you a gun, and we'll see if you'll really shoot."

"They may have knives too," says Estrecho.

"Knives, pistols," says Bigote, touching his skull belt buckle. "You walk out here. You see a bunch of people. You don't know who they are, or what they're carrying, or whether they bear you ill will. You could have a criminal element who know very well how to take you down."

"Over here," Revel orders Ray, pushing him suddenly over close to the Bronco. "Put your hands on the roof—that's the way—and spread your legs," he orders, kicking Ray's spread legs, one at a time, closer to the SUV. That's it," he says, as Ray fumbles into position.

Ray can't tell whether they are serious. Are they arresting him? Finally? After keeping him prisoner all day?

"Like in the movies, eh?" says Bigote, walking behind Ray as if he's going to frisk him. Instead he says, "Jab me with your arm and try to reach for my gun."

"You serious?" asks Ray. Then he jabs Bigote with his elbow, releases his hands from the top of the Bronco, and grabs for Bigote's gun nestled in its leather holster.

"Ouch," says Bigote. "See? It's not possible. Now stand with your hands interlocked on top of your head," he says.

Revel stands by, watching, a half-amused, half-bored smile on his narrow face, nothing much in his small eyes.

Bigote comes up behind Ray from a weird angle and grasps Ray's hands hard.

"You can put yourself at ease at any time," he says, squeezing Ray's fingers as if in a vise.

Mouth open, Ray's immobilized with pain. He's sure Bigote has broken his fingers. He's heard them crack.

Suddenly he lets go. "I'm not angry," Bigote says, "I'm just showing you something."

"Where are we going now?" Ray asks, rubbing his fingers, unshed tears painfully stinging his sinuses, his still-swollen nose, now running.

In the back seat of the Bronco, speeding along both on road and off, Ray's exhausted, almost too wiped out to be scared, though he does know he's in the hands of two lunatics. The agents may be exhausted too, as they've both been silent for a change.

"We're going to a motel," says Revel.

"What?" says Ray.

"You say 'what' an awful lot," Revel laughs, ominous, as does Bigote. His deep laugh with its high-pitched finish.

"What do you think?" asks Revel. "We're going to finish you off."

"What?" yells Ray. But he's not surprised. Isn't this what he expected all along?

AS REVEL PULLS IN AT AN EL PASO RED ROOF INN, Ray hyperventilates until the top of his head pounds and he is dizzy.

So this is where it will happen? He's so terrified he can't even begin to think of an escape.

"Have a good night," Revel says as they practically have to pull him, limp, out of the Bronco, and lead him, each holding an arm, through the lobby to the sign-in desk.

They laugh when they let go of him and he sways, nearly falling.

"We'll be back for you tomorrow," says Bigote, stroking his disgusting mustache. "Don't go anywhere." They laugh again.

Ray feels in his pants pocket with a shaking hand—of course—no wallet—no nothing. Just some change maybe left over from coffee this morning—eons ago.

Revel turns and throws Ray's wallet at him. "Catch!" he says, like some idiot kid, as he throws a phone, too.

The desk clerk, a young boy with a blue Mohawk looks up at Ray, ready to help him.

The phone, Ray sees, is Felix's.

RAY SINKS INTO THE LARGE GREEN BED, relieved, completely limp and exhausted, but feeling so fantastic to be alone, his life extended, given back to him as a gift. Yes, he has no vehicle. But he has a phone. And he has his wallet, which he checks out. Unexpectedly, nothing is missing.

Where had Revel come by Ray's wallet, and Felix's phone? Hadn't he left them in the hotel room at Lajitas, with Stella? He's sure he did. But he's much too tired to think.

There's a bottle of fresh cold water on the dresser near the bathroom, and he has his wallet, and Felix's phone. He feels that he has everything he needs to live, and a bolt of joy fills his chest.

If he's lucky Felix's phone still has some charge left, enough anyway for one call.

He should call Stella. How must she be feeling? Would she be in a panic?

He decides to call someone he's seen a recent message from on Felix's computer, and his phone.

"Cervantes," says a hoarse voice after four rings.

THIRTY~SEVEN

*And sisters the two towns may have been. They certainly did share
a certain painful, awkward resemblance. The aluminum and glass
of high-rise, commercial El Paso seemed an ugly mockery of Juarez's
broken sidewalks and muddy alleys. Whining for dimes on the
international bridge, the ragged kids just south of the midpoint seemed
a reductionist, half-satiric version of the brokers and lawyers in
summer-weight suits who ambled through El Paso's central plaza.*

Philip Garrison, *Augury*

RAY'S TAKEN A SHOWER, but he's wearing the same dirty royal blue shirt and grimy tan chinos from the day before.

He feels somewhat rested in spite of dreams he can't fully recall, some of them with Felix. Not that he actually saw Felix, but while he was dreaming he felt that Felix was Felix. Or Felix in combination with someone he doesn't quite recognize. He's left with a sense of emptiness, an inchoate despair.

He misses Stella, though he doesn't necessarily wish he were with her now. But his body, his skin, longs for her. He also thinks about the panic she feels when she finds him gone, disappeared without a word, just like Felix.

Or maybe that's just his imagination. Maybe she's fine—relieved even. And she has the car, and all the baggage and clothing.

Someone gave Revel and Bigote Felix's phone, and Ray's wallet. It had to be her. Maybe she was part of their plan?

Then he thinks maybe they broke into their room and tied Stella up, and she's frantic. Maybe they hurt her. Two psychopaths. He wouldn't put it past them.

Then he pictures the back of her head as she knelt in front of Bigote, his head back, mouth open.

THERE'S A KNOCK AT HIS DOOR. He checks his watch—exactly nine, just as he'd said. He'd been about to turn on the local news, and so, when he opens the door to Mr. Cervantes, who holds out a ruddy hand at the level of Ray's stomach, he almost places the TV remote in it, instead of his own hand.

"You'll have to excuse me," Ray says. Things are happening. I don't know what's going on—my life's a mess. I need help." He runs his hand through his hair, embarrassed.

"Let's get some coffee," says Cervantes, who is quite short but stands very straight. "We can talk then." His onyx eyes, with their long, straight eyelashes, look straight into Ray's. He'd told Ray on the phone last night that he knows Felix, has worked with him, has given Ray some hope. Cervantes, standing before him, short and stocky and looking like a stone pre-Columbian statue, is very real.

In the bright coffee shop across the highway from the motel, Ray orders coffee and an enormous breakfast, feeling his wallet inside his pants pocket to reassure himself it's still there.

Cervantes, across the orange Formica table, asks, "So you have no vehicle?" He sips his coffee, the "not-Starbucks" coffee as he calls it.

"I don't know where to begin," Ray says, "it's an unbelievable story, and this is only the most recent event."

He hesitates, studying Cervantes' large round face, his copper skin.

"I'm listening," Cervantes says. "So, you've already told me on the phone that Felix is your friend, you were on a trip together and he went missing?"

"Yes," says Ray. "Yesterday morning I was kidnapped from the restaurant in Lajitas, where Felix's wife and I were staying, by a couple of Border Patrol agents who pretended they knew where Felix was and were going to take me to him. I didn't believe them, and didn't want to go, but one of them dragged me to the car where another was waiting. They wouldn't let me go back to my room. I had nothing with me, and Stella didn't know where I was going. And they left Felix's notebooks on the table. They wouldn't let me grab them."

Ray stops, and wipes his forehead. He's still enraged and upset about the loss of the notebooks.

"You were staying in a resort with Felix's wife, Stella?" asks Cervantes.

"Yeah," says Ray, surprised that that's what Cervantes has noted from his story.

"I mean, nothing's going on," he lies. "We were all on a trip, and now that Ray's missing, we're searching for him. I have his phone—that's how I got your number."

Cervantes nods.

"So, these guys, the BP agents, they drove me around all day, showing me the border, enjoying themselves making me think they were either going to arrest me, or murder me, and after what seemed like a year, but was probably most of a day, they drove me to this Red Roof Inn, threw my wallet and Felix's phone at me, and left me there, pretending they'd be back today."

Ray shifts on his orange molded plastic chair. "They said they wanted to scare me, to show me things. Things I needed to see. But why me? Why? I just don't get it."

Cervantes looks into Ray's eyes. His are so black the pupils are invisible.

He runs his hands through his very long crew cut that stands straight up again after his hands have passed through. His sharp-edged lips curve into a wry smile. "I'm not the least surprised," he says. "Many Border Patrol agents are too arrogant. They think they are above the law. Some of them are former military. Others are just in that job because they love violence. Their education requirements are minimal. They like to think they can get away with anything."

His stubby fingers tighten around the orange coffee mug.

"Can we generalize like that about thousands of BPs?" Ray says.

"I said, 'some.'"

They move back in their seats to allow the waitress to place their steaming platters in front of them: three-egg omelets, bacon, sausages, and home fries, shiny with grease, and garnished with tiny bits of onions and green pepper.

Ray is starving, and begins eating, ravenously.

"You look as if you haven't eaten in weeks," says Cervantes, laughing, placing his orange napkin on his lap.

"I feel as if I haven't."

After Cervantes has eaten a small amount of his food, he says, "Most of the Border Patrol have an intelligence that is shrewd but uneducated. They have a gang mentality—a turf way of thinking. They have an old fashioned code of revenge, and a code of silence."

He cuts his food methodically, pushing it with his knife on to the back of his fork. His small teeth are very white, and he chews for a long time before swallowing.

"Felix," says Ray, forking the last of his home fries into his mouth.

"Ah, yes. Felix," Cervantes says. "I haven't seen Felix in quite a while now, but he did help me whenever he could. He was a lover of justice, very rare, and of course he had enemies."

Ray is avid to hear more.

"I work for the American Friends Service Committee, a Quaker organization." Cervantes cleans his teeth with his tongue. "We monitor civil rights along the border. I thought you knew that when you called."

He motions to the waitress, and points to his coffee cup.

"I have an office, a phone and a computer, and trouble finds me," he says.

"As I said, your number and name came up on Felix's phone," says Ray.

"I'm no lawyer," Cervantes says, "but people who are beaten by Americans or people who have their rights trampled, have recourse, unlike people beaten by Mexican authorities. And I'm the recourse, or resource. People can call me and I will make every attempt to obtain justice for them."

He speaks slowly and carefully, as if he's making an effort to be understood, yet he speaks perfect English with no accent.

"The agents of law enforcement, the Border Patrol, police, lawyers, customs officers, judges, all scorn me because I'm just a witness who has come up from the streets. But I'm persistent, I agitate, and I sue. I publicize, and I complain. I won't be intimidated. Those people who need help find me—my name is out there," Cervantes says.

"Law enforcement detest me," he adds. "They are often in difficult situations to begin with and I make things harder for them."

He notices Ray studying the plastic toothpick he's placed in the corner of his mouth. "I used to be a smoker," he says, showing his bright teeth, "so this is my substitute."

"There are an awful lot of former smokers around here," says Ray, smiling, taking the last piece of buttered toast from the dish, china, but made to look like a straw basket, in the middle of their table. He breaks off a small piece, and runs it along the remaining grease on his plate.

"He is very intense, Felix. No?" asks Cervantes.

Felix. So far, an enormous shadow. Everywhere and nowhere. Doing good and doing evil, possibly running drugs, demonstrating against the defilement of the atmosphere, loving justice, but perhaps a murderer of a Mexican. Known or not known by the Border Patrol, and unknown to someone who has sent emails to him—it has begun to seem that maybe Felix is more an idea or a myth than a corporeal human. Ray is beginning to doubt the few days he's spent in Felix's company before he disappeared.

"Felix is very driven when he gets an idea," says Cervantes, cleaning his teeth with the toothpick. "He cannot stand injustice. Especially involving others. He gets very angry. This is very different from getting mad when things don't go your way."

Cervantes leans back against his molded seat back. The toothpick is back in his mouth, bobbing as he speaks. "He makes many enemies while he pursues his idea of justice, no? I have warned him he will get killed one day."

That sounds like Felix," Ray says. "At least the Felix I spent a bit of time with a few days ago."

HIS DOWNTOWN OFFICE IS SMALL, but well lit and orderly. Cervantes indicates where Ray can plug in Felix's phone, and pulls some fat books, the size of art books, from some shelves along one side of the office, bidding Ray to sit in a saggy, but comfortable easy chair.

When he carefully places the fat books on his spotless glass-covered, old-style public school desk, the color of new-born infant stool, Ray sees that they are photo albums. He gets up, and goes over to see better.

"These are my clients," Cervantes says, putting on a pair of half-eyeglasses with thin black frames. "Men and women, who have been beaten, or even shot."

Cervantes turns the pages for Ray. The photos are mostly all gruesome, in acid colors, of people with broken bones and bruised faces and bodies, some pointing to their livid gunshot wounds.

The albums begin to look like some glossy Mexican magazines that specialize in photos of the horrifying, such as piles of bodies executed by drug cartels, or murdered by corrupt government officials, and hideous car wrecks.

The mestizos (Cervantes' word) in the albums look miserable, stunned, and terrified.

"They all have stories," he tells Ray. "This man was caught just as he came over the fence. Border Patrol chased him down."

He turns the page. "This one was only sixteen when he was shot in the stomach for picking up a rock. Another," he turns the page, "they caught at a checkpoint up north. They tried to get him to sign a 'voluntary return.' He refused and said he wanted a hearing with an immigration judge. So they brought him into a back room and beat him till he signed."

He continues turning pages with stubby tanned fingers. "Nowadays I photograph with my tablet, or my phone, but there's more dignity with these real photos in the albums," he says. "They are here. They are real." He holds up his phone. "Where are the photos when the phone is closed? Or when you aren't looking at them?"

Ray's back aches from leaning over to see Cervantes' battered clients. At first he is sick and incredulous. His huge breakfast remains undigested, and he has a greasy taste in his mouth. His nose still aches, and he's aware of a persistent unpleasant odor that is probably in his own body.

After too many more photos, they don't elicit the same disgust and anger, but a low level buzz of rage remains, like the buzz of the old fashioned fan that's been turned on.

Maybe this is what Felix endures. Though it would be worse to just get used to the photos, and what is going on, and not really see them anymore, to the point where their impact is the same as ads for bridal gowns, or cars.

Cervantes pulls off his reading glasses. His ears stick straight out now that his hair is flattened at the sides of his head from his glasses.

"I can go on forever with this," he says. He turns a page. "They assaulted this woman sexually, spread-eagled her on the ground and said they were doing a body search for drugs, right? Right in front of her two young sons."

He looks up at Ray, who is thinking about Felix seeing these photos, seeing these people.

"I can tell you don't want to see any more," Cervantes says. "That's my problem."

He searches Ray's face for signs of boredom, or a surfeit of disgust, and brushes back his hair, which stands straight up again after his hand's passed over it like a field of wheat passed over by a breeze.

"The stories become repetitive. People get tired of bad news. Local TV and radio, newspapers, refuse to cover my hearings in court, trying to get justice for these people. Not because they don't care about justice, or because they are bad people. But they've heard it all before. They become numb. 'Oh, it's just Cervantes again,' they say."

"Yeah," says Ray, standing straight, getting the kinks out of his back. "You're right. How many more of these can I see—do I need to see? But that doesn't mean I don't get it. But what does Felix do about this abuse? What can I do?"

"The victims are reluctant to testify," continues Cervantes, placing the albums on one of his bookshelves with the care one might give to an album of family photos, of loved ones, one's children. "These are people who come from countries where police abuse is the norm. And they did try to enter the States illegally. They're scared to make the effort to get justice."

He takes a small plastic case from a drawer in his desk. Ray hopes it is Tic Tacs or something like that for the bad taste in his mouth, but Cervantes draws a plastic toothpick from the opening in the little case, and places it between his lips.

"For all my trouble, this is what I get—threats, by phone and by email. Listen to this." He presses a button on his phone. Here are some of the messages I get. Very nasty, very abusive, and sometimes scary.

"Diego, you fucking greaser. You better not open your mouth about your grease tribe coming over the border. You beaners got no business defending this illegal crossing that's been going on. The cops are going to start shooting you Mexicans soon. The white man built this nation and you greasers are guests. We will decide what to do with you. Stop criticizing the Border Patrol and our whites who are trying to save our white country. We are going to cut off all your patchoukos. White power is going to get you, Chuko."

"Is that message from a Border Patrol agent?" Ray asks. "I can't believe it. And you are a U.S. citizen."

"One of my greatest fears is of the Border Patrol," says Cervantes. "They are the most uncontrolled, unsupervised, and undisciplined law enforcement agency in the country. I don't recall if that particular message is from an agent. I save them all in case something happens to me."

He picks up a blue mug from his desk and looks in it, as if it might have been magically filled with coffee, checks his phone and puts it back in the pocket of his loose pale blue jeans that seem to be more work jeans than fashion statement.

"Can I tell you a story?" he asks.

Ray is impatient to hear more about Felix. He sits again in the comfortable chair, but really would like to leave. He looks at his watch but doesn't register the time—it's just a habit. He's about to say he should go, when Cervantes says, "This is something Felix got involved with."

Cervantes sits beside Ray, not behind his desk, on a molded plastic chair that might have come straight from the restaurant they had breakfast at.

"About thirty miles north of the border is a country store that got famous because it has a giant sculpture of a chicken on its roof. I have no idea what it's made of—maybe fiberglass. The store has been there for a long time, since the land was once chicken farms that employed Mexicans to do the dirty work. There's a lot of cheap development going on."

He crosses his legs and leans back a bit. "I wish we had more coffee." Cervantes' straight dark eyelashes leave shadows above his cheekbones.

"Anyway, the store, called La Gallina by the immigrant workers, the thousands of Mexicans living in squatters' camps between the housing developments, sells processed groceries like cookies, deli meats, banana, coffee and sandwiches. Many of the workers are impoverished Mixtecs from Oaxaca. Some of them walk miles to the store and hang out in the parking lot where trucks driven by farmers, or contractors who need workers come by to hire them for temporary cheap labor. They might be dirty from the fields, but they are, for the most part very respectful customers for La Gallina."

Cervantes leans back in his chair and shakes the plastic toothpick case. "The owners of La Gallina, Ash and Theron Taggert, are huge and nasty, unlike their dad, Edgar, and often run Mexicans out of their store with baseball bats, or even rifles. They won't let them use their bathroom, or their public telephone." He sighs. "One day Juan Martinez, who'd crossed the border illegally about four months before, and had been working in the fields, came into the store for a cup of coffee. Taggart accused him of stealing, and Ash and Taggard dragged him, kicking and screaming, into the back of their store, where they bound him up with duct tape, and handcuffed him to a pipe, and allegedly beat him. I say 'allegedly' but his face and body were all bruised. A neighbor saw him tied there during the day, and a Border Patrol cop came in for a sandwich and saw him, and neither did anything to help Martinez. Later that day, Ash and Taggart put a bag over Martinez' head and wrote, 'no mas acqui' on it. They marched him, still bound, to wander blindly around in a field till someone finally found him."

He continues, "This had happened before, but all the others kept quiet about it, afraid they'd be sent home, or even killed. But not Martinez. In spite of being illegal he went to the El Paso Times and told a reporter there his story. He said some day someone is going to get killed if I don't tell my story.

After Martinez complained, the Taggart boys were arrested, but they had friends on the force. One detective testified that the Taggarts were frustrated by the illegals, and that they weren't racist. They were just protecting their business. Though Martinez hadn't stolen anything, there were no charges filed against the person who'd seen him tied up and didn't report it. The complicity of the Border Patrol guard who'd seen Martinez being abused was investigated internally but it went nowhere. The Taggarts copped a misdemeanor for false imprisonment."

"How does Felix fit in here?" asks Ray.

Cervantes looks at Ray, somewhat disgusted. "Didn't you hear this story?"

"I do care," says Ray. "It's horrible."

Cervantes' black eyes bore into Ray's a spark of light reflected in each. "In this atmosphere and with these crimes condoned, teenagers hunt, beat and kill Mexicans. Gangs of schoolboys near the squatters' camps armed with baseball bats, beat and rob Mexicans because they don't like them. When they grow up they graduate to more serious weapons."

Cervantes rubs an invisible stain on his neat desk.

"Felix worked on the Martinez case with Lina Castino. He got too involved. Maybe too little separation. Or uncontrollable anger. It was the last case he worked on. I haven't seen him since."

"I'm enraged just hearing about this," says Ray. "It's unbearable. But the Felix I know, which is obviously not the current Felix—well, I'd be hard put to describe him as someone who can't control his rage."

EARLY THAT EVENING they drive toward a border to watch for the first large groups running north.

The ground is dark with mesquite, dense with desert scrub. In spite of some spotlights that make the border look like a stage set, there are plenty of dark, unlit areas. The sky is a deep royal.

They've driven past cinderblock houses, fences of ocotillo cactus. An old green Ford pickup passes, swirling dust. Cervantes looks at the driver. "Where's she coming from?" he asks.

The road grows rougher, potholes full of water from a short rain. The fence at the border is just barbed wire. Cervantes follows dirt roads, sometimes narrow paths, very slowly, checking for tracks. "If you study the tracks at dusk they appear luminous," he says.

He parks near the wire fence.

"I don't come here anymore," he says. "Especially after dark."

A white and green Border Patrol van, large enough to hold a batch of illegals, cruises by. Cervantes pales, his muscles tense.

"My wife worries that I won't come home," he says. "Some of them recognize me, and would love nothing better than to get me out here alone."

"Do you think it would solve anything to eliminate them?" Ray asks.

"No. We should reduce them. And disarm them. Right now there are more than twenty thousand. Every election the Republicans and Democrats add more agents to the border. If there's a threat from ISIS in the Middle East, they add more border patrol."

Another car's headlights illuminate Cervantes' face, which is yellow, eyes startled wide, shadows of his lashes on his high cheeks, like barbed wire. "If they get you, you have to do what they tell you. You don't run. You don't talk. You don't argue."

"Even if you are a citizen," he continues, "you have no rights."

THIRTY-EIGHT

Every time I see it, I realize that I've forgotten again how the fence on the international bridge bends, at the top, at a nasty oblique angle. It reminds me how the United States means to discourage even the most avid prospective immigrant, even somebody willing to jump a hundred feet to the river trickling under us, down its concrete trough.

Philip Garrison, *Augury*

RAY'D NEEDED TO PISS SO BADLY THAT, finally in the bathroom at the Red Roof Inn, the tips of his fingers tingle when his bladder releases its noisy stream into the toilet.

He's exhausted, his eyes burn from sun and dust, his skin is reddish and tender, the hair on his arms turning pale against his darker sunburnt skin.

He now has many more names of people Felix has worked with. When he checks out the phone, he sees that Stella has called eight or nine times. Was she calling Felix, or Ray on Felix's phone. He sees that the calls are for him.

He's thought of Stella all day, and all yesterday, an undercurrent to whatever he'd been doing. He wants to hold her close, and feel and smell her—but not just sex, he worries that she's alone and terrified. Or maybe he's the one who's frightened. But now that the phone is charged, and that she is calling him, he has no desire to talk to her. Or maybe he's afraid to call her because he has no confidence in his ability to stay away.

She is trouble. How did Revel get Felix's phone and Ray's wallet? From their room, when Stella was maybe in the bathroom? Or from Stella? Questions about her roil in his head. Desire roils his body.

After a shower, he looks in the mirror and is startled. He is darker, and thinner.

This room he's inhabiting for the second night feels like home. He gets into the tightly made bed with its cool sheets on his hot skin; the airconditioner rattles for a few seconds every ten minutes or so in a regular rhythm that is comforting, rather than annoying. And the car, the silver Toyota he'd rented while being driven by Cervantes, is reassuringly parked right outside his window.

When he turns on the TV, he once again thinks of the bacteria on the remote, but is soon distracted by a pair of newscasters sharing the screen, a pale-haired male and a woman with long straight blonde hair that curls at the ends. They share the telling of bad news—Trump's tweets, car crashes, domestic disputes, and deaths.

There is no news about a couple wanted by the FBI or the El Paso police. There's no news about anyone found beaten or shot in an El Paso house. And there is no news about a dead white male found in a motel, and who had been carried out on a stretcher, one scuffed white running shoe sticking out from under the pale sheet covering his body and his head. He is almost happy.

RAY IS WITH STELLA. At least it seems to be Stella, though something strange about her makes him unsure. They are traveling, and are in a mall, or a small street with a lot of shops, in what looks like Amsterdam, and are arguing because Stella wants to shop for clothing, and he wants to check out some strange geological structures that line part of the street near a canal or river. He walks away from her and strolls along the canal enjoying himself until he begins to feel anxious, realizing that he is now miles from the mall, and that he has no money with him, and no passport. He can't recall the name of the hotel they are staying at, nor how to get there, and he doesn't speak the language.

In a state of panic, he is nearly immobile. People walk past him and stare. What could they be looking at? Is he so terrified he's drooling or something equally embarrassing? Do they think he's a homeless person, a beggar?

One good thing he remembers is that he's to meet Stella at the airport at seven, in time for their flight. He looks at his watch. It is so late, after six, and, he doesn't think he'll be able to get there in time.

A man wearing striped overalls and a backwards baseball hat stops near Ray. "Are you okay?" he asks.

Ray doesn't understand the language he speaks, but he gathers, after some talk and some sign language, that the man will drive Ray to the airport for a fee. When Ray accepts the offer, thinking he'll get the money from Stella at the airport, the man calls some of his friends over to help out.

They get into a strange looking metal vehicle, like a trolley on tracks. Some of the men are driving, and some are sleeping. They all wear overalls.

The trolley is moving very slowly and Ray worries that they won't get to the airport in time for his flight, or to pay these guys. He sits near two sleeping men, whose heads flop around as they move forward jerkily, feeling his stomach cramp.

He asks the driver, the person who'd stopped to ask if he was okay whether he thought they'd make it in time.

"Your plane leaves at seven-thirty. It's six-thirty now." He doesn't take his eyes off the track. "We have to cross a border," he says, still looking ahead, but turning his hat so the brim points toward Ray.

Ray closes his eyes, hoping to nap, but his body remains tense and tight.

All of a sudden there's an explosion of light behind his closed eyes. He jumps.

What happened? Have I gone blind? He doesn't know any doctors here, wherever he is. He opens his eyes slowly, terrified, and finds that he can see, but there's a gauzy gray film over everything. As his panic subsides a bit, the gray melts away like mist when the sun rises. He notes that he will get his eyes checked by his Cambridge ophthalmologist, the minute he gets home to Boston.

"We're here at the airport," the drivers tell him, and open a metal door. Is it the same one he'd walked into earlier? And it doesn't look like an airport. When he looks around to hail the drivers in their striped overalls, the metal trolley is gone.

There is no main entrance. Or any other entrance, and he prepares himself for a long hike. The upside? No one has asked for the fare they'd decided upon.

Walking briskly in the direction of a huge, flat area for airplane landings, a slinky yellow dog walks beside him. Ray realizes that he's leading him in the right direction. The dog is skinny, and lopes faster and faster, looking more and more like a coyote.

He follows at the coyote's speed, which is sometimes quite fast, almost running. The coyote has led him to an area full of stray dogs of every breed, all of them skinny, and some with skin diseases, and someone dragging a large food bag is trying to feed them, but they surround him, threatening to throw him over. He goes closer to see whether he can help, and he's surprised to see that it's Felix.

There's a huge mud puddle gleaming like an oil slick, between them. Felix puts out his hand to help Ray across, smiling with joy at seeing him there. Somehow Ray misses Felix's hand, and Felix falls into the mud. Ready to help him out, Ray stands there waiting for Felix to get a foothold, his arm out. But instead Felix sinks as if the pool of mud is a quicksand bog, the dogs crowding around. The coyote stares at Ray with his yellow eyes.

WHEN RAY WAKES, he's surprised to be alone. The motel curtains closed, he has no idea if it's morning, noon or night. He lies there, trying to remember the dream. He recalls Oskar saying that Stella is a coyote, a trickster. In his dream he was lost. The coyote was leading him. Where? The airport? Away from the airport? The coyote led him to Felix. Only to lose him again.

THIRTY-NINE

RAY DRIVES HIS NEW RENTAL, the silver Corolla, windows closed, and air on, to visit Lina Cardenas, the person Cervantes told him about who had worked with Felix.

Though he's showered, he's still wearing the only clothing he's had for the last couple of days, and feels itchy and sweaty.

Cervantes hadn't told him much about Lina, except that she'd done fabulous work, was brilliant, and that she probably knows how to find Felix. She also, apparently, knows Stella.

Ray's decided to continue his momentum in his search for Felix. He thinks about Stella far too much, but thinks he's making progress this way—solo.

Yesterday the desire to reach her, to respond to her calls, had been a steady electric current just under his skin. Keeping in motion helps, but maybe not enough. She has stopped calling him, and even though that makes him happy, it causes him to desire her more.

But he makes up a tale of rejection—she's not calling and no longer wants to see him, be with him, or talk to him. He can feel sad, and deserted, but think there's nothing he can do, or has to do about it.

Now that he's not with Stella almost every minute, he sees that their sexual intimacy hasn't taught him much about her, or who she was.

And how much had he really known Olivia? Had he ever known her? What did she think of the irony of her cancer at age thirty-eight? Cells of death growing instead of cells of life—the baby she'd wanted. And what did he do? Deceive her about wanting a child? Did that cause her not to conceive? No. But who is he? A man who didn't want a child. A man who lies.

Having a child might have been okay too. He's always been inclined to try things out, usually other peoples' ideas. Even something as irrevocable as having a child. He's often been super agreeable, allowing others to lead him, interested in seeing what would happen, rather than finding out what he needed and wanted. Is that passivity to the point of insanity? But even though willing to be led, he sees that he's led a rather circumscribed life. Not even seeing what he wasn't seeing.

He'd thought he was helping Stella find her husband, his friend. But now he's not sure.

Now he thinks about whether this mission is something he needs or wants to continue. Is he really free to decide? He may be trapped in a series of events, where one thing leads to another, until choices are made that lead to fewer and fewer options, until there's one path.

The longer he lives, the more he drags a past that constantly informs a present. He ponders the quote that he thinks may be from Lampedusa: "If you want everything to stay as it is, everything needs to change."

THE BRICK, STEEL AND GLASS BUILDINGS of the growing city of El Paso shimmer in Ray's windshield like a mirage as he drives over potholed roads lined with ocotillo, prickly pear, and chollo. He senses the snake, armadillo, and coyote disappearing south as he drives north towards the banks, shopping malls and condos.

He has a quick breakfast at a fast-food wagon parked between two buildings, and he eats in the car, unwrapping the foil encasing his quesadillas, stuffed sparsely with cheese and chicken and orange grease, and drinks his coffee, which had been brewed—he saw the pot—but which tastes like powdered Nescafé.

At exactly nine, Ray takes the elevator to the fifth floor of an already shabby, but built to look elegant, building of concrete and glass. The elevator has the chemical odor of new carpeting, but there's no carpet. It shakes horizontally as it moves slowly up.

At the fifth floor, relieved to be out of the elevator alive, Ray looks for Room 57, the narrow hallway buzzing with white fluorescent light. The door opens just as he reaches it.

"You are Ray?" a woman asks, in a husky voice. She holds out her hand, which feels cool; her blackberry eyes study him.

She looks Mexican, with perfect latte skin and long, black straight hair, partially off her face in a large barrette, the rest to her shoulders.

Ray's surprised that she is so young—in her twenties maybe—but the hand she holds out to him has visible veins, thin fingers with enlarged joints, like the hand of an older person or someone who has done years of physical labor. Incongruously, her fingernails are long, and polished red.

"Would you like some coffee?" she asks, turning and walking into the large open room with its three large windows facing the street. She stops at a large, neat desk near the center window, and turns to face Ray, who's followed, as she's expected.

"I'd love some," says Ray. "I just had a meal from a food cart, but the coffee wasn't great." He's sorry he's said that, in case her coffee is bad too.

He looks around. This office is very different from the other offices he's been in lately, which had seemed like the underground caves of people doing underground work.

At a nearby desk a woman, totally undistracted by Ray who is just standing around nearby, doesn't even look up from whatever she's working at. Her dyed blonde hair, very short on one side, much longer on the other, and covering that side of her narrow face to her jaw line, flows gently like a smooth curtain whenever she moves her head from side to side.

"Sorry about the mug," says Lina, returning, with one in each hand. "All our cups seem to be chipped. Do you like milk? The only cream we have is powdered." She crinkles her small nose.

"This is fine," says Ray, sitting across from Lina. "More than fine, this is great. Just what I needed."

"Felix," she says.

"Yes, Felix," says Ray. He's holding his mug between his legs because there are too many papers on his side of the desk. Strange, with everything digitized, why is there still so much paper everywhere?

"I've worked with Felix on and off," Lina says. "We worked together on some environmental issues, and then also when I joined the *Comite Fronteriza de Obreras,* or The Border Committee of Working Women. You have heard of us?"

Ray shakes his head.

We are a group, but unlike unions we don't collect dues from members. We keep a low profile, and just work in small groups to inform *the maquila* workers, the factory workers of their rights. Our organization is known to thousands who work along the lower Rio Grande. We teach them, after we teach ourselves, what their rights are under federal labor law, and about the occupational dangers of working in the factories."

"Why are you The Border Committee of Working Women?" Ray asks, his cup radiating heat into his thighs.

"You mean because it sounds like a union of prostitutes?" Lina's smile is wide and her teeth large and shiny.

"No," Ray says, blushing. "I didn't mean that. What about male factory workers?"

"Factory owners prefer women workers. You might say it's because they can pay them less, and that's true, they do pay them less, but also because women work harder, and are generally more dextrous. With women there is less absentee-ism—even though some have children—less drunkenness, and there's little violence."

"For instance," she continues, "there's a Phillips company in El Paso that has a factory across the border in Juarez that hires only Mexican women. So you have to fight for their rights, or else the workers will not get breaks, they won't be able to go to the bathroom, they won't have fridges or microwaves in the lunchrooms. They wouldn't even have lunchrooms. Instead of paying factory workers enough for them to buy their lunches, the factory would provide food, but would charge the workers high prices for it, making a profit on that too. And the workers would have no choice but to buy their food at the factory because there is too little time allotted for eating. Things are so bad that after working in a factory for many years, if a family member of yours dies, you may get one day off for the funeral. If you are lucky."

Maybe she's picked up on his impatience, or his anxiety, because she says, "So, back to Felix."

He actually feels pretty comfortable with her. If he thinks about it, though he's never thought about it before, he almost never feels comfortable.

"Felix got involved with environmental issues in El Paso, mostly involving the copper smelter near where he and Stella lived. He organized his neighbors to complain in a group about the devastating ever-present odor and the poisonous air. So the company built a longer smokestack so that most of the waste blew into Juarez. If that wasn't enough, the company was cited so many fines for not cleaning up their waste they had to close down. The city of El Paso ended up paying billions to clean up the factory's waste. Then it opened again."

"Now that Juarez is full of factories, the pollution is uncontrollable," she says. "El Paso is right across the river from all those pollution-creating factories. We can't ignore it."

She drinks some coffee, and makes a face. "Cold already," she says. "Is yours okay?"

"Yes, it's fine," Ray says. He's mesmerized by her bright fingernails.

"When over fifty women factory workers went missing, some still in their teens, and many of their bodies were finally found, mutilated and raped, and somehow the police couldn't find out who did that, Felix sort of went crazy, and he began helping people more directly." She looks at Ray with her light brown eyes to make sure he's paying attention. "I mean not always legally," she says. "Though I'm not sure how. I didn't see him involved anymore in our organization."

"What about Stella?" he asks. "Do you know her? What is she involved in?"

"I have seen Stella a number of times, but I don't know her very well. She never got involved in these issues. Maybe other ones? I don't know." She touches the rim of her mug, feeling the chip with a perfect red fingernail. "I got the feeling from Felix that she was not a woman who appears weak but underneath is very strong, especially when there's trouble, but that she appears self-sufficient, but underneath is weak." She is still for a moment and Ray is too, as he thinks about that.

"Don't get me wrong," she says, "Stella has done an amazing job of recording and transcribing indigenous tales of the area … but I think she was always upset that Felix's empathy was elsewhere. A place she didn't want to go."

Lina smiles and fiddles with the mug. "Some think Felix is a very angry, a very crazy person, but I think he is a very passionate person. Some are afraid of him and don't want to work with him because he can be unpredictable. But I think he's very controlled. This controlled passion is very attractive," she says, looking up at Ray in a way that suddenly causes him to see her as very sexual. Were they involved? Lina and Felix? Was Lina just jealous of Stella? Certainly Stella wouldn't have cared, if Ray were to believe Stella.

"No," says Lina, laughing, running her tongue over her shiny teeth. "I can guess what you are thinking. No. Felix may be very attractive, but he's not a good prospect for a relationship."

Ray thinks about that and laughs too.

"So, you haven't seen Felix in a while. But, knowing him as you do, where do you think he might be? Is he a drug smuggler, as someone implied? Could he have gotten in trouble with a bad bunch? Last time we saw him he'd been beaten up by Mexicans, so he said, who were strangers, drunk, and they got into a fight. So he said. And he thought he might have hurt one of them badly while fighting them off. He said he thought he killed one of them. Then he disappeared. Could he have been kidnapped? Murdered in revenge?

Stella thinks she saw his body on a gurney, on TV news. The body was almost completely covered, but Stella thought she recognized a sneaker ... at first I thought she was nuts, but it could have been him."

"As I said," says Lina, her forehead crinkled with worry, as if Ray's anxiety were a contagious virus, I haven't seen Felix in at least six months. I don't think he's a drug smuggler." She smiles. "I've been working more with the *maquiladoras*, to make things better for the workers, and Felix had moved to helping migrants get across the border, and into the U. S. alive and safe. I can connect you with someone from the Sanctuary Movement, or some other agency or group who help migrants cross the desert."

"Don't coyotes do that? Isn't that their job?"

Lina looks at Ray sidelong, as she's also looking through a small desk drawer, which, from where Ray sits, looks disorganized compared with everything else in the office. Along with papers, people's cards, and large paper clips, she seems also to have some food items wrapped in foil, and a half eaten apple in a small plastic sandwich bag.

"Coyotes are a necessary evil. They get paid a huge amount, and are supposed to get their clients safely to their destinations, but when things get tough, and they often do, they take the money and run. You must have read about trucks found in the desert full of dead and dying migrants, left by drivers, deserted by guides?"

She looks up at Ray. "If it gets too hot, if too many are getting dehydrated or sick, if the Border Patrol is on their trail, they're out of there. They are not murderers. But they will save themselves first. They are a business. That's their morality."

"If they leave people to die after taking all their savings, aren't they murderers?" Ray asks.

Lina doesn't answer. She shakes her hair back over her shoulder, and looks up. She's found something. A card, and something else. She stuffs everything back into the drawer, shuts it, and holds something out for Ray, who suddenly feels so dizzy and weak he has to hang on to the desk. If he takes what she gives him, he is committing himself, not only to finding Felix, but to doing Felix's work.

"Here's the info for the Salvation people. They know all the other organizations that do similar work." She picks up something else she's taken from the drawer.

"Here's Felix's phone. And his charger. I've been keeping it for him," she says.

"You can return it to him when you find him."

FORTY

We sit and talk quietly,
with long lapses of silence,
and I am aware of the stream that has no language,
coursing beneath the quiet heaven of your eyes, which has no speech.

William Carlos Williams, *Paterson*

RAY RENTS A ROOM IN A LARGE, clean El Paso hotel that has
six stories, an elevator, and rambling hallways. And windows
that open, though they look out on other rooftops.

The hotel has a restaurant, and, while the phone charges,
he goes downstairs, sits at one of the sleek glass tables, and
orders a steak and a baked potato.

How many phones does Felix have? Ray wonders.

"This is Felix's," Lina had said. "You can return it when
you find him." Not "if" you find him. That one word gives
him hope.

He's bought a backpack, a pair of jeans, two long-sleeved
t-shirts and some underwear, a razor, some soap, and other necessary cosmetics, which should be fine until he leaves for home.

His vacation time is nearly over, and he has to plan his
classes for the coming semester. There will be meetings he'll
be expected to attend. His usual vacations were spent thinking about new ways to penetrate most of his undergraduates'
impermeable cocoons of un-interest and boredom, but lately
he hasn't given a thought to his work.

He doesn't feel that hungry, but when his dinner arrives it looks and smells delicious, and he eats more heartily than he has in days—since his dinner in Lajitas with Stella, during the storm. No, he had dinner after that with Cervantes. Still, every day seems a long time ago. Each day seems another world, and a new time zone that he has to get used to as if he has jet lag.

LATER, IN BED, he tries to stay awake by watching TV news while the phone charges. It's an old model, a cheap Sendo, a brand Ray's never heard of, and seems to take extra long to charge. It could be that the battery is dead.

He checks the other phone, and sees that there is no message from Stella. In spite of being relieved a dark bubble of disappointment settles somewhere between his lungs and his stomach. He's strongly tempted to call her, an impulse he can't get rid of, but so far he hasn't given in to it. He pictures her as he'd last seen her, sleeping beside him on the big bed in Lajitas, wrapped in the pale blanket like an enormous chrysalis about to hatch, just a bit of her face, a coil of reddish hair, and one big toe, emerging.

Or, no, the last time he saw her was a bit later, before he'd left for the restaurant after carelessly hugging her, not bothering to look at her, as if he'd be seeing her in less than an hour.

BEFORE THE PHONE HAS ENOUGH CHARGE TO GET A SIGNAL, Ray's practically asleep, involved in a movie he'd been watching that is now part of his half-asleep dream. The story and the characters from the film have been grafted into his dream that he is sick with a bad sore throat, and he is going to need an operation that will be performed by his friends.

He is upset, because his friends—and it isn't clear who they are—may not be skilled enough. In fact, none of them are surgeons, or even doctors. What's worse, they haven't checked out his throat to see whether he really needs the operation. They haven't even looked at it. One of the friends looks like someone on the faculty in Boston, and another looks something like Lina Cardenas, but with her hair short and black, like Olivia's. They are all hoping that the operation will be a success. They've operated successfully on Felix, so they're pretty sure they can do a good job on Ray.

Perhaps because his throat is so sore he can't talk, or because he doesn't want to upset them, he hasn't been able to tell them that he doesn't want them to operate on him.

Ray would like to have complete confidence in them, but watching them plan, he's pretty sure they're going about it the wrong way. However, without his voice he can't tell them that he doesn't need or want the operation, or voice his doubts about their skill.

"I don't need an operation," he squeaks unintelligibly. "I just need something to drink."

He wakes himself with his own strange and strangled sounds. His throat burns. He gets himself some water and vaguely recalls that the film he'd been watching while falling asleep had something to do with a man going into the hospital for surgery. The doctor is sure the man is the murderer who killed his wife a few years before.

Ray tries to remember how the operation in the film turned out. Did the doctor murder his wife's murderer? Or did the doctor follow his Hippocratic Oath and try his best to save the man. Or did he discover that the man he was operating on was not the man who murdered his wife?

Ray is still exhausted, but wants to check out Felix's phone. He's not sure how this old phone works; he's generally not great with communications technology. He tries to find Felix's contacts, but it soon becomes clear that Felix has no contacts in this phone. Nor any messages. It's clear that he didn't use this phone as a phone. But when he touches the photo gallery icon, a batch of tiny photos load, maybe as many as fifty, or more tiny squares on the small screen. He touches the top left photo, as the rest fall away.

For a moment it looks as if Felix has kept the same photo record as Cervantes, of migrants who've been abused. Ray soon realizes that these are photos of migrants who have been crossing the desert.

The first is a picture of a group of people lying on the ground in a variety of positions, clothing half off and strewn around them, as if they couldn't get it off fast enough.

Another, close-up, shows a woman, eyes swollen shut, lips cracked, with what look like needles in her hands and face. Acupuncture, Ray thinks. He soon realizes they are cactus spines.

All the photos are of people with dirty, swollen faces, some, many, appear to be dead. Some are of groups of four or five, lying amongst their own filthy discarded clothing, old empty water bottles, and old food wrappers. Some of the women are stripped to underpants and bras, the men to their undershorts.

There are photos of sleazy-looking men, some of them looking like teenagers. Perhaps these are the coyotes? Were these photos taken as evidence? What did Felix hope to do with them? And how did he take them? He must have been there. Were some of these the people he saved? Did he suffer with these people, cross the desert with them, in order to photograph them?

Was this what Stella meant when she'd told him that Felix had too much empathy? "Yes," she'd said. "Empathy is crucial, but you can have too much. You can let your feelings for others lead you straight into their deplorable situations. You can be destroyed. How can that help?"

He decides he will return to Lina Cardenas in the morning. Could it be that she hasn't seen Felix's photos? He hopes that maybe she'll recognize someone. Though when he thinks more about it, he's not sure how that will help find him. He's beginning to be unsure about whether any of this is relevant.

HE WASHES HIS BRIEFS AND HIS CHINOS in the shower, hangs them over the shower's glass door, shaves, and brushes his teeth. He feels cleaner than he's been in a while.

Once in bed though, when he closes his eyes he sees the swollen, sunburned faces, the cracked, bleeding lips, the sores, the cactus spines like arrows, the greasy hair, the bodies, thin, or fat, in their underwear, their eyes open or closed. Their bruises look like rotten fruit.

And the sneakers, sandals, or running shoes, on or off, some white, others purple and green, all filthy, scattered around in a tableau of violence.

He remembers that in the Holocaust Museum in DC on one of his dates after Olivia had died, the photos were disturbing, horrifying beyond belief. But when he'd seen the pile of shoes, men's, women's, children's—shoes shaped by feet, shoes that had been put on in the morning by people who thought that they would take them off in the evening and wear them again the next day—he'd had to slink into the corner of the room to weep.

When he opens his eyes for relief, he can't help thinking about Stella. He wraps his arms around a pillow, as if it's her.

He breathes in deeply. The pillow smells fresh and clean. He tries to remember her smell of citrus, or coconut, and all the other unidentifiable molecules.

Leaving her the way he did, dragged away by Revel from the restaurant in Lajitas, not having said goodbye, and later, not having answered her messages, he feels bereft, lost. And worried. What is she doing? Where is she now? Home? Has Felix returned? Has she been arrested?

He pictures her fucking Bigote, or Oskar, or some other asshole. The men are nearly nude, wearing some portions of their uniforms, like caps, or the green shirt of the Border Patrol. They have mustaches, and hairy butts. They smell of sweat. And the thing he hates most is that Stella, white next to their darker skin, voluptuous and round next to their stringiness, moves animal-like, but gracefully, her bracelets tinkling, emitting familiar purrs of deep, pure pleasure.

He can no longer keep from pressing her telephone number, her home number on Felix's phone—the first one they'd gotten from their home—his heart pounding into his throat so that he wonders whether he'll be able to speak.

The phone rings five times, and then he hears Stella's voice, higher and softer than he remembers. "Hello?"

His blood roiling like a hurricane in his ears, he hangs up.

FORTY-ONE

Everywhere you went, you left something behind.
Benjamin Alire Saenz, *In Perfect Light*

ONCE AGAIN IN A DREAM STATE, very nearly asleep after thinking about getting home to Boston and to his job, he dreams that he is in a resort, but this time he can tell by the vegetation and the architecture that he's in the northern part of the United States. Perhaps he's already home, and is continuing the few days of vacation he still has in an area outside of Boston.

He's barbecued some steaks in the large grassy yard, and leaves them on the grill, perhaps longer than he should, in order to search the rooms of this sprawling resort for some plates to put them on before they've dried out.

He's not sure who he's preparing dinner for—Olivia? Stella? And maybe only once before in his life has he barbecued outdoors.

All the dishes are on high shelves in the large rooms. He's about to take some white dinner plates from shelves in one of the rooms when a man with a large belly hanging over his beige shorts that reach his reddish knees, stands in the doorway.

"This is my room," he says, pointing at the door.

"Can I borrow these plates?" Ray asks.

The man continues to point at the door, so Ray leaves, not wanting to take the time to argue.

Picturing the steaks curling at their edges, he hurries to find his own room which perhaps has dishes too, on shelves that he's never noticed, and a maybe if he's lucky a table, but he is soon lost amongst doors that look the same in the labyrinthine hallways that he usually loves in these old houses.

Sitting for a moment on the wide gray painted wooden steps up to the porch, still holding the long-handled spatula for turning the steaks, he notices how much these stairs resemble the stairs outside the house he lived in as a child, and which the neighborhood kids called a "stoop."

A woman he's never seen before, wearing very short shorts and a pink halter top, is seated on the top step, half under the porch overhang and half in the open, playing with a baby lying on a small yellow blanket, or towel. The baby is tiny, but supported by the woman's hands, she stands up, and takes a few steps.

"That's great," Ray says. "How old is she?"

The woman places the baby on her back on the blanket, where she begins to kick.

"She's three months," says the woman.

"Amazing," says Ray. "I've never seen a baby walking at three months. Even with support."

When he looks again at the infant she has a soft coat of greenish-yellow fur, and at the ends of her flailing arms and legs are padded paws.

From the corner of his eye he sees Stella walk right past him down the porch steps in her white Capri pants and Olivia's royal blue blouse. She's moving so fast that she's already way past the house, and down the street.

Ray can't believe she didn't say anything, or even greet him. Where is she going, and why is she leaving without him, or without telling him when they were supposed to eat the steaks?

"Stella," he calls, running after her. But she's too fast for him, and soon she's out of sight.

Hurt, and disappointed, he decides to go home rather than remain at the resort. Even though his apartment is in the city and he's in the country, there is a subway train only half a block from the resort.

When he gets down the very long flight of stairs to the train, he realizes that he hasn't got his jacket or his wallet, and has no change in his pockets. He's ashamed that he doesn't even remember what the fare is.

Desperate, he manages to get up the courage to ask a couple of well-dressed people near the turnstiles if they could help him with the fare. "It's just one-way," he says, humiliated, wondering whether they believe that he wants the money for a drink instead of the train.

A man wearing a suit and tie, and a woman dressed for work, ignore him, walking right past him through the turnstile as if he's invisible.

For a moment he's really afraid he won't get home, and even though it's a number of miles to his home, he decides to walk. He ascends the long flight of subway stairs and is back out on the street.

"I can do this," he says out loud to himself, elated, walking briskly, enjoying the evening coolness, the rolling clouds, the breeze.

He feels the rain, first just a few drops, that sizzle and fizzle in the air leaving only dust, but then it gets darker, and starts to rain hard.

Soon it is pouring and has become pitch black, the dark cut every few minutes by jagged lines of lightning and eardrum-busting thunder.

The streets run with rainwater. It runs down into his collar. It's in his eyes; his hair is dripping, and his sneakers, full, squish with every step, especially when he walks faster.

The rainwater flows faster along the curbs, and soon the street looks like a river. Large boards and furniture parts among other detritus float along on the current, which is getting stronger, and it gets tricky dodging all the stuff so that it doesn't smash into him.

He's not so sure he's going to make it home, and feels his strength waning as he struggles against the current. Soaked, he is also freezing. His nose and his hands icy, deep chills run through him regularly, leaving him weak.

He manages to cross the street, the current pulling hard at his legs, which he has to raise high at every step in order to make any progress.

Once on the other side of the street it's easier to walk. It's not raining so hard, and it's a bit warmer.

He's thirsty, and thinks it would be great if he can stop off somewhere for a short rest and a drink of water, or beer, but now that he's looking for a luncheonette or a store, or even a bar, he no longer sees any. Not even any houses.

Most likely he's miscalculated because he realizes that he's still at least fifteen miles from home, and with the landscape having changed so radically, he's afraid he may really be lost.

It's a relief that the rain has stopped, but it's getting hotter. His clothes having dried right on him, he's sweating huge globules of liquid that leave large dark stains like bruises on his shirt, under his arms, around his neck, and in the center of his chest. The smell of his own body, a bit sweet and a bit sour, familiar, yet somehow alien, assails him now and again.

The ground too has changed, nearly unnoticed, from a concrete street and blacktop road to gravel and sand. Stunted trees are sparse, and creosote bushes with the waxy coating on its leaves to keep it from dehydrating, are now, after the rain, abloom with zillions of tiny yellow flowers.

His shoes have dried, too, grey with dried mud, and stiff, and he notices he's tripping over small pebbles. Perhaps he's already somewhat dehydrated. If so, that could be why he's lost his sense of direction. He begins to breathe hard, nearly in a panic.

He's reassured that there are others walking beside him, as if on a city street, though without the speed or sense of purpose. They are all walking slowly, the same speed, heads lowered, like wind-up toys that are running down. Like zombies. Somehow, that calms him.

They wouldn't be here if they weren't going somewhere, he thinks. And suddenly, strongly, he desires to be home. He wants to find Felix. But more than anything, he can't wait to get home.

"Hay agua?" asks a man walking beside Ray. The man's mouth is so dry his tongue flips like a fish out of water, and he can hardly get words out.

"Wish I did," Ray says, and becomes aware that he really needs some water, that he's feeling some of the strange effects of dehydration. He wishes he'd brought some.

"How can it be so dry now, after so much rain," he says, but the man has disappeared.

Some of those shuffling beside him look like the people in Felix's phone photos, with similar cracked lips, maroon sunburns, mauve and olive green bruises. The same sand in their eyelashes, swollen eyelids, black circles underneath.

Someone up ahead has fallen, and soon all are passing the man, whose arms and legs are spread as if he's making a snow angel.

Ray prepares to stop, to see whether he can help, to see what the man needs, but the crowd is pressing him on, and truth to tell, he has no energy.

"You must save yourself," the man near him says. "It's too late for him anyway."

They are passing more bodies, some of them women. Some are naked, and some have faces open to the sun that blackened them, mouths open and full of sand, as if they'd tried to drink it.

The more bodies they walk past, the less startling or disturbing the sight. As if the fallen are part of the organic scenery, the landscape, like the yucca, saguaro, the low mesquite trees, the cholla.

They follow tracks of tennis shoes, soccer shoes, huaraches, boots, then the shirts, pants and socks highlighting the sandy landscape with bits of bright red or orange, or blue.

Next the empty boxes of peach juice, and orange juice, the small cereal boxes, the tuna fish cans, and water bottles, as they continue on, moving stealthily around low hills dunes, and dry bushes.

They have reached some rock tanks, probably built ages ago by Indians, that still hold small amounts of rainwater. Almost everyone has enough strength to bend down and drink, or help someone else get access to some water, or to fill any plastic bottle they might be carrying.

This is a good place to rest, he thinks before realizing that around the tanks is a graveyard, with low or ground-level markers, most covered with and masked by scrub. It seems strange that water and death can be so close, living together. As if water was the end goal of the traveler who is now free to die.

Ray's shoulders and back ache as if he's carrying a heavy backpack, but he has nothing more to get rid of, and no way to relieve his pain. He bends over, allows his knees to hit the sand, then lies flat on his stomach on the ground. From a low tank he drinks and drinks, but can't assuage his thirst.

He fears he's at the point where you can no longer drink liquid fast enough to make up for the rapid dehydration. Soon he will begin to walk in circles, to hallucinate, and to see mirages.

Which is what he thinks he's seeing when he spots Felix in the distance, ministering to some children. The stance is Felix's. The bald head too. Finally!

He's excited and even musters enough energy to pull himself up, and totter.

But as he approaches the man and looks again, Felix is gone—he's either disappeared or it wasn't him.

Ray rubs his eyes, but he's rubbing them with sand. He's got no more adrenaline. He's got nothing left.

IT'S GETTING DARK. All the pink and orange streaks have shredded and disappeared, leaving the sky a clear deep royal blue. Lights twinkle in the distance, but Ray knows they are much farther away than they look. Many miles.

He hears a wolf's howl, way too close for comfort. Chopped near the middle, it sounds like the war cry of an Indian.

"Are there wolves here?" he asks a woman with short, very curly hair, who looks otherwise like Dory.

"That's a coyote," she says, standing still for a moment. "Listen."

Ray stands still and listens, but now all he hears is the crying of a baby. Loud. A baby in distress. How like an animal it sounds. He looks around. Surely no one would bring a baby on a journey like this? But he knows they do. How could a mother, or even a father, leave a baby behind? He knows many have to do that too.

He finds the woman with the baby. She has a blanket tied around her shoulders, making a supported pouch, part of the throw left to cover the baby completely, including its face. She is thin, with dark, absolutely straight hair cut evenly along her jaw. She reminds him of Olivia. In that case could all this be a dream?

But Olivia never had a baby, with Ray or anyone else.

"The baby is thirsty," says the woman, "but I have no more milk."

She pulls the blanket down and then the corner of a shirt, and shows Ray a beautiful round breast with a caramel-colored nipple, as if offering it to him.

"I have a small amount of water," Ray says, holding out the bottle he'd filled at the rock tanks. There's about an inch at the bottom.

"Giving away your last ounce of water," says a woman with a fat, curly ponytail. "You have an excess of empathy."

"Stella," says Ray, thrilled. "What are you doing here? I've missed you."

"Me too," she says. "I've missed you so much."

Ray searches her face for signs of irony. Her hazelnut eyes have tears pooling at their bottoms, about to overflow.

"Don't cry," says Ray. "We have to conserve the liquid in our bodies."

"Sit with me a while," Stella says.

"But how did you find me? Did Felix return? Where are you going now?"

He sits next to Stella, gingerly, careful of his stiff back, on a chunk of old mesquite tree trunk, trying to keep away from the hole that ants are marching from, checking the sand nearby for scorpions or snakes. He smells her familiar hair scent and wants to rest his head on her shoulder.

"It feels so fucking good to rest," he says, "but it might be a mistake not to continue on while it's dark, and getting cooler." Reluctant to stay any longer, but reluctant to leave Stella, he's not even sure he has the energy to go farther.

He removes his sneakers and filthy socks and checks his feet for blisters. He hadn't noticed much pain, but his feet are swollen and bruised, and there are a few blisters near his heel, and large ones on the front bottoms of both feet. The blister on one heel has broken, and he worries about infection.

The sky becomes purple, then black. He knows he should be moving toward the shimmering lights ahead, but he feels so good. Too good. Maybe death will arrive, painless, like when you take a walk in the snow and lose your way, get tired and cold and desire more than anything to go to asleep. Ray can see that it's possible to be so tired you just don't care.

This scares him and he tries to move, to feel some energy.

"This journey changes people's values," he says to Stella. "Clothing, water, money—everything becomes too heavy and becomes something to get rid of."

The moon begins to spread its light.

Stella says, "Coyote can go great distances without food or water. Many Indian tribes believe he created the earth—but then, because of some stupid mistake—he also gave us death."

"Are you saying you can go far without food or water?" he asks. "It seems that Coyote is only human after all. And why are you thinking about death?"

"I'm not thinking in particular about death. I was thinking about creation. You are the one thinking about death."

Ray thinks about that for a moment, but everything he can think of to say sounds trite. So he says, staring into the endless space of the desert, "I'd love to make a big bonfire, and roast some marshmallows."

"Hot dogs even better," says Stella.

Ray's salivary glands ache, but produce no liquid.

"I'll tell you a story," Stella says, putting her arm around him, "about how Coyote learns to make fire. He goes to the people, and says, 'Teach me to make fire.'"

"How does he know what fire is if he can't make it?" Ray asks.

Stella continues, "The people didn't trust Coyote, but they gave him their flint stones anyway, and showed Coyote how to rub them together until they sparked. Coyote tried and tried, but got nothing—not even one spark. Everyone laughed at him, so Coyote, being Coyote, had a huge tantrum, and threw all the flints on the ground. This started a fire so huge and so hot that the earth split open. People were thrown to one side or the other of the giant split. Water Pourer, in order to stop the flames and the smoke, poured as much water as he could into the enormous crack or crater left by the fire—"

"I get it," says Ray, "that's how the Grand Canyon came to be."

Ray turns to see Stella better. This is the Stella he loves.

Now she looks well, and fresh, as if she's just showered. She's wearing a white Mexican blouse with red, orange and magenta flowers hand-embroidered around the square neckline.

He's surprised—this is not a style of clothing he's ever seen on her before. And, in spite of her looking so well, her fingernails have been bitten so far down that some have sharp new moons outlined in rust-red blood.

Ray's determined to ask again about Felix, but doesn't know how to change the subject from Coyote. "So, you have this laughable character …" he says. He realizes then that Stella has disappeared, and he's talking to himself.

He looks around, in a panic. She's gone. Disappeared. There's nothing nearby but a skinny cholla.

"Come on," he says, thinking she must be somewhere around, "quit fooling around. I'm half dead. This is no time for silly games."

It takes a few moments for him to realize she's really gone, and when he does he is bereft, devastated. Deserted. Fear laced with dread—he recalls these feelings from childhood.

He begins the process of pulling on his socks, but his feet sting at the mere touch of the rough, sweaty cotton. Blisters he hadn't felt before have risen and are painful to the touch. He thinks about walking barefoot, but he knows walking without shoes in the desert would be a disaster, as proven by all the discarded shoes he's seen, so he makes an effort in spite of the pain.

"We go on merging with the heat and the exhaustion as if there's no other world for us," a man who has stopped to watch Ray's efforts, says.

Ray realizes that there probably are a few better ways to get to his destination, but he'd allowed himself to be convinced that crossing the desert made it less likely he'd be stopped by the Border Patrol, as the Border Patrol didn't like being out there in the desert either. But shouldn't he have realized how dangerous this route is?

A man walking faster than most, head down and partly hidden by a brown hoodie, sleeves rolled a few inches above his wrists, is about to pass Ray.

"I saw you at the rock tanks, right?" Ray asks him. "Have you seen this man?" He pulls a folded photo of Felix from the back pocket of his chinos, a photo he hadn't remembered even having until this moment.

The man looks up, surprised to be spoken too, as if in another world. "Hey, man, he says, squinting at the photo. His light blue eyes look strange as his skin is so dark. "It's hard to see at night, and my vision ain't too good neither." He looks at the photo again, surprised.

"That's Soldado Juan," he says.

"Who?" asks Ray. "It's my friend Felix, who is missing. Who's Soldado Juan?"

"He's the patron saint of Mexicans crossing the border," says the man. "He guides us across the desert. He blinds the Border Patrol. Haven't you seen chapels and shrines to Soldado Juan, where people leave flowers, candles and photos of family members who are crossing? They even leave copies of green cards. And shoes."

"Never heard of him," says Ray, walking beside the man.

"Soldier Juan was a private in the United States Army who was convicted by a military tribunal for the rape and murder of an eight-year-old Tijuana girl. A crime he did not commit. His friends thought he'd been framed by a superior officer—but anyway, no one's happy until someone takes the blame. Right or wrong."

The man pulls his hoodie closed in front, and wipes his nose with his hand. "Here's how the *Ley de Fuga* worked," he continues, trudging next to Ray, head down, bobbing a bit like a chicken's. "Soldado Juan is supposed to run for the border while a firing squad—not sure how many soldiers—shoot at him with their rifles. Before he reached the border with the U. S. he took—who knows how many bullets—in the back and fell dead on Mexican soil. When his friends tried to clean up the blood it couldn't be removed. Blood continued to seep from his grave, and voices can still be heard coming from it."

He blows his nose through his fingers, and onto the sand. "Will you look at this?" He points to a wad of thick black mucus. "I'm eating, drinking and breathing sand."

"Anyway, it was declared a miracle, not sure by who, and a shrine was build right there in Tijuana. There are chapels all over dedicated to Juan Soldado, where traffickers and those crossing the border pray. A gringo saint," the man says, shaking his head.

"No, no," says Ray, "it's my friend Felix. He helps people stay alive crossing the desert."

"Why would he do that?" the man asks. "Can I see that photo again?" The man's forehead is burnt rust, and his lips have deep cracks. "Looks a lot like you," he says.

Ray doesn't know how he looks now, but he does feel different—thinner, firmer. His expression feels different too, as if he's changed from inside out. He runs his hand over his skull to see whether he still has his hair.

The man holds up a tiny piece of a mirror. Ray bends painfully into a position in which he can see himself. It's impossible to see all his features at once in such a tiny fragment.

His features are familiar, but they all possess aspects of Felix. He looks again. The mirror is merely a sliver, a shard, and it's dark out. From a different angle he doesn't recognize himself at all.

Perhaps he's gone beyond some boundary but he no longer feels the pain of his shoulders and his back. Even the aggravating pain of his open blisters is gone. No longer limping, or feeling the heaviness in his thigh muscles, the heat, the sweat, the thorns, the weight of his arms, he takes pleasure in crashing ahead.

Continuing on has nothing to do with thought or will, just movement. He's just a part of movement, of air, of the heat rising from the center of the earth.

Surprised at the silence, he raises his head. There is not a sound, only the black mountains ahead, bare rock, thousands of years old. And the millions upon millions of stars above them. The sand is marked with Arthur Murray-type dance diagrams, thousands of footprints going in all directions, human and animal.

"Stella?" says Ray, startled to see he's accompanied by a woman, moonlight on her loose and bushy hair. She has the lithe grace of an animal, like a panther or a young puma. When she turns, instead of Stella's face, Ray sees the face of a coyote, soft and lovely, with its tan velvet fur, soft canine shapes, and moist glistening nose.

"I should have known," Ray says.

"Come," invites the coyote, with a graceful lope, a little like a dance step.

Ray goes through all he's been told about not trusting a coyote. Is this Stella trying to trick him? For what purpose? But even if Stella is playing a trick on him, what would be the harm of walking with the strangely appealing coyote for a while, side by side?

The coyote turns her large orange eyes toward Ray.

"I know it's you," he says. Though it doesn't seem to matter.

"Isn't it ravishing," he says, looking up. The jagged mountains have become shimmering lights, clusters of them nestled in, and festooning the foothills in the distance, as if the world has been turned upside down and they are the constellations, twinkling and teasing, appearing closer than ever before.

LYNDA SCHOR is the author of five collections of short fiction, including *The Body Parts Shop* and *Sexual Harassment Rules.* Her prizewinning fiction and nonfiction has been published in many anthologies, magazines, and literary journals, including, *Playboy, GQ,* and *Ms.* She has taught fiction writing at a number of colleges and universities, among them, Florida International University, Western Washington University, and Pratt Institute.

She was a faculty member of the Lang College of The New School for twenty-six years. She is currently living in San Miguel de Allende, Mexico. *DEARTH* is her first novel.

OTHER BOOKS BY THE AUTHOR:
Appetites
True Love & Real Romance
The Body Parts Shop
Seduction: Stories of Love & Art
Sexual Harassment Rules